The Crossing

M.M. Riches

The Crossing

Acknowledgements

The Crossing has been many years in the making and would never have happened without the support of some very special people to whom I am eternally grateful.

First and above all, I am in awe of the courage and deeply indebted to those dear friends who can no longer be named. They walked with me, taught me, and shared with me their personal histories, encouraging me to tell their stories. To them this work is dedicated with love and deepest respect.

To Professor Mick Dodson, for your interest and enthusiasm and the exciting endorsement that gave me the courage to proceed with publication, many, many thanks.

To Roger Stoddart and Irene Warfe, my wonderful teachers, thank you for believing in me right from the start.

To Heather Whitford Roche, fellow writer and friend, many thanks for your constant support and encouragement – always there for me!

To Suzanne Gatz and Mary Melcherts, my dear friends and fellow travellers on the writing journey, thank you both for the friendship and faith that kept me going.

To Dr Jill Blee, friend, teacher and mentor, thank you for the valuable workshops and assessments that moved the work along.

To Kate Ryan Writers Victoria, many thanks for your early encouraging assessment and advice.

And to the Victorian Police and Victorian Railways Historical Societies, my thanks for valuable research assistance.

The Crossing
ISBN 978 1 76041 982 0
Copyright © M.M. Riches 2020
Cover image: dayene.designer from Shutterstock

First published 2020 by
GINNINDERRA PRESS
PO Box 3461 Port Adelaide 5015
www.ginninderrapress.com.au

This book is dedicated to the children of the Stolen Generations, their families and communities. To those who inspired this work by sharing their stories with me, I am eternally grateful.

One

On a hill above the city, woodlands sheltered St Magdalene's convent from Melbourne's bustle. In the bluestone corridors of the Mother House, white-veiled novices waited to kneel before Mother Anna. The Provincial Superior received the young nuns one at a time, assigning them the work they would undertake as they left St Magdalene's to face the world for the first time in two years.

As she waited, nineteen-year-old Sarah Norton ran her rosary through nervous fingers. 'Please God,' she prayed, 'send me to St Martin's.'

At St Martin de Porres Hospital, the Sisters of St Frances Cabrini trained their nurses and Sarah had wanted to be a nurse all her life. Finally, it was her turn to tap on Mother Anna's open door.

'Ah, Sister Anthony. Come in, my dear.'

Sarah crossed the floor, one hand clutching the large wooden beads that hung from her waist, muffling their rattle. She lifted them clear of her knees as she knelt before her seated Superior.

Mother Anna's smile and cultured voice belied the coming thunderbolt. 'Sister Anthony, we are sending you to Liguori College. I know you will do well there.'

Sarah dropped her eyes and drew breath as quietly as she could. Liguori College was the order's teacher training academy. When she looked up, there was an obedient smile on her face. 'Thank you, Mother.' But as soon as she had spoken, she lowered her eyes again.

Mother Anna leant over the head bowed before her. 'I'm sorry, my dear, but we are not sending any trainees to Mother Basil this year. The need of the order at present is for teachers. It may still be possible for you to study nursing in the future. Since you hope to go to the New Guinea Mission, it would be well for you to be qualified in both areas.'

'Yes, Mother.' Sarah swallowed a sigh. Doubling her qualifications made mission work seem so far away. A small comfort came from the implied promise that eventually Mother Anna would send her to New Guinea.

'You will not be alone. Sister Patricia and Sister Whilomena are also going to Liguori College.'

Sarah bowed her head again. Mother Anna could hardly have assigned her two more different companions. Patricia was fun. Whilomena was, well, Whilomena.

The chapel bell echoed through the monastery, sounding the Angelus.

'Mother, would it be…may I have permission to spend extra time in chapel this afternoon?'

'Of course, Sister. Prayer should be our refuge in times of trial. Prayer always helps.'

'Yes, Mother. It does. Always.'

*

In March, Sarah became a student at Liguori College and in November she wondered where the year had gone. She smiled, remembering her resistance to teaching. Already she loved it. These days she looked forward to her time in the classroom, even though she was awed by her responsibility to trusting young minds. She especially loved working with the smallest children. They brought her their secrets and scraped knees, always confident of a little sympathy.

Her first year ended with everyone eager for the summer holidays. They passed quickly, as holidays do. As she prepared to return to Liguori, Sarah was again summoned by Mother Anna.

The Superior was seated at a quaint little secretaire. She looked up through her open door as Sarah approached, and said, 'Come in, Sister.'

She waited until Sarah knelt before her. 'Sister, Mother Sebastian, the Superior at St Cuthbert's, is in need of extra hands. As you know, St Cuthbert's is one of our orphanages. I'm told you are good with children. St Cuthbert's needs you, my dear. Sister Daniel has organised everything. You and Sister Whilomena will leave for Cobbs Crossing on Monday.'

Outside the Superior's parlour, Sarah allowed herself to sigh. Hurrying through the corridors and out into the grounds, she found Patricia throwing hoops on the basketball court. The skirt of her habit was buttoned behind her waist, her veil thrown over her shoulders.

'An orphanage? But you were doing so well at Liguori.'

'Enjoying teaching too, which surprised me. I'd only ever wanted to be a nurse.'

'And with Whilomena.'

They grinned at each other. Serious, self-disciplined Whilomena. Her uncompromising interpretation of every rule set a standard Sarah despaired of reaching.

'I won't mind working in an orphanage. The poor kids need someone to take care of them, don't they? But at this rate I'll never get to New Guinea.'

Patricia threw her the ball. Sarah hoisted it towards the basket. It circled the rim and fell back down.

'It's funny. When people talk about the vows we take as nuns, they always seem to think chastity or poverty will be the hardest to live with.'

'And they're wrong?'

'For me they are. Obedience! It's obedience that's really hard.'

'Where on earth is Cobbs Crossing?'

'Search me. It's not in New Guinea, that's for sure.'

'You're really keen on New Guinea, aren't you? Why?'

'Have you ever heard of the Kokoda Track?'

Patricia shook her head.

Two

On the same day that Sarah accepted her appointment to St Cuthbert's, Lachlan Harris was visiting Mother Sebastian at the orphanage.

Harris was the owner of Mullanurra, a sheep/wheat station in the Cobbs Crossing district and the largest property in the Mallee. He touched his fingers to his Akubra and gave the Superior a charming smile as he said goodbye. He strode down the convent steps and crunched his way across a gravelled drive to where his late-model Land Rover waited in the shade of peppercorn trees. The nun watched her benefactor depart with a satisfied smile.

The smile disappeared as she caught sight of the vehicle pulling into the driveway to take the Land Rover's place: a 1956 FJ Holden utility, which would have been a creamy yellow if it was clean. With a sniff of contempt, the Superior folded her hands and waited to receive the editor of the town's only newspaper.

A young man in jeans and an open-necked shirt emerged from the dusty ute. He crammed a battered hat on top of unruly brown hair, patted the notebook in his shirt pocket and headed through the suffocating noon heat to the convent steps. He was followed by a mongrel dog with long legs and floppy ears. It was part whippet, part anybody's guess. The grounds were still and quiet, as if even the birds found it hard to breathe, but Bronko bounded about, sniffing the air and snapping at flies.

Mick reached the veranda and stepped out of the scorching sun. 'Morning, Mother. What's Harris after? Trying to buy you out?'

'Mr Harris is a generous Christian gentleman, Mr O'Mara. His patronage is greatly appreciated by St Cuthbert's.'

Mick grinned. 'That's a bunch of adjectives I've never heard applied to Harris before. Come on, Mother, if Harris is supporting St Cuthbert's, there has to be something in it for him. He doesn't believe in anything but Mullanurra.'

'I'm sure you didn't drive all this way to debate Mr Harris's beliefs, Mr O'Mara. How may I help you?'

Three

The Railway Hotel in the centre of Cobbs Crossing was a popular meeting place. When Mick headed into his favourite watering hole ahead of the lunchtime crowd, a couple of locals were already propping up the bar.

'Good game last week, Mick.'

'On ya, Mick! Carn the Tigers!'

Football was a passion in the Mallee and good players were the town's heroes. Every Saturday, Cobbs Crossing emptied and Victory Park filled with fans. Flying high above the pack, Mick kept the opposition's scores low, while at the other end of the ground Majik, his best mate, thrilled fans with safe marks and long kicks that drilled the big sticks with deadly accuracy.

Mick placed his order at the bar and called for a beer. In one of the pub's cosy booths, he spotted Arthur Lawrence, almost invisible behind a copy of the *Chronicle*. Mick scooped up his change in one hand and a well collared beer in the other and took a thirst-quenching sip. He moved away from the bar, balancing his beer against the press of men now manoeuvring to be served. The clamour of male voices and the smell of free-flowing beer filled the room.

Mick made his way to the doctor's table, grinning at the head still buried in the newspaper. 'Riveting stuff that, eh, doc?'

A head of white hair appeared from behind the paper. 'Ah, O'Mara, sit down, sit down.' Doctor Lawrence was a large man with a cheerful face. His sedate suit was challenged by the bold, striped tie of his beloved Cobbs Crossing Tigers. He tossed his newspaper onto the seat beside him. 'I see there's to be an orphanage outing to Mullanurra. The children will enjoy that.'

Mick gave the doctor a between-the-lines version of what Mother Sebastian had told him. Welfare inspectors would be in Cobbs Crossing on St Patrick's Day. Lachlan Harris was to host them at Mullanurra. He had invited the orphans of St Cuthbert's to a picnic, which the inspectors would also attend.

Doctor Lawrence smiled at his beer. 'Ah, I see.'

A young waitress lingered at their table, arranging Mick's fish and chips in front of him. She met his wink with a grin as she left.

'Mother Sebastian tells me that Harris is a "generous patron" of St Cuthbert's. Any idea why, doc? I mean, it's hard to believe it's out of the goodness of his heart.'

'Well, no, not exactly. There's a story there all right.' The doctor looked up as a shadow fell across their table. 'And here's just the man to help me tell it. Will you join us, Sergeant?'

Ed Buchanan dumped the doctor's newspaper onto the floor and seated his solid six-foot frame at their table. His uniform pants stretched tight across his belly, betraying the Sergeant's fondness for the local lager. Without benefit of knife or fork, he began wolfing the two meat pies he had brought to their table.

Mick drained his glass and picked up the doctor's empty one. 'My shout.' He returned juggling three beers. 'Now, about Harris and all the money he's pumping into St Cuthbert's.'

'I said you could shed some light on that, Sergeant.'

'God, that's goin' back a bit. Must be fifteen years ago.'

Lawrence nodded. 'Yes, about that. Amelia Harris had just given birth to their Cynthia. I attended her and the same evening I was called back to Mullanurra because their housekeeper had also gone into labour. Pearl was only fourteen. Amelia had been more annoyed at the inconvenience, than shocked that a fourteen-year-old was having a baby. Every time I saw her, she complained about the morals of "those blacks". But when Pearl's baby was born, the child was almost white. As soon as she saw the baby, Amelia realised it wasn't one of the Aboriginal workers who was responsible.'

13

'And that's when the shit hit the fan.' Buchanan smirked at Mick, who ignored him and raised eyebrows at the doctor.

'Well, yes, in a manner of speaking. Pearl refused to say who the father was. The baby was packed off to the orphanage. Poor little beggar.'

Mick wasn't sure if the doctor was expressing sympathy for the baby or the young mother.

'That's when Harris called me in,' Buchanan picked up between mouthfuls of pie. 'Things were easier back then. All Abos were wards of the state. Now they have to be charged with neglect, or we have to muck about convincing the parents their kids are going to get a great whitefella education.' He pulled a handkerchief from his pocket and wiped his mouth, dabbing at a small Charlie Chaplin moustache.

Mick and Doctor Lawrence exchanged tight-lipped glances. The doctor looked at the glass he had raised halfway to his lips. He put it down again without drinking and pushed it away.

'You're OK with that?' Mick's voice was low.

The doctor shot him a warning glance.

Buchanan produced a packet of cigarettes and shoved one between his lips, lighting it without offering the pack to his companions. 'It's not my fault if they haven't got the bloody brains to know what's good for 'em. Anyhow, it's the law. I'm just doing my job.'

Watching the storm brewing on Mick's face, the doctor hurried the conversation back to safer ground. 'But fifteen years ago you didn't need a mother's consent?'

'That's right. I wasn't surprised that the kid had to go to the orphanage. But what was surprising was that Harris handed me a huge wad of cash. He reckoned he had to accept responsibility for his staff.'

'Didn't you think that was strange?'

'I just do what I'm told, mate.'

'And Harris has been supporting the orphanage ever since? For fifteen years?'

'Suppose so.'

Mick turned to the doctor. 'The child wouldn't still be out there, surely. Don't they farm the kids out as soon as they can?'

'It depends. St Cuthbert's trains its own labour force. Some of the older girls are kept on to nursemaid the babies.'

'So it's possible the girl is still there?'

'Maybe. But there's no way of knowing. Pearl called her Tallara, but Mother Sebastian would have none of that. She'd have given the child a suitable Christian name, and she enjoys concocting surnames from the date of their arrival.'

'Well, that was the twenty-first of September,' Buchanan chuckled. 'I remember because I was in the doghouse with the missus. I'd forgotten our wedding anniversary.' He scraped his chair back as he rose from the table. 'Doctor, O'Mara.'

Doctor Lawrence lowered his voice as Buchanan left them. 'God, Mick. I thought you were going to hit him.'

'So did I. Just doing what he's told. Where have we heard that before?'

'Always comes in handy, the old Nuremberg defence. Did you see how he tapped the table with his left hand whenever he mentioned Majik's mob, and with his right when he talked about anyone else?'

'I did.'

'Building fences with his hands to match the fences in his mind.'

'He's just a bully with a badge. And yeah, he hates…well, you heard him…"Abos". Majik can't go anywhere without Buchanan searching his car. He watches him like a hawk after the Saturday match. Even week nights after training, just in case one of us sneaks him a beer. And of course, Majik doesn't dare show his face at the pub.'

'But Buchanan loves his footy, Mick. Surely he'd never lock up one of the Crossing's star players just for –'

'I wouldn't put it past him.'

'Majik's well regarded, though. He could get a certificate of exemption. I'd put my name to his application…give him a good character. Plenty of others would too.'

'I suggested that to him once. He said, "No bloody fear, mate! I'd rather die of thirst than jump through whitefella's hoops."'

They sat staring at their beers.

Mick's thoughts returned to Pearl's baby. 'Anything special about the twenty-first of September?'

'Not that I know of. You're not thinking of looking for the child, Mick? Surely it's better not to interfere after all this time.'

'What do you think Pearl would say about that? She must be what, twenty-nine by now? And probably still looking for her daughter. Are you sure there's no way the child could be identified?'

'Oh, she could be identified all right. She had a little, blue-grey patch on her shoulder shaped like a cloud.'

'A birthmark?'

'Yes, I know, but Mick, we can't go around searching the bodies of fifteen-year-old girls.'

'No, I suppose not. Is Pearl still...'

'Working at Mullanurra? Yes. She had several miscarriages after that first baby. I thought she'd never carry another child full term. Then about five years ago, she had a little boy. She called him Jamarra.'

'And he's at the orphanage too?'

'Well no, he's still at Mullanurra with his mother.'

'How come?'

'I'm not sure. It's strange considering how smartly her first baby was disposed of. Jamarra was darker. Maybe that's why he survived inspection. Or maybe Harris likes having a boy around to torment Amelia. It's no secret he wants a son of his own. I've heard him taunt his wife with her failure to give Mullanurra a male heir. Pearl takes good care to keep the boy out of Amelia's way. Wisely too, if you ask me.'

Mick couldn't let go of a story. 'Do we know where Pearl came from?'

'I doubt she knows herself. She was only about nine when she arrived at St Cuthbert's, and she might have been moved many times before that. They do it on purpose, you know, move the poor little blighters as far from their families as possible. Australia's a big country and they don't always keep records of their movements.'

'Yeah, I've noticed.' It wasn't the first time Mick's journalistic nose had been frustrated by a dearth of documentation in Aboriginal affairs.

Four

Escaping the commotion of Spencer Street station, Sarah and Whilomena boarded their train. They found a compartment with only one occupant, a boy of about fourteen who appeared to be travelling alone.

When the nuns entered, he jumped to his feet. 'Good morning, Sisters.' He hoisted their cases into the overhead racks and remained standing while they seated themselves opposite each other in the window seats.

Sarah acknowledged his courtesy with a nod. 'Good morning. What is your name?'

'Billy, Sister.'

'Well, thank you, Billy.'

Billy seated himself at the other end of the compartment, pulled a *Batman* comic from his pocket and buried himself in it.

Sarah resigned herself to the long journey ahead. The train shunted off and soon Melbourne's suburbs gave way to the farmlands of the west. From time to time, the engine belched black smoke, clouding the windows and blurring the landscape. Whilomena had long ago opened her prayer book. Sarah attempted to follow her example but her eyes kept wandering to the window.

Ballarat was a welcome three degrees cooler than Melbourne. The train hissed to a standstill and Billy dashed off to the cafeteria.

He returned with a bottle of Coca-Cola and a steaming bundle of chips wrapped in newspaper. 'Chip, Sisters?' he offered.

'No, thank you, Billy.'

Sarah and Whilomena exchanged droll glances as the tantalising smell of salty chips filled the compartment. It was already several hours since breakfast.

Sarah's prayer book lay unread in her lap while the landscape claimed her attention again. Having sped express from Melbourne to Ballarat, the train now stopped at every tiny town. At Maryborough, an opulent railway station in the middle of nowhere mystified travellers. Then Dunolly, St Arnaud, and the flatter, drier landscape of Donald, Birchip and Woomelang, towns Sarah knew only by name, and some she had never heard of.

As they moved into the vast north-west, massive wheat silos loomed against the skyline witnessing the mainstay of the Mallee. Below them, sheep grazed on wheat stubble in the wake of the harvest, their wool tinged with red dust.

Sarah closed her book and gave herself up to the distractions beyond her window. The white trunks of eucalypts soared into vast blue skies. They dangled waxy leaves that glistened, reflecting the sun. Parrots flittered through their branches, and on the ground cockatoos competed with sheep for the leavings of the harvest.

Since leaving Ballarat, the heat had gradually increased and their compartment was now quite stuffy. Sarah used her prayer book as an ineffectual fan. Her habit was uncomfortably warm in this climate, and the starch surrounding her face had a nasty way of becoming limp and sticky and moulding to her jaw. Glancing to make sure that Billy was still absorbed in the adventures of Batman, she eased a finger between her chin and her coif. Aided by the prayer book fan, a faint scrap of air reached her invisible throat. She stretched her back, easing stiff shoulders. In the opposite window seat, Whilomena sat tall and still, her eyes on her prayer book. Her body was motionless, except when a finger turned a page. Sarah sighed. How disciplined Whilomena was.

Billy jumped up and stepped between the skirts of the nuns. 'I'll get you some nice fresh air, Sisters,' he promised, tugging at the window.

Sarah realised too late what he intended. 'Oh, no Billy, don't.'

They choked and spluttered as smelly black smoke filled the compartment.

Red-faced, Billy slammed the window down again. 'Sorry, Sisters,' he apologised as both of the spluttering nuns now enlisted their prayer books as fans.

It was past five o'clock by the time they reached their destination. They had left Melbourne at ten minutes to eight that morning. Sarah steadied herself for the jolt as the train braked.

As it shuddered to a stop, Billy leapt to his feet and offered his services again. 'Luggage, Sisters?'

'Thank you, Billy.' Sarah nodded to where he had stowed her suitcase beside Whilomena's.

He appeared to have no luggage of his own. With his comic stuffed in his hip pocket and a suitcase in each hand, Billy led the way to the rear of the train. Depositing the cases side by side on the platform, he offered his hand to Sarah and Whilomena in turn as they stepped down from the train.

Cobbs Crossing merited a railway station only because it was on the line between Mildura, queen city of the north-west, and Melbourne, the state capital in the south. Six sets of train lines and two towering wheat silos at one end of the platform suggested that the station's expansion had more to do with the Mallee's movement of produce to the south than with a constant flood of passengers. A weatherboard waiting room, restrooms and a ticket office squatted on a long platform. A steep cement ramp led down past large water tanks to an unsealed car park, where peppercorn trees spread their branches like weeping umbrellas. A dusty billboard with a tall glass of foaming beer at either end of the lettering advertised the Railway Hotel. Sarah glanced about for another religious habit but their self-appointed escort had already spied two nuns waiting by a van in the car park.

'This way, Sisters.' Billy was off. He had their luggage in the van before Sarah and Whilomena had introduced themselves to the sisters from St Cuthbert's.

When Sarah turned to thank him he was gone. As the train pulled away, she spied him back on board, leaning dangerously from an open window, smiling and waving his comic at them.

Sister Matthew introduced herself and Sister Leo. She gave the novices an encouraging smile as she seated herself behind the wheel. 'St Cuthbert's is twenty miles from town, Sisters. We'll be there by six o'clock, in time for dinner.'

The van lurched off at a pace which showed little respect for its fragile condition or, Sarah suspected, for the speed limit. They headed away from town onto an unsealed road that followed a wide arc into the north-west. The little van appeared to know its way around potholes fairly well. The speed did not decrease despite the bumpy ride.

Sister Leo intoned the opening lines of Vespers. After more than nine hours of train travel, Sarah welcomed the soothing cantata. The psalms allowed her to lose herself in the landscape with no need to concentrate on conversation.

Through trees that lined the road, she could see more sheep in summer dried paddocks. Now and again, there was a dam almost dry, its low water ringed by the red earth of the Mallee. Hills stretched along the horizon. At one point, the paddocks on their left were broken by an avenue of cypress trees. They stretched to where chimney tops were visible a mile from the road. Sarah thought they had reached the end of their journey but the van hurtled on, skimming the tops of the corrugations. As they passed the cypresses, bluestone pillars and iron gates proclaimed Mullanurra.

Sarah stretched her aching limbs as best she could. Vespers ended. Still they hurtled along, red dust streaming behind the van like the tail of a fiery comet. Polite attempts at conversation floundered. St Magdalene's seemed a world away. Sarah closed her eyes. When the van turned off the road, reduced speed and the crunch of gravel under their wheels alerted her to their arrival.

St Cuthbert's was situated at the top of a slope so gradual that its considerable height was at first hardly noticed. Sarah had Spartan expectations of a convent almost in the wilderness. As they drew nearer, she gaped at a grand, two-storeyed, bluestone structure, its verandas and balconies trimmed with iron lace. On either side of its imposing façade, conifers planted long ago cast long shadows over the disappearing summer afternoon. A little to the south and almost hidden by a forest of eucalypts was a modest weatherboard church. It stood like a poor relation forced to attend a grand function and trying to hide shabby attire from the host. The convent and the church both faced east, so that their altars greeted the rising sun.

The van stopped at the top of the driveway in front of broad, bluestone steps. Sister Leo helped Sarah and Whilomena unload their luggage. As Sister Matthew and the van disappeared around the building, Sarah rotated on the spot, suitcase in hand, admiring another unexpected surprise. On their left, a path of white quartz neatly raked and weed-free, extended from the convent to the forlorn little church. On their right, it wound out of sight behind the main building. A third fork wandered off into the trees. Every path was bordered by a blaze of red geraniums. The flowers nodded above neatly trimmed mounds of green foliage. The massed tricolour was dramatic.

Sarah remembered helping her father weed rose beds. 'Someone here is a great gardener, Sister. This is beautiful. It must take a lot of work.'

Sister Leo didn't turn her head towards the romping parade of flowers. She spoke over her shoulder as she headed up the convent steps. 'Yes, indeed, a lot of work, Sister. We should keep moving. Mother Sebastian will be waiting.' She led them under a bluestone arch and across a mosaic tiled veranda.

Through cedar doors with stained-glass surrounds, they passed into a foyer framed by a second arch. It opened into a long, wide hall. As she and Whilomena followed their guide, Sarah stared at her surroundings. Cream walls above a mahogany dado were topped by gold trimmed cornices. The vast floor space was polished oak. A crimson carpet led them through the hall and disappeared up a broad staircase.

As they started to climb the stairs, Sarah stared up at a life-sized painting of the order's foundress. Saint Frances Cabrini looked down on them from the landing.

Sarah blessed herself in the sign of the cross. 'Please help me to be a good nun, Saint Frances, and to accept hardship cheerfully'. Despite her heroic resolution, by the time they reached the first floor, a travel-weary Sarah was hoping she would not have to carry her suitcase much further.

At the top of the stairs, Sister Leo indicated a short, well-lit passage to their right. 'That is the way to the chapel, Sisters. You'll find it easily from the top of these stairs.' She led them into a gloomier passage running through the north wing.

They passed a series of small closed doors.

Sister Leo pointed out bathrooms at either end of the passage before showing each of the exhausted novices to one of the prepared bedrooms. 'I will wait at the top of the stairs for you, Sisters.'

Left alone for the first time that day, Sarah dumped her suitcase with relief. It seemed to have doubled its weight since that morning. Her room was a replica of the one she had occupied at the Mother House – white walls and an uncovered floor, a single bed, a wooden chair and a small wardrobe. On the wall facing the bed, a crucifix hung high on the plaster wall. A tiny window overlooked an enclosed quadrangle. Across the quad she could see another row of small windows. Without unpacking, she made a speedy visit to the bathrooms, glad to rinse away the dust of travel. When she returned to the top of the stairs, Whilomena was already waiting.

Sister Leo conducted her charges to the opposite side of the landing and into a long community sitting room. A row of French windows stood open onto the balcony, their curtains motionless in the heavy summer evening air. Three more nuns sat around in armchairs.

Sister Leo introduced the newcomers. 'Mother Sebastian, here are Sister Anthony and Sister Whilomena.'

Sarah smothered a gasp of surprise as the Superior rose to greet them. Mother Sebastian was an Amazonian woman, her extraordinary height accentuated by a slender frame. Her black habit did nothing to relieve the severity of her appearance.

She stared down on the new members of her community. 'Welcome to St. Cuthbert's, Sisters.' There was no enthusiasm in the greeting.

Sarah was determined to start well. 'Thank you, Mother. What we have seen so far looks wonderful…this beautiful building…and all those lovely flowers.'

Whilomena was content to let Sarah speak for them both.

'Ah, yes. We are very proud of our geranium paths, Sister.'

Sister Matthew had joined them again. At the mention of the geranium paths, Sarah noticed glances exchanged between her and Sister Leo.

Mother Sebastian took over the introductions in the same bored tone. 'This is Sister Innocent.' She nodded towards an elderly nun in black-rimmed glasses with very thick lenses.

Sister Innocent nodded and smiled at them and turned back to her needlework, which she held almost at the tip of her nose.

Mother Sebastian indicated the last nun in the room. 'This is Sister Augusta.'

Sister Augusta leaned back in her chair and examined the novices without finding anything to her liking. 'Teachers, are you?' she demanded, as if they were deaf.

'We will be, Sister. We have not yet completed our –'

'Humph! You'll be more work than help, then.' She returned to the book in her lap, shaking her head in disgust.

Mother Sebastian started towards the door. 'Come, Sisters. Sister Monica has kept dinner for us.'

She swept out of the room at such a speed that Sarah wondered if hunger explained her curtness. She and Whilomena stood aside while the other nuns followed their Superior. The novices then joined the procession down the staircase, through the great hall and into the nuns' dining room.

Twelve high-backed chairs lined a long table. There was a sideboard at the bottom of the room and a crucifix above the head of the table. The cook, Sister Monica, joined them. She was a cheerful soul, not at all put out at having had to keep dinner waiting. They took their places at table in order of rank, standing behind their chairs. Minutes passed, until Sarah realised what they were all waiting for, and what was required of her, now being the junior of this little community.

'Please, Mother, a blessing,' she invited in an unsteady voice.

'May the food we are about to eat give us strength of body, mind and spirit, to the greater glory of God.' Mother Sebastian did not sound as if her humour had been improved by the extra wait.

As soon as chairs were drawn back and the nuns seated themselves, the food began to appear.

Sarah had expected that the nuns would take turns to wait on each other at table, as they had at St Magdalene's. She was surprised when two girls of about fifteen began carrying food and teapots to the table. They were identically dressed in shapeless, brown shifts and white aprons. White headscarves hid almost all of their hair. They did not speak to the nuns or to each other as they placed plates on the table and poured cups of tea. They moved softly around the room, disappearing every now and then and reappearing with more food and teapots or trays to collect empty dishes.

The end of the meal was signalled by the tinkle of Mother Sebastian's bell. Pairs of black habits bobbed their way back upstairs for night prayers, the white veils of Sarah and Whilomena contrasting in the rear.

The novices blinked as the chapel doors opened onto a gallery that stretched a good half of the north wing. Sarah was too tired to take in much detail, but the thought occurred that surely all of this was never designed for just six or eight nuns. As they chanted the evening prayer, she gave herself up to the hypnotic rise and fall of their unaccompanied voices.

Devotions ended, they bowed to the altar in a deep genuflection, touching one knee to the floor and bending heads and shoulders low. They filed out of chapel and moved down dark corridors, where each one disappeared behind her own door.

Five

At five o'clock the next morning, the convent bell ordered the sisters of St Cuthbert's out of their beds. In dressing gowns and short night veils, Sarah and her sisters moved to and from the bathrooms, silent shadows passing each other with downcast eyes.

In fifteen minutes, they were in chapel for Matins and Lauds, private prayer and meditation. When the Superior signalled the end of devotions with two sharp knocks, they filed downstairs, through the great hall and outside onto the geranium paths. Here the air was alive with the tang of eucalyptus. The only sound in the still morning was the crunch of sixteen feet on the gravelled path, as the procession headed towards the little church next door. Sarah's spirits soared as they were greeted by a joyful chorus of chortling magpies heralding the sunrise.

In the light of morning, she could see that the third branch of the flower-trimmed path stretched thirty or forty yards north, to spread under clumps of stringybarks and weeping peppercorn trees, creating a car park for visitors. Every inch of it was raked, weed-free and lined on both sides with the same vibrant red geraniums.

On the steps of the church, Sister Matthew waited to whisper to Sarah and Whilomena. 'Mother Sebastian would like to see you both after breakfast.'

They nodded in acknowledgement and followed the other nuns inside.

Sarah ran her rosary through nervous fingers. Summoned by the Superior already? Surely she had not had time to transgress.

The interior of the little church was painted a blistering white. Windows well above head height admitted light but allowed no distractions.

The altar was white. The pulpit and lectern were both white. On the sanctuary, only the geraniums protested the relentless white, splashing their startling red from large brass vases.

Sarah knelt with the other nuns on unpadded kneelers at the back of the church and blessed herself. Soon the sounds of shuffling feet and subdued voices announced the arrival of the orphanage children. She turned toward the aisle as her future charges filed into the church. Her glance became a stare as a sea of brown and black faces filled the pews. Here and there, a face as pale as her own stood out against the darker ones. Among them, Sarah recognised the two girls who had waited on the nuns at table the night before.

The children squashed against each other until the pews were bursting and settled into their seats, awaiting the arrival of the priest. Sarah smiled as small hands covering faces in an attitude of prayer spread fingers through which big eyes could peek.

After breakfast, Sarah and Whilomena hurried through the great hall to Mother Sebastian's study. They made their way past comfortably furnished parlours whose doors stood invitingly open. When they reached the Superior's door, it was closed. Sarah tapped twice.

'Come.' Mother Sebastian's curt command penetrated the heavy door.

The Superior was seated behind a businesslike desk. On the wall behind her, her martyred namesake, Saint Sebastian, was portrayed tied to a tree, his naked body pierced by arrows.

Sarah and Whilomena knelt on the floor, their beads clattering on the boards.

Mother Sebastian waved them onto chairs and addressed them without preamble. 'I understand that you have not completed your training, Sisters, but we are short-staffed, so I will have to put both of you into a classroom immediately. You will be monitored by the teachers but you will have to manage on your own much of the time. You will also take turns on yard duty, dormitory monitoring, and share portress duties between you.' She clutched a large, white handkerchief in one hand as if expecting to be seized by a fit of sneezing at any moment. She waved it about as she spoke. 'You have seen your charges this morning at Mass. Boys are only with us until they are seven. After that, they go to one of the farm schools run by the brothers. Girls stay on until we find placements for them. By that time, they should have acquired good domestic skills which will make them useful to society and give them a place in the community. The schooling of Aboriginal children is difficult, Sisters. They are not well suited to academic learning. Our task is to make them into good Christians and capable workers. One of the most important rules is that English is the only language spoken.'

Sarah frowned. 'Do they all know how to speak English, Mother?'

Whilomena, sitting stiffly on the edge of her chair, stared at the floor and held her breath.

'They can learn, Sister.' Mother Sebastian directed a raptorish glare at Sarah. 'We cannot prepare them for civilised society if they do not. English is the language of their future. Without it, they can never be employed. Surely you can comprehend that.'

Sarah nodded. Yes, that made sense. Severe perhaps, but it made sense.

'Also, there is to be no dancing or singing other than the hymns we teach, and they are never, never to have contact with full-bloods. Our job is hard enough without being undone by the outlandish stories they tell the children. It is important to keep the upper hand, as you will discover if you make the mistake of leniency. The children know the rules and expect to be punished if they disobey them.'

Sarah thought that the rules were harsh. As soon as the principal paused, she asked, 'What happened to all their parents, Mother?'

Mother Sebastian regarded her outspoken novice for a moment before replying. 'Not all of their parents are dead, Sister, but they are without exception unable to look after their children. They live in appalling conditions. You'll see for yourself before long.' She continued in a more persuasive tone. 'Many Aboriginal parents simply don't want their children. They are happy for us to take them off their hands, and the children are far better off with us. It's for their own good.'

Sarah nodded again. 'I see. And the white children, Mother?'

'Good heavens, Sister, there are no white children at St Cuthbert's! The children you saw were light-skinned Aborigines, mixed-race children of unfortunate alliances. They fall into various classifications – half-castes, quadroons or octoroons, depending on the mix of their parentage, but they can never be classified as "white", no matter how pale their skin may be.' Mother Sebastian delivered the information with unflinching detachment.

She seemed to remember her handkerchief again and sniffed into it, then sighed. 'Sisters, I have a chronic condition. No child is ever to be admitted into my presence if he or she has a cold or, indeed, any illness. I have a delicate constitution and if I catch a cold, bronchitis or even pneumonia is sure to follow.'

Sarah wasn't sure if that was likely but she replied a respectful, 'Yes, of course, Mother.'

Whilomena bowed a silent acquiescence.

Mother Sebastian stood up. Her intimidating height was still a little unnerving to the novices, but for the first time since their arrival, she managed a small smile. 'Given your long journey yesterday, I have not assigned you any classroom duties today, only some playground supervision. This being Friday, that will give you three days to rest, and more importantly, get to know St Cuthbert's. We don't want you getting lost.'

Sarah glanced up, a quick smile on her lips, but saw nothing to suggest that the Superior was joking.

A distant bell sounded.

Mother Sebastian waved a dismissive handkerchief. 'There is morning recess, Sisters. A chance for you to find out what you're in for.' They were almost out of the door when she called after them. 'One more thing, Sisters. Frugality is a virtue anywhere, but an essential practice at St Cuthbert's. There is never enough money to do all that's expected of us. I rely on your support in avoiding waste and husbanding our meagre resources. That is all. You may go.'

The novices had no difficulty finding the playground. The shrieks and laughter of children at play guided them to the quad Sarah had seen from her bedroom.

As they moved about the playground together, Sarah smiled at the faces that surrounded her and whispered to Whilomena, 'I would have classified them as children.'

When the bell rang again and the children disappeared into their classrooms, Whilomena excused herself. Left alone, Sarah decided to follow Mother Sebastian's advice and take herself on an orientation tour. She turned about, looking at the three wings and the colonnade which enclosed the quad. The east wing she already knew. It housed the grand entry hall, Mother Sebastian's study, the parlours, the nuns' dining room and that great staircase. Behind the staircase, a passage ran the full length of the east wing, giving access to the other two wings. The north and south wings ended in the colonnade which joined them across their west face.

Young voices floating on the warm air drew her towards the north wing. She recognised the sing-song chant of a class being prepared to make their first confession.

'Through my fault, through my fault, through my most grievous fault,' the children chorused.

Sarah smiled and sighed in sympathy, thinking that Catholic children were probably the only seven-year-olds in the world who knew what grievous meant. Seven. Every child educated in a Catholic school made their first confession at seven, learning the chant that would become the mantra of their emotional lives. From then on, the process was repeated every month.

Sarah remembered kneeling in her parish church and shuffling closer to the end of the pew, as one by one her classmates disappeared into the darkness of the confessional box. While she had waited, trying not to think about the sick feeling in her stomach, she would be examining her conscience, searching for mortal and venial sins of which to accuse herself before the priest, then repeating her sins over and over, so that she would not leave anything out, because making a faulty confession was another sin.

To guard against such a misfortune, they would be prepared in the Grade Two classroom before being paraded into the church. Eyes closed and heads down on desks over folded arms, they were encouraged to memorise any thoughts, words or actions that needed confessing. They maintained this posture with a minimum of fidgeting, while Sister moved between the desks, listing all the wrongs of which they might be guilty, and pausing after each, to give them time to reflect. 'How long has it been since my last confession?' Pause. 'Did I make a bad confession at my last confession?' Pause. The heads resting on wooden pillows raked their consciences to see if there was a bad confession looming in their past. 'Have I missed Mass on Sundays or Holy Days?' Pause. 'Have I eaten meat on Fridays?' The sharp smell of varnished desktops assaulted their nostrils but the heads to which they were attached remained still. 'Have I broken my fast before Holy Communion? Have I disobeyed my parents or teachers? How many times? Have I told lies? If so, how many times? Have I cheated in games or schoolwork? Have I spoken disrespectfully to my parents or teachers or others placed over me? Have I entertained impure thoughts?' Sometimes a fly flew in through the open window, buzzed over their heads and flew out again but the heads would not move. 'Have I read any books against faith or morals? Have I taken anything that was not mine? Have I sinned against purity, alone or with others? Have I taken the Holy Name of Jesus in vain?'

On and on went the list, delivered in a soft monotone and always the pause for reflection at the end of each suggestion. Often they did not understand the sins held up for their scrutiny. For the scrupulous, this caused further fear. What does that mean? Did I do it? Will I make a bad confession if I don't accuse myself of that? Will I have a black soul? Will I go to hell forever?

A black soul. Shaken, Sarah froze and stared at the horizon. Teaching white children to abhor a black soul might well have further connotations than the avoidance of sin. And what did holding up blackness as the essence of evil do to children whose skin was black?

She frowned towards the classrooms. Could it be deliberate? She couldn't be the first one to have had such a thought. With a soft little laugh at herself, Sarah shook her head. She was imagining things. No. There was nothing deliberate or sinister in this use of language. It was just the way people – well, white people – spoke.

Leaving her quandary and the heat of the quad behind, Sarah entered the north wing, stepping into a long, much cooler corridor. The first Confession class had ceased their chanting, and in their place younger voices now piped a sing-song alphabet. In the first room, some of the older girls were sewing by hand or pedalling away on a couple of ancient sewing machines, unsupervised but absorbed in their work.

A door opened opposite and Sister Leo appeared, closing it behind her. Despite the hubbub from the classrooms, her voice was almost a whisper. 'I saw you crossing the courtyard, Sister. Are you finding your way about?'

'I'm just exploring, thank you, Sister. Are these your rooms?'

Sister Leo nodded, still whispering. 'Yes, the infirmary and day nursery. I keep my doors closed during classes.' She rolled her eyes towards the jumble of sounds from across the hall. 'I have fifty-five toddlers on my own while the seniors are in class…quite a handful. I'm hoping Mother Sebastian will assign one of you novices to me.'

'I'm free today, Sister. Would you like a hand now?'

Sister Leo gave Sarah a tired smile. 'That's very kind, Sister Anthony, but you enjoy your day off. We'll put you to work soon enough.' She slipped back behind the nursery door and closed it, leaving Sarah alone again.

In the next room, Sister Augusta was covering a blackboard with chalk, her back to a large number of students who certainly weren't responsible for any disturbance to Sister Leo's little ones. The children's heads were bent over exercise books and pencils were copying what was being written on the blackboard.

In the third room, elderly Sister Innocent was tapping an alphabet chart with a wooden ruler. Three taps on each letter. Three energetic shouts as her juniors sounded them out. 'A, a, a! B, b, b! C, c, c!'

31

Sarah smiled. Most of the children were paying attention.

In the last classroom, Sister Matthew's senior girls were engaged in some sort of debate.

Having come to the end of the corridor, Sarah followed the colonnade into the south wing. This was Sister Monica's province, an enormous kitchen and scullery, a huge pantry, cool room, and the students' refectory. The plump little cook's rosy complexion was not improved by the heat of her domain. The kitchen was not only the place in which meals were prepared but also one of the senior girls' classrooms. She was surrounded by her students, white aprons over shapeless orphanage dresses, sleeves rolled up above their elbows and hair hidden under white scarves. She smiled as Sarah peeped into the kitchen.

Sarah watched as Sister Monica set her charges to this task and that, then she offered to help. 'What would you like me to do, Sister? Perhaps I could peel those?' She indicated a pile of potatoes.

Sister Monica's eyes rounded in alarm. She plucked at Sarah's sleeve and pressed a floury finger to her lips. Stepping back into the huge pantry which ran the length of the kitchen, she beckoned Sarah to follow her. Safely insulated by the pantry's shelves, Sister Monica whispered in breathless staccato bursts. 'Never do any of the chores ourselves, Sister. Only teach. Supervise. Girls do everything. Learning to be domestics, hmmm? Learn by doing, Mother says. Teach the girls what employers expect. Mother says, help the girls remember their place, by remembering our place.' She nodded in confirmation of her little lecture and directed a closed-lipped smile at Sarah.

Sarah nodded.

The little cook looked ill at ease delivering these instructions. She called to one of the students. 'Lily, would you peel the potatoes today, please?'

A girl of about fifteen shuffled forward and began washing the mountain of potatoes. Lily was tall for her age, and slender, with a crop of glossy black curls. She was one of the students Sarah had mistaken for a white child. Her skin was the light, golden brown Sarah would have thought of as a good suntan, the colour pale-skinned girls envied. She had sapphire eyes, long lashes and well-defined black eyebrows. Sarah thought she might have taken Lily for Irish, if she had met her anywhere else.

'Lily is my best student. She helps Sister Leo in the infirmary too. You like to work with Sister Leo, don't you, Lily?'

'Yes, Sister.' Lily's eyes didn't leave the potatoes.

'Lily would like to be a nurse, I think, Sister Anthony.'

Sarah glanced back at Lily as they moved away. 'Any chance of that?' she whispered.

'No, oh no.' Sister Monica shook her head. 'It's a shame too. Sister Matthew is in charge of the senior girls. She works hard to help them get ahead. She says Lily is very bright.' The little cook shrugged and shook her head, turning away from Sarah. She managed one last breathless sentence. 'But that's not the problem, you know?'

Six

On Monday morning, Whilomena was dispatched to help Sister Leo in the nursery. Sarah was assigned to Sister Matthew's classroom, and to supervising the children at mealtimes. In the refectory, she watched boys and girls of all sizes pushing against each other's backs as they queued at the servery. Breakfast was a bowl of porridge, which the children carried to the tables. Wooden stools clattered against floorboards as they sat down. When they had scraped their bowls clean and started licking their spoons, Sarah asked Sister Monica if there was any toast. The little cook only fixed despairing eyes on Sarah and shook her head.

A girl of about eight raised her hand.

'Yes? What is your name, please?'

'Betty, Sister.' Betty had big eyes and coarse hair that stuck out like the fur on a frightened cat. She was a kind little girl but as often as not, her forays into helping landed her in trouble. Her greatest achievement was to get through the day without being punished for something.

'What did you want, Betty?'

'Can we go please, Sister? We have to do our jobs before school.'

'What job do you do, Betty? Don't pick your nose, dear.'

Betty's hands disappeared behind her back. She twisted her shoulders back and forth as she spoke. 'I work in the laundry, Sister.'

'Thank you, Betty.'

As Betty sat down, her stool crashed to the floor. Her hands flew to her mouth. 'Whoops!' She rolled her eyes and waited to hear her punishment.

'Tut, tut, Betty. Gently, dear gently.'

Betty blinked back at Sarah, her mouth open in disbelief.

'What other jobs do you do, children?' Sarah looked around for the only girl she had met. 'Lily, you help Sister Leo in the nursery, don't you?'

Lily stood when spoken to but there was sulky defiance on the face that met Sarah's. 'Yes, Sister. I feed the babies, make the little ones' beds and take their sheets to the laundry.'

Sarah hid a smile as Betty heaved a sigh.

'After that, I go to the convent and do the sweeping and dusting.'

Sarah stared at Lily. This young girl did all these jobs before nine o'clock, on one bowl of porridge. Seeing that the new sister seemed impressed, hands shot up everywhere. As a laughing Sarah nodded at this one and that, they came to their feet and introduced themselves.

'I'm Peter, Thithter. I feed the chookth an' get the eggth.'

'Thank you, Peter. How old are you?'

'I'm five, Thithter!'

'I'm Tommy, Sister. I pick up fruit in the orchard and bring in the wood for Sister Monica's fire. I'm seven.'

'I'm Helen, Sister. I'm twelve. I help Sister Monica in the kitchen until the bell goes.'

As child after child boasted of their responsibilities, Sarah remembered grizzling because she had to make her bed before she left for school. She dismissed the children and they trooped out, returning bowls and spoons to the servery as they went.

Seven

Sarah found Sister Matthew in Sister Innocent's empty classroom.

The assistant principal was a forty-year-old woman with a pleasant face and gentle eyes. She was laying out pencils and paper on rows of wooden desks. She looked up at the sound of Sarah's step. 'Good morning, Sister Anthony. I can't tell you how glad we are to have your help.'

Sarah took some paper and a handful of pencils and started on the other side of the room. 'I'm happy to be useful in any way I can, Sister.'

Sister Matthew grinned. 'Never fear, Sister. Those ways will be legion. So many children and so few of us.' She beamed at Sarah. 'It would be wonderful if you could help Sister Innocent with her little ones. She's not young, you know. If I didn't have to watch out for her, I would have more time for advanced work with the senior girls.'

Sarah raised her eyebrows. 'Advanced work? So you don't think —'

'That they're "not suited to academic learning"?'

Sarah laughed with delight at the way Sister Matthew pursed her lips and glared down her nose as she mimicked their Superior.

'No, Sister, I do not. In fact, some are quite bright. Take Lily, for example. Lily could be anything she wants to be, given the chance. It's a crime to be telling her she's only fit to serve others all her life.'

'So we can teach them more than the basics?'

'It's never easy, Sister. We need to be careful. But yes, together I'm sure we could manage a little extracurricular tutoring. What do you say?'

A breeze wafted through the open window.

Sarah smiled at her new ally. 'I'm sure we could, Sister. I'm sure we could.'

Sister Matthew attacked the blackboard with a duster, speaking over her shoulder. 'What do you think of St Cuthbert's, Sister?'

Sarah picked up another duster and started on the opposite end of the chalk-covered blackboard. 'I'm surprised it's so big, Sister. It's like a mansion, isn't it?'

'That's exactly what it was. It was built in the nineteenth century by a miner who made his fortune on the goldfields. The chapel used to be a ballroom and the bedrooms we use were the old servants' quarters. The family rooms are far too grand for people who've taken a vow of poverty.' She put down her duster and brushed chalk from her fingers. 'In the 1940s, the house was used by the army as a prisoner-of-war camp. That little church next door was added during the war for the prisoners. They built it themselves, I believe.'

'I thought it looked a bit odd beside all this.'

'Yes. The dormitories appeared about the same time for the same reason.'

'I haven't seen the dormitories yet.'

'They were also built by the prisoners. In fact,' Sister Matthew laughed and Sarah raised her eyebrows, 'when we first came here, the children were always running away and we couldn't work out how they were getting out. They were locked in at night but every now and then one of the little scamps would disappear. They never got far. The police soon returned them but they kept getting out. It was a great mystery until we discovered...' Sister Matthew broke off, shaking her head in amusement.

Sarah was laughing in anticipation. 'What? What were they doing?'

'The Italian prisoners had burrowed escape tunnels during the war, and our little rascals had found them.'

Sarah gasped. 'Are they still there?'

'Oh, no. We had them sealed off long ago.' Sister Matthew stopped laughing. 'At least, I hope there are no more. Mother Sebastian has a short fuse with runaways. She has threatened to be quite severe with the next child who runs away. I hope there are no more tunnels.' She gave herself a shake. 'After the war, the government gave the building to our order and it became St Cuthbert's Orphanage. We have almost two hundred acres, most of which feeds our neighbour's sheep.'

'Our neighbour? That's Mullanurra?'

'Yes. We have a small dairy and a vegetable garden. The Italian prisoners gave us a good start with that. There's also an orchard and a great many chickens. The children love the hens. I think they've named every last one.'

Sarah smiled, remembering how she and her siblings had made pets of the family's hens.

Sister Matthew continued. 'There used to be a stable, but long before we came it had been converted into a garage. I suppose that happened when the army was in residence. Have you found the library yet, Sister? You must see the library.'

The bell interrupted their conversation. Sister Matthew hurried into the quad and Sarah followed. Children jostled, spacing themselves at arm's-length from each other in a flurry of obedient activity. Sister Matthew waited for them to come to order. At her signal, a scratchy rendition of the Colonel Bogey march blared from a weathered loudspeaker. The children trooped into the classrooms knees high, arms swinging to the infectious military music.

With a nod to Sister Matthew, Sarah followed Sister Innocent into her classroom and stood beside her as her charges sorted themselves into desks. Through the open doorway, she watched Lily and Helen move past to Sister Matthew's room. When the children had found their places, Sister Innocent led them in making the sign of the cross for morning prayers. Sarah blessed herself with the children. When the prayers were done, Sister Innocent began unrolling the alphabet chart. The children were hushed, curious eyes watching the newcomer.

Remembering the sleeping babies across the corridor, Sarah leant down to whisper in the old nun's ear. 'Sister, I wonder if I could borrow the children. I would like them to show me the grounds. We could practise the alphabet in the orchard perhaps?'

A smile lit Sister Innocent's face. She nodded at Sarah. 'That would be so kind, Sister. I could supervise the sewing room.'

Since Sarah had observed that the girls in the sewing room were in little need of supervision, she thought that would be an ideal occupation for the old woman. Sister Innocent handed her the chart and disappeared.

Sarah turned to the children, who were still watching her in wide-eyed silence. 'Good morning, boys and girls.'

'Good mooooooorning, Sister and God bless you,' chanted the children.

Sarah smiled around at them. 'I heard a rooster crow this morning. Does anyone know where the chickens live?

Every hand in the room shot up to a chorus of 'Sister! Sister!'

Sarah put a finger to her lips and lowered her voice to a whisper. 'We would have to go out very quietly, so that we don't wake the babies across the corridor. Let's pretend we're mice. If we make any noise, the cat will catch us!'

The children shivered with delight.

'Now, mice, show me the chickens.'

They crept towards the door on their toes, grinning at each other and pressing fingers to their lips. Down the corridor past Sister Matthew's room tiptoed the mice, over the colonnade and on through the vegetable garden. They crossed a gravelled drive that disappeared into the stables-cum-garage. Through its open doors, Sarah could see the little van that had met her in Cobbs Crossing. Parked next to it was a stately white sedan, trimmed with shiny chrome. The van looked extra shabby beside it. The mice led Sarah through an orchard of apple trees, their neglected branches growing in unruly tangles. Beyond the orchard, a wire fence surrounded a shed with a rusty roof and a yard with a scorched-earth appearance. Hens scratched and clucked to their chicks. A rooster flapped his wings.

'Chooks, Thithter,' Peter announced proudly. He took charge, showing the way to where nesting boxes protruded through the wire.

Lifting the lid of one, he shooed a hen off the nest and stretched bare arms into the straw, emerging with a smile and a warm egg in each hand. He continued foraging and soon his arms were full.

Sarah was about to suggest a basket when Betty rushed forward. Holding out the skirt of her dress with one hand, she began transferring eggs from Peter's arms into her basket. An egg rolled out on each side of Betty's skirt, and both landed on her bare feet with a splattering of yellow yoke.

'Whoops!' Betty froze. Her lower lip trembled. She stared up at Sarah.

'It's all right, Betty. It was just an accident. We'll take the eggs. You go and wash your legs.'

As the other children rescued the remaining eggs and a relieved Betty scampered off to the bathrooms, Sarah looked to one of the bigger boys.

'Tommy, could you find me a spade in the garden shed?'

'Yes, Sister. What for?'

'We need to bury the broken eggs.'

The children stared at Sarah. 'Why, Sister?'

Sarah's grandfather had instructed her on the mischief of magpies when she was only Betty's age. 'If we leave them here, the magpies will start looking around for more eggs. And when they find the nests, no more eggs.'

'Ahhh,' whispered the children, as if Sister Anthony had imparted some secret wisdom.

Tommy returned with a spade and dispatched the broken eggs. Betty came back with clean legs and a basket.

Sarah pointed out a patch of juicy milk thistles growing on the edge of the orchard, telling the children, 'Chickens love thistles.'

In seconds, every thistle was hoisted over or pushed through the wire fence. The children were rewarded by a flurry of activity as the hens clucked and scratched and led their chicks to feast on the treat. The laughing girls and boys forgot to be mice.

Sarah led them back to the orchard and seated herself on a fallen log. Gathering the children around her on the grass, she heard their letters. One after the other they rattled the alphabet off without any difficulty. 'Very good. Now, can you count in twos?' They could. 'In fives? In tens?' They could.

Sarah raised her eyes over their heads to the dark bulk of St Cuthbert's. Where were the unteachable children she had heard about in Mother Sebastian's study? She read them the only fairy story she had found in the classroom and her mice giggled when the fairy godmother worked her magic on Cinderella's mice.

The school bell rang. Sarah dismissed her pupils and returned to supervise the midday meal. Lunch was soup made from vegetables grown by the children themselves. Mother Sebastian's budget did not allow meat for their meals. Sister Monica sometimes killed a chicken, but it disappeared with little effect in the huge cauldrons of her kitchen.

When the children's meal was over, Sarah and Sister Monica ate in the nun's dining room. Some senior girls were clearing the table vacated by the other nuns. They placed clean plates before Sarah and her companion and poured them each a cup of tea.

As soon as they were left alone, Sarah leaned across the table and whispered, 'All this being waited on, Sister. It's not how I expected to live as a nun.'

Sister Monica put down the fork she had just picked up and shot a furtive glance towards the door before answering. 'They learn by doing, you know, Sister.' Her rosy complexion deepened further. 'Mother says we have to let them wait on us. Good practice, you know? Only work they'll get. Domestics, hmmm?'

Sarah shook her head. 'But Sister Matthew doesn't believe –'

She got no further. Sister Monica had raised a finger to her lips and was shaking her head in alarm.

Eight

After lunch, Sarah hurried upstairs. The library, she hoped, might yield some books suitable for reading to the children.

Following Sister Matthew's directions, she found a long gallery of book-lined walls, the floor space scattered with inviting leather armchairs. The smell of furniture polish filled the air. Two senior girls hurried out, their arms full of cleaning cloths and dust mops. Only the most trusted girls and no boys were allowed above stairs. Sarah drifted along the rows of books, reading titles on the shelves. It appeared that they had been added to by every owner of the house. There were military volumes, which she supposed had belonged to army officers stationed here during the war, and volumes in German and Italian, perhaps left by prisoners-of-war.

'You look pleased with our library, Sister Anthony.'

Sarah almost dropped the book she was holding. Mother Sebastian had appeared between the open doors, her head almost touching the architrave.

'Oh, yes, Mother. It's beautiful.'

'It has been my pleasure to restore this building.' The Superior's eyes swept the gallery with a smile of satisfaction. She ran a finger along the nearest shelf, inspecting it for dust. 'I believe we have an extensive selection, Sister, but if you cannot find what you are looking for, let me know. If I approve your choice, I'm always happy to expand our collection.' She swept away along the landing.

Sarah watched her disappearing figure with a puzzled frown. She continued to peruse the shelves and was about to leave when she spied a familiar title almost at eye level. Smiling, she eased the book from the shelf. The bell clanged below, echoing through the building. Sarah hurried downstairs, the library book tucked under her arm.

Children were running into the quad from all directions. As Sarah arrived, Tommy came tearing across the colonnade, racing against the other boys. He looked back over his shoulder, laughing and collided with a thud into Mother Sebastian. He reversed a few quick steps and stiffened, his eyes fixed on her shoes.

Mother Sebastian gasped. 'Thomas Larkins!' The white handkerchief flew about in her hand as she brushed herself down. 'Thomas Larkins, you will –'

Tommy clapped both his hands over his face and produced an enormous sneeze. Mother Sebastian stepped backwards, the handkerchief covering her face. Tommy sneezed again louder than before.

The Superior spoke from behind her handkerchief. 'Get away from me, you dirty little urchin! Go, boy! Go!'

Tommy didn't need telling twice. He scampered off into the assembly lines, where the sneezing ceased.

Hiding her amusement, Sarah called Tommy out of line as the children filed past her. 'That's a very mysterious allergy you have there, Tommy. You weren't sneezing in class this morning.' She was greeted with a broad grin.

'No, Sister.'

'Do you think you had better see Sister Leo for some medicine?'

Tommy looked horrified. 'I'm better now, Sister. See? No more sneezing.'

'Are you sure?'

'Yes, Sister. All better.'

'Very well. Hurry along then.'

Tommy disappeared into the classroom, leaving Sarah chuckling to herself as she followed.

Sister Innocent arrived, struggling under a pile of books.

Sarah hurried forward. 'Let me take those, Sister.' She unburdened the frail arms. 'I would consider it a favour if you would tell me when there is anything you need moved about, Sister. It would make me feel useful.' She was rewarded with a tired smile. She set the books down on the old nun's desk, a variety of junior readers at different levels. 'Are the children reading this afternoon, Sister?'

'Yes, dear. I can't always hear them all. There are so many of them. But they know which book they are up to. Oh, Sister Anthony, perhaps you could hear some of them read?' Sister Innocent sounded as if it had just occurred to her that she had a new assistant.

The children shuffled around the desk, sifting through the readers. As each child found the book they were looking for, they went to their seats, tripping over a foot stuck out in the aisle or squawking as someone's hair was pulled. When everyone had been heard with time to spare, Sarah whispered to Sister Innocent, who once again made off for the sewing room.

Now every eye was on Sarah.

Lowering her voice, she stressed each word in a suspenseful whisper. 'Who likes stories?'

Every arm shot up.

Sarah smiled around the room at the excited faces. 'I found a book today. It's a book my mother read to me when I was little. It's called *The Little Black Princess*. Would you like to hear it?'

'Yes, Sister,' shouted the children.

Sarah's finger went to her lips. 'Can we be mice again?'

'Yes, Sister,' whispered the children.

Sarah stood on the platform and opened her book. The room was still enough to hear the children breathing. 'Bett-Bett must have been a Princess,' Sarah began, but she hadn't read far when she stifled a gasp and stared at the page. She didn't remember that word. Her mother must have skipped it, or substituted it. She forced a smile for the waiting children, every neck craning to see what the problem was. Sarah started again, eyes darting ahead along the lines, so that she would not be caught out. Jeannie Gunn's *Little Black Princess* was after all, it seemed, still a 'nigger'.

Sarah read on, censoring the offensive word. The ignorance of the 'Missus' and the adventures of Bett-Bett delighted the giggling children. These little ones, most of whom had never owned a pet, took for granted the love between Bett-Bett and Sue the dog.

'Aren't we clever? We know how to manage things, don't we?' Bett-Bett told Sue, and a sea of smiling faces nodded. The children cheered when Bett-Bett fought the station dogs off little Sue, and grinned when she gave away all the clothes the Missus had made for her. But not everything Bett-Bett believed could go unchallenged. No 'Debbil-debbil' would kill them for wearing a red dress, Sarah assured the children.

When Bett-Bett explained that she preferred to sleep on the floor instead of the 'Too much jump' of the Missus' spring mattress, Tommy had his hand up.

'What's a spring mattress, Sister?'

'It's a mattress with springs inside it, Tommy. The springs make it very bouncy.'

Another hand went up. 'Do you have a spring mattress, Sister?'

'Um, yes, Betty. I do.'

Five-year-old Peter thought spring mattresses sounded like fun. 'Can we bounth on your mattreth, Thithter?'

Sarah hid a smile. 'My mattress is in the convent, Peter. You aren't allowed in the convent, are you?'

Peter had a solution. He fixed hopeful eyes on Sarah. 'Can you bring it outthide for uth, Thithter?'

*

When Sarah entered the nuns' dining room for afternoon tea, only Sister Matthew was at the table. 'I hear you have mice in your classroom, Sister Anthony.'

Sarah grinned. 'Yes, me and Cinderella.' She poured herself a cup of tea and sat opposite Sister Matthew, helping herself to scones and jam. 'Speaking of Cinderella, I think she left her coach in the garage.'

'Oh, you mean the Falcon.' Sister Matthew glanced at the door and lowered her voice. 'A visiting bishop passed through once. The car he was driving looked almost presidential. Not long afterwards, Mother Sebastian decided that it was undignified for the Superior of St Cuthbert's to be seen behind the wheel of our little van. The Falcon uses ten times the petrol it takes to keep the van on the road. Meanwhile, the children live on soup without meat and windfall fruit.'

Sarah frowned. But then, for the second time that day, she accused herself of pride in having questioned the actions of her Superior, if only in thought. They finished their scones in silence.

At six o'clock, Sarah was waiting at the head of the tables again when the children trooped back into the dining room. Pancakes were common for dinner but not the plump pikelets Sarah's mother served, dripping with butter and smothered in golden syrup. These were pale concoctions of flour and water sometimes seasoned with whatever bits and pieces Sister Monica could spare. The children saw sweets only on Sundays, when jelly and custard with the evening meal was a treat that made mouths water. But there was never enough. Despite Sister Monica's best efforts, their tummies rumbled.

Nine

Mother Sebastian looked down her dining table and spotted one of her novices staring at her plate, her knife and fork untouched. 'Is anything wrong, Sister Anthony?'

'I'm sorry, Mother. I'm not hungry. May I be excused?'

'Are you ill?'

'No, Mother.'

'See me when we have finished.'

Sarah walked out through the darkness of the great hall. As she crossed the veranda into a warm autumn evening, she was greeted by the scents of pines and eucalypts, and a chorus of cicadas. She looked up at a sky ablaze with stars and, as she looked down again, her glance fell along the path towards the little church. Prayer should be our refuge. Prayer always helps.

The door was not locked. Sarah opened it and gave a gasp of pleasure. Empty and silent, the little church by night was enchanting. Moonlight filtered through the high windows. The sanctuary lamp cast a ruddy glow.

Sarah moved slowly up the aisle and knelt at the communion rail. She closed her eyes and blessed herself. 'Dear Heavenly Father, please help me to be a good nun. Forgive my pride and make me humble. Teach me to obey without question, even if I don't understand. You have placed my Superiors over me and it is not for me to question their actions. I give my life to You. Thy Will be done.'

When Sarah presented herself in Mother Sebastian's study, the Superior was standing in front of her desk, shaking a small clock and checking it against the chained pocket watch in her other hand. She looked up. 'Do you have the right time, Sister? My clock disagrees with my watch.'

Sarah produced a weighty silver watch and held it against Mother Sebastian's hand. The Superior's watch looked shabby beside the beautiful gift that Sarah's twin brother, Harry, had given her when she entered the convent.

Mother Sebastian's eyes glinted. 'That's a very fine watch, Sister Anthony. You must come from a wealthy family.'

Sarah's mouth opened and closed again. Was this a test to see if she would talk about her background, in defiance of the rules? She chose her words with care. 'Thank you, Mother. Yes, it is a beautiful watch. I'm lucky to have it.'

Mother Sebastian sniffed, adjusting her watch and returning it to her pocket. She sat behind her desk and waved Sarah into a chair. 'Now, Sister, this business of not eating...'

'It's the food, Mother.'

'What's wrong with the food?'

'Nothing is wrong with it, Mother.'

'You are not making much sense, Sister.'

'No, I know. I'm sorry, Mother. It's just that, well, we eat so plentifully, and the children...' Sarah's voice trailed off.

Mother Sebastian fingered her spectacles back up her nose. 'I'm sure Sister Monica does her best, Sister.'

'Oh yes, I'm sure she does, Mother. It's just that our meals are so much better. I feel guilty eating meat every day when –'

Mother Sebastian raised an impatient hand. 'It is necessary for us to eat well, Sister. We cannot afford to get sick.' She sniffed into her handkerchief. 'You know how hard we have to work, how difficult it is to teach these children.'

An eager smile lit Sarah's face. Her words tumbled out unchecked. 'Not all are difficult, Mother. In fact, some are very bright. Lily, for instance. Lily is quite smart. Some of the sisters believe she can do more than housework.'

Mother Sebastian scowled at her reckless novice. 'Lily Matthews is a freak, Sister. I've tried to convince Sister Matthew that encouraging her is a waste of time. She won't ever be accepted in any position that requires higher learning. Proficiency Certificate indeed!' Sarah opened her mouth, but before she could say another word, Mother Sebastian raised her hand again to stop her. 'Believe me, Sister, no good will come of educating Aboriginal children above their station. They will be better off if they are not encouraged to forget their place. And I expect to see you eating properly in future. You may go.'

As Sarah climbed the staircase on her way to chapel that evening, she conceded with a sigh that Mother Sebastian had a point. Was it not futile, cruel even, to encourage children to aspire to positions which society would never allow them to occupy?

She continued to supervise the children at their meals, unable to sound enthusiastic as she intoned the Grace. 'Bless us, oh Lord, and these Thy gifts which of Thy bounty we are about to receive, through Christ Our Lord.'

'Amen,' chorused the hungry children.

Ten

Mother Sebastian sat beneath the melancholy painting of her patron and allowed Sarah and Whilomena to kneel before her. 'Tomorrow is the first Sunday of the month, Sisters, Chapter Sunday.' She eyed Sarah much as a spider might regard a butterfly caught in its web. 'Sister Anthony, as the junior here, you will lead us. Please be prepared.' She smiled with smug satisfaction.

Sarah kept her eyes on the floor and steadied her lower lip. Chapter Sunday! She had thought that that humiliating practice had been left behind at the novitiate.

At two o'clock on Sunday afternoon, the children of St Cuthbert's were left in the care of the big girls, while the nuns closeted themselves in the convent chapel. Even the kitchen and infirmary were left in the care of trusted senior students, so that Sister Monica and Sister Leo also could attend Chapter.

Mother Sebastian's bell signalled the beginning of the exercise. Sarah rose from her knees with great care, but as she lowered the seat of her stall, it slipped from her nervous fingers and crashed like a sledgehammer, echoing through the chapel. Red-faced, she descended the two tiers of stalls and knelt alone in the vast open space of the chapel floor. Her heart thumped so hard it hurt. Mother Sebastian, Sister Matthew, Whilomena and all her sisters waited above her.

In a voice subdued but unflinching, Sarah forced out the words she had memorised. 'I accuse myself of rebellious thoughts against the Holy Rule; of arguing with my Superior, of tardiness in obeying the bell and of breaking silence by speaking before chapel. I beg of God our Father the strength to overcome all my faults and I ask my sisters to pray for me.'

Rising from the chapel floor demanded Herculean resolve. Sarah bowed to the tabernacle and walked on wooden legs towards the chapel doors. As she drew level with Mother Sebastian, she inclined head and shoulders in the direction of the Superior's chair. The bow was acknowledged with a condescending smile and Sarah continued towards the doors. Only a few more steps, but they seemed so far away. She left the chapel, closing the doors behind her and coaxed her cold legs down the staircase, her hand hovering above the bannister.

As she wandered outside, the warm afternoon revived her spirits. She walked between rows of weed-free flowers and waited for Whilomena to join her. The resentment that she felt told her that nothing about this ritual had helped her to conquer her pride. She was not feeling humble, only humiliated. She shrugged, deciding to dismiss the theatrics of Chapter Sunday as a pointless practice which she was unable to avoid. Then she sighed and made a mental note to accuse herself of rebellious thoughts again the following month.

Eleven

The welfare inspectors arrived in Cobbs Crossing on the fifteenth of March and accepted the standing invitation of Lachlan Harris to stay at Mullanurra.

Amelia Harris always enjoyed playing hostess, but on this occasion she greeted her visitors with barely concealed eagerness. Her long blonde hair was swept up into a French roll and lacquered into submission. A cocktail dress of pink taffeta emphasised her curves and made the most of the tan she spent hours achieving. As Harris poured drinks for his guests, one of the inspectors gave Amelia the chance she was waiting for.

'That was a wonderful meal. You are a splendid cook, Mrs Harris.'

'Oh, it wasn't me, Mr Chandler. Our Pearl is a real jewel in the kitchen.'

Harris raised his eyebrows and turned back to the sideboard with a puzzled grin, but he said nothing.

'Pearl? That's the one who served us tonight? She's your cook as well?'

'Yes, and Pearl has such a lovely little boy. Would you like to meet him?'

Harris's eyes narrowed, now aware of the game. His mouth tightened in a way that would have warned his wife if she had been paying attention. 'Jamarra will be in bed by now, Amelia,' he growled.

'Oh no, I don't think so. Not yet.' Amelia tinkled the bell beside her hand.

The young woman who had been waiting at table hurried into the room. She stood before Amelia, her arms at her sides, her fingers linked together in front of her apron.

'Pearl, our guests would like to meet Jamarra. Could you bring him in, please?'

Pearl turned a face of desperate appeal towards Harris, who quickly looked away.

'Jamarra's in bed, Missus Harris.'

'That doesn't matter, Pearl, just this once. Go and get him.'

Pearl started towards the door, still looking at Harris, who continued to avoid her eyes. Amelia became aware of the silence at her dinner table. She glanced at her husband and for the first time she saw the storm in his eyes. She tried to resurrect her party, chatting with her guests and checking their glasses. A wall clock ticked away the minutes.

'Where on earth has Pearl got to with that child?' Amelia was about to go in search of her cook, when the sound of footsteps running along the veranda reached the dining room.

'Someone's in a hurry, Mrs Harris.' Mrs Pierce, the only woman in the welfare group, had a talent for stating the obvious.

Harris leapt up. He strode out of the room and opened his front door in time to confront Pearl with a sleepy Jamarra in her arms.

'Don't be silly, Pearl. Where on earth could you go? Come back inside.'

Pearl shrank away from him, lurching backwards down the veranda steps. She held the child so tightly that he began to protest and wriggled to be free. Harris took a step towards her.

She backed down another step. 'They'll take him away, boss.'

'No, they won't, Pearl. I won't let them. Now come inside this instant.'

He reached out towards her and she backed down several more steps, keeping her eye on Harris. She missed her footing and disappeared into the darkness with a scream. Ignoring her hurts, she scrambled to where Jamarra had landed. He sat bawling indignantly.

She pulled her son to his feet and gave him a push. 'Run!'

Jamarra, now wide awake and alert to the urgency in his mother's voice, took off into the trees that surrounded the house. Pearl started after him but Harris had her by the wrist before she had moved more than a few feet.

'Now that was silly, Pearl. He's just a little boy. There's only one place he'll go. You get back inside this minute or I'll ring Sergeant Buchanan and you can spend a while in the lock-up.'

'Please, boss, please don't let them take my baby away.'

He released her arm. 'I won't, Pearl. Not if you behave and go inside this minute.'

He watched her drag herself back along the veranda, peering into the darkness as she went. He reached inside the front door and fished inside Amelia's umbrella stand for the torch he knew was kept there. Moving through the darkness on familiar ground, he made his way through the trees to the bottom of the home paddock. An old Chevy with its doors removed and its wheels sunk into the earth had long served as a comfy cubby house for the children of Mullanurra. It was Jamarra's favourite hideaway.

Harris shone the torch into the interior and startled eyes blinked back at him like a possum caught in the headlights of a car.

'It's all right, Jamarra. You can come back to your mother now.' He held out his hand and the child scrambled over and walked back to the house beside him.

In the dining room, Jamarra peered around for his mother. She was not there. The room was full of strangers, all of them staring at him. He was small for a five-year-old. He dug his toe into Amelia's Persian rug and twisted thin arms together in front of his body. His eyes darted from one face to the next with a nervous smile.

Mrs Pierce made a fuss of him. 'What a beautiful little boy. Those lovely long lashes! And I didn't know Aborigines could have such blue eyes.'

'Full bloods don't,' Amelia smirked.

The inspectors couldn't ignore what Amelia had put under their noses. In Mullanurra's library after dinner, they tackled their host about Jamarra.

The grazier frowned. 'There's no question of neglect while he lives on Mullanurra.'

'That's not the point, Harris. It's obvious that the child has white blood.' Mr Chandler's opinion was backed by murmurs from the group around him. 'These half-castes strengthen a race nature intended to disappear long ago, and that could be dangerous. Remember what happened in the Congo.'

Mrs Pierce shivered.

Harris grinned at his guest. 'You think Jamarra's about to stage a bloody uprising, is that it, Chandler?' He refilled the inspector's glass.

'Thank you. No, of course not, but hell, Harris –' Chandler remembered there was a lady present. 'I'm sorry, Mrs Pierce, but Harris, you know what I mean.'

Harris bristled. 'I won't have it, Chandler. No one living on Mullanurra can be charged with neglect.'

'No, of course not, Harris. I'm sorry. I didn't mean to cast aspersions.' Chandler retreated into his glass.

The other delegates allowed Harris to replenish their supply of Mullanurra's good wine. In the comfort of their host's library, Jamarra was forgotten. Amelia abandoned her listening post outside the library door and appeared full of smiles to show her guests to their rooms. She startled Chandler by closing the door of the room she showed him into. He relaxed as her purpose became clear in a whispered confidence.

'Mr Chandler, I share your concern about the boy, Jamarra. He should be with the sisters, of course. But I also understand my husband's wish that no scandal should attach to Mullanurra. What if his mother didn't work here any more? Didn't have a job at all?'

Chandler smiled his compliance. 'You're right, Mrs Harris. The child should be with the nuns. And after what we saw here tonight, we know his mother is not going to give her consent. But unemployed, she and the boy would end up in that shanty camp on the river. Then we could send the police down there to charge the boy with neglect, without any reflection on Mullanurra.'

Twelve

On the seventeenth of March, St Cuthbert's issued every child with a silver medal of the Virgin Mary in honour of the feast of St Patrick. Outside the little church, Sarah stood with dozens of medallions suspended from her arm on bright green ribbons. She and Sister Matthew placed one over the head of each child as they filed in for mass.

The festive ribbons made a pretty display against fresh white dresses and spotless shirts. Today, every child had shoes and socks and the girls had ribbons in their hair. The welfare inspectors stood beside the nuns and beamed on the immaculate children.

Mrs Pierce took a handful of ribbons and helped the nuns distribute the medals. 'The children look as if they've been polished, Sisters. How do you keep those white dresses and shirts so spotless?'

Sarah and Sister Matthew exchanged uncomfortable glances. Dresses, shirts, shoes and socks had been taken out of storage and distributed in the early hours of the morning. Nuns and older girls had been kept busy straightening neckties and tying shoelaces, wardrobe accessories the children only saw at inspection time.

Under cover of Mrs Pierce's preoccupation with the children, Sarah whispered to Sister Matthew, 'Wouldn't it be better to let Welfare see that we can't afford to dress the children properly?'

'Mother Sebastian wouldn't dare risk it.'

'They wouldn't close us down?'

'It would have the same effect if they withdrew funding.'

'Funding? You mean the government pays –'

'A per capita sum for the support of each child. We wouldn't survive without it.'

Thirteen

St Mary's Parish in Cobbs Crossing had acquired an enthusiastic young curate happy to include St Cuthbert's in his flock. This morning, Father Conway embarked on a dramatic rendition of St Patrick's voyages, designed to captivate his young audience. Despite his enthusiasm, young bodies fidgeted and impatient legs swung under wooden pews. The children of St Cuthbert's welcomed welfare inspections like other children looked forward to Christmas. They knew the inspectors would be joining them for meals. They knew they would eat well all day. No need to search the orchard for fallen fruit or risk Mother Sebastian's wrath scavenging scraps from the kitchen.

After Mass, the older girls helped Sister Monica and Sarah prepare breakfast. Tommy arrived from the orchard with a basket brimming with crisp apples.

Lily called out to Sarah, 'Look, Sister Anthony, the boys have picked good fruit today, straight off the trees, not the fallen stuff. They've got no bruises or grubs or anything. After breakfast, we're going to help Sister Monica make apple pies for the picnic.'

Sarah smiled. It was good to see Lily excited about something. The children chattered to Sarah and to each other as they laid the tables for their once-a-year real breakfast.

'Look, Sister, sugar for the porridge.'

'I'm not having porridge. We can have corn flakes if we want. Sister said.'

'And toast with marmalade. Yum!'

'Yes and there will be milk on every table.'

Twelve-year-old Helen had arrived with a tray. She placed it on the first table and picked up a jug of milk in each hand. Swinging around in excited haste, she bumped into Sarah, splashing milk all over the skirt of her habit. Lily ran to the kitchen for a mop. Helen froze, both milk jugs still in her hands and horror on her face.

Recovering from the shock of an unexpected milk bath, Sarah looked up and saw the child's distress. 'Never mind, Helen. It was just an accident. You know what they say, it's no use crying over spilled milk,' she smiled. 'Still, I'd better go to the laundry and sponge this off straight away.'

Helen dumped the jugs on the nearest table and raced after Sarah. 'I'll come with you, Sister Anthony. I'll help.'

Sarah was about to say it wasn't necessary when she thought better of it. For Helen, it was necessary. They crossed the colonnade to the laundry, Helen apologising all the way and Sarah trying to reassure her.

The laundry was a rectangular building with openings at both ends in place of doors. It had cement walls and a cement floor, half of which was covered in water. Along one side, deep troughs, also cement, were too high for most of the girls leaning into them. Betty was there, perched on a wooden crate, up to her elbows in soapsuds. Sarah watched the little laundress with a sad smile as the child pulled clean items out of the soapy trough, struggled to wring them out and dump them into the rinse water. Betty's hair was hanging limp around her face. With every item she transferred to the rinse, she managed to add more soapy water to the front of her dress.

Along the opposite wall, a clothesline stretched the length of the laundry. Two of the older girls were there, pegging out panties. On the last two lines, hidden behind the underwear, Sarah stared at squares of cotton cloth with brown stains that left no doubt what they were used for.

She looked through the laundry opening at a perfect sunny day. 'Girls, why on earth don't you hang everything outside? It's much better, more hygienic, to dry your clothes in sunshine and fresh air.'

Helen was busy dabbing away at Sarah's habit with a clean cloth and cold water. 'Oh no, Sister. Not these things. The boys might see.'

Sarah almost laughed. None of the boys were more than seven years old. 'Won't they see them anyway, when they come in here?'

'Boys aren't allowed in the laundry, Sister.'

Sarah shook her head. Madness. 'So, all of you girls use these cloths, and they're never aired outside?'

Helen nodded, embarrassed. She looked as if she thought she had done something wrong again but this time she didn't know what. 'No, Sister.'

Sarah looked down at her damp habit. 'That's lovely. Thank you, Helen. You've done a great job.'

Helen beamed. 'Sunshine now, Sister – sunshine and fresh air!'

Sarah laughed.

Fourteen

During the morning, the welfare team inspected the classrooms. Sarah was alone with the children when they arrived, Sister Innocent now having made it her regular habit to supervise the sewing room. Sarah was conducting four spelling bees at once. Rows of spotless children in white clothes and green ribbons were applying their pencils to paper as she walked between them, calling out different words for each group to write down.

Mother Sebastian appeared in the doorway. She had to lower her head as she entered the room. She was followed by a woman and three men, none of whom were taller than she was. The children sprang to their feet unprompted.

'Good morning, Mother, and God bless you,' they chorused.

Mother Sebastian favoured them with a smile and they wondered how they had managed to deserve it. 'Good morning, boys and girls. You may sit down.'

Sarah nodded across the room at her visitors. 'Thank you for your help this morning, Mrs Pierce. Would you or the gentlemen like to talk with the children?'

A horrified expression swept the smile from Mother Sebastian's face. She coughed, replaced the smile and found her voice. 'I fear we have interrupted your lesson, Sister Anthony. You must excuse us.' She swept out of the room with the inspectors scrambling to keep up, the gentlemen tipping their hats to Sarah as they rushed after their guide.

Fifteen

Outings at St Cuthbert's were as rare as snow at Christmas, but by late morning everyone knew about the picnic. The children were buzzing like bees. They assembled bareheaded in the heat of the quad, waiting for the walk to Mullanurra.

Mother Sebastian arrived, intent on a last-minute review of faces and fingernails. As she walked between the rows, children surrendered their hands. She stopped in front of Peter. He produced his hands and held his breath. He did not breathe again until she had passed down the line.

'Lily, is that you talking back there?' Mother Sebastian shrilled across the ranks of chattering children.

Sarah stared around the quad. The excited youngsters were all babbling away.

Mother Sebastian did not need a reply. 'Get your apron and go to the kitchen, Lily. Sister Monica will find work for you to do while we are away.'

The hubbub in the quad ceased as if someone had thrown a switch. Lily stalked away, her head held high and her chin jutting out, her blue eyes blinking back tears she refused to let fall.

*

The homestead at Mullanurra was an oasis of green, a haven from the dust and heat. An avenue of cypress trees wound in from the road, providing shade so dense that it was comfortable beneath them, even on the hottest day. They opened upon a park-like expanse of mown grass, garden beds, shrubs and smaller trees. A two-storey house of red brick was separated from the park by a low picket fence. At least five chimneys were visible, raising their terracotta tops from the slated roof.

The children sat in groups on the dry grass. They feasted on home-made lemonade, sandwiches, cold chicken, sausage rolls and lamingtons provided from Mullanurra's kitchen, and the apple pies baked by Lily and the senior girls at St Cuthbert's.

Amelia Harris invited the nuns onto the broad veranda that encircled the house. Her smart cream culottes and silk blouse were highly visible among the black habits, ensuring that their hostess would be the centre of attention.

The welfare inspectors were already seated in comfortable chairs, surrounded by food and drink. The gentlemen rose as the sisters climbed the veranda steps. Harris offered his hand to each of the nuns as Mother Sebastian introduced them. He was taller than everyone except Mother herself and in his open-necked shirt, moleskin pants and riding boots, he looked the magazine image of a country squire. As Sarah took the hand he extended, she looked up into a handsome face and charming smile.

Cynthia Harris, the fifteen-year-old daughter of Mullanurra, appeared from time to time. She smirked at orphanage girls her own age in frocks that were years out of date and paraded like a model on a cat-walk, in a mint- green mini and knee-high boots of white patent leather.

During the day, the sisters took turns to leave the comfortable shade of the veranda and walk in twos among the children, who were eating or playing across the grassy spaces.

In the early afternoon, a ute inched its way up Mullanurra's drive, the driver alert to the large number of children darting between the trees. Harris excused himself and left the veranda to greet his visitor. Mick hoisted the strap of a camera case over his shoulder and waved a notebook at his host. Bronko romped away after the children, revelling in pats from eager hands.

Harris extended his hand to the journalist. 'How are things on the farm, O'Mara? Slow, I guess, like the rest of us, but I suppose Frank doesn't have the staff problems we have at Mullanurra.'

Mick was wise to the Lachlan Harris lord-of-the-manor persona. He refused to be baited. 'Staff giving you problems, are they, Locky? Gee whiz! Aren't you paying them enough, mate?'

Harris ignored the mockery and continued his baiting. 'When are we going to lose you to the big smoke, Mick? I thought you'd have shaken the Mallee dust off long ago, got yourself a desk in Melbourne by this time, old son.'

Mick's writing talent had been discovered while he was still in high school. Old Tom Guthrie had kept the *Chronicle* alive for decades, working out of a shopfront on Memorial Square. Looking to his retirement, Tom had sponsored a series of story writing competitions for local students. Young Mick had been a consistent winner, and as a result Tom had offered the boy an apprenticeship with the *Chronicle*. Mick had accepted, eager to learn all that the old man could teach him. He had even endured being the only boy in the school to take shorthand. Tom encouraged and tutored him until one day he handed the whole office over to his protégé. Mick had taken the reins, dreaming of the big story that would be his ticket to Melbourne or Sydney. Cobbs Crossing, it turned out, was short on dramas of national interest and Mick's brother, Pat, was still a few years shy of being old enough to take on the family farm. Their widowed father remembered longing to leave the bush himself and understood Mick's dreams. In the meantime, Frank O'Mara was grateful for the strong arms and broad shoulders of his eldest son, even on a part-time basis.

'One day, Harris. Melbourne will be there a while yet.'

'But meantime you're stuck on the farm. Don't you resent that?'

Mick was beginning to lose patience. 'Well, it seems it won't be for much longer. My father has another son who just can't wait to take over the farm.'

His barb was well aimed. A black scowl clouded the face of the heirless owner of Mullanurra. Grinning with satisfaction, Mick turned his back on his host and headed towards the more agreeable atmosphere of the veranda. Amelia introduced him to the inspectors.

He jotted down names in his notebook and started setting up his camera. 'Now then, ladies and gentlemen, how about some photos for the *Chronicle*? And the children, Mother?'

Mother Sebastian's eyes lit up. She surveyed the laughing children. They were a sea of white in their once-a-year good clothes, and full of smiles as they frolicked in the grounds of Mullanurra. She inclined her head towards Mick with a condescending smile and then turned to her novices. 'Assemble the children in front of the house, please, Sisters.'

While Sarah and Whilomena gathered the children, the inspectors and the nuns posed along the veranda. Mother Sebastian placed herself in the centre of the group, taller than either of the men who stood on each side of her. The children arrived and Mick asked them to sit on the wide veranda steps. They filled the steps and flowed down onto the grass and into the garden. The novices stood at either end of the veranda. Their white veils stood out against the dark brick of Mullanurra, framing the picture.

With one or two directions to those on the veranda, Mick positioned his cast and took his photos. 'That's it, Sister, all done. The kids can go now if you like.' He had directed his remarks to the nearest novice, barely glancing in her direction as he strapped his camera away.

Sarah blinked at her sudden promotion and looked up to the veranda. Mother Sebastian still at the rail, nodded. There was no sign of the handkerchief today, Sarah noticed.

The children, not so respectful of rank or protocol, had started to move away as soon as the man with the camera said they could go. His dog went with them. As Mick sauntered back to his ute, he gave a shrill whistle. Bronko skidded to a halt, his four feet almost touching each other as he turned in one movement. Then he was racing back to his human, his ears streaming behind him. Mick opened the cabin door and Bronko leapt onto his privileged front seat. As the ute turned down the driveway, the children chased it waving, and Bronko barked goodbye through the open window.

Back on the veranda, the company settled into their chairs again.

The three women who waited on the tables were all Aborigines. They trudged back and forth between the kitchen and the veranda under Amelia's watchful eye. Mother Sebastian greeted a St Cuthbert's graduate among them, an attractive woman who Sarah judged to be about thirty.

The Superior presented her to the inspectors. 'Pearl was about nine when she came to St Cuthbert's,' Mother Sebastian informed the company, 'and Mrs Harris offered her employment at Mullanurra when she had just turned thirteen. Pearl is a very satisfactory worker, Mrs Harris tells us.'

Pearl seemed to shrink from the limelight. She stood with her head lowered, her eyes downcast and a shy, embarrassed smile almost hidden.

'Yes, we met Pearl during dinner last night. It's nice to see you again, Pearl.'

Pearl seemed even more embarrassed by Chandler's greeting. She picked up an empty tray and hurried into the house.

The Superior of St Cuthbert's had not chosen the name Pearl. If a child arrived on her doorstep on the feast of a certain saint, then that was the name the child received. If the liturgical calendar failed to inspire her, she followed the example of Mr Bumble in *Oliver Twist* and chose from the next letter of the alphabet. The phone book came in handy on such occasions. Since Pearl had come into her care on the eleventh of August, she was named Philomena in honour of the saint of the day, and since Mother Sebastian had reached the letter M in search of surnames, her finger had prodded the phone book and landed on Marsh. Philomena Marsh. That, however, was too sophisticated and possibly too complicated a name for a domestic in the employ of Amelia Harris. So upon her arrival at Mullanurra, Pearl she had become. She did indeed have eyes like black pearls, but Sarah doubted that would have motivated Amelia's choice.

As well as catering to the guests on the veranda, the serving women carried trays to the grassy areas where the children were eating. They were kept busy replenishing the disappearing supplies of food and drink. The children were not used to eating under so little supervision. Although the sisters walked among them, numbers and space were on the children's side. With big eyes and eager hands, they demolished the food as fast as it appeared.

Amelia, the consummate hostess, had provided a separate dining room inside the house for the nuns. Sarah had just returned from enjoying a private cup of tea when Harris leapt to his feet and startled her with a loud shout.

'Pearl!'

Pearl, who had been carrying a tray to where the children were eating, wheeled about and headed back to the house.

As she returned to the veranda, Harris barked at her again. 'I told you to stay here! You're supposed to be serving our guests. Don't let me see you wandering off down there again, do you hear me?'

Pearl nodded. 'Yes, boss,' she murmured.

Sarah was astonished by the change that had come over Harris. The eyes that had been so attractive as he played host were now blazing down on Pearl's head, his handsome face ugly with anger.

'Bring out some more sandwiches and stay up here and help.'

'Yes, boss.'

As Pearl traipsed off to the kitchen, Sarah stared at three untouched plates on the tables in front of them. Mother Sebastian rose from her chair and moved behind Harris, bending low over his shoulder to murmur in his ear.

Harris breathed out a gentle 'Ah,' and nodded to her, smiling again.

Pearl returned with another plate brimming with sandwiches and forced a shy smile for each visitor as she offered the platter around. Sarah had a strange feeling that she had seen Pearl before, but she knew that was unlikely.

As the afternoon wore on, Pearl watched from the kitchen window as Jamarra romped with some of the visiting children who had discovered the old Chevy. The back seat had long ago been pulled out of the

66

car and left on the grass beside it. Jamarra, in proud possession, was showing off to the other children, bouncing up and down on its ragged upholstery as if it were a trampoline. As Pearl grinned at his antics, a bounce too high took him over the edge. He landed sprawling on the grass, spreadeagled and winded.

By the time Pearl reached the kitchen door wiping wet hands on her apron, one of the white-veiled novices was already helping Jamarra to his feet. Pearl paused on the veranda and watched the young sister brush her son down, bending over him and patting his head. Jamarra smiled and nodded at something the sister said to him. As he scrambled back to the bouncing seat, the novice straightened and noticed Pearl watching her. The two women nodded at each other with silent smiles. Pearl returned to her kitchen. Sarah joined the company on the veranda.

Sixteen

The St Patrick's Day picnic had been such a public relations success that Mother Sebastian was almost jovial at dinner that evening.

As the nuns left their dining room Sarah caught up with her, determined to take advantage of the Superior's good mood. 'May I have a word with you please, Mother?'

Mother Sebastian turned so quickly that Sarah almost collided with her. 'Yes, of course, Sister.' She stood with her hands clasped in front of her and a benevolent smile, waiting for Sarah to speak.

Sarah's whisper was innocent and confidential. 'Mother, I'm sure you're not aware that no one is supplying the older girls with sanitary napkins for their, um, their time of month. They're using rags, which they wash by hand and hang up inside the laundry. Not very sanitary in such a large community of women, I'm sure you'll agree. If you like, Mother, I could ask Sister Leo to order supplies and distribute them to the girls from the infirmary. I would be happy to help.'

The smile disappeared. 'Sanitary napkins?' Despite her agitation, Mother Sebastian kept her voice low, aware of the way sound carried in the great hall. 'Sanitary napkins, Sister? What ridiculous extravagance!' Her hand delved into her pocket and emerged clutching her handkerchief. 'It is good for the girls to learn thrift. Home economy is, after all, part of their training.'

'But Mother, we use them.'

'Sister, will you please stop comparing what we do with what they do. As if there is a comparison. The girls are lucky to have their rags.' Mother Sebastian smirked. 'It's a step up for them, Sister. What do you think they did in the bush?'

Sarah blinked. 'In the bush?' she stammered. 'Mother, I don't think any of our girls have ever lived in the bush, have they? But if they did, well, I suppose they must have had their own way of...' Sarah knew she was floundering, '...their own methods of, of hygiene.'

Mother Sebastian gasped. 'Hygiene?' A mirthless laugh mocked the idea. 'Sister, you are talking about Aborigines,' she snorted. 'I will discuss this no further.' She turned her back and swept away, shaking her head.

Sarah stood for a moment, staring at the darkness gathering in the great hall. Then she followed her Superior.

Seventeen

The day Welfare left Mullanurra, Amelia called her housekeeper into her sitting room. Pearl left the dishes and hurried to stand before her mistress, wondering what she had done.

To her surprise. Amelia indicated a chair. 'Come over here, Pearl. Sit down.'

Pearl sat with her eyes downcast, twisting her fingers into knots. She had never before been invited to sit in the presence of Mrs Harris.

'Pearl, we have a problem. Those people from Welfare, they want to take Jamarra away.'

Pearl's head jerked up, panic on her face.

Amelia raised a pacifying hand. 'Don't worry, Pearl. I have a plan. If Jamarra stays here, those Welfare people will know where to come and get him, and they will come, Pearl. But if you and Jamarra don't live here any more, they won't be able to find you, will they?'

As Pearl's whole world crumbled, she grasped at the sliver of hope in Amelia's words, fixing desperate eyes on the last person she had expected to be concerned with her child's safety. 'Where will we go, Missus?'

'Majik will know what to do, Pearl. I'll give Majik a call tomorrow.'

Eighteen

Bronko lifted a sleepy head from his armchair. He gave a half-hearted 'Woof,' as his human greeted a cheeky faced grin that appeared around the office door.

Mick acted as Majik's unofficial secretary, letting him use the *Chronicle*'s phone to take orders for his delivery business.

'Mullanurra, mate. Mrs Harris has a job for you.'

'Ta, Mick. Catch ya later.'

Majik contracted small local jobs around the Mallee and sometimes drove as far as Melbourne or Adelaide, saving for the big fleet of shiny transports he dreamed of owning one day. His faded, used-to-be-red Dodge truck was barely roadworthy and attracted much attention from Sergeant Buchanan. Minutes later, it arrived in Mullanurra's driveway.

Majik jumped out of the cabin, the image of the flashy heroes in the western films he loved. His handsome face and black curls were half hidden under a broad-brimmed hat. He wore a chequered shirt and a red scarf knotted at the back of his neck. The long legs and athletic body that thrilled fans when scorching the oval at Victory Park, were today clad in denim jeans and silver-studded cowboy boots.

Amelia was waiting on the veranda as Majik loped up the steps.

'You got a job for me, Mrs Harris?' It wasn't until he reached the veranda that Majik noticed Pearl clutching a battered suitcase in one hand and Jamarra by the other.

'Pearl needs somewhere to live, Majik.'

'Where do you want me to take her, Mrs Harris?'

'I don't know, Majik. I was hoping you would know. If she stays here, Welfare is going to take her boy from her and she'll never see him again.'

The pretended solicitude worked just as well on Majik as it had on Pearl. As far as either of them knew, Pearl wasn't so much being dismissed from Mullanurra, as hidden from Welfare.

*

Majik's truck left the highway, trailing a cloud of red dust as it sped over the unsealed corrugations of the river track. Just over twenty miles to the east of town, on the banks of the Murray River, a cluster of oddly assorted dwellings housed a dozen or so Aboriginal families. The truck slowed to a more respectful pace as it entered the camp. Pearl peered at the place Majik had suggested as their best chance. Some structures were little more than shacks of canvas, corrugated iron and kerosene tins beaten flat. Others were modest weatherboard homes that shone with house-proud tidiness and sometimes even boasted a garden, in which flowers romped between beds of vegetables. Pearl pulled Jamarra close and crossed her fingers.

At the end of the row, they stopped outside a small house set back among the gums, a little separate from the others.

Majik pointed to a fallen tree trunk, long part of the communal camp furniture. 'Maybe you wait, eh?'

His passengers clambered out of the truck. Before they reached the designated waiting room, the front door of the house opened. A woman of about sixty emerged, shielding her eyes from the sun.

Majik shouted a greeting. 'Aunty Mary!'

The woman, a matronly figure in a sleeveless frock, appeared to recognise him. She waved him forward, at the same time peering behind him at the strangers sitting on the tree trunk. Pearl watched Majik talking to the woman, now and then raising an arm to point in her direction, but she could not hear what they were saying.

After a few minutes, Majik beckoned them down and introduced them. Aunty Mary's skin was the colour and texture of leather. Her grey hair was twisted into a plait that reached the small of her back. A stern demeanour put the world on notice. She nodded at Pearl with the barest hint of a smile. It turned into a real one when Jamarra's head peeped from behind his mother.

She raised her no-nonsense eyes to Pearl. 'Need a bunk, do yer?'

'I don't have any money, Aunty, but I could do your housework. I'm a good cook too.'

Aunty Mary snorted. 'And what would I be doin'? Just see yer clean up after yerself and the boy, fetch some water now and then. We'll call it a deal.'

Aunty Mary Johnson had herself been raised on a mission and she had no idea where her own two children were. They had been taken from her while their father was serving his country at Tobruk during the war. Jim Johnson had built the little house for his family before he enlisted. Now twenty years a war widow and childless, Mary would not have lived anywhere else, even if the good citizens of Cobbs Crossing had made her welcome in town.

Majik waved goodbye and Aunty Mary shooed her guests inside.

'There's only two bedrooms, so yer'll have to share, unless the boy wants to sleep on the porch?'

Pearl put a hand on Jamarra's shoulder. 'We'll be happy to share, thank you, Aunty. We're very grateful.'

Aunty Mary frowned. 'Maybe the boy wants to go outside and play?' It was more an order than a request.

At a nod from his mother, Jamarra ran out, leaving the women alone.

Aunty Mary beckoned Pearl into a tiny kitchen. 'Yer welcome here, you and the boy. But be warned, girlie. This place is no safer for that boy of yours than any other. In fact, it's a darn sight more dangerous in some ways.'

Pearl glanced towards the door through which Jamarra had disappeared.

Mary waved a dismissive hand. 'No, I don't mean this mob, though yer might like to keep yer distance when the old buggers smuggle their grog in at night. They can get bloody noisy when they get on the grog. They can be dangerous then all right with their bloody drunken rows an' half-killin' each other. But as long as yer keep yerself and the boy out of their way, yer'll be all right.'

Aunty Mary eased herself onto a kitchen chair. 'No, I'm talkin 'bout them bloody coppers. They're a lot worse. They're always turnin' the place upside down. It's a national sport with them.' Aunty Mary snorted. 'The good thing is, there's always plenty of warnin' that they're comin'. They roar into camp, sirens wailin', lights flashin', the works. Scary as the devil, the bastards!'

Every muscle in Pearl's body tensed. Her clenched fists forced their fingernails into her palms. 'What should I do?'

'You and me, we keep that boy out of sight. We teach him where to hide when those good-for-nothing coppers come prowlin' round.'

'Where?' Pearl wanted a miracle.

'Yer know that old tree trunk yer been sittin' on?' A conspiratorial smile hovered in Aunty Mary's eyes. 'That old log's holler as a boy before breakfast. Come on, I'll show yer.' She started back to the door, still talking over her shoulder. 'Yer got any important people friends? Doctor? Priest? Know anybody like that?

A bewildered Pearl wracked her numb brain for important people friends.

Aunty Mary was still walking and talking. 'Yer need letters. Letters from important people, tellin' that yer a good mother.'

'Oh, references!'

'Yeah, references. Got any?'

'No.'

'Get some. Get some pronto.'

Nineteen

Pearl was on the lookout the next time Majik's truck returned to the river camp. As soon as it pulled up outside the hut Majik shared with his father Old George, Pearl begged a ride to St Cuthbert's. The old Dodge was soon crunching its way up the gravelled drive of the orphanage.

Majik waited in the truck. Pearl forced herself up the convent steps and asked Whilomena, who answered the door, if she could speak with 'the other sister who wears a white veil'. Sarah was summoned and the two women recognised each other.

'I'm Pearl, Sister, from Mullanurra.'

'Yes, I remember you, Pearl. Please come in.'

Pearl seemed horrified at the thought of crossing the convent threshold. She shook her head, so Sarah stepped out and led her guest to one of the wooden veranda seats.

'My name is Sister Anthony. We saw each other, didn't we, Pearl, when that little boy was hurt?'

'That was my boy, Sister, my Jamarra.' Slowly at first, then with more confidence as she saw that she had the young nun's attention, Pearl told Sarah about her move from Mullanurra and Aunty Mary's suggestion.

'Oh, Pearl, I'm so sorry. Of course, I'd be happy to write you a reference.' Sarah bit her lip, remembering Mother Sebastian's disparaging description of the river camp. 'I'll have to visit you, Pearl. Sister Matthew and I will come after class today,' she promised.

Pearl started to leave. She had almost reached the steps when she looked back at Sarah.

Sarah hurried towards her. 'Pearl? Was there something else?'

Pearl hesitated. 'No. Thank you, Sister. Goodbye, Sister.'

*

Sarah and Sister Matthew took care to make their visit to Aunty Mary's house look as little like an inspection as possible. They did not open drawers or poke into cupboards. They didn't wander about the house. They accepted armchairs in the faded, but clean and tidy lounge room, and found compliments for their hostess.

'What pretty cushion covers, Mrs Johnson. Did you make them yourself?'

Sarah had not been able to shake the feeling that there was something more that Pearl had wanted to ask her. She tried to provide an opportunity. 'Where is that beautiful little boy of yours, Pearl?

'He's outside, Sister. Would you like to see him?'

As they strolled towards the hollow log, which Jamarra was now using as a balancing beam, Pearl took the opportunity Sarah had provided. 'Sister, do you know where Tallara is?'

Sarah stopped walking. 'Tallara? I don't know anyone called Tallara. Who is Tallara, Pearl?' She inclined her head towards Pearl, waiting.

Pearl turned her face away. Her head hung down and her voice came over her shoulder so low that Sarah only just heard her answer. 'My other baby, Sister. My little girl. They took her away.'

Sarah stifled a gasp. 'Oh, Pearl.' She took one of Pearl's hands in her own. So Pearl had already had a child taken from her. No wonder she wanted testimony that she was a good mother.

*

On the way back to the orphanage, Sarah questioned Sister Matthew. 'How long have you been at St Cuthbert's, Sister?

'Nine years, come this September.'

'Have you ever known a child named Tallara?'

'Tallara? I know the name well but I've never met the owner of the name.'

'Tallara is Pearl's daughter, taken from her some time ago. Pearl believes that she's at St Cuthbert's. What do you know about Tallara, Sister?

'Pearl's daughter? Well, that makes sense. I'm in charge of the mail, you know, among other things.' Sister Matthew dismissed her many duties as deputy principal lightly. 'We receive all these letters addressed to "Tallara Marsh". The sender's name has always been Pearl Marsh, Mullanurra. I've never had the heart to tell Pearl that we can't forward them on anywhere. Mother Sebastian doesn't know, or won't say, where Tallara is now — if she ever was at St Cuthbert's. Mother told me long ago to destroy the letters but I just can't. I have a box full of them stashed away on the top shelf of my classroom cupboard.'

*

Over the next few days, the river camp was bewildered by an unprecedented stream of important-people visitors. Sarah and Sister Matthew had visited as Sarah had promised. After which the nuns enlisted Father Conway and then Doctor Lawrence to visit and write references for Pearl. Pearl was embarrassed by all the attention. Aunty Mary was unfazed. Jamarra practised diving into the hollow tree trunk every time a car appeared. Aunty Mary watched as the important-people letters piled up. She gave Pearl a tin tea caddy to keep them in.

Twenty

On the steps of the police station, Ed Buchanan rocked on the balls of his feet. He rubbed freckled fingers over his close-cropped scalp before placing his uniform cap on his head. Looking down the length of Memorial Square, he surveyed the comings and goings of Cobbs Crossing. It was his town. He gave his belly a congratulatory pat. A nice touch, he thought, sending his junior to make the report. Constable Beaver would be an independent witness to the squalid conditions in that festering river camp. With the report in hand, he could issue a charge of neglect and grab the kid. Job done.

*

As the young Constable opened food safes and poked into cupboards, Pearl whispered to Aunty Mary, 'I'm sorry for bringing this on you.'

Behind the policeman's back, Aunty Mary shrugged. 'Don't you worry, girl. We're used to it.'

Pearl watched every move. She remembered the tea caddy. 'I have letters, sir.'

'Constable. It's Constable, not sir. What letters?'

Pearl didn't see Aunty Mary's warning eyes. 'References to say I'm looking after my boy. That I'm a good mother.'

'The boy, yes. Where is he?' Pearl froze.

Aunty Mary grabbed the tea caddy. 'Here are the letters, Constable. Yer can read 'em if yer like.'

'I should show them to my Sergeant. I'll take good care of them, OK?'

Pearl nodded helplessly as the policeman shoved her precious references into the pocket of his uniform jacket.

*

Sergeant Buchanan sat at his desk with a pile of paperwork in front of him and a frustrated scowl darkening his face. On top of the papers was Constable Beaver's report on the living conditions of Pearl and Jamarra.

'A well-kept vegetable garden. Their own chickens and eggs. A small, two-bedroom house, modest but clean and well maintained. Adequate food stocks. No indication of neglect or danger to the boy. A young man the mother trusts will take the boy to school in town next year.'

Under the report there was a pile of letters all of which said more or less the same thing. The boy, it seemed, was well cared for and there were no grounds for a charge of neglect.

'Constable eager-bloody-Beaver! Christ Al-bloody-mighty. Save me from bloody bleeding hearts!'

Twenty-one

A pale pre-dawn stretched across the river. Along the bank, white-trunked gum trees caught the light and stood like ghostly sentinels against the darkness of the bush. A blue van slipped into the camp. It moved between huts, shacks, and small silent houses as if taking part in a funeral procession. Sounds of the waking bush, the laughter of kookaburras and the chortle of magpies, helped mask the slow crunch of tyres.

A dog barked, then retreated into sulky silence as a stream of abuse was followed by an empty boot. The van moved on. It stopped several yards from the last house. The men didn't close the doors as they crept out of the vehicle. Buchanan waved Beaver towards the front of the house and then disappeared, looking for the back door.

The constable's knock produced a flurry of sound. A curtain moved in one of the windows. Behind the door, urgent commands were issued in loud whispers. Someone was running. Jamarra, half asleep but sensing his mother's fear, let the back door swing with a bang and bolted into Buchanan with a thud. Buchanan grabbed him and Jamarra sunk his teeth into the policeman's arm. While Buchanan swore and nursed his hand, Jamarra took off around the house. The sergeant started after him, shouting to his subordinate. Constable Beaver dashed to cut off the retreat but Jamarra dodged him and kept running. Pearl tore through the house and burst through the front door. Aunty Mary raced after her, clutching a straw broom. Her long hair not yet plaited, flew about her shoulders in wild disarray.

At the sight of his mother, Jamarra abandoned his course towards the log and ran back to Pearl.

'No, baby! Go back! Run! Run and hide!'

'Mummy! Don't let them get me!'

Before he could reach his mother, the two men had him cornered. Jamarra jigged up and down, sobbing. Tiny fists pounded his chest in desperation as he ducked first one way and then the other. Pearl ran towards him but Buchanan grabbed her. Constable Beaver had hold of Jamarra now.

'Careful! The little buggar bites,' Buchanan warned. 'Get him in the van, quick.'

Aunty Mary smacked the business end of the broom across the Constable's shoulders, sending his cap flying. He wrenched the broom from her and threw it away. The distraction allowed Jamarra to wriggle free but Beaver soon had him again. Jamarra threw himself on the ground, kicking and calling for his mother.

Buchanan had released Pearl.

Without thinking, she grabbed his arm. 'Don't take him, Sergeant. Please don't take my boy,' she begged.

Buchanan shoved her away, sending her sprawling to the ground. She jumped up and ran pleading after Beaver, who was bundling a screaming Jamarra into the back of the van.

Buchanan caught up with her. He held her upper arm in a vice-like grip and shouted to the Constable, 'Get the bloody thing started.'

The sound of the van doors slamming shut behind Jamarra ripped through Pearl. She stopped pleading and screamed at Buchanan, kicking and scratching. The back of his hand slammed against the side of her face and she hit the ground again, her head exploding with pain. The Constable jumped behind the wheel and the engine roared. Buchanan leapt in beside him. As the van began to move, Pearl jumped up and raced after it, pounding the back of it with both fists.

Jamarra appeared in the rear window. He jiggled the handle and banged tiny hands against the glass, screaming hysterically.

Pearl stretched out her arms, calling to him. 'Jamarra! Jamarra!'

With a screech of tyres, the van accelerated and sped forward in a cloud of dust. Pearl staggered, fell and leapt up again. The car disappeared. She stumbled on until even the dust of the van was no longer visible. Her head throbbed, her throat hurt, and she could hardly see.

A clap of thunder rolled across the river and the soft Mallee earth turned to mud in a sudden downpour. Pearl sank to her knees, still calling hoarsely down the track. Aunty Mary plodded through the rain and urged her to come inside. Pearl didn't seem to know she was there. She rocked back and forth, her tears washed away as the storm raged round her.

Her screams had woken the camp. Figures emerged and gathered around, ignoring the rain. Gentle hands helped her to her feet and guided her back to Aunty Mary's house.

Twenty-two

The mansion that had become St Cuthbert's Orphanage had once boasted a grand ballroom. The Sisters of Saint Francis having little use for a ballroom, it had been converted into a splendid chapel. The original oak floor was polished for prayer more perfectly than it had ever been for dancing. Large stained-glass windows filled the sanctuary with colour and light. The altar was covered in white linen, the tabernacle flanked by candelabra and fresh flowers.

Elevated above the hurly-burly of the orphanage, the chapel was on most days the peaceful haven it was meant to be. This morning, however, the sisters' prayers were challenged by crashes and eerie moans as the storm drove rain across the balconies and rattled the windows.

Struggling against the distractions of wild weather, Sarah was reading the same page of her Imitation of Christ for the umpteenth time, when the doorbell rang. First on portress duty this morning, she hurried downstairs. As she approached through the great hall, she could just make out, through the stained-glass surrounds of the front door, the police uniform standing in the storm-darkened morning.

Sergeant Buchanan removed his cap and introduced himself. He pushed forward the child at his side. 'His name's Jamarra, Sister.'

'Jamarra?' He was still in his pyjamas and they were soaked.

Buchanan mistook Sarah's surprise for shock at such a heathen name. 'Don't worry, Sister. Mother Sebastian'll think somethin' up for 'im.' The officer grinned. 'Somethin' a bit more godly than Jamarra, I wouldn't mind bettin'.'

Sarah wasn't paying attention. 'But I know this boy, Sergeant.' She placed a reassuring hand on trembling shoulders. 'Jamarra is not an orphan. He is cared for and loved, not neglected in any way. Oh, dear Lord! Pearl. Sergeant, what about his mother? She will be out of her mind.'

'I wouldn't worry too much about the mother, Sister. These boongs –' Buchanan pulled himself up with a smirk. 'I mean, these Aborigines don't feel about their kids like white mothers do. She'll soon forget 'im.'

Sarah had been bending over Jamarra trying to reassure him with the sight of a familiar face. At the Sergeant's words she reared up to face him. 'Excuse me, Sergeant, but that's just not true. At least, not in Pearl's case. Mrs Marsh is a most loving mother. She came to us asking for references because she has been afraid of this very thing happening.

'Comes here pesterin' the nuns, does she? Well, just you let me know if she turns up again, Sister. I'll let her cool her heels in the lock-up for causing a nuisance.'

Sarah gasped. 'Heavens, Sergeant, there's no need for that. Pearl is not a nuisance. She is just a mother trying to keep her son safe…trying to prevent this very thing from happening.'

Buchanan fidgeted and looked away. Turning his cap in his hands, he stared at the deluge beyond the veranda. 'Well, Welfare wants 'im here. I'm just doin' what I'm told. Mornin', Sister.' He replaced his cap and clumped down the convent steps ignoring the rain. The blue van disappeared down the driveway.

Sarah looked at the child that had been dumped in her charge like abandoned rubbish. She bobbed down on her heels, lowering her face to his and taking his tiny hands. Even wet with tears and swollen from crying, Sarah thought Jamarra's blue eyes with their long lashes were the most beautiful she had ever seen. 'Hello, Jamarra.' She ached to comfort him with promises of home and his mother, but she had no idea how long it might take to sort out his situation. Better not to make unkeepable promises. 'I suppose we should get you warm and dry, and find you something to eat. Would you like that? Have you had breakfast?'

There was no response. Jamarra shivered and gulped big, convulsive sobs.

Sarah tried again. 'Will you come with me, Jamarra? You'll feel better when you're warm.' She took two steps over the threshold and turned with her hand held out.

Jamarra, not having budged an inch, was still on the other side of the door where Buchanan had left him.

'Come with me please, Jamarra, that's a good boy.'

The child dropped his head and murmured something into his heaving chest without moving.

Sarah lowered herself again, vainly seeking eye contact, and whispered, 'I didn't hear you. What did you say, Jamarra?'

'Want me mum.'

The whimper tugged at Sarah's heart. She scooped the child up in her arms and held him against her shoulder, hugging him to her and patting the damp little head. When she stood him down again, he let her take his hand. She led him without further protest to the infirmary.

Sister Leo had not returned from chapel but Lily was there, keeping watch over five sleeping babies. Sarah wondered what time this poor girl must rise in order to relieve the infirmarian for morning devotions. Lily didn't seem to find anything surprising in the unannounced arrival of another child. She helped Sarah get Jamarra into a warm bath. While Lily watched over him, Sarah stepped across the corridor to the sewing room. She searched the shelves where finished work was stored. Much-mended shirts and shorts were neatly stacked in graded sizes. Sarah grabbed one of each.

When she returned to the infirmary, Lily was towelling Jamarra dry.

'Thank you, Lily. You're very good with children, aren't you?'

Lily flushed with pleasure but she said nothing.

*

'Wait here, Jamarra.'

In the great hall, Jamarra, in clean dry clothes, stopped on the exact spot Sarah indicated. He had eaten no more than a mouthful of the breakfast she had found for him in the empty kitchen. Back in the infirmary, he had fallen into a restless sleep. It was now past nine o'clock and Sarah wanted to get to the bottom of this terrible mistake.

Two knocks on Mother Sebastian's door and Sarah obeyed the summons to enter. The Superior was bent over her work. Sarah knelt at the side of her chair.

'Yes, Sister?' Mother Sebastian did not look up.

'Mother, Sergeant Buchanan left a child here this morning. But there's been a mistake. It's Jamarra, Pearl Marsh's son. You know Pearl, Mother. We can tell Welfare –'

Mother Sebastian's pen paused but she did not lift her head. 'Tell them what, Sister?'

Sarah gasped in disbelief. 'We can tell them what a good mother Pearl is. That Jamarra is not a neglected child. That he doesn't belong here, he belongs with his mother.'

Mother Sebastian said nothing.

Sarah insisted, 'Mother, he keeps asking for her, poor little mite.'

The Superior sighed. She raised her head at last and pushed her spectacles back up her nose. 'Bring him in and wait until I have spoken with him, please, Sister.'

Sarah returned to the hall, half expecting to find that Jamarra had bolted. He was where she had left him, swaying back and forth and staring at the faraway ceiling.

Sarah led him into the study. As soon as he caught sight of Mother Sebastian, he tried to hide behind Sarah. When she went to leave the room, he tried to follow her.

She bent down and whispered to him. 'Mother Sebastian wants to talk with you, Jamarra. I will be waiting right outside the door.'

Big eyes pleaded with Sarah. She wished she could stay beside him.

As she left, she winced as Mother Sebastian addressed the child in very unmotherly tones. 'Come here, boy.'

Through the door she left ajar, Sarah heard Jamarra mumble something she could not make out.

Mother Sebastian's voice was clear enough. 'Well, your mother does not want you.'

Listening from the hall, Sarah gasped. Jamarra began wailing.

Mother Sebastian shrilled above his cries. 'Stop that dreadful noise at once. At once, do you hear?'

Jamarra's efforts to stop crying only resulted in noisy sobs. A damp patch appeared in the front of his shorts.

Mother Sebastian backed away. 'Oh, you dirty child! Now look what you've done!'

Sarah burst through the door. 'I'm sorry, Mother. I forgot to tell you. This boy was sneezing when Sergeant Buchanan left him with me.'

Mother Sebastian covered her face with her handkerchief. 'Get him out of here. Out!'

Sarah scooped Jamarra up in her arms and fled down the hall. She swept into the quad without putting him down. He clung to her and she carried him across the playground, dodging puddles left by the recent rain and glad of the deserted grounds, all the other children now at their lessons. Between the laundry and garage they went and on to the dormitories.

The six iron-roofed dormitories, built as barracks for prisoners-of-war, were freezing in winter, and at the height of summer they were like walking into an oven. They were designed to sleep twenty. Bunks and cots had been squashed between every bed, until there were forty children crowded into each hut. Situated behind the main buildings, they did not interfere with views from the convent and were never seen by visitors.

The only dormitory allotted to boys over three was at the far end. By the time they reached it, even a bundle as fragile as Jamarra was starting to feel heavy.

Sarah set him down and walked from bed to bed, lifting pillows until she found one with no pyjamas under it. 'Tonight you will sleep here, Jamarra. In the morning, watch the other boys. Follow them. Do what they do. Now come and we'll get you some morning tea. You must be hungry by now.'

For the rest of the day, Sarah had a pint-sized shadow. Jamarra refused to leave her side even when the other children were at play. If she disappeared into the convent, she found him sitting on the steps, cuddling the convent cat and waiting for her return. At the end of his first day at St Cuthbert's, Sarah visited the sewing room again. She found a pint-sized pair of pyjamas and led Jamarra back to the dormitory.

Twenty-three

When the bell startled sleepy heads awake the next morning, Jamarra had not long been asleep. He had spent the night huddled under his blanket, sobbing for his mother and jumping at every strange sound from inside or outside the dormitory.

Boys tumbled out of beds around him in too much hurry to give the newcomer more than a glance. Jamarra watched them strip off their pyjamas and stow them under their pillows. They pulled their blankets up to the pillows and scrambled into day clothes left at the foot of their beds.

Tommy nudged Peter as he recognised the boy they had played with in the old Chevy at Mullanurra. Jamarra stashed his pyjamas as he had seen the others do and pulled his blanket up, more or less straight. He wriggled into shorts, tugged a shirt over his head to save struggling with buttons and followed the bathroom queue.

*

Mother Sebastian beckoned Sarah aside as the nuns left the chapel after morning prayers. 'We will call the new boy Joseph May, Sister, after the stepfather of Our Lord and the month of Our Lady.'

'A new name? Mother forgive me, but surely –'

The Superior stopped Sarah with a raised hand and an exasperated sigh. She spoke with slow, deliberate emphasis. 'Please see that he knows his new name, Sister Anthony.'

As she watched Mother Sebastian's back disappearing, Sarah remembered Sergeant Buchanan saying something about Mother changing the child's name. She had not been paying attention at the time, but now she thought it was as if he knew. As if it had happened before. What was it he had said? 'Something more godly'? Would Mother Sebastian have considered Tallara a godly name? Sarah doubted she would. Jamarra was to become Joseph. Could Tallara's disappearance be explained as simply? A name change? If so, was she still at St Cuthbert's? How old would she be? Probably just a few years older than Jamarra, Sarah guessed. About Betty's age perhaps, or maybe Monica's.

*

Sarah pulled a sympathetic face at a puffy-eyed Jamarra as he followed Tommy, Peter and the other boys into her classroom.

When morning prayers were done, she announced a game she hoped would help him. 'Girls and boys, let's see if I can remember everyone's name. If I don't know every name, we will have extra story time today.'

Giggles greeted the new game, everyone hoping Sister would make a mistake.

Sarah started with the boys' row. She walked from desk to desk, ticking off names on her fingers. 'Tommy, Peter, Jamarra...no, I'm wrong!' Sarah raised her hands to her face in mock consternation. 'Jamarra has a nice new name, everyone. His new name is Joseph. Joseph May. Tommy, can you do better than I did? Stand up please, and call out the name of each boy.'

Tommy began with cocky confidence, each of his mates grinning and jumping to their feet as he named them. He was wise to the game and remembered not to say Jamarra. 'Joseph May!' he shouted.

Jamarra was staring out the window. He didn't turn round when his new name was called.

At recess, Jamarra found himself the centre of a crowd of curious children. He twisted his arms together in front of his body and stared back at them.

'Can you do tricks?'

Jamarra rolled his eyes and the children laughed. Encouraged, he wriggled his nose and pulled his mouth this way and that with his fingers.

'Joseph May! What on earth are you doing?'

The other children scattered, leaving Jamarra, who still did not recognise his new name, standing alone with his back to the speaker. A sharp rap on his upper arm reminded him.

'Joseph! Look at me when I'm speaking to you.'

Rubbing his arm, Jamarra turned to face the speaker and immediately looked everywhere else.

Mother Sebastian towered over him, tapping her palm with a blackboard pointer. 'I asked you a question, Joseph. Why were you making those ridiculous faces?'

Jamarra swallowed. 'Makin' uver kids larf.'

'Speak properly, Joseph. Say, "I was making the other children laugh, Mother."'

'I...I...w...woz...'

'Hurry up, Joseph, I haven't got all day.' Mother Sebastian swished the pointer against her skirt with a loud smack.

Jamarra jumped. He tried again, eyes glued to the pointer. 'I...I... I...' He had forgotten the words. He began to cry, and again a humiliating puddle formed at his feet.

Mother Sebastian lurched back and raised the pointer. It fell across Jamarra's shoulders. 'You dirty, dirty boy! Go and wash yourself.' Mother Sebastian delivered a stroke with every second word.

Jamarra took off sobbing, not knowing where he was supposed to go, but glad to be gone. He ran into the corridor that led to the classrooms, the only part of the building he remembered, and thumped into Sarah. He screamed and shrivelled against the wall.

'What's the matter, Jamarr – oh dear, I mean, Joseph? Oh!' Sarah spotted the damp shorts and wet legs. 'It doesn't matter, Joseph. Come with me.' She held out her hand but he did not move. She crouched down on her heels. 'Jamarra, your name is Joseph now,' she whispered. 'We'd better have a wash, don't you think?'

He nodded and took her hand. As they walked towards the bathrooms, the little fist fastened on her fingers so tightly it hurt. Sarah made no effort to release them.

*

In the afternoon, the children were quick to remind Sarah that she had made a mistake with Joseph's name. She owed them extra story time. *The Little Black Princess* was opened again but before Bett-Bett's adventures continued, Peter's hand was up. He had remembered something.

'Marra'th got a thpring-mattreth, Thithter...in hith car!'

Sarah paid particular attention whenever Peter spoke. His inability to pronounce 's' was difficult to decipher. 'Try again, Peter, and remember, we call Jamarra Joseph now.'

Before Peter could start thithtering again, Betty hurried to help. 'Sister, he said –'

'Thank you, Betty, but if we let Peter try for himself, one day he will be able to say s just as well as we can.'

Peter beamed at the prospect of such improvement. 'Jotheph got a thpring-mattreth in hith car, Thithter!' He smiled so triumphantly that Sarah wondered if he thought he was getting it right already.

'Very good, Peter, thank you. Yes, I've seen it. Joseph, would you like to tell us about the spring-mattress in your car?'

Jamarra's head hung down on his chest.

'Joseph?'

He rocked back and forth but didn't look up.

Compassionate little Betty rushed to the rescue again. This time she got it right. 'The mattress is at the big house, Sister. You know, the picnic place where he used to live.' She lowered her voice to a whisper. 'It might be, maybe it makes him think about his mum.' Betty blinked sagely.

Of course. Sarah nodded gratefully at the thoughtful little girl.

Sarah continued to challenge Bett-Bett's belief in Debbil-debbils and their terrible punishments. Not all the adventures of *The Little Black Princess* had a positive effect on her class. When Bett-Bett covered herself in mud to ward off mosquitoes, some of the children copied her. Sarah spent that afternoon with her sleeves rolled up, rushing them through the showers before Mother Sebastian saw them. When Bett-Bett threaded ticks on a string like beads, Sarah found it disgusting. The children were delighted and tried it with whatever bugs they could find. As for the passage that explained that blood was good for sticking feathers to your body, Sarah left it out entirely, having visions of an infirmary full of cut fingers and a hen house full of denuded chickens.

Twenty-four

One afternoon, the boys' row in Sarah's classroom was almost empty.

'Where is Tommy? Where are Peter and Joseph?'

'They're weeding, Sister. They went in the paddock with the sheep and Mother said they have to weed until dinner time.'

Leaving what was left of her class drawing pictures of Bett-Bett and Sue, Sarah hurried along the corridor between the classrooms. Holding her beads against her side, she sped through the great hall and out over the veranda.

In the garden, her missing pupils were struggling with implements never designed for children. The afternoon sun blazed down on hatless heads. Gloveless hands carted water, raked, wheeled barrows and hoed endless rows of flowers. Some were weeding between sharp quartz stones, kneeling on gravel paths with bare knees and knuckles.

Jamarra was with them, small shoulders hunched as he struggled with a watering can. He had followed the other boys because Sarah had told him, 'Go where they go, do what they do,' and he was puzzled to find himself in trouble for doing what he was told.

Sarah turned on her heel and in a few strides knocked on the door of her Superior's study, bursting in without waiting for an invitation. 'Mother, they're only children! They could get sunstroke working out there all afternoon or, at the very least, badly burnt.'

Mother Sebastian's pen hovered over the work in front of her. She sighed and shook her head, abandoning a lecture on decorum as futile. 'They are disobedient children, Sister, and as such they are being punished.'

'But Mother –'

'And I do not expect to have to explain myself to a novice.'

'But Mother –'

Mother Sebastian slammed a hand down on her desk as if trying to frighten a naughty child. 'Sister Anthony! What on earth made you think of becoming a nun?'

Twenty-five

The sisters had just sat down to their lunch when the doorbell echoed through the great hall. Sarah hurried to the bottom of the table and bowed head and shoulders towards Mother Sebastian. Seconds later, she opened the front door to a breathless, dust-covered Pearl.

Pearl struggled to breathe and speak at the same time. 'Sister…I want to…see Mother…please.'

'Good grief, Pearl. Sit down. Let me get you some water.'

As Sarah turned to go, Pearl grabbed her arm.

She withdrew her hand as if she had touched the queen. 'No. Mother Sebastian. Please, Sister.' She sank onto the veranda seat.

The Superior was not overjoyed at being called to the door as she was starting her meal. As Sarah returned with a glass of water, Mother Sebastian's voice floated down the hall.

'I'm sorry, Pearl. Those children are not at St Cuthbert's. I don't know where they are.'

Sarah could hear Pearl pleading, her soft voice rushing on, stopping for breath and starting again, then sobbing.

'It's no use getting upset, Pearl. I cannot help you. If you come here again, I shall have to complain to Sergeant Buchanan. Those children are not here. We have no one called Tallara and no Jamarra.'

Sarah froze.

Mother Sebastian closed the front door and started back down the hall. She frowned at Sarah's flustered face. 'Yes, Sister?'

'Mother, I beg your pardon, but I could not help hearing and I thought you might have forgotten. The child you named Joseph May used to be called Jamarra.'

Mother Sebastian fixed cold eyes on her troublesome novice. 'Come with me, Sister Anthony.' She stalked into her study and stood at one of her windows, watching Pearl trudge back towards the road.

Sarah followed. She set down her glass of water and lifted her beads to kneel. Mother Sebastian waved her onto a chair.

Sarah perched on the edge of it, stood up, sat down and stood up again. 'Will I see if I can catch Pearl, Mother?'

Mother Sebastian stretched out her arm, indicating the chair once more. A frustrated Sarah sank back down.

The Superior glared her impatience. 'Sister, have you forgotten what I told you when you arrived at St Cuthbert's? We do not, under any circumstances, allow the children to have contact with other Aborigines. It unsettles them. They cannot progress if they are allowed to continue their tribal associations.'

Sarah spluttered and almost laughed. 'But Mother, Pearl's not tribal.'

Mother Sebastian glared. 'As you very well know, Sister, Pearl worked at Mullanurra, where many other Aborigines are employed. And now I believe she lives at that river camp. Who knows what peculiar notions she may have picked up from her kind? Please try to understand. Our mission is to bring these children to Christ. We cannot do that if they are told that the land was created by a giant serpent and such nonsense. Is that what you want, Sister? Is that the sort of pagan superstition you think Our Lord wants Aborigines to believe?'

'I think, if Jesus was here today, He'd be an Aborigine.'

'You blasphemous child!'

'Oh, no. I didn't mean any disrespect, Mother.'

Mother Sebastian regarded Sarah with suspicion. 'Well, what did you mean, Sister?'

Sarah swallowed. 'Mother, I was only thinking that when Jesus was born a Jew, the Jews were slaves. He was the Son of God. He could have been born to a Roman centurion or even a Caesar. But He chose to come as one of a dominated race. Doesn't that tell us how He would have related to the Aborigines?'

The Superior only snorted.

Frustration made Sarah reckless. 'Mother, isn't it, um, untruthful, to tell Pearl that Joseph is not here?' Despite her distress, Sarah stammered at the audacity of calling her Superior a liar.

Mother Sebastian gasped. 'Good grief, Sister Anthony. Do you really think you belong in the convent?' She walked behind her desk and sat down as if someone had pushed her into her chair. 'As for that, technically I wasn't lying. I didn't say that Joseph May is not here. I said that no one called Jamarra is here.' Mother Sebastian shifted in her seat and shrugged as if not even she found the fine distinction convincing. 'Just remember, Sister, contact with other Aborigines is not in the children's interest, and under no circumstances is information about any child at St Cuthbert's to be given to any native, no matter what relationship he or she may claim. That is the rule and the rule is to be obeyed. You may go.' The Superior picked up her pen and started writing as if Sarah had already left the room.

Sarah paused with her hand on the doorknob. 'Mother, Pearl mentioned another child, a little girl. Was there ever a child named Tallara at St Cuthbert's, Mother?'

Mother Sebastian's pen hovered over her work. Without lifting her eyes she repeated, 'I said you may go, Sister Anthony.'

The loud clang of the playground bell greeted Sarah as she hurried through the great hall, her thoughts racing. If Mother Sebastian didn't know who Tallara was, would she not have said so, just as Sister Matthew had done? And if Mother had renamed Pearl's daughter, would she not justify denying Tallara's existence, as easily as she had denied Jamarra?

Yet, Sarah reminded herself, Mother Sebastian was her Superior, appointed by God. No matter how difficult she might find Mother's rules, she was obliged to obey them. Her cheeks warmed at the memory of Mother's reprimand. This was the second time her Superior had questioned Sarah's fitness for religious life, but she so much wanted to be a good nun, go to the missions, make a difference. She shook her head.

She must do better. She must. She must subdue her pride and govern her impatient tongue. She clutched the crucifix at her waist. 'I will, Jesus. With Your help, I will do better,' she promised. Sarah quickened her pace. Her students would be waiting.

As she crossed the quad, an unruly commotion reached her ears. Hoots and laughter were erupting from one of the classrooms. Sarah shook her head. The noise would be waking the babies. Entering the corridor, she gasped and hurried forward. The uproar, she realised with horror was coming from her own classroom. Sarah was mortified. Sister Leo's little ones would be disturbed. Sister Matthew would wonder at her lack of classroom control and Sister Augusta – Sarah didn't want to think about what Sister Augusta would say. She rushed to the door of her classroom. At the blackboard, Betty was perched on a stool, dusting off an amusing caricature of Mother Sebastian.

'Betty!' Sarah's voice was loud and angry.

A startled Betty whirled around, wobbling and almost falling from the stool. She dropped the duster. It fell to the floor in a puff of chalk dust.

Sarah grabbed Betty's arm and delivered two hard smacks to the back of the little girl's bare legs. 'Go and stand in the corner. We don't want to see your naughty face.'

Betty stared at Sarah in bewilderment. Her lip trembled. By the time she was standing in the corner, Sarah regretted that she had acted in such haste.

Tommy's hand shot up. 'Please, Sister, it wasn't Betty. It was here when we came in. Betty was just cleaning it off.'

Tommy's words added to Sarah's remorse.

Twenty-six

Night after night, Jamarra pulled his thin blanket over his head and tucked his knees into his tummy against the empty ache of missing his mum. His body heaved with sobs muffled into his pillow, until he fell into an uneasy sleep. He often slept through the bell and woke to Peter's urgent lisping, 'Jotheph! Jotheph!' reminding him that he was no longer Jamarra.

One morning, he woke to a problem more serious than remembering his new name. Still under his blanket, his eyes darted about but no one was looking at him. He was a big boy now he told himself, and he hadn't done this in a long time. He pulled off his pyjama pants, screwed them into a ball and shoved the damp, smelly bundle under his pillow in a lump.

*

Sarah's pupils sprang to their feet as Mother Sebastian marched into the room. They 'God blessed' her in an energetic chorus and she ordered them to sit.

She feigned speaking to Sarah but she was glaring at the children. 'I'm sorry to interrupt you, Sister Anthony, but I'm afraid there is a very wicked boy in this room.'

The children almost stopped breathing. They sat like little stone statues as Mother Sebastian moved closer, searching face after face. Mouths gaped. Eyes were glued to the blackboard pointer she was slapping against her side. They shrank into their desks, making themselves as small as possible.

The raptor eyes fixed on the boys' row. 'There is a wicked, dirty boy in this room, Sister. A boy who leaves dirty, smelly things in his bed. A boy who wets his bed, Sister.'

A room full of frightened faces swivelled towards Sarah.

'An accident I'm sure, Mother, while he was asleep.'

The faces swivelled back to Mother Sebastian with just a shadow of hope.

'It was not an accident to put dirty pyjamas under a pillow, Sister. It was not an accident to pull a blanket up to cover a wet, smelly bed.' The Superior's voice rose loud and shrill. 'The boy who wet his bed last night will stand up now.'

Seconds dragged like hours. The room felt hot and stuffy despite the open windows. Every boy's eye was on the floor. Every girl's eye was on the row by the windows, the boys' row. At the back of the hushed room, a leg inched into the aisle. It was followed by another leg and a small, unsteady body. Jamarra stood with shoulders drooped and arms dangling at his sides. His head hung down, his eyes on the floor. Sarah ached at the sight of him. Once more, she wished she could pick him up and run away.

Mother Sebastian swished the pointer against her habit. Her voice now low, was more menacing than the shrieking of a moment ago. 'Come here, boy.'

Jamarra moved forward as if he was going to his execution. As he reached the front of the room, he raised his head for the first time and looked straight at Sarah.

'Mother,' Sarah's mouth was dry. 'Mother, I will keep this boy back after class and see that he is punished.'

Mother Sebastian flashed Sarah a scornful smirk. 'I think not, Sister Anthony.' She skewered back to Jamarra, using the pointer to indicate a chair standing against the wall. 'Bring me that chair, boy.'

Jamarra struggled with the chair, half lifting, half dragging it into the centre of the room. When he had manoeuvred it into place, Mother Sebastian slapped the pointer across its seat with a crack that made the whole class jump.

'Up!'

Jamarra clambered onto the chair. On finding himself at eye level with the Superior's cold stare, he almost fell off it again.

'Face the class.'

Jamarra wobbled as he turned on the chair. He came face to face with a roomful of eyes, some sympathetic, some simply curious, and he hung his head.

Mother Sebastian pointed at Jamarra. 'Sister Anthony, this boy is to stand here for the rest of the afternoon. After school, he will remove every weed on the geranium path, and he will do it on his own. If he is not finished before the dinner bell rings, he can go without his meal.' She swirled about, elbows jutting her veil out like the wings of a very large bat, and she was gone.

Jamarra's head was almost on his chest. The other children began to breathe again but they sat staring at Sarah. She wondered how to help without openly defying her Superior. At the back of the room, the sympathetic way in which Betty was gazing at Jamarra gave her an idea. She had long since apologised for losing her temper and hitting the little girl, and she took every opportunity to make amends by promoting Betty in front of the other children.

She addressed her shaken pupils. 'I need to go to the sewing room. Everyone, please take out your readers and practise your next two pages. I will hear you when I come back. Betty, please bring Jamarra his reader. You could help him with the hard words.'

Soon every head was pretending studious interest in the pages of the Victorian Primer and Sarah left the room.

For a few seconds, the heads remained focused on the readers. Then eyes began to dart around the room.

Betty left Jamarra's side and moved to the door. She leaned into the corridor and looked left and right. It was empty. She ran to the lonely chair and patted Jamarra's leg. 'Yosef, sit. Sit.' She tapped the seat of the chair. Jamarra stared at her. Betty insisted. 'Sit. I'll watch. I'll tell you when Sister comes.'

At last, Jamarra understood. He sat down, brushing the tears from his face. Betty took up her post. She squatted in the doorway, her reader forgotten except to swat a fly that challenged her watch. A hushed buzz of childish voices soon sounded behind her.

Sarah spent as long as she could manage in conversation with a puzzled Sister Innocent in the sewing room. Returning to her classroom, she made no effort to muffle her footsteps or control the clatter of wooden beads at her side. Her approach was greeted with scuffles and she smiled to herself at Betty's urgently hissed 'Yosef! Yosef!' She found every head buried in a book and Jamarra standing upright on his chair. During the afternoon, Sarah found it necessary to visit the infirmary, the kitchen, the laundry and the library.

At four o'clock, Mother Sebastian looked from her window. She nodded in grim satisfaction at the small boy kneeling on the gravelled path. Beside him was a cane rake; behind him, a pile of weeds. As she rose from her desk, more of the path came into view and the smile froze. The boy was not alone. On the other side of the path, one of the girls was on her knees with a hoe and another pile of weeds. Snatching up her blackboard pointer, the Superior strode from her study and swept down the bluestone steps to the kneeling children.

Betty had no time to register the threat before she was hauled to her feet.

'What do you think you are doing?'

Dangling in Mother Sebastian's grasp, Betty gulped. 'I, I was just, just helping Yosef, Mother.'

'Did I not say he was to do this by himself?' She shook Betty as if the child was a rag doll. 'Seeing you are so anxious to help, you can do the rest by yourself. Joseph, go.'

Jamarra scrambled to his feet but he lingered, looking up under his lashes at Betty. Mother Sebastian frowned at his legs. Just above his knees, the pockets of his short pants were sticking out sideways at a most peculiar angle.

'What have you got in your pockets, boy?'

Jamarra plunged both hands into his pockets and produced a number of stones in each.

'And just what do you intend doing with those, Joseph May?'

'Nuffin', Muver. Jus' savin' 'em.' He was proud of his collection. He kept only the smoothest stones or ones with interesting marks and colours.

'Saving stones? What nonsense.' Mother Sebastian's free hand raised the pointer and it landed on the seat of Jamarra's pants. 'Throw them away at once.'

He jumped out of reach of the pointer. Opening his fingers, he let the stones fall in a pile at his feet, hoping he might be able to find them later.

'Now go.'

With a rueful glance at his would-be helper, Jamarra slipped away.

Mother Sebastian was still clutching Betty's arm. 'You are a very disobedient girl,' she said, giving the child another shake. You will not leave until every weed is gone. I will inspect this path in the morning.'

With a final shake, Betty was released. She lost her balance and tumbled over, spreading her hands to break her fall. With a convulsive sob, she picked herself up, brushing gravel from grazed palms and knees. She retrieved her hoe and set to work.

Betty missed dinner and went to bed hungrier than usual that evening.

Next morning, Mother Sebastian searched for weeds on the section of path she had allotted. She searched in vain. Jamarra found most of his stone collection on top of his desk, tied up in a scrap of cloth from the sewing room. There had been red jelly at dinner, Jamarra's favourite. He had wrapped his in his handkerchief to save for Betty. Red jelly, he discovered, did not save well in a boy's pocket.

Betty appeared in class with a sunburnt face, scraped knees and blistered fingers. Sarah led her to the infirmary. She exchanged glances over the child's head with Sister Leo, while the nurse applied ointment and bandages. In the classroom, Sarah turned a blind eye as Betty's tousled head kept flopping onto her chest and jerking up again as she struggled to stay awake. Sarah watched as the child made a determined effort to write something on a scrap of paper.

By the time the bell rang, Betty had lost her battle with wakefulness and slumped forward onto her desk. When she and the sleeping child were the only ones left in the room, Sarah prized the paper from under Betty's hand. The words blurred before her eyes:

deer mummy
>   i miss you pleez cum an get me i promis i will be good
>   luv from Betty

Sarah buried her face in her hands.

Twenty-seven

The Little Black Princess had become the most-loved book in the junior classroom, and the children's favourite games imitated the adventures of Bett-Bett and Sue.

Sarah laughed along with them and encouraged their inventiveness. When she read them the chapter in which Bett-Bett unravelled cloth to make string bags, she surprised them with scraps of coloured fabric salvaged from the sewing class. They took them into the orchard and tried their hands at unravelling, rolling and knotting, with more laughter than success.

Sarah read on. When Bett-Bett and her dog cuddled under their blankets to eat biscuits in bed, Peter's arm shot up. Sarah laughed.

Without waiting for his question she told him, 'No, Peter, I'm sorry. I can't bring you biscuits when you go to bed.'

When Bett-Bett and the women were rewarded with treacle after doing the laundry at the river, Bett-Bett declared that she liked washing days.

Sarah looked up from the book to smile at the little laundress in her class. 'Do you like washing days, Betty?'

'No, Sister,' Betty sighed. Then she brightened as an idea occurred to her. 'Maybe on the hot days, we could take our laundry to the river, and maybe we could have a big jar of treacle when we finished. I think I would like laundry days then, Sister.'

The story still presented Sarah with challenges. When the Old Man said that everyone had the spirit of some animal inside them, she hastened to offer the children a more Christian version. She explained that the real Spirit they had inside them was the Holy Ghost.

This time, Peter gasped without even raising his hand, 'We got a ghotht in uth, Thithter?'

Another character, old Billy Muck made fire without matches. Sarah decided to censor again. Perhaps it was not wise for children who imitated everything and lived in a hot, dry country to hear how to make fire.

She did, however, tell them about Bett-Bett hatching a crocodile egg under a broody hen, confident that they would not find one of those in the grounds of St Cuthbert's. Peter thought a crocodile would make a wonderful pet and spent a lot of time searching for an egg to hatch.

Twenty-eight

Sister Leo did not sleep upstairs with the other nuns. In case of an emergency during the night, her bed was behind a screen in one of the dormitories. Before she retired, she padded her way between stretchers and cots, checking that her charges were all where they should be. She had almost reached the end of the first dormitory, where the senior girls slept beside the babies.

She stopped, staring at an empty bed. Its blankets were tucked in place, its pillow unoccupied. 'Where's Lily?'

In the darkness of the dormitory, bodies in brown-blanketed beds were as still as death.

Louder and more urgently, Sister Leo demanded, 'Does anyone know where Lily is?'

A baby sat up in its cot and started to wail. One of the older girls came to life and laid the little one down again, cooing it back to sleep.

Sister Leo pounced on her, too concerned about her missing charge to worry about waking the baby. 'Helen! Helen, where is Lily?'

'Don't know, Sister. She was here before.'

The convent came to life faster than it had retired. When a search of school and convent buildings had not produced Lily, torches combed the night-time bush, long fingers of light bobbing through the darkness.

Mother Sebastian picked up her phone. The headlights of Sergeant Buchanan's van probed the night as it wound up the slope towards the orphanage.

Mother Sebastian opened the door herself. 'There was a woman here today, Sergeant. Pearl Marsh. I'm sure she has something to do with this.' Mother Sebastian stalked the great hall as she spoke, her handkerchief clutched to her bosom.

'Pearl Marsh? Isn't that the mother of the kid I brought here a couple of days ago? Is he missing as well?'

'No, thank goodness. That was the first thing I checked. Joseph May is still in his bed.'

The sergeant scratched his head. 'So the Marsh woman's kid is still here, but you think she's helped this other girl to run away? What makes you think that, Mother?'

Mother Sebastian turned her face to the darkness beyond the open front door.

Buchanan didn't wait for an answer. 'Don't worry, Mother. They can't get far on foot. We'll have the woman in the lock-up and the kid back here before breakfast. Mind if I use your phone?'

Mother Sebastian paused in her agitated pacing, and waved her handkerchief towards a recess under the stairs.

Buchanan picked up the phone. 'If you're right about Pearl helping the runaway, I'd better let Locky Harris know. She's lived on Mullanurra most of her life. She might try to hide the kid out there.'

Mother Sebastian sniffed. 'I think that's most unlikely, Sergeant,' she snapped. She was halfway down the hall again by the time the phone was answered at Mullanurra, but she could hear Lachlan Harris barking at Buchanan.

The sergeant put the phone down, unperturbed. 'Locky's mad as hell about that woman comin' here pesterin' the nuns,' he grinned. 'Evenin', Mother.'

*

The convent phone started ringing before even nuns were out of bed. In the course of the morning, a besieged Mother Sebastian answered her phone to the *Chronicle*, to Father Conway and to Mullanurra, as well as several calls from inquisitive town gossips. They all received the same answer. 'No, there has been no news of the missing girl.'

By the time Mick turned up hoping to get more information in person than he had on the phone, Mother Sebastian was in no mood to deal with journalists. When Sarah returned to tell him that her Superior could not see him, he decided to try his luck with the young novice.

'Sorry, Sister, I didn't introduce myself properly at Mullanurra. I'm Mick O'Mara from the *Cobbs Crossing Chronicle*.'

Sarah accepted the hand he held out to her. 'Yes, I remember. You were taking photos at the St Patrick's Day picnic. I'm pleased to meet you again, Mr O'Mara. I'm Sister Anthony.'

He loved the way she spoke, convent school of course, elocution compulsory. He wondered what colour her hair was and tried to picture her without the veil and coif that shrouded her face and shoulders. Conscious of his gaze, Sarah turned her head.

Bronko ran back and forth on the path sniffing, chasing insects and every now and then running back to nudge Mick for a pat.

His owner introduced him. 'And this is Bronko.'

'I saw Bronko at the picnic too, but we haven't been formally introduced.' Sarah smiled, extending her arm. 'Hello, Bronko.'

Bronko sniffed her hand then raced away down the path, going nowhere in particular.

Mick had his notebook out. 'What can you tell me about the missing girl, Sister Anthony?'

'Nothing, I'm afraid. We haven't heard anything yet.'

'Well, what's her name? How old is she?'

Sarah began to understand why Mother Sebastian hadn't come to the door. 'Her name is Lily Matthews and I think she's about fifteen. I really don't know any more than that, Mr O'Mara.'

'Sergeant Buchanan is questioning that woman who used to work at Mullanurra.'

'Pearl?'

'That's it, Pearl. Lily and Pearl, eh?' He grinned, blue eyes full of mischief. 'Nobody could say we're not doing our best to make good whitefellas out of them, could they, Sister?'

Sarah saw the incongruity for the first time. She pressed her lips together, supressing the smile that threatened to condone his irreverence.

Mick tapped a pencil on his notepad as if trying to remember something. 'Pearl, Pearl, let's see, her surname was, um…'

'Marsh, Pearl Marsh,' Sarah supplied innocently. 'But why is Sergeant Buchanan questioning Pearl?'

'It seems she was here asking about some children the day before Lily disappeared.'

'Oh, well, yes, she was, but that was just a coincidence, I'm sure. Pearl wasn't asking for Lily. She was looking for someone called Tallara. We don't have a Tallara here, and Mother Sebastian told Pearl that. I heard her.' Even as she spoke, Sarah heard the echo of Mother Sebastian's lies in her own words. Hadn't she already wondered if Pearl's Tallara might be here, having had her name changed, just as Jamarra's had been?

The newspaper man was looking straight at her, as if he could read her thoughts. 'Just a coincidence, Sister?'

Sarah felt a guilty blush heat her face. 'I'm sorry, Mr O'Mara. I can't help you. I must go.'

'Thank you for your time, Sister.' Mick tipped his hat to Sarah and flipped his notebook shut. His story-hungry nose loved a coincidence, especially when so many people were jumpy about it.

*

'Lily's gone! She's run away!'

It was whispered from child to child, sometimes in fear, sometimes with a hint of triumph. That afternoon, the unsettled youngsters in Sarah's class were more than ever eager to escape into the make-believe world of Bett-Bett and Sue.

The children held their breath as Sarah picked up *The Little Black Princess* again. They laughed with Bett-Bett when the Missus declared that hide-and-seek was no fun, because the Aboriginal women could track her so easily. Even Bett-Bett could track her. The women made fun of the Missus because she could not recognise her own husband's tracks in the bush. When Sue, Bett-Bett's dog, broke her leg on a hunting trip, Sarah looked up to a sea of tearful faces.

At last, they reached the end of the book. Sarah had doubts about telling the children the real ending. She worried that it might encourage hope where there was no hope to be had, or make their reality harder to bear. But they loved Bett-Bett and her little dog. They would, she was sure, rejoice with her. So she read the final chapter. Bett-Bett became ill because she was bush-hungry. Leaving the Missus, she returned to the bush and her own people.

'The end.'

There was not a sound in the room. Forty dejected faces watched Sarah close the book.

'Maybe we can read it again sometime.'

The faces broke into smiles. Sarah was about to set them to drawing pictures of Bett-Bett and Sue, when a heavy footstep turned every head towards the door.

Mother Sebastian stormed into the room, her face red with rage, her eyes blazing at Sarah. 'Are you mad, Sister Anthony? No wonder we have runaways! They have you to encourage them.'

Sarah blinked. 'No. Oh, no, Mother. This story is just –'

'I know what it's about, Sister.' Mother Sebastian stalked across the room and snatched the book out of Sarah's hands. '*Black Princess*, indeed! It's about everything I warned you not to encourage in these godless little heathens.' Mother Sebastian waved her handkerchief in a gesture of despair. 'It's about an exaggerated sense of their own importance. It's about pagan, ungodly beliefs,'

Ignoring the staring children, Mother Sebastian shook the little volume in the face of her most difficult novice. 'And it's about a child turning her back on civilisation and choosing to live like a savage!' She began tearing pages from the book. She tore page after page, flinging them out in front of her. Pages fluttered between paralysed rows of frightened children, landing on the floor like oversized confetti.

*

It was late afternoon when Sergeant Buchanan returned a dishevelled Lily to St Cuthbert's. Mother Sebastian and Sister Matthew were paying a dutiful call on Father Conway, so Whilomena reported their arrival to Sister Augusta, who ordered tea to be served in the front parlour. She then bustled downstairs to receive the sergeant and the runaway. Ignoring Lily's battered appearance, Sister Augusta delivered a lengthy lecture and a detailed description of what was in store. She finally dismissed Lily to await her fate at Mother Sebastian's hands. Lily stumbled down the great hall and out into the quad. Crossing the colonnade near the kitchen door, she came face-to-face with Helen bearing a tray of tea and cakes.

'Lily!'

Lily pushed past her and kept on towards the dormitories. As soon as Helen had delivered her tray, she went in search of Sister Anthony.

Sarah found Lily on her bed, face to the wall. 'Lily?'

There was no answer. The thin body stretched out on the bed did not move. Sarah put her hand on Lily's shoulder. The child seemed to shrink from her touch.

Sarah seated herself on the edge of the narrow bed. 'I'd like to help you, Lily. Why did you run away? Are you so very unhappy with us?' She frowned as she caught sight of a large bruise on the side of Lily's face. 'Who hurt you, Lily?'

Lily twisted around, turning an indignant glare on Sarah and the young nun gasped. One of Lily's eyes was closed. Her lips were swollen and there was a cut on the left side of her forehead. Dried blood from the cut caked Lily's cheek.

'Oh, Lily!'

Lily had turned away again. 'I kicked him.'

'Kicked who? Sergeant Buchanan?'

Lily did not answer.

'Lily, we should go to the infirmary and see Sister Leo. Come. I'll take you.'

When Lily appeared at the door of the infirmary on Sarah's arm, Sister Leo rushed towards them.

She led Lily to a chair by her dispensary with a gentle, 'Dear, oh dear. It looks like you've been in the wars, my girl. Let me have a look at you.' Her tone was light-hearted, but she exchanged grim glances with Sarah, shaking her head.

While Sister Leo attended to Lily's injuries, Sarah tried again to get the girl to talk. 'Lily, do you know an Aboriginal woman called Pearl?'

'I got lost. They found me near the river, Pearl and Aunty Mary. They took care of me. It was nice till those bloody coppers came.'

'Language, Lily, language. But you had never met Pearl before you ran away?'

Lily screwed her bruised forehead into a puzzled frown. 'No.'

'Well, Lily, why did you run away?'

'Mother was mean! All the kids were talkin'. Why didn't Mother let me go on the picnic?'

Sarah sighed. So it was just a coincidence. Pearl had nothing to do with it until afterwards. 'I'll see if Sister Monica can spare a cup of tea and a scone. Would you like that, Lily?'

Lily nodded. Sarah sped away to the kitchen and returned with a covered tray. At the infirmary door, she almost collided with Mother Sebastian.

The Superior lifted the cloth that was covering the tray and scowled at the teapot and single buttered scone. 'And who is this for, Sister?'

'For Lily, Mother. She is –'

'Come with me.' Mother Sebastian whirled away, scattering children who would rather not be seen.

Leaving the tray with Sister Leo, Sarah hurried after her Superior. In her study, Mother Sebastian rounded on Sarah. 'So, Sister! Children who break the rules are rewarded with tea and scones. You have a very unusual approach to discipline, Sister Anthony.'

'Mother, Lily ran away because –'

'Sister, I don't care what heartbreaking story that ungrateful creature has fed you. Do you know where Sergeant Buchanan found her?'

'Yes, Mother, Lily told me. I know the camp isn't ideal, but Pearl and Aunty Mary had taken her in. She was safe with them. Their house is clean and tidy and quite comfortable and Mother,' Sarah took a breath, 'forgive me, but isn't Lily nearly sixteen? If she wants to be with her people –'

'Her people! Are you starting to believe the rubbish you read to the children, Sister? Her only future is to be assimilated into white society without which she has no future. Her father understands that and he wants her here, with us.'

'Her father?' Her father is alive? Where is Lily's father, Mother?'

Mother Sebastian clamped thin lips together, too late to recover her words. 'That is confidential. The point is, she ran away. If she is allowed to get away with it, others will admire her, copy her. I cannot allow that to happen. We will make an example of her. Ask Sister Augusta to bring her to me. Then help Sister Matthew assemble the children at the laundry end of the quadrangle.'

'Mother, I beg you –'

'Immediately, Sister Anthony.'

Twenty-nine

Assemblies were held in the mornings and always facing the classrooms to the north. The children made curious faces at each other when Sarah and Sister Matthew marshalled them along the west-facing colonnade in the late afternoon. On this side of the quad, at this time of day, standing still with nothing to look at but the cement walls of the laundry was boring and uncomfortably warm.

Mother Sebastian and Sister Augusta appeared, leading Lily between them. The Superior seemed oblivious to Lily's injuries. She pushed her in front of the assembled children. All fidgeting stopped. Even the little ones were still. Every eye was on Lily. She refused to hang her head. She stared out above the other children and they gaped at her bruised and swollen face. Sarah's hand moved over the crucifix she wore at her waist.

Mother Sebastian dominated the assembly, a tower of black garments and gesturing arms. She pointed a finger at Lily and her voice echoed down the colonnade. 'This is a very wicked girl. She has run away and caused a great deal of trouble. She is going to be punished.' Her narrowed eyes darted about. 'You will see what happens to children who run away.' She grabbed Lily's arm and bundled her off the colonnade towards the laundry.

Sister Augusta followed and all three disappeared. The unwilling witnesses heard their footsteps on the concrete floor, then scuffling sounds and a sudden scream. The children outside froze in terrified silence. At the sound of a second scream, some flinched but none moved from their places.

Mother Sebastian's voice could be heard above the scuffling. 'Stand still, you wicked creature, stand still! Hold her, Sister.'

There followed several loud slaps and the screaming became hysterical. Sarah's lower lip was clenched between her teeth. Her fingers tightened around her crucifix. Some of the little ones started to cry. As the commotion inside and outside the building increased, Sarah began to move among the children, touching small heads and patting shoulders, all the time fighting an urge to run into the laundry and spirit Lily away.

Sister Leo was rocking on her heels and glancing up and down the rows of children, as if counting that no more were missing. Sister Innocent was threading her rosary beads through frail fingers, her lips moving without sound. Sister Matthew stood in front of the assembly with downcast eyes. Sister Monica's eyes were shut tight. Lily's screams turned into chilling howls and shrieks, louder and louder. Some of the children covered their ears. Most of the little ones were crying now. The sun was in their eyes, hanging low in the west but the day was still warm. Odours spread from puddles formed at small, bare feet. The air was heavy with perspiration. Flies buzzed about the yellow puddles.

The screaming stopped and they could hear Lily sobbing great exhausted, gulping sobs. One of the children collapsed a few yards in front of Sarah. She was about to help Sister Leo, who had rushed to the child, when gasps from the others turned her head. Mother Sebastian had reappeared, pushing Lily in front of her.

Lily? Sarah stared in open-mouthed horror. The girl who stood before them no longer looked like Lily. Head lowered at last and eyes fixed on the ground, Lily was paraded before them. Her arms were pinned behind her back so that she could not cover her shame. Her head of lovely black curls had been cropped bare. Jagged tufts showed how roughly her hair had been hacked. Cuts bled onto her forehead. Many of the children started crying again.

Mother Sebastian eyed the assembly in triumph. She put a finger under Lily's chin and forced her face upwards. 'When children run away, this is what happens,' she threatened.

Exposed for all to see, Lily trembled, her eyes puffy and red, her face swollen. Sarah leant one hand against the warm bricks of the colonnade, blinking against the stinging in her eyes. For one frightening moment, she could not draw breath.

That night, Sarah tossed in her bed. Sleep would not come. She was unable to shut out the image of Lily's shorn head, an image that gave rise to uncomfortable questions. What had happened to Lily today could not be right. It could not be right that she, Sister Matthew, Sister Leo, all of them, had stood by and let it happen. But what could she have done?

She stared across the foot of her bed at the crucifix on the opposite wall. She would never be a good nun if she did not learn to accept the authority of her superiors without question. Obedience was the hardest thing, she had always known that. And obedience wasn't obedience if one only obeyed rules one approved of. Yet how could the pain and humiliation of a child be the Will of God? 'Oh, Jesus, help me.'

Sarah tried to think of beautiful things, like sunsets on the beach at home. Her mind kept returning to her reception day. St Patricks Cathedral, where they had entered as Brides of Christ and left in the habits of the Sisters of St Frances Cabrini. And then came the night. After the incense and flowers and her mother's wedding dress, after the great pipe organ and Gregorian chant, after the euphoric, medieval ceremony and happy celebrations with family and friends, then had come that night.

*

In the morning, Sister Augusta gave Lily one of the dresses the girls wore on inspection days and a pair of black shoes and white socks. With cold indifference, she ordered her to bundle up her meagre belongings. Then she marched her charge down the great hall, Lily's recent humiliation hidden under the scarf she wore on kitchen duty.

Sarah was leaving the dining room on her way to class. She stepped right into Lily's path and stared at her Sunday best clothes. 'Lily! Where are you going?'

Lily stared back sullen and silent, eyes dark ringed after a sleepless night. There was no pleading in those eyes, no expectation. She stepped aside to let Sarah pass.

Sarah reached a hand towards her. 'Lily –'

Sister Augusta scowled Sarah out of the way and prodded Lily on towards Mother Sebastian's study. Through the open front doors, Sarah could see the Superior's flashy white Falcon. Whilomena was waiting in the front seat. Sister Augusta disappeared into Mother Sebastian's study, leaving Lily to wait outside. Sarah started towards her again but stopped as the study door reopened. Mother Sebastian stalked out with Sister Augusta behind her. Lily was bundled into the back seat and the car turned down the drive. When it returned shortly before Vespers, Lily was not with them.

*

In the semi-darkness of late evening, Sarah moved along silent corridors to her long empty classroom in search of a pen she had mislaid. The vow of poverty she was preparing to take prevented her asking for another until she had made every effort to find the one that was lost. On her desk, a strange-looking bundle was perched on top of her books and papers. It was wrapped in a scrap of material from the sewing room. She turned it over, unwrapping it. As the last fold of fabric fell away and the contents were revealed, she gasped.

The Little Black Princess had been patched, glued, stitched and taped. The cover looked like a jigsaw puzzle, but the title and author's name were correctly in place. Every page was pintucked into a spine of cotton fabric. Sarah began turning the pages as if she was reading the Bible then stopped, choking down a sob. Her tears would not be blinked away. Between the mended pages, lay a red geranium.

Thirty

Harriet Muller looked her new help up and down and up again. Harriet was short and much overweight. She had lank hair, a pallid complexion and dull eyes. With all of her children grown and flown, she was none too pleased to find herself pregnant again at the age of forty-nine. She launched into a catalogue of duties. 'I need the fire in the kitchen lit by six each morning. Do you know how to tell the time, girl?'

Lily stood with eyes lowered and hands behind her back as drilled at St Cuthbert's. 'Yes, Missus Muller.'

'You'll have to speak up, girl. I don't hear too well. Can you set a fire that will burn without filling the house with smoke?'

Lily spoke louder as requested. 'Yes, Missus Muller.'

'When the fires are lit, you will prepare and serve breakfast. Do you understand?'

'Yes, Missus Muller.'

'Your work will finish when you have cleaned up after the evening meal, unless I have extra jobs for you. Mother Sebastian says you're good with babies.' Harriet patted her swollen belly.

'Yes, Missus Muller.'

'Good. You'll have a couple of months to settle in and then you can look after this 'un as well. Your wages will be paid into the bank. You won't need money here. You'll have a roof over your head and all your meals. Best to save your pay for a rainy day.'

'Yes, Missus Muller.'

'Come, I'll show you where you sleep.'

Lily followed Harriet's broad beam as she waddled towards the back of the house, at least two inches of petticoat dangling below her skirt.

They followed a threadbare carpet runner down a dingy passage of peeling wallpaper. As they passed the kitchen, Lily saw dirty dishes piled on the sink. A marmalade cat was helping itself to something in a mixing bowl. Another cat, black with white socks, ran out of the kitchen between Lily's legs.

Harriet showed Lily into a shabby sleepout on the back veranda. Its only door was a battered fly screen. Holes rendered it useless as a fly screen, and a catch that wouldn't close rendered it useless as a door. In place of a window, a length of corrugated perspex ran along one wall. On a nail in the opposite wall dangled a single coat hanger. Beneath it, there was a camp stretcher with a thin mattress and a blanket covered in cat fur. The culprit, a white Persian, was curled up on the pillow with its tail around its body, washing its paws.

'Put your things away and come and see me in the sitting room. Do you have work clothes and an apron?'

'Yes, Missus Muller.'

Harriet heaved herself back up the passage.

Lily sat on the bunk and the cat climbed onto her lap. It purred like a motor idling when she stroked it. Every part of her body ached. She longed to lie down but she didn't dare. The woman would be waiting. She wanted to cry but she didn't dare do that either. With all the tears stored up inside her, she was sure she would never be able to stop. She put the cat back on the bunk and changed into her work shift, hanging her white dress on the coat hanger. She put on her apron and went in search of her new boss.

In a musty sitting room at the front of the house, Harriet was lounging by the radio with a tin of biscuits in reach of her fat fingers. Her legs were propped up on a stool. 'Clean up the kitchen and get dinner started,' she ordered when Lily appeared.

In the kitchen, Lily looked about her, shaking her head. There seemed little point in Sister Monica's home craft lessons or Sister Leo's hygiene classes to end up working for this lazy layabout. In the river camp, Aunty Mary and the woman called Pearl had kept a much cleaner house. She hardly knew where to begin. There was one window, shut tight, its glass opaque with grime. Lily unlocked it and threw it open. She chased the cats away and cleared the benches. She filled an iron kettle and started the fire. After she had done the dishes, she scrubbed the benches, washed the window and then looked for a broom and a mop. With the floor clean at last, she returned to the sleep-out and sank onto her bunk.

The screen door opened without ceremony. Lily lifted her head to see a heavily built man of about fifty filling the doorway.

He leered at her. 'Well, well. Who do we have here?'

Lily guessed who this must be. She forced her aching limbs to stand up again. 'I'm Lily, Mister Muller.'

'Here, here. None of that "Mister" stuff. Call me Sid, sweetheart.' A wide grin split his fleshy face.

Lily lowered her eyes. 'I don't think I should do that, Mister Muller.'

'Please yourself, sweetheart. 'Ere, 'ave a lolly.' Muller pulled a brown paper bag from the pocket of his pants.

Lily shrank in disgust from the dirty fingernails that held out the sweets. 'No, thank you, Mister Muller.'

'Don't like peppermints, eh? Well, I reckon they might be a bit hot for little girls. I bet you like chocolate, though, don't you, eh?'

'I don't know, Mister Muller. I've never had chocolate.'

'Never had chocolate? Well, we'll have to fix that, sweetheart.' He gave Lily a lecherous wink and ambled away, letting the door bang behind him.

Lily sped down the passage to ask Harriet what she wanted for dinner.

Thirty-one

On a warm November afternoon, Sarah waited on the convent steps for the community's van to crunch its way around from the garage. Sister Matthew needed to collect some books, and Sarah was to accompany her into town. They turned down the geranium drive, Sarah shaking her head as they passed children at work in the garden.

Sister Matthew claimed her attention. 'Have you been into Cobbs Crossing yet, Sister Anthony?

'Um, no, I haven't. Is the town very big?'

'It's growing all the time. There's a high school now, two churches, a football oval, and at least four hotels that I know of.' Sister Matthew laughed, then as another thought occurred, she sobered. 'There's also a swimming pool.'

Sarah raised her eyebrows at the subdued tone as the pool was mentioned but as Sister Matthew did not elaborate, Sarah changed the subject. 'Doctor Lawrence was at the orphanage yesterday. Does he come to St Cuthbert's often?

'Doctor Lawrence is a saint. He comes out whenever Sister Leo calls him and sometimes when she doesn't. Sister says he never charges us a penny. His wife is a lovely lady too. Mrs Lawrence is the president of the Cobbs Crossing Ladies' Guild and she sees to it that a lot of the guild's fundraising finds its way to us.'

'I'm sure Mother Sebastian welcomes their donations.'

'I'm sure she does. There always seems to be plenty to do with the money. Young Father Conway is generous to us as well. He makes a regular gift on behalf of St Mary's parish.'

Sarah frowned. So many sources of funding, not to mention free medical services, and yet the children could not eat meat and the older girls, young women really, had to do with rags instead of sanitary napkins. Sister Matthew was still talking, pointing out landmarks and properties as they hurtled along.

They entered the town through the same streets of weatherboard houses and picket-fenced gardens that Sarah had seen on her arrival. Turning east, they crossed the train tracks and veered onto the Calder Highway. They passed the railway station and the van turned off the road under a wrought-iron arch that announced 'Victory Park'. In the distance, Sarah could see a football oval and, immediately in front of them, the swimming pool. She gasped at what Sister Matthew had no doubt brought her here to see. On the wire fence that surrounded the pool, a sign announced 'WHITES ONLY'.

'Never seen anything like that in the south?'

Sarah shook her head.

'I'm not surprised. They get away with much more than they could in the bigger towns, being way up here in the never-never.'

'Is it legal?'

'I'm not sure, but it wouldn't matter much. I have a feeling that the law in Cobbs Crossing would sympathise with the sentiment.'

With the mighty Murray River flowing clean and free less than twenty miles from town, the swimming pool might have struggled for patronage if it were not for the Aboriginal camp sprawled along the river bank. As the river flowed north, town families intent on a picnic and a dip, drove well south of the camp.

Family men, especially men with daughters, knew they had to be extra vigilant. 'A man can't be too careful. Bloody boongs. They might, y'know, in the water. Next thing, some nice white girl's got a swollen belly.'

Most people laughed at the absurdity of such a notion, but there were always those who nodded and shuddered as their imaginations ran riot.

Sister Matthew turned back into town along Anzac Avenue and

parked at the top of Memorial Square, the civic and social centre of town. Every schoolkid knew that the square was not a square but a very large rectangle, a long expanse of lawn with a war memorial at its centre. The cenotaph was flanked by giant jacaranda trees that blazed lavender-blue every November, in time for Remembrance Day.

The lawn was the topic of many council debates. The mayor many times proposed paving the entire square, as a water-saving economy.

The Misses Klein just as often argued in alternate phrases.

'It would be a disgrace –'

'– if a town that had given so many sons –'

'– could not spare enough water –'

'– to keep a patch of grass green in their memory.'

Though neither had ever been married, the town afforded Miss Constance Klein and her sister Mary the respectful title of war widows, both having lost their fiancés at El Alamein. The names of their lost loves were inscribed on the cenotaph and the sisters were champions of Memorial Square maintenance.

From opposite ends of the Square, St John's Church of England and St Mary's Catholic church faced each other in bluestone solidity. Between them, the police station and the clubrooms of the Returned Services League, small shops, eateries, the Railway Hotel, and the *Chronicle* office overlooked the cenotaph and the jacarandas.

Joe, the grocer, declared the square to be 'All-a-most a piazza!'

Majik's father, Old George, was less enthusiastic. 'Whichever way you turn, you got them damn devil-dodgers watchin' you.' Old George still wore his faded army uniform, hoping that the reminder that he had served his country as well as any man might keep Sergeant Buchanan off his back. It didn't. Nor did it get him across the threshold of the RSL clubrooms.

When the van was parked at the end of the square, Sarah put her hand on the door but Sister Matthew shook her head.

'No need, Sister. I won't be long.' She disappeared, leaving Sarah alone.

Sitting in the sun, the little van soon became stuffy. Sarah wound down her window and turned towards the cooler air. On the footpath, a middle-aged man in a navy suit sat behind a collapsible table. The table was covered in artificial poppies and every now and then, someone stopped to buy one. They dropped donations into a tobacco tin, fixing the blood-red emblem into their lapels as they walked away.

Today was the eleventh of November, Remembrance Day. On this day as on Anzac Day, Sarah's thoughts of home and her father would defy her efforts to discipline her memories. This would be the third year that she had not worn a Flanders poppy in remembrance; next April would mark the fourth year that she had not watched her father marching with his mates and then standing as if cast in bronze as the bugle sounded the Last Post.

In the Norton home, Anzac Day was sacred. No matter how many bills were waiting to be paid, Sarah's mother, Vera Norton, always squirreled away a few shillings for the two-up game that would be held after the march and a few more for Henry to buy a round of drinks. She wouldn't see her husband shamed in front of his mates, for want of a bob or two to shout a digger a beer. On the morning of the march, she would be up early to polish Henry's medals and pin them in a straight line across his chest. Henry was allowed one day a year to feel proud. One day a year, his wife and children joined the crowds that lined the streets to watch the march. One day a year, flags waved and people cheered, while the nation ensured that the next generation would be just as keen to troop away to war. One day a year, the veterans paraded to the applause of a grateful country and, while the law turned a blind eye, played two-up in exclusive camaraderie 'lest we forget'.

'Sister Anthony?'

Sarah was startled out of her daydream. She looked up to see Mick striding towards her, Bronko romping in front of him.

Mick draped an arm along the top of Sarah's window and leant into the van. 'This is a bit of luck. I was on my way out to the orphanage but you can save me a trip.'

As he bent down to speak to her, his chest was so close to Sarah's face that she could smell the sun on his skin. It conjured a memory of the day he had introduced himself at St Cuthbert's. She felt again the firmness of his handshake. She put her hand on the car door, intending to open it, step out and put a more modest space between them. She realised that to open the door, she would have to knock him over.

She took refuge in formality. 'How can I help you, Mr O'Mara?'

'Oh, I just thought the Sisters might rest easier if they knew that the scoundrel that's been encouraging orphans to run off in the night has been arrested.' There was a twinkle in his eyes. 'In fact, she's in the lock-up.'

'She?'

'Pearl Marsh.'

'Pearl?'

'Yes, but surely you read about it in the *Chronicle*, Sister Anthony?'

'I'm only a novice, Mr O'Mara. I'm not permitted to read newspapers.'

Mick raised an eyebrow and drew back a little, unwinding his body. 'Next you'll be telling me you don't listen to radios either.'

'Well, as a matter of fact, we don't.'

Mick gave a gasping laugh. 'It must be like living on another planet. How do you keep up with what's going on in the world?'

His amusement rankled. Sarah mustered her dignity and answered him in a superior tone, intended to suggest that she belonged to a world he wouldn't understand. 'To tell you the truth, I haven't missed knowing everything that's going on in the world. It's been peaceful.'

'And convenient?'

She didn't know what he was getting at but thought it wiser not to ask. 'About poor Pearl, Mr O'Mara. She shouldn't be in jail. She didn't have anything to do with Lily's disappearance. Lily said she ran away because –' Sarah caught herself just in time.

'Because?' Mick hinted hopefully.

Sarah avoided the trap. 'I guess it's Lily's business. She deserves some privacy, don't you think?' She wondered if privacy was a concept a journalist would understand.

'Sergeant Buchanan says Mother Sebastian is convinced Pearl had a hand in it. I wonder why she thinks Pearl is involved.'

Sarah wondered so too.

The town hall clock began to chime the eleventh hour of the eleventh day of the eleventh month. The man in the navy suit turned his portable radio up full blast and the notes of a bugle floated loud and clear. Cars and shops turned their radios up too and the square was filled with the strains of the Last Post. The poppy salesman stood to attention and shoppers stood motionless. Old George appeared from under one of the jacarandas and came to attention, saluting the cenotaph. Sarah stared at the old man's chest, recognising on his faded uniform medals from the African and Pacific campaigns, the same medals her father wore.

The Misses Klein, the only people moving in the square, came out of their fashion boutique carrying between them a large wreath of red poppies. They walked up the steps of the cenotaph and disappeared from view. Mick stepped back from the car, not at attention but tall and still, his long legs planted apart. Sarah escaped the car at last and stood in respectful silence.

Sister Matthew appeared in a shop doorway, her arms full of parcels. She too waited till the bugler had finished. As the last notes died away, Mick sprang to meet her and helped load her bundles into the van. While Sister Matthew arranged her parcels, he tossed Sarah a salute and a cheeky grin before he sauntered off.

Sarah told Sister Matthew about Pearl's arrest and the nuns hurried off on foot, to the other end of Memorial Square. The front office of the police station was unattended, but from somewhere behind it, they could hear a voice they recognised. Pearl was begging to know how she could get her child back, one minute screaming angry demands, the next pleading and making tearful promises. They heard Sergeant Buchanan's harsh growl, followed by a scream from Pearl as a metallic door slammed shut with a clang. Footsteps came towards them. From behind the safety of his counter-topped desk, Sergeant Buchanan found himself confronted by two indignant nuns.

Sarah glared across the counter. 'Do you still think Mrs Marsh will soon forget her son, Sergeant?'

His disdainful grin displayed nicotine stained teeth but no humour. The stale smell of his last cigarette hung about him.

Sarah demanded to know what charges had been laid against Pearl.

'No charges, Sisters. Just lettin' her cool her heels for a bit. Just a warnin' like.'

Sarah lifted her chin. 'I give you my word, Sergeant, Pearl Marsh had nothing to do with Lily Matthews's disappearance.'

Buchanan placed his palms on the counter and leaned towards her. He raised shaggy eyebrows. 'Oh? And how can you be so sure, Sister? I found them together, you know.'

'You found them together, Sergeant, because Pearl found Lily lost in the bush and offered her protection. Is this the reward she gets for being a Good Samaritan? Besides, if Pearl had encouraged any child to run away, it would have been Jamarra, her son. That makes sense, doesn't it? Pearl has never shown any interest in Lily.'

Sister Matthew offered her support. 'I don't believe they'd ever met before either, Sergeant. Lily wasn't even allowed to go on the St Patrick's Day picnic at Mullanurra.'

Sarah nodded. 'That's right! There's just no reason to keep her locked up.'

Buchanan raised surrendering hands. 'Enough, Sisters! Enough! If you're happy to vouch for the woman, I'll turn her loose before the day is over. How's that?'

Sarah lifted her chin. 'How about to us, right now, Sergeant?'

Thirty-two

Rachel Steiner, the district nurse, was a smart, no-nonsense forty-year-old. She wore a blue uniform and kept her brown hair netted in a tidy bun. Every few weeks, Rachel called to check on the progress of Harriet's pregnancy.

At each visit, Lily served her own home-made scones in Harriet's sitting room and Rachel watched the girl go about her work. In such a short time, she observed, the child had converted the Muller household's chaos into a reasonable standard of order and cleanliness. Rachel knew enough of Sid and Harriet Muller to believe that there wouldn't be much leisure in Lily's life.

One day, after examining Harriet, Rachel accepted a scone and a cup of tea and asked, 'When is Lily's day off, Mrs Muller?' She sipped her tea. 'Sundays, perhaps?'

The question seemed to bewilder Harriet. 'Sunday? Ah yes, Sunday,' she stammered, clutching her belly. 'That is, Sunday afternoon…um… until four o'clock.'

Rachel smiled and glanced up as Lily collected their cups. 'Would you like to come out with me on Sunday, Lily, and meet my Katie?'

Lily stared at Rachel as if she had invited her to Outer Mongolia. Her eyes darted towards Harriet.

Rachel followed her glance. 'Oh, Mrs Muller won't mind, will you, Harriet, seeing it is Lily's day off? I could pick her up after lunch and have her back by four.'

Harriet spluttered but she couldn't think of a way to say no. 'As long as she's back on time, Mrs Steiner. I need her, you know.' Harriet spread her hands across her belly as if the baby was about to pop into the world at any minute.

'Yes, I know you do, dear. We'll be back by four, I promise.'

*

For the next three days, Lily scrubbed, cleaned and cooked like never before. Harriet picked and found fault. Lily bore the grumblings in silence and looked for ways to please. She cut flowers from the neglected garden and arranged them on the little table beside Harriet's chair. She sweetened Harriet's tea with honey and baked her favourite cakes. When Harriet continued to complain, Lily tried harder. She had not forgotten Mother Sebastian's spite and she was determined not to give Harriet an excuse to cancel her outing.

On Sunday, Harriet dawdled over her lunch. When she was finished at last, Lily cleared away the dishes and changed into her one good dress. She put on the orphanage socks and shoes and went outside to wait for Rachel. When the nurse's little blue Beetle arrived in the driveway, Lily ran to meet it. She stopped, puzzled. There was another girl sitting beside Rachel and the car only had front doors.

The girl jumped out, laughing at Lily's confusion and pushed her seat forward. 'You have to climb over.'

Rachel made the introductions. 'Lily, this is my Katie. Katie, this is Lily Matthews.'

Katie had the same cheerful face as her mother and the same green eyes but she had blonde hair cut in a short bob. 'C'mon, Lily. We can both sit in the back.' She climbed into the back seat, pulling the front seat upright again when Lily had clambered in after her.

'No giggling back there, mind,' Rachel teased.

The Steiner home was a large, well-preserved heritage house surrounded by broad verandas. It was set in a well-kept cottage garden. Katie rushed Lily to her bedroom. It was a pretty, girly room of dolls, dresses and posters and a dressing-table cluttered with perfume bottles, make-up and jewellery. It was clean but so untidy, a glorious chaotic mess of teenage trappings. The walls were covered with photos of film stars, cut from magazines. The chopped-up magazines were still on the floor. On a bedside table, a doll in a crinoline was holding a lamp. Pink chintz curtains had more film stars pinned to them.

Lily stared around her. 'All this is yours, Katie? You have this whole room, all to yourself?'

'Yep.' Katie flopped on the floor. She pulled a record player from under her bed and put a record on the turntable. '*Jailhouse Rock*,' she announced with a grin.

Lily had never heard anything like the music that came out of that little machine.

Thirty-three

Sarah and Whilomena still rotated portress duties between them. It was Sarah's turn the following day when Mick arrived again. He turned his most charming smile on her. He preferred talking to the novices when he was fishing for information. Mother Sebastian was too cagey to let anything slip. Not as attractive as this one either.

Sarah stepped onto the veranda. 'I'm actually glad to see you today, Mr O'Mara.'

He grinned and Sarah blushed, realising how he'd interpreted her words.

She turned her head, grateful for the breeze that floated across the hill and hurried to explain. 'I wanted to tell you that after we talked about Pearl being arrested, I remembered that Lily told me she had never met Pearl before she ran away.'

'And you believe her?'

'Yes, I do. Children don't lie as easily as adults do, Mr O'Mara.' Sarah patted the head of a little boy who had run up and hidden his face in her habit. 'What's the matter, Peter?'

'Thithter routhed on me.'

'What were you doing to make Sister rouse on you?'

'Nuffin.'

'Nothing? Sister roused on you for nothing? Poor Peter.'

Mick looked on as Sarah dug out one of the large white handkerchiefs peculiar to nuns and dabbed at Peter's damp eyes. 'You really like these kids, don't you, Sister?'

'Of course. They're children. Would you like to come to the kitchen, Peter, and see what Sister Monica has for us?'

Peter beamed, his tears forgotten.

Sarah sighed over his head and murmured as if speaking to herself. 'It won't be much. There's never enough for meals, never mind snacks.' She realised she had spoken aloud and reddened. 'I don't mean to sound ungrateful to our benefactors, Mr O'Mara. The Ladies' Guild, Father Conway and St Mary's, they're all very generous.'

'The Ladies' Guild supports St Cuthbert's? St Mary's Parish as well?

'Yes, I believe so.'

'And Harris of course.'

'Mr Harris? From Mullanurra? I didn't know that he –'

'For the last fifteen years at least, it seems, and of course, there's Welfare too. These kids should be eating like kings, Sister. Where do you suppose all that money is going?'

Sarah gasped. 'I'm sure there has been no misuse of funds, Mr O'Mara. It's just that, well, food must be so expensive.'

'It isn't that expensive, Sister. I admire your loyalty,' the tone of Mick's voice implied 'your naivety', 'but sooner or later questions are going to be asked about this place and the authorities will want answers.'

They were interrupted by Whilomena. She did not look well. Her eyes were inflamed and her face was flushed. She took a moment to catch her breath before speaking. 'Excuse me, Mr O'Mara. Sister Anthony, Mother Sebastian asked me to remind you that we need to pack our cases today, as we'll be leaving very early in the morning.'

'Thank you, Sister. Whoops!' Sarah was almost pulled off her feet by Peter, who had shuffled around to the other side of her at Whilomena's appearance, dragging the skirt of Sarah's habit with him, his face hidden in its folds again. She laughed as she steadied herself.

Whilomena frowned at Peter. She turned away coughing, and disappeared inside the convent.

Sarah leaned down and whispered to Peter, 'Go and wait for me by the kitchen door, Peter, that's a good boy. I won't be long. Wait. Have you fed the chickens today, Peter?'

'No, Thithter.'

'Well, why don't you ask Joseph to help you? I'm sure he'd like the chickens. Then you can both wait for me at the kitchen.'

'Yeth, Thithter.'

Her eyes followed him as he scampered away.

Mick had waited, watching Sarah as she tended to Peter. Whilomena's words had made him curious. 'Packing? Had enough of St Cuthbert's, Sister Anthony?'

Sarah managed to keep a straight face. 'Sister Whilomena and I are returning to the novitiate to take our vows, Mr O'Mara. We'll be back after Christmas.'

'Glad to hear it…that you'll be back, I mean. Taking your vows, eh? That means you'll be trusted with worldly temptations like newspapers?'

She nodded with a small smile, flattered that he had remembered.

His expression sobered and a frown furrowed his brow. 'Sister, I hope this won't sound disrespectful, but I don't know many true believers and there's something personal I'd like to ask.' He spoke with uncharacteristic hesitation and started down the veranda steps while he was speaking, so that she was obliged to follow.

She threw him a guarded glance. Lay people were often curious about religious life and this man was a journalist. What on earth was he going to ask her?

They were now walking along the geranium path towards his car.

He took her silence for permission to ask his question. 'What is it that makes you so sure of your faith, Sister? I don't mean what you've been taught to believe, but –'

'One isn't taught to believe, Mr O'Mara. Faith is a gift from God.' As soon as she had delivered the catechism answer, Sarah wished she had ignored him or at least come up with something more original, more clever. Too late.

'Not taught, eh?' Mick shook his head. 'Come on, Sister. Isn't it just a bit suspicious, don't you think, that all the kids you teach will end up with Catholic "faith" and those who go to the synagogue will end up with Jewish "faith" and so on for Muslims, Baptists, Mormons, Hindus, and the high Church of England?'

Sarah stopped walking. She stood with one hand over the crucifix at her waist, trying to think of something to say.

135

Mick seemed not to notice. He pressed on. 'If faith is not taught, Sister, how do you explain the Christian mission to take the gospel "to the whole world"?' Lost in his argument, Mick had continued striding forward when Sarah had stopped. Now he looked around and noticed her discomfort. He walked back towards her. 'I'm sorry, Sister. I guess I can get a bit carried away sometimes.' He lowered his voice. 'But really, Sister Anthony, if it's not to teach faith, how do you justify keeping all these poor little non-orphans at St Cuthbert's?'

Sarah turned startled eyes towards the convent, glad to be out of earshot but conscious that they were in full view of the front windows and the balcony. She glanced up. There was no one there. 'Someone has to prepare them for the outside world, Mr O'Mara.'

Mick's intense expression relaxed into an infuriating grin that suggested he suspected Sister Anthony's knowledge of "the outside world" wouldn't fill a thimble. Sarah could not hold his gaze.

'The children are here to get a good education, Mr O'Mara.'

'A good education? Qualified to be labourers and domestics? Respectable occupations for sure, but is that what your parents would have called a good education, Sister? How many of these kids do you expect to go to university, Sister Anthony?'

Sarah wondered how she could turn this conversation off. For a moment, she thought of simply walking away. 'Well, what do you expect me to do about it, Mr O'Mara?' she retorted.

Mick raised his eyebrows at her tone but the desperation in her voice made him merciful. He spoke more gently. 'The question is, what do *you* expect you to do about it, Sister Anthony?'

They had reached his ute. It looked at home under the stringybark and peppercorn trees. Mick leaned his back against it. Bronko's head appeared through the open window and rested on Mick's shoulder.

Mick raised an arm above his head to rub the dog's ears, his expression sober. 'How well do you know Pearl, Sister?'

Sarah welcomed the change of subject. 'She comes here often, always looking for a child she calls Tallara. She won't believe that we don't have a Tallara.'

'Have you never known of a child's name being changed at St Cuthbert's, Sister Anthony?'

Sarah's mouth opened and closed again. He knew. He knew that Mother Sebastian changed the children's names.

'Well, don't you think that's probably what happened to Tallara?'

She bit her lip and nodded. Yes, that was exactly what she had suspected ever since Jamarra's name had been changed. However, questioning Mother Sebastian had not produced a result. She reddened. He must think her very stupid or even untruthful.

Mick didn't wait for a reply. 'Pearl had Tallara when she was only fourteen. The baby was packed off to St Cuthbert's.'

Fourteen! Then the child would be much older than Sarah had supposed.

'Do you know anything special about the twenty-first of September, Sister?'

Sarah blinked. 'Well, yes. Sister Matthew celebrated her feast day two months ago. The twenty-first of September is the feast of Saint Matthew.'

'Is that so? Well, I'll bet you anything, Sister Anthony, that if there is a fifteen-year-old girl at St Cuthbert's surnamed Matthew or perhaps Matthews, her file will show that she arrived on the twenty-first of September. What?' The colour had left Sarah's face. He straightened up, reaching out a hand towards her shoulder but dropping it before he touched her.

'Lily! Lily is Lily Matthews.'

He whistled. 'Yes of course, the one that ran away. And she is about fifteen?'

'Yes, that's right.'

'Pearl's Tallara has a cloud-shaped birthmark on her shoulder.'

'I've never seen a birthmark on Lily. Well, of course I've never looked for one.'

'I would love to know what the date on Lily's file is.'

'Lily isn't at St Cuthbert's any more. She was sent away. I doubt Mother Sebastian will tell us where she was taken.'

'All the more reason for getting a look at those files. They might say where she is. It would be cruel to get Pearl's hopes up if we can't tell her where her daughter is.'

'Not much chance of seeing the files. They're kept under lock and key in Mother Sebastian's study.'

Mick's eyes twinkled. 'Well ,Sister, you'll have more than your vows to think about while you're at the novitiate, won't you?'

'I'll pray about it, Mr O'Mara, every day.'

Mick snorted and shook his head. 'Is that really how you're going to tackle problems for the rest of your life, Sister Anthony? Pray about whatever is wrong?'

Sarah stiffened. 'Prayer is very powerful, Mr O'Mara.'

'It doesn't seem to be working at St Cuthbert's.' Mick moved around the car and slipped behind the wheel, tipping his hat to Sarah.

She stepped back as the ute circled on the gravel and headed down the driveway leaving her staring after him. How uncomfortable this irreverent man could make her feel. Despite the fact that he seemed to enjoy shocking her with his atheistic views, she suspected a closet humanitarian lurked beneath the surface. But he was so superior, and altogether too sure of himself.

She headed back to the convent, still fuming as his challenges repeated themselves in her head. Some of his accusations she had to admit were undeniable. St Cuthbert's curriculum would not take students to high school, let alone university. Yes, her father had insisted that his children's schooling would be their path out of poverty. Henry Norton didn't challenge the status quo for himself. His church taught him to accept the will of God. The traditions of his class and station taught him that knowing your place was important. You didn't rock the boat. You didn't challenge authority, no matter how much you privately griped about its power over your life. Anyone who did was 'just a bloody stirrer'. In Henry's code, you accepted the cards life dealt you and blamed no one but yourself for your failures. But he certainly wanted better for his children, and education, he believed, would provide it. 'Is that what your parents would have called a good education, Sister Anthony?' Mick had touched a nerve.

Sarah quickened her pace. Little Peter would be waiting for her. As she reached the veranda, a basketball hurtled around the corner of the building and bounced down the driveway pursued by a bunch of rowdy children. Laughing and distracted by their game, they tore after the ball as it rolled straight towards the forbidden geranium path. To Sarah's horror, at least a dozen children headed after it. She scooped up her habit and raced towards the ball. The children skidded to a halt at the sight of Sister Anthony, her skirts up around her knees and running. She placed a hushing finger on her lips. At the sound of a door opening, eyes darted down the veranda towards Mother Sebastian's study.

Sarah tossed the ball to one of the children. 'Go!'

Alert to the danger now, they sped back the way they had come and disappeared. Coming to investigate the commotion, a puzzled Mother Sebastian arrived at the end of the veranda to find only Sister Anthony praying her rosary on the geranium path.

As Sarah prepared for bed that evening, her thoughts strayed to her conversation with the newspaper man. She slipped between the sheets remembering that he had known all along about Mother Sebastian's name changes. She resented having felt obliged to keep silent on that score and burned at the thought that he must consider her very naïve. She saw again the amusement in his eyes when she talked of the power of prayer. Uncomfortable with the realisation that his good opinion was important to her, Sarah accused herself of pride. Yes, she confessed to herself, and more than pride. Although Mr O'Mara irritated and annoyed her, he also stirred feelings inconsistent with her impending vow of chastity. She leapt out of bed and knelt on the bare floorboards, her face buried in her hands. 'Dear Jesus, help me to be worthy of Your Love. Take these feelings from me. Help me to be a good nun.'

Thirty-four

Lily now lived for her Sunday afternoons, every one spent with Rachel and Katie. In December, she helped them decorate the first Christmas tree that she had ever seen. The more time she spent with the Steiners, the more her servitude with Sid and Harriet disgusted her. Sometimes, life with the Mullers also alarmed her. Unwelcome gifts of chocolate had started appearing on her pillow. Without knowing why, Lily sensed that these gifts were wrong and dangerous.

Harriet's job list grew and grew. Lily was now expected to work in the garden as well as the house. One morning, she knelt on a goat track path behind the house, attacking weeds with her bare hands. Harriet's radio was turned up so loud that Lily could hear it where she worked.

At the bottom of the garden, a rusty gate creaked as Sid Muller opened it. He lumbered along the path towards the house and paused to watch Lily work. 'Not like that, sweetheart. It'll take a month of Sundays like that. Use a hoe.'

'A hoe, Mister Muller?'

'Don't you know what a hoe is, sweetheart? There'll be one in the shed. Come on, I'll show you.'

He stretched out his hand to help her up but Lily jumped to her feet before he touched her. Muller trudged back the way he had come, through neglected beds of spindly cabbages. Lily followed well behind. Just before the garden gate, he disappeared into a small, tin shed. Lily waited by the open door.

Muller bellowed against the radio they could still hear. 'Well, come on in. I can't show you the tools with you out there, sweetheart.'

Lily wished he wouldn't call her that. He always called her 'girl' when Harriet was present, she noticed. She stepped inside. The shed was stuffy and dark and smelled of mildew. There were piles of hessian bags and stacks of empty planters against the back wall. Along the side walls, implements she had never seen before were propped in disarray.

Muller selected a pronged tool with a long wooden handle and held it out. 'Well, come and get it, sweetheart.'

Lily reached for the hoe.

Muller put it behind his back. With his other arm, he grabbed Lily around the waist. 'First, how about a kiss for old Sid, eh, sweetheart?' He leered at her, his eyes roving over her body.

Lily struggled. She wrenched free and ran towards the door. Muller dropped the hoe. He pulled her back, trapping her in sinewy arms and holding her close against his body.

'No, Mister Muller! Let me go! Let me go!'

The nauseating smell of stale sweat and body odour made her gag. She struggled to break away but he crushed her to him.

'Now, don't be a silly girl. Just a little kiss. Don't I give you all those nice chocolates? You have to be nice to old Sid, sweetheart.' One hand moved over Lily's breast and squeezed.

She screamed. Muller covered her mouth with his own. She twisted her face away from the slobbering lips. The rough stubble of his un-shaven face grazed her cheek like sandpaper. She kicked hard against his shins and he let go with a howl.

Lily sprang for the door again.

He cut her off and slammed it shut. The cajoling smile was gone. 'It's time for you to learn how to be nice to old Sid, sweetheart.'

Lily backed away breathing hard. Eyes wide with panic, she stared about the shed like a cornered animal. There were no windows. No other doors.

'Missus Muller! Missus Muller! Help me!' She screamed so loudly that she hurt her throat.

Muller chuckled. 'The missus won't hear you, sweetheart. It's just you and me.'

He lumbered forward and pushed Lily backwards onto the pile of sacks. He lowered himself to his knees in front of her and pushed her legs apart. With one hand at Lily's throat, he fumbled with his belt. Lily drew her legs up to her chest and kicked. Muller went sprawling backwards. He clambered back to Lily, dragging her legs down towards him so that her head and shoulders thumped onto the earthen floor.

Kneeling on her legs, he slammed his hand hard against the side of her face. 'So that's how it's going to be, eh? You bloody little boong! I'll teach you, you bloody black bitch.'

He lifted his hand again and again. Lily's head exploded with pain. Her whole world had shrunk to the repeated hammering of his angry fist. Her arms flayed about in a futile effort to ward him off. One hand fell on something hard on the floor beside her. She grabbed the handle of the hoe and swung with all the strength her fear mustered, bringing the iron prongs smashing against the side of his head. Muller crumpled to the floor, blood pouring down the side of his face. This time, he stayed down.

Lily dragged herself up. Every movement hurt. She pushed herself to her feet, gasping for air. Even breathing hurt. Muller had not moved. Blood was pooling around his head. Lily realised she was still holding the bloodstained hoe. She dropped it as if it was a poisonous snake and rushed at the door, wrenching it open.

The sunlight was blinding. She leaned forward, her hands on her knees, sobbing and struggling to breathe. She looked back into the shed. In the flood of light that streamed in from the open door, Sid Muller's lifeless body bled into the dirt. Lily choked down the scream that rose in her throat. A gulping sob burst through her clenched teeth.

Forcing her aching limbs to move, she ran. Through the garden she ran and on past the house, then down the treeless, gravelled drive towards the highway. She had no idea where she was going, only that she must be gone. The image of Muller's bleeding body forced every other thought from her mind. She ignored the pain that protested every move. Propelled by the horror of what she had done, blinded by tears and the sweat that poured into her eyes, Lily ran.

Thirty-five

Mother Sebastian summoned Sarah. She did not offer a chair, leaving her novice to kneel before her. 'Joseph May is to be transferred, Sister. Tell Sister Whilomena to be ready to leave with me in an hour.'

Sarah caught her breath. In her mind, she saw Pearl's pleading face. As long as Jamarra stayed at St Cuthbert's, there was a chance for their reunion. 'But Mother, Joseph has just started to make friends here. Don't you think –'

'You are not yet the Superior of this convent, Sister Anthony, and I do not need to explain my actions to you.'

'Please, Mother. There are empty beds in the boys' dormitory. With Lily gone, the children are already uneasy.'

'You are wasting your breath, Sister. You are the very reason we are sending the boy away.' Mother Sebastian smirked as the colour drained from Sarah's face. 'Your friendship with his mother, oh yes, Sergeant Buchanan told me, not to mention your little chats with this newspaper man. Whatever you tell him is certain to be misconstrued. You have made it dangerous for the boy to be here, Sister, and you can explain that to his mother, next time she comes weeping at our door.'

Thirty-six

In November of their third year as Sisters of St Frances Cabrini, it was time for Sarah and Whilomena to return to St Magdalene's. Novices who had, like Sarah, entered as girls of seventeen, would be returning to the Mother House as twenty-year-olds to take their first vows.

Mother Sebastian would be submitting a report to the Provincial Superior, Mother Anna. Whilomena's report, Sarah supposed with a sigh, would be glowing with enthusiasm. Sarah made every effort to display a humble heart to her Superior, offering up her thoughts, words and deeds and begging God for the grace to be a perfect nun.

When the time came for them to leave, Whilomena's cough was much worse and she was being cared for by Sister Leo in the infirmary. Mother Sebastian, taking advantage of the opportunity to see Melbourne and St Magdalene's again, appointed herself as Sarah's travelling companion.

In the early hours of Wednesday morning, Sarah and Mother Sebastian waited on the Cobbs Crossing railway station. Every few minutes, Mother Sebastian was seized with a noisy fit of coughing. Despite the prospect of ten hours closeted alone with her Superior, Sarah scanned the horizon with eager eyes. She loved train travel. A distant whistle increased her excitement and within minutes the platform erupted as the Mildura Sunlight thundered into the station.

Mother Sebastian headed for the train, leaving her suitcase sitting on the platform. Sarah picked up both their cases and followed. Once the nuns had installed themselves in an empty compartment, it stayed empty. None of the other passengers appeared eager to spend a day watching their language and engaging in wholesome conversation.

Not that much conversation was required. Mother Sebastian's handkerchief didn't leave her face. Sarah found the perpetual coughing tedious but by the time the train steamed into the windswept chill of Ballarat, she was accusing herself of failing in charity. Mother Sebastian was leaning into one corner, her eyes closed, her mouth slack and her face a sickly, putty grey. Beads of perspiration dotted her upper lip. The starch of her coif was damp across her forehead.

Sarah stepped into the passage and returned with a paper cup full of water. Mother Sebastian took it in an unsteady hand. She hesitated, glancing towards the corridor.

Sarah knew what the problem was. 'It's all right, Mother. I'll stand in the doorway. No one will see you drinking.'

Before they reached Melbourne, it was obvious that Mother Sebastian was seriously ill. Mother Eymard and Sister Daniel, who met them at Spencer Street Station, decided to take her straight to Mother Basil at St Martin de Porres Hospital. As Mother Sebastian was settled into bed, Sarah watched the nurses going about their duties with a twinge of envy.

Thirty-seven

Sarah followed Sister Daniel along the main gallery of the Mother House, where large windows overlooked a landscaped courtyard. The garden's well-maintained lawns were a lush green at this time of year. Ash trees umbrellaed over walkways, spreading splashes of gold and claret. Hundreds of sparrows twittered in their branches, enjoying the spring sunshine. Down in the courtyard, Sarah could see other returning novices renewing acquaintances, their excited chatter challenging the sparrows.

Sister Daniel led Sarah to one of the rooms that had been prepared for the novices. Sarah hardly glanced at the familiar white walls and simple furnishings. She stood clutching her suitcase in both hands as Sister Daniel crossed the tiny room and opened its only window. As soon as she left, Sarah hurried to close the door, standing with her back against it and her suitcase still in her hands, as if shutting out something she was afraid of.

Over the next few days, every returning novice was scheduled to meet with the Mistress of Novices. Mother Eymard was a cultured gentlewoman in her mid-seventies. Dedicated to her vocation, she imposed as much discipline on herself as she did on her novices. Her face was as lined as the crumpled paper in her wastebasket but her back was straight and her head erect. Her businesslike office was the opposite of Mother Anna's gracious parlour in every respect.

When Sarah went to kneel, Mother Eymard pointed with her pen, indicating a chair on the other side of her desk. 'Welcome back to St Magdalene's, Sister Anthony. It is a pity that Sister Whilomena was not able to accompany you. How have you found St Cuthbert's?'

'Quite surprising, Mother. I didn't know our order ran a home for Aboriginal children.'

'More than one. And you're happy working with the children, Sister?'

'Yes, Mother.' Sarah hesitated. 'I do like the children, Mother. I love them and I am happy working with them, but Mother, they aren't happy.'

Mother Eymard raised her eyebrows. 'What makes you say that, Sister?' She laid down her pen and pushed her papers away, folding thin, age-spotted hands in her lap.

Sarah edged forward on her chair and whispered as if she was telling a secret. 'Mother, the younger ones cry most of the time. I've heard them at night, crying for their mothers and found them in corners during the day, sobbing their little hearts out.' Sarah paused.

Mother Eymard waited in silence.

'The older ones don't cry. They just stare with big, empty eyes. Sometimes I think they hate us. Of course they don't say that, but they aren't happy, Mother. They all want to be with their families and they don't understand why they can't be.'

Sarah paused again but still Mother Eymard said nothing, so she went on. 'That's another thing, Mother. Most of them do have families. They aren't orphans at all. I know one of the mothers well. She is a good, capable woman and she wants her children back.'

Mother Eymard heaved a weary sigh. 'You say they don't understand, Sister Anthony, and you are right. They don't understand how difficult it will be for half-caste children to make their way in the world. If they're not educated, how will they survive?'

'But Mother, no real education is offered. They are only trained to be servants.'

Mother Eymard's face creased into a dry, mirthless little laugh. 'Sister, I worked on a mission many years ago. Like you, I wanted to help Aborigines better themselves. But after fifteen years of hard work, there was no progress to speak of. I came to accept that they are simply not capable of higher learning. Believe me, I know. I've tried. We would be wasting our time trying to turn them into doctors and lawyers.'

Sarah stared across the desk. This sounded disturbingly familiar.

'Besides, Sister, where do you think educated Aborigines would work? Who would employ them? Household duties and farm labour is their place, and separating the children from the adults is the best way for the children to be assimilated. It is for their own good.'

Sarah slumped on her chair. She wasn't sure what she had hoped for from Mother Eymard, but she might as well have been talking to Mother Sebastian.

Mother Eymard waited for Sarah's acknowledgement of what she had said. She heard none. 'Sister Anthony?'

Sarah swallowed. She took a deep breath and raised an earnest face to her Superior. 'Mother, forgive me, but I don't believe that all Aborigines are incapable of benefiting from real education, if only we would give them the chance. And I don't believe it can possibly be "for their own good" to take children away from parents who love them.' Sarah dropped her eyes again, her outburst hanging in the air.

In calm silence, Mother Eymard filed through a pile of manila folders on her desk and removed one, laying it open before her. 'Mother Sebastian has mentioned how much difficulty you are having accepting religious obedience, Sister.' She looked across her desk at Sarah, who was eyeing the folder with a glum expression. 'Mother also reports that you are very proud and that you value your own opinion, as we have just seen. Sister, you are about to take vows that require your perfect submission.'

Sarah looked up with anxious eyes. 'Oh, I know, Mother, and I've prayed and prayed and prayed about it.'

'If all that prayer has not worked, Sister, a little extra penance may help. Come.' Mother Eymard indicated the floor by her chair.

Sarah moved around the desk and knelt before her Superior, her head bowed.

Mother Eymard reached into the bottom drawer of her desk. As she straightened, Sarah stared with parted lips at the object in her Superior's hand. Half a dozen strips of knotted leather dangled from a plaited handle. 'It is called a discipline.' Mother Eymard let the lashes fall down in front of Sarah's pale face. 'You should visit the infirmary if the skin is broken.' She wound the tails around the handle and handed it to Sarah. 'Like any penance, it is not to be discussed with others.'

Sarah opened a reluctant hand to receive the discipline and buried it deep in her pocket.

*

Evening recreation was lively as the professed-elect shared their stories. Sister Scholastica joked about the way children pronounced her name. Sarah forced a smile, her mind full of thoughts she could not share. The conversation around her seemed to be coming from the other end of a very long tunnel. How many of her sisters examined their consciences every night and decided how many lashes they deserved? How could she do that? She glanced around the room. It was like being in one of the dramatic films she had seen about convent life, only she had never believed for a minute that nuns really did such things. She had always thought it was just Hollywood being, well, Hollywood. This was the twentieth century, for goodness sake!

At nine o'clock, chatter ceased as the bell intoned the Great Silence. Within minutes, sixty women, nuns, novices and postulants had assembled in chapel for the evening prayer. Sarah loved the ancient chant but tonight the psalms did little to soothe her. Her mind kept wandering from her hymnal to her pocket. At Mother Anna's knock, the sisters rose in turn, one from each side of the chapel. Meeting in the centre of the open floor, they genuflected to the altar in pairs. Returning across the dark but still warm courtyard, the procession of veiled heads bobbed its way along the cloister in the moonlight, seen only by the sparrows in the ash trees.

That evening, Sarah lingered longer in the showers than a strict observance of her pending vow of poverty dictated. Returning to her room at last, she climbed onto her bed, and sat on her pillow, knees up under her chin, arms hugging her legs. She stared at the twisted leather object she had dropped on her chair as if a rodent had found its way into her room. After several minutes, she picked it up between finger and thumb, opened the wardrobe and dropped it behind her suitcase as if she was tossing a dead rat into an incinerator. There would have to be another way. No matter how desperate her need for discipline, self-flagellation was not an option Sarah could espouse.

In bed, her eyes wandered around the spartan room recalling another night at St Magdalene's. Mother Anna had extended the celebration of their reception ceremony by granting the novices permission to be up late. On that night, the magical atmosphere of the chapel at eventide had delighted Sarah's bubbling spirits. In the semi-darkness, two larger-than-life seraphim arched the tabernacle with monstrous marble wings, raising in their hands lamps that sent lights and shadows dancing across the sanctuary and down the dark chapel floor. By the time she had torn herself away, she was alone, and the lights of St Magdalene's had dwindled to an odd window here and there. As she had crossed the courtyard that night, Melbourne's misty drizzle was again soaking the hill, a chill wind driving it.

Sarah tossed in bed, remembering how happy she had been. She had hugged her new robes to her body, delighting in wearing the habit for the first time. Climbing the stairs, she had crept out onto the balcony. Wind and rain had swept in between the arches. Melbourne had blazed below, spreading out from the base of St Magdalene's hill. She had peered down at the speeding traffic and neon lights of the big city and shivered. A muffled sound had mingled with the elements and she had strained to listen. Was someone sobbing? Wind had whistled around her veiled head and rain pattered at her feet. After a moment, she wasn't sure she had heard anything. She had left the balcony and turned into the deserted corridor, tiptoeing past the closed doors of her sleeping sisters until she reached her own. Preparing for bed, she had been startled by a knock. According to the most rigid rule, the sisters did not intrude upon each other in their one private domain.

Now two years later, her memory of that night, that Bride of Christ night, became a dream in which she walked towards the door with wooden arms that did not want to open it.

*

The following day, the novitiate chaplain visited so that the professed-elect could confess before their retreat, a ten-day period of prayer and meditation during which they would prepare for the very serious step they were about to take.

A troubled Sarah had a question to ask. 'Father, will my vow of obedience be binding even if my conscience tells me that I am being required to do wrong?'

From the other side of the curtained grill, a disembodied voice answered her, fatherly but firm. 'Your vow of obedience applies only to your Superiors, Sister. To decide you know right and wrong better than they do would be failing in humility, don't you think? If we only obeyed rules we approved of, there wouldn't be much point to a vow of obedience, would there now?'

Not even Sarah could argue with such logic. She left the confessional box feeling none of the euphoria which was the usual reward for dumping one's guilt at the altar. This was not like the satisfying confessions of her childhood, when her gravest 'sins' were eating a meat pie on a Friday, or those of her adolescence, when she had crept into the confessional like a scarlet Mata Hari, to whisper shamefaced to the priest that she had 'let a boy touch me', emerging shriven and full of grace. There was no comforting metamorphosis today. Only a persistent, mocking challenge to her search for peace: 'What do *you* expect you to do about it, Sister Anthony?'

If, in the days to follow, Mother Eymard looked for and failed to find a more penitent Sister Anthony, no mention was made of it. In

December, Sarah and the professed-elect took their vows in the monastery chapel, with only the community and their families as witnesses. There was none of the pomp and finery of their very public reception ceremony to distract from the serious nature of their undertaking. One by one, they knelt before the bishop and pledged themselves to poverty, chastity and obedience for one year.

Thirty-eight

On a farm outside Adelaide, a small boy crouched in an orchard watching a snail slime its way over a fallen apple. The bucket he was supposed to be filling was empty. He stretched out on the grass, propping himself up on his elbows. His chin rested on his hands and his legs waved in the air behind him. The dry grass tickled his nose. It was his sixth birthday but he didn't know it. There had been no presents and no cake. No one had said 'Happy birthday'. He held his breath as the snail made its way up one side of the apple and down the other. The world beyond the orchard had ceased to exist. He had found a friend.

'You lazy little sod! How many apples have you picked?'

Jamarra jumped to his feet and grabbed the empty bucket. He backed against the tree as the owner of the scary voice loomed over him.

Alf Braachs wasn't that big. In fact, he was puny. But he was a noisy, impatient bully and Jamarra was only six. 'What have you been up to, eh?' He spotted the apple at Jamarra's feet. 'Bloody snails! They're not bloody pets, you know. This is what we do with snails.' Alf lifted a muddy boot and smashed the snail and apple into a combined pulp. 'Now get up there and get those apples, you bloody little monkey. She's waitin' for 'em.' He cuffed the back of Jamarra's head.

Jamarra hooked the bucket over one arm and scrambled up the tree. He liked climbing, and apples trees were easy. Their branches, pruned so as to provide space for air and sun to penetrate, worked just as well for small boys desperate to escape an angry boss. He was out of Alf's reach in no time.

'Mind you get good ones now, no grubs.' Alf ambled back to his tractor. At St Bartholomew's Home for Boys he had been glad to take the scrawny runt off Brother Leonard's hands. He reckoned he could get enough work out of him and not have to lay out much in food. The boy had turned out to be a dreamer and Alf was beginning to rethink his decision.

Jamarra perched on a branch and looked down at the slushy mess that had been the snail. He scowled towards the paddock where the tractor had started again, potatoes popping up behind it. He inspected every apple before adding it to the bucket. It was harder to climb back down when the bucket was full. Almost on the ground, he missed the last branch and thudded to the earth spilling the apples and scraping his knee. A trickle of blood ran down his shin unnoticed. Reassured by the distant drone of the tractor, he sprang after the fallen fruit. With the bucket full again, he headed to the house.

Ida Braachs presented the defeated appearance of a woman who expected little from life and had settled for less. These days, though, there was sometimes a smile behind her tired eyes. They lit up now as Jamarra arrived in the kitchen. 'Hello, Jo Blo. Have you got my apples?'

Jamarra held up his bucket with a triumphant smile. 'Yes, Missus Braachs.'

'Good boy. There'll be apple pie tonight. I'll save a nice big piece for you. Would you like that?

'Yes, Missus Braachs.'

She smiled her faded smile and noticed his bleeding leg. 'Oh, Joseph, what have you done to your knee?'

Jamarra inspected his leg. 'Blood,' he announced with pride. 'I didn't cry.'

'You're a brave boy.' Ida washed the little leg and put a plaster over the cut.

After lunch, Alf ordered Jamarra to help him bag potatoes. As they left the house, Alf sniffed the air. A siren wailing across the countryside told him that his nose was right. He shaded his eyes with a calloused hand and scanned the horizon. A plume of dense white smoke was headed their way. Not a big fire but it could destroy his fences. The best bet was to stop it at the dam.

He started to run, calling to Jamarra, 'Get on!'

Before the boy had reached a safe hold on the back of the open tray, the truck took off with a screech. Jamarra lay flat and clutched the edge with desperate fingers, terrified of being flung into the trees as they whizzed past. The truck bumped down a dirt track to a big, galvanised-iron shed. It was as large as the house and in much better condition.

Alf jammed on the brakes and Jamarra rolled across the tray. 'Here, boy, help me get these sacks onto the truck.'

Jamarra picked himself up, jumped down and ran into the shed after Alf. He stretched small arms as far as they would go and picked up a bundle of potato sacks as big as himself. He tottered to the back of the truck, dumped the sacks and ran back for more.

When they were all loaded, Alf ordered him back onto the truck. Jamarra burrowed down between the sacks as the truck took off again, bumping over the paddock towards the dam.

Alf placed half the sacks at each end of the dam. 'Now see here, boy, the fire is not to get past the dam, understand? I'll be on the other side and I want you here. What you do is, you wet your sack in the dam and belt the fire out with it. Just keep hitting the grass wherever the fire gets past me. Understand, boy?'

Jamarra's eyes darted from Alf to the approaching fire. He nodded. Alf took up a position across the dam.

Jamarra began wetting sacks, soaking them in the dam and piling them on the bank. He looked across at Alf, who was already wielding a wet sack. Flames forked through the dry grass like something alive. Jamarra picked up one of the sacks and tried to copy Alf. Full of water the sack was much heavier. His thin arms protested but he managed to throw the sack down on the flames. Then there were more flames. His wet sack was soon a dry sack and then a smouldering sack. Smoke filled his nostrils, stung his eyes and burned his throat. The sack caught alight and Jamarra threw it into the dam.

Soaking another sack, he smacked it down, almost losing his balance under its weight. He jumped back screaming as his bare feet stood on charred grass. Burnt and frightened, he dropped his sack and started to run, wincing with every step. A loud splash on the other side of the dam stopped him. Alf had fallen into the dam. He was struggling to climb out, skidding and falling back, unable to get a grip on the steep slope of wet clay. His clothes and big boots weighed him down, sucking him into the mud.

Jamarra ran around the inside of the dam, where the flames had not reached. He picked up some dry sacks and spread them over the slippery bank. He piled others over the first lot. Soon there were enough sacks for Alf to clamber out over them and sit panting on the bank.

As soon as he could speak, he turned on Jamarra. 'Now, how the hell are we supposed to put the fire out with your sacks all burnt and mine all covered in mud?'

Jamarra was returned to St Bartholomew's without warning or explanation. He was neither sorry nor glad to be back in Brother Leonard's care. The cane replaced Alf's boot and his bed in the dormitory didn't guarantee a better night's sleep, but he missed Ida's smuggled treats and kindness. Although the image of his mother's face had faded, he remembered the feeling of being mothered and thought of the carefree days at Mullanurra with longing. In the mornings, his little hands would turn the pillow to hide a wet patch in the middle. A wet patch in the middle of the mattress was a bigger problem, but his hands were too small to turn the heavy kapok sack and save himself from another merciless caning.

Thirty-nine

'Welcome back, Sister.' Whilomena's tone was deferential. She still wore the white veil of a novice, while Sister Anthony was now a professed nun in the full black habit of the order.

As Sarah stepped across the threshold, carols from distant classrooms echoed through the great hall. The children of St Cuthbert's were preparing for Christmas.

Sarah's nose twitched, tickled by an outdoorsy aroma. Halfway down the hall, a papier mâché 'stable' made by the children housed Mary, Joseph, and the Christ Child. Fresh straw filled the manger and covered the floor.

Sarah wrinkled a freckled nose at the straw and her eyes sparkled with amusement. 'Perhaps it's just as well Mother Sebastian isn't here, Sister.'

Whilomena did not smile. She handed Sarah an unopened letter. 'This arrived while you were away, Sister.'

Sarah glanced at the envelope, recognising the handwriting on her first mail that had not been read by anyone else. She buried her uncensored letter in her pocket, savouring this privilege of her new status.

Whilomena hovered. 'How is Mother Sebastian, Sister?'

'Oh yes, Mother is not at all well, Sister. She has pneumonia. She is in hospital. Sister Matthew's not back yet?'

At the train station, Sarah had been astonished to find not the little convent van but Mother Sebastian's sleek white Falcon Futura waiting to collect her.

Behind the wheel, Sister Augusta had explained that Sister Matthew had taken the van to Mildura. 'The Mercies have invited St Cuthbert's to talk to their children about the work of our orphanage. Sister

Matthew drove up there this morning with Sister Innocent. So we had to roll out the limo for you, Sister.' Sister Augusta's tone implied that this was a great extravagance and was somehow Sarah's fault.

Whilomena shook her head. 'No, Sister Matthew is not back. I'll let you know when she returns.'

'Thank you, Sister.' Sarah started to leave then turned, as if a random thought had occurred to her. 'Oh, Sister, can you tell me where Joseph May is now? I remember that you accompanied Mother Sebastian when he left St Cuthbert's.' Sarah examined her letter again, as if the answer to her question was of no great importance.

Whilomena's voice remained respectful but her smile held a hint of triumph. 'I'm sorry, Sister. I'm not sure I should say. Perhaps, if you were to ask Mother Sebastian?'

'Yes, of course. Thank you, Sister.' Sarah hurried up the wide mahogany staircase. Hmm, nicely foiled, Whilomena. She made herself a cup of tea and sought the privacy of the balcony to open her letter.

Dear Sare,

I wish you didn't have to be so far away. I wish we could still visit you like we did when you were in Melbourne. Mum has been in hospital and with you gone, guess who gets to do all the housework? I never knew Dad and the boys were such babies around the house! I'm forever picking up after them. I miss you, Sare, even though I get the *School Friend* and *Girls' Crystal* all to myself now but I guess you wouldn't want to read kid stuff like that any more, eh?

Sarah looked up as Whilomena found her again. 'Has Sister Matthew returned, Sister?'

'No, not yet. Someone else is asking for you, Sister. It's Mr O'Mara.' Whilomena's disapproval was written all over her face.

Sarah frowned. What did he want now? She descended the stairs again still reading Julia's letter:

Sare, would you please send me a letter all for myself, with just my name on the envelope?

Love from Julia

PS: Harry is in the army now. Dad is real pleased. He says the army is a good life for a young bloke when there is no war on.

Sarah found her visitor propping up one of the veranda posts, a roll of newspapers under his arm. Bronko was patrolling the geranium paths as usual.

Mick tipped his hat as she appeared. He grinned at her black veil. 'Congratulations, Sister. Welcome back.'

'Thank you, Mr O'Mara.' She felt the colour rising in her cheeks and fingered her crucifix in awkward silence, remembering their last conversation.

He didn't seem to notice. 'Bet you thought I wouldn't remember these?'

Sarah relaxed a little, laughing as he offered her the newspapers. As she reached to take them, Julia's letter fluttered to the ground. Mick swooped to retrieve it.

He handed it back with only a glance at the page. 'Letters too now, eh? I bet that's a welcome change?'

Sarah put the papers on a veranda seat and accepted her letter. 'Oh, we've always been allowed to receive and write letters, Mr O'Mara. But it is good to know that at least my incoming mail isn't read now.' As soon as the words were out, she fumed at herself. *When will I learn not to answer him so quickly? He is just too clever at asking questions.* She smiled to herself. *What a surprise, Sarah, that a journalist should be good at asking questions.*

Mick shook his head in disbelief. 'You mean to say that your letters home are censored? That's a bit grim.'

Sarah bit her lip. He had such a talent for making her say more than she meant to say. He had hit the nail on the head, though. It was, indeed, grim. 'I'm sorry, I shouldn't have mentioned it.'

'Tell you what, Sister. I'll bring a few newspapers around every now and then. I know you're not interested in what's going on in the world,' he teased, 'but now that you can read papers again, you have a lot of catching up to do. And if you ever want to send uncensored letters home, just give them to me. I'd be happy to post them for you, no trouble at all. You can trust me to treat them like the Royal Mail, no peeking, I promise.' This time, the smile he gave her was kind and sympathetic, with none of the usual stirring in his eyes.

'Thank you, Mr O'Mara, that's very generous, and of course I know I could trust you with my mail.' She was surprised to realise that she really did feel she could trust him, 'But it wouldn't be at all appropriate, you know.'

'Well, if you ever think it would be appropriate, Sister Anthony...' Mick tipped his hat goodbye, the laughter back in his eyes.

Sarah watched him stride away to the car park, slapping his thigh to bring Bronko to his heels.

*

As Mick's ute disappeared, the convent van bumped its way up the drive. Sarah waved a happy hello as Sister Matthew crunched past towards the garage, with Sister Innocent clutching the door as if she was on the Ferris wheel at Luna Park.

Sarah hurried through the convent and down the schoolroom corridor to meet them. She held the cloakroom door open as the travellers crossed the colonnade.

'Welcome back, Sister Anthony. How does it feel to be a professed Sister of St Frances Cabrini?'

Sarah laughed. 'I don't think I'm used to it yet.'

Sister Innocent nodded a frail little smile and excused herself.

Sister Matthew headed towards the convent, beckoning Sarah to follow her. 'I'm glad you're back, Sister. I need to talk with you.'

Through the corridors they went, into the great hall, past the nativity tableau and along to Mother Sebastian's study, where Sister Matthew offered Sarah a chair. '

Sit down please, Sister, there's something I want to ask you.' She paused and stepped over to the door they had left open, pushing it shut. She sat down, not behind the desk, but in a chair beside Sarah.

'I'm happy to help of course, Sister. I imagine you must be up to your eyeballs, having your class to teach and being in charge now as well.'

'That's just it, Sister. When Mother Sebastian left, she gave me her keys, saying that I should leave the mail on her desk and she would catch up with everything when she returned.' Sister Matthew pointed to bundles of rubber-banded mail on Mother Sebastian's desk. 'Of course, she expected to return in a few days. Now it seems it may be weeks, or even months.' Sister Mathew shook her head, pulling a comical face. 'I'm no administrator, Sister. Bookkeeping, well, I don't know a ledger from a lamington, so I was wondering if you've had any experience at this sort of thing?'

Sarah thought she might on this occasion, safely mention her background. 'Well, yes, Sister. I did bookkeeping in school and our home is also the family business, a guest house in Lorne, called Margaret Rose. I helped my parents in the office.'

Sister Matthew clapped her hands. 'Wonderful.' She whisked a bunch of keys from her pocket, thrusting them at a startled Sarah. 'The books will be here somewhere, I suppose. You'll have to open any letters addressed to "The Principal" or "The Superior". Keep Mother's personal mail aside. There will be cheques to be banked and people to be paid. See me when you need cheques signed. I'm a signatory to our account with Mother Sebastian, either to sign. Sister Monica and Sister Leo will be able to help with information about our suppliers.' Sister Matthew was breathless but smiling. 'Thank you, Sister Anthony, you're a godsend.'

Her black skirts swirled out of the room, leaving Sarah staring at the mail cluttered desk, Mother Sebastian's keys in her hand.

As Sister Matthew's footsteps echoed through the great hall, Sarah hurried to the filing cabinet. She tried key after key. The cabinet refused to betray its secrets.

*

A few days after Sarah's return, Pearl climbed the bluestone steps and knocked on the intimidating front door of St Cuthbert's.

Whilomena, now the only novice and so on permanent portress duty, answered the door. She didn't wait for Pearl to speak. 'Yes, yes. I'll get Sister Anthony.' She left Pearl standing and found Sarah where she knew she would be these days, behind Mother Sebastian's desk, surrounded by paperwork. She announced the visitor with a shade of irritation. 'That woman is here again, Sister. Can't you discourage her? How many times is this?'

'Mrs Marsh is a mother searching for her children, Sister. She comes here at the risk of being arrested again. It is very brave of her.'

Despite her sympathy, Sarah approached the veranda dreading the questions for which she did not have an answer. Knowing Pearl would not enter the convent, Sarah stepped outside and seated herself on one of the garden benches, patting the space beside her. Pearl hesitated then sat down, leaving a respectful distance between herself and Sarah.

It was only nine o'clock but already warm even under the veranda. Beyond its shade, the day was heating up. The air was heavy with the sweet scent of wattle and bees droned from flower to flower. Sarah was glad to see a truck parked beyond the paths. A young man in a cowboy hat was sitting in its shade. Thank goodness Pearl hadn't walked today.

Sarah listened to questions she had heard before and still had only one answer for. 'I'm sorry, Pearl, they aren't here. I give you my word. I have never met anyone called Tallara. Jamarra was here but not any more. I'm terribly sorry.'

'Where is he, Sister Anthony?'

Sarah had never seen eyes so full of hope and despair at the same time. She dropped her own eyes and shook her head. 'I don't know that, either.'

Pearl frowned. She stood up facing Sarah. 'Somebody knows, Sister Anthony.' Her voice was only slightly raised but it was passionate. 'My baby came here, now he's gone? Somebody took him. That somebody knows where he is. Who took my boy away, Sister Anthony?'

Pearl had every right to be angry, Sarah acknowledged, but naming Mother Sebastian would not be useful. She stood up, touching Pearl's bare arm with a gentle hand. 'I wish I knew where he is, Pearl. I really do.'

'Sister, you know I'm a good mother.' Pearl's voice trembled. 'You tell them, Sister, like you wrote in the letter. Please, Sister, please help me.'

A tornado churned inside Sarah. She grasped Pearl's hands. 'I will, Pearl. I'll find Jamarra…and Tallara too if I can.'

As she closed the convent doors, Sarah slumped against them with a weary sigh. That was a bit rash, Sarah Norton. How exactly do you intend to keep such a promise?

Forty

After Mass on Christmas morning, the children of St Cuthbert's chattered unchecked as they crocodiled out of the church. They made their way to the refectory, where the noisy chatter turned into awed whispers.

'Corn flakes!'

'Toast!'

'Marmalade!'

'Fruit salad and ice cream!'

'And look, lollies!'

The chatter resumed noisier than before, as scores of laughing girls and boys rushed to their seats and found their spoons. They passed bowls and platters, giggling with delight as they helped themselves and each other to the mouth-watering Christmas fare.

No one rapped a cane or rang a bell for silence.

Forty-one

The sisters of St Cuthbert's were becoming accustomed to the luxury of current newspapers with their morning tea. Mother Sebastian had taken no interest in the world outside St Cuthbert's. Therefore the convent had never received papers, unless a visitor thought to drop one off. Now they had worldwide and local news several times a week. Every time Mick delivered the papers, he asked for Sister Anthony. Whilomena wondered if he thought Sarah was the only nun who could read.

On the morning of the fifteenth of March 1962, Sarah walked down the great hall in obedience to such a summons. Mick had made a special effort today, driving out to the orphanage with papers tossed off the train only that morning. Whilomena had left the front door open, and as Sarah approached she could see him lounging against his adopted veranda post. As she drew closer, he straightened and held up a newspaper in both hands. Splashed across the front page of *The Age* she read, 'Bill Grants Vote to Aborigines'.

Mick grinned, confident that Sarah would be excited. 'This means that all Aborigines have at least the Commonwealth vote now. Western Australia and Queensland are dragging the chain on state rights, but it looks as if the west will cave in soon.'

Sarah's forehead puckered into a puzzled frown. 'You mean they… Aborigines, couldn't vote until now?'

Mick shook his head.

No wonder governments got away with murder.

'See what happens when you don't read newspapers, Sister Anthony.' He shot her one of the cheeky smiles that confused her so much and grinned as she looked anywhere but at him.

Mick continued his deliveries to the convent and Sarah continued to accept them with a formality that amused him. *The Age, The Melbourne Herald* and the *Cobbs Crossing Chronicle* became her link to the world she had left behind. It surprised her to find so many mysteries in so little time. Who were the Beatles? What was a miniskirt? She skimmed the national papers for world events but spent longer with the local one. She liked the opinion pages, intrigued by the debates that heated a small town newspaper with nothing earth-shattering to report.

One morning, among the letters to the editor, she read one that stopped her teacup halfway to her mouth.

> Dear Sir
>
> I read with interest your article on the recent Welfare inspection of St Cuthbert's Orphanage and the glowing report which the institution once again received.
>
> No one questions the good intentions of the Sisters, or the need to take into care children who are orphaned. However, many of the children at the 'orphanage', I have discovered, are not in fact orphans but still have living parents.
>
> Surely these children would be better cared for by their own parents, even if the circumstances in which they live are not all we might wish?
>
> Anon

Sarah read and reread the letter. She would like to answer it but she doubted if even Sister Matthew, now acting Superior for three months, would encourage one of her sisters to take part in a public debate.

Forty-two

Sarah examined the ledger for the umpteenth time, running her finger down column after column, her brow puckered into a puzzled frown. She looked up and rose from her chair as Sister Matthew appeared in the doorway. 'Thank you for coming, Sister. I would have come to you only,' she gestured towards the books and documents spread all over the desk.

The acting Superior waved Sarah back to her seat and pulled another chair up to the desk. 'Now then, Sister, remember I'm not an accountant. I don't know how much help I can be.'

Sarah reversed the ledger so that it was facing Sister Matthew. She tapped the open page. 'It will be a big help, Sister, if you can tell me what these mean, all these payments to an account called "Maintenance", with no supplier details. My question is, what maintenance? I thought you might know.'

Sister Matthew frowned. 'Perhaps the chequebook has more details?'

'You'd think so, but I've searched it for carpenters, plumbers, anything that might be called maintenance. I even went back through the earlier chequebooks. All I found was more mystery, regular large cheques written out to "Building Fund", and I do mean large, Sister… hundreds of pounds at a time and the amounts seem to tally with –'

'With the "maintenance" payments?'

'Yes.' Sarah handed the current chequebook across the desk. 'Do we have a building fund, Sister?'

Sister Matthew scanned the chequebook stubs and her frown deepened. 'I don't know, Sister, but I know who would know. Sister

Whilomena is ready to take her vows. She will need a travelling companion. It seems like the perfect opportunity for you to discuss this with Mother Anna.'

Their eyes met. Sarah understood.

Forty-three

It was mid-April before Sarah accompanied Whilomena back to St Magdalene's. Sister Matthew had asked them to wait until the end of term so that their absence would not be such a burden on the little community.

At the Mother House, Whilomena went into retreat, leaving Sarah free to enjoy her holiday, free except for the unpleasant duty that was the real reason for her return to Melbourne.

*

Mother Anna was standing by the open windows of her pleasant parlour enjoying a perfect April morning. The novitiate gardens were a riot of autumn colour. Her cultured, Queen Mother voice floated over her shoulder to answer Sarah's query.

'Building Fund? Oh, that would be ours, Sister, the St Frances Cabrini Building Fund. All of our institutions support our building fund out of their surplus.'

Sarah blinked. 'Surplus? There is no surplus at St Cuthbert's, Mother. The children are often cold, they're poorly dressed and they're always, always, hungry.'

Mother Anna turned away from the window. 'Perhaps Mother Sebastian has been overzealous on behalf of our work, Sister.' She raised startled eyebrows. 'Good heavens! Surely you don't suspect Mother of embezzlement, Sister Anthony?'

'Mother, this is worse than embezzlement. This is taking food from hungry children.'

A shocked gasp escaped the Superior. 'Sister Anthony, surely we need to deal charitably with our poor sister's perhaps misguided enthusiasm.'

Sarah stared, open-mouthed. Misguided? To starve children? And for what? To build more institutions in which more children could starve?

'Mother, if Welfare knew about this, or the police –'

'Sister, I implore you! Think about the children.'

'I am thinking about the children, Mother.'

'I will speak with her.' Mother Anna patted Sarah's sleeve. 'You are bound by a vow of obedience, Sister. I trust that vow is still sacred to you?'

'I made another vow, Mother, to the mother of one of those children. That vow is sacred to me also.'

Mother Anna sank down into the window seat. She gestured to the space beside her. Sarah sat, her back very straight.

Mother Anna leaned towards her. 'I can see that you feel strongly about this, my dear. I have a suggestion. Why don't you take the time to make a retreat yourself while you are with us? I'm sure Sister Matthew can spare you for a few more weeks. Ask Our Lord to strengthen your commitment to your vows and let yourself be guided by the Holy Spirit.'

Sarah opened her mouth and closed it again without saying anything. The Holy Spirit, she thought, would never counsel her to steal from children.

Mother Anna was anxious for a truce. 'And Sister, what if you remain in charge of the budget and bookkeeping, until a permanent Superior can be found for St Cuthbert's?'

*

In June, Sarah and Whilomena, now both wearing the black veils of professed members of their order, left the novitiate for the long journey into the north-west. The Mallee looked different at this time of year.

On both sides of the train tracks, mile after mile of young wheat swayed in soft winter sun, as if the land had been covered in pea-green silk.

Sister Matthew was more than happy for Sarah to hold the purse strings. Sarah understood that her new status as Sister Bursar was designed by Mother Anna to pacify her outrage. Nevertheless, she saw and snatched an opportunity for happy change at St Cuthbert's. She conferred with Sister Matthew, Sister Monica and Sister Leo on ways to improve conditions for the children. Milk appeared at every meal. The astonished children found custard and red jelly after dinner during the week and, on Sundays, ice cream or chocolate pudding. The lunchtime soup had meat in it now and little bread rolls for dipping. Big eyes opened wide to a treasury of new storybooks and workbooks suited to every grade level. The senior girls had access to a well-stocked cupboard in Sister Leo's infirmary and they threw away their rags.

Forty-four

Late one chilly afternoon in early spring, Sarah and Sister Matthew waited on the Cobbs Crossing railway platform. The day was dark with threatening rain.

Sister Matthew cast a wary eye skywards. 'I think we'll be glad of the brollies. Our new Superior might not be in for a very good first impression of Cobbs Crossing.' She looked along the empty track. 'I wonder what she'll be like.'

Sarah was wrestling with the mechanism of her rarely used umbrella. 'I hope she approves our budgetary changes.'

'They seem to be working well. I can't imagine she would find fault with your system, Sister.'

The day before, a phone call from the Mother House had delivered instructions. Sister Matthew reread Whilomena's neatly written note for the umpteenth time: MOTHER SUPERIOR ARRIVING COBBS CROSSING 5.15 P.M. WED 11 SEPTEMBER PLEASE MEET TRAIN.

Wind whistled across the platform. Dark clouds, low and gathering fast rolled towards them. The rain started as the train pulled into the station, lazy fat drops splashed down at first, becoming a torrential downpour in minutes. The nuns raised their umbrellas and held the back of their veils down against the tugging wind. Lightning lit up the station and the darkness was banished for a few startling seconds of blazing light. As a deafening clap of thunder filled the blacker darkness left in its wake, Sarah gasped at an Amazonian figure in windswept robes stepping off the train. She stared in horrified disbelief at the figure striding towards them through the rain.

'So much for Mother Anna,' she hissed. 'What hypocrisy. I was sure –'

Sister Matthew raised a warning finger to her lips. She hurried forward and placed her umbrella over the 'new' Superior's head. 'Welcome back, Mother. I hope you're feeling better.'

Her hypochondria reinforced by a genuine illness, the big white handkerchief never left Mother Sebastian's hand. In the days to come, Sarah seethed as every 'luxury' she had introduced was done away with and the budget tightened again.

Forty-five

On the convent balcony, a cosy corner caught the mid-spring Mallee sun. Placing her teacup on a table beside her, Sarah opened a letter penned in her own hand. She would write it only to clear her mind, she had told herself. She would never post it, with or without Mr O'Mara's assistance. When it was written, however, she found she could not tear it up. It remained in her pocket for days, being read over and over.

Dear Sir

Anon asks if the children at St Cuthbert's would not be better off cared for by their own parents. In some respects I agree. There are aspects of life in the institution which are harsh and sometimes even cruel. Children are severely punished, are not well fed and suffer many privations. With welfare inspections occurring only once a year, it is easy for the establishment to camouflage these short comings.

Unfortunately, the children's parents are not able to give them the education they need in order to find a place in a world so different from their own. Assimilation, it seems is their only way forward. Despite the hardships created by this necessity, I believe it will be for their own good.

I only wish that the system could be administered with more compassion.

Signed, Concerned.

Sarah put the letter back in its envelope and tapped it against her lips, deep in thought. No, of course she could never post it. She glanced at her watch and picked up her teacup, hurrying downstairs just as the bell ended morning recreation. From under trees and around the corners of buildings, children poured across the colonnade and into the quad.

Mother Sebastian appeared and watched them shuffle into formation. 'Right hand on the shoulder of the person in front of you. Left hand on the shoulder of the person beside you.'

There was some confusion while the little ones sorted their right hand from their left. Once in place, they stood like little barefoot soldiers and waited for the order to march.

Mother Sebastian began striding back and forth across the assembly, directing threatening glances up and down the rows of nervous children. They were careful to avoid her eyes.

'Sister Augusta tells me that some of you have been asking to write to your parents.'

Heads popped up in the ranks.

'I cannot imagine why your parents would want letters from you.'

The heads dropped down again.

Mother Sebastian's voice reached every corner of the quad. 'How many times do I have to remind you that you are here because your parents do not want you?'

Sarah smothered a gasp as the tirade continued.

'Your parents have given you to us because you are difficult, naughty children. They don't want you. There is no need for you to write to parents who don't want you.'

Every time Mother Sebastian spat out 'don't want you', Sarah winced. Behind her, one of the little ones was crying. She stepped back and laid an arm about the child's shoulders. All around her, children were sniffing or brushing tears away with the backs of their hands. The military perfection of the assembly had dissipated into slumped shoulders and drooping heads. The older ones were standing in sullen silence, refusing to cry. The little ones were sobbing and trembling, not attempting to hide tear streaked swollen faces.

There was a lump in Sarah's throat as she gazed down row after row of distraught children. She sighed and shook her head. She wanted to gather every one of them in her arms and tell them that it was not true. Surely it wasn't pride or disobedience to question such cruelty? Christ would never speak to children like this. 'Jesus, help me. Please give me a sign. Show me what I should do.'

As the dispirited youngsters were dismissed, Whilomena approached Sarah and announced with a bored sigh that Mr O'Mara was waiting to see Sister Anthony. She raised her eyebrows when Sarah responded with a mirthless little laugh.

Mick was leaning on his favourite veranda post, his battered Akubra pushed to the back of his head, his hands shoved into the pockets of his jeans. The usual bundle of newspapers was rolled up at his feet. Why couldn't he just give them to Whilomena?

'Good morning, Mr O'Mara. More papers? Thank you. The sisters appreciate your kindness. Aren't we a bit out of the way for regular deliveries, though?'

'It's no trouble, Sister. I'm always on the road. Besides, I like our little chats,' he teased.

Sarah's head was still full of Mother Sebastian's rant and the sobs of the children. She looked so grave that the laughter in Mick's eyes disappeared.

'Sister?'

'Mr O'Mara,' she began. Her confusion was obvious, her expression artless.

He straightened and waited, watching her without a trace of the teasing of a moment ago.

She plunged her hand into her pocket and pulled the envelope from its hiding place. 'Mr O'Mara, I wonder if…that is, I was thinking, I mean, you once said –'

Mick nodded at the letter. 'Would you like me to post that for you, Sister?' His tone was as casual as if this was something they did every day.

'Well, not post exactly. I haven't addressed it or sealed it. It's for the *Chronicle*, so you'll have to read it, as the editor of course,' she stammered.

Mick took the envelope. 'Nothing easier, Sister. Consider it delivered. Safe as the Royal Mail.' Despite the light-hearted words, there was no mockery in his voice or in his eyes. He saluted Sarah and sauntered down the steps, stowing the envelope in the breast pocket of his shirt.

Sarah did not know if she dreaded or looked forward to his return.

The next time Mick delivered papers to St Cuthbert's, the first one contained Sarah's letter in print. An answer, dated two days later, challenged everything she thought she knew.

Dear Sir

'Concerned' represents the most dangerous of do-gooders: those who mean well but act in ignorance or stand by and watch evil being done. By the writer's own admission, conditions in the institutions are appalling. Yet 'Concerned' justifies this by claiming that these measures are intended 'for the children's own good'. I would like to draw your readers' attention to the real motive behind the removal of Aboriginal children from their communities.

In an address to the Conference of Commonwealth and State Aboriginal Authorities held in Canberra, April 1937, Mr A.O. Neville, then Commissioner for Native Affairs, brought forward his objective for the taking of children and the control of Aboriginal marriages:

'Are we going to have a population of one million blacks in the Commonwealth, or are we going to merge them into our white community and eventually forget that there ever were any Aborigines in Australia?'

Every Australian should be ashamed of the genocidal intent implied in this statement, which is recorded in the archives of our national parliament.

Signed, Ashamed.

Sitting in her balcony hideaway, Sarah stared at the newspaper spread out before her on a wrought iron table. A rereading did nothing to ease the mind-numbing shock of those words. She tore the letter from the page, folded it several times, and tucked it into the deep pocket of her habit.

A movement in the distance caught her eye. A solitary figure had left the highway and turned down the drive towards St Cuthbert's. Pearl. Sarah jumped up and hurried down the broad staircase, glad of the carpet that softened hasty footsteps. She might as well answer the door and save Whilomena the bother of looking for her.

Forty-six

From the pile of newspapers, Sarah separated the copy of the *Chronicle* that contained her letter and the one from which she had torn the answer from 'Ashamed'. She hid them at the bottom of the fire-starting pile beside Sister Monica's stove. The rest she delivered to the community room.

She kept the letter that had shocked and challenged her, reading it over and over. Perhaps it wasn't true? It was such a long time ago. 'Ashamed' might be mistaken. How could she find out? If only she was back at St Magdalene's. As a professed nun, she would now be permitted to visit Melbourne's great libraries. It was unlikely that the Cobbs Crossing Library ran to records of Canberra parliamentary conferences. Then an idea occurred. Of course! Mr O'Mara! A journalist would know, or at least know where to find out. But as soon as the idea popped into her head, Sarah backed away from it. If what the letter asserted was true, it was the sort of thing that people working with Aboriginal children should know. Telling him that she didn't know would prove that she was, indeed, 'acting in ignorance'.

Before mid-morning, she was accusing herself of pride. Before the day was over, she had admitted to a more uncomfortable truth – how much she wanted him to think well of her. In chapel that night, Sarah prayed to be delivered from temptation. She decided to tell Whilomena that whenever Mr O'Mara called in future, he was to be told that Sister Anthony was unavailable. By morning, she was asking herself other questions. If she avoided Mr O'Mara's company, how would she find out the truth of the claims made by 'Ashamed'? Besides, wouldn't she become stronger by confronting temptation, rather than running away from it? Would not her vocation, her habit, her vows, protect her?

When Mick turned up again, Sarah pulled the crumpled newspaper cutting from her pocket. 'This letter, Mr O'Mara, do you know if what it claims is true?'

He only glanced at the paper in her hand. He knew which letter it would be. He looked from the piece of paper into big, troubled green eyes. Those eyes! They were so lively on the rare occasions that he had seen her laugh. Now, defenceless and pleading with him to deny something she didn't want to believe, they were enchanting. Why on earth, he wondered, would such an attractive young woman become a nun?

'It's true all right, Sister. An unhappy fact of our history. But I understand that you need proof in black and white –' He cut himself off, shaking his head. 'Pardon, Sister, unintended, I promise.' Colour flooded his tan cheeks. 'I meant, I understand that you need to know the facts before you act.'

Her eyes widened. Act? What on earth did he expect her to do?

'You could ring or write to the Parliamentary Library in Canberra, requesting a copy of the record. Or if you prefer, I could contact them and have the extract forwarded to you.'

Sarah rewarded him with an unhappy smile. 'Thank you, Mr O'Mara. I would appreciate that. What a dilemma. I'll be looking for something that I don't want to find.'

*

In Mick's next parcel of newspapers, Sarah found a bundle of books. She was tempted to rush them upstairs and hide them in the library but honesty got the better of her. She knocked on Mother Sebastian's door and asked permission to read them.

Seated behind her desk, the Superior left Sarah kneeling as she flicked through the first book, *Simply Human Beings*. She pushed her spectacles up her nose, observing with satisfaction black-and-white photos of ramshackle fringe-dwelling camps. 'Yes, Sister, read it. You might learn what we're trying to save them from.'

She passed the book to Sarah and picked up the next one. She didn't even open Auber Octavius Neville's blueprint for child removal. She just nodded at the title with grim satisfaction, *Australia's Coloured Minority...their place in the community*. 'You see, Sister, Mr Neville knew how important it is that they, and we, remember what "their place" is.'

Sarah bit back the reckless response that almost escaped her. The book was handed across the desk and Mother Sebastian picked up Gordon's *The Embarrassing Australian*. She blinked at the cover photo: a handsome young Aboriginal man in the uniform of an Australian army officer.

While Sarah held her breath, expecting this book to be rejected, Mother Sebastian looked amused. '*The Embarrassing Australian*. Yes, indeed. No doubt they are embarrassing when they forget their place. This story will no doubt compliment Mr Neville's argument that they must be kept in their place. Take it, Sister, take them all. I never thought I'd say it, but I'm grateful to Mr O'Mara. Through all this reading, you may learn a thing or two. You may go.'

Rising from her knees, Sarah accepted the last book, backed out of her Superior's study and fled down the great hall.

*

A few days before the arrival of Sarah's books, Mick's FJ had hurtled down the Calder Highway at a speed that would have had Buchanan's siren wailing if the sergeant had been there to see it. Mick had made a few phone calls and a Melbourne dealer had unearthed a tattered copy of Neville's work from the dusty shelves of a second-hand bookshop. He had agreed to hold it for one day. *Simply Human Beings* Mick had no trouble locating, having only recently been released.

Majik had lent him *The Embarrassing Australian*, bursting with pride in Old George's service record. 'Dad was in Greece with this bloke,' he said of Captain Saunders, whose cover photo had startled Mother Sebastian. 'He was the first Aboriginal officer commissioned in the Australian army.'

In her first spare moment, Sarah settled herself in her favourite balcony corner with the book she expected to be most challenging. Reading inside its faded dust jacket, she shook her head: 'Mr Neville states unhesitatingly his belief in an unpopular solution of a contentious problem, nowhere shirking the truth lest it might give offence'.

She hoped there would be no proof that Neville's views had been widely accepted as 'Ashamed' asserted. When photocopies of the documents Mick had requested from the Parliamentary Library arrived, Canberra crushed her hopes with evidence that Neville's proposals had been accepted at the highest levels of government, become official policy, and put into practice with the support of the police, welfare and institutions such as St Cuthbert's.

And you, Sister Anthony Norton, and you too, Sarah chided herself.

Forty-seven

The next time Mick visited St Cuthbert's, Sarah handed him another letter and invited him to read it.

He scanned the lines and whistled. 'Holy cow! Are you sure you want this published? I mean, with your name and everything?'

'I thought you'd be pleased, Mr O'Mara. It should cause a sensation. Isn't that what you've been after?'

'I've been after the truth.' He sounded hurt. 'But have you thought about what a hornet's nest this will stir up, Sister?'

She gave a grim little laugh. 'I've done little else. There will be consequences of course, but my name, my title, will not be easy to ignore.'

Mick stared at the defiance in her eyes, her letter still open in his hand. He felt as if he was talking to a different person. What guts. 'Right-oh, Sister, I'll publish your letter.' There was new respect in his eyes.

As his FJ crunched down the drive, dark clouds gathered on the horizon, moving towards the orphanage hill.

*

Two days later, Mother Sebastian was storming to and fro beneath her martyred namesake. During the morning, she had received volatile calls from Sergeant Buchanan claiming that her convent was harbouring a dangerous radical, and from Lachlan Harris, demanding Sister Anthony's immediate dismissal. She had received a call from that wretched newspaper man, seeking an interview, fielded enquiries from Doctor Lawrence and taken messages from people she didn't even know. On her desk, a copy of the *Chronicle* rushed to her by an alarmed Father

Conway, lay open at the page that had every tongue in the Crossing wagging.

Dear Sir

Not only are most of the children at St Cuthbert's 'Orphanage' not orphans but they are continually told that their parents don't want them, when in fact I have seen parents who never cease searching for their children, questioning whoever will listen and even risking imprisonment, trying to find daughters or sons who have been to all purposes kidnapped from their love and care. The local police, press, doctors and landholders all know that what I am saying is true.

Sister Mary Anthony Norton,
Sisters of St Frances Cabrini
St Cuthbert's Orphanage

The culprit was kneeling on the floor, the skirt of her habit consuming much of the limited pacing space. Mother Sebastian poured out her rage, asking questions to which no answer was required, expounding apologetics without logic, bent only on excusing the inexcusable. The white handkerchief fluttered in the air and Sarah suffered the tirade in silence.

'Your familiarity with that, that newspaper man, not to mention a complete disregard for your vows, makes it impossible for you to remain here, Sister. I am going to arrange your return to St Magdalene's this minute!' The Superior swept out of her study, leaving Sarah kneeling on the floor.

Sarah was not surprised by the verdict. From the moment she had given Mick her letter, she had been waiting for the sky to fall. As she rose to leave, she placed a hand on Mother Sebastian's desk and knocked a bunch of keys onto the bare floor with a clatter. Bending to retrieve them, she noticed a key that had not been among the others when she had kept the ledgers for Sister Matthew. Across the desk, her eyes fell on the filing cabinet. In seconds, she had opened it, pulling out the middle drawer.

From the phone alcove beneath the stairs, Mother Sebastian's raised voice echoed through the great hall.

Sarah's fingers trembled as she leafed through the files. March, Marston, Matthews! Lily. Female. Quadroon, almost white. Born 21 September 1945. There was no reference to a birthmark, nor did the file say where Lily had been assigned.

Mother Sebastian could still be heard on the phone.

Sarah continued to finger through the files. Jamarra's file was not there. The phone clicked back onto the receiver and swift strides sounded in the hall. Sarah forced leaden fingers to hurry the files back into place and wriggle the key into the cabinet again. Locked! She put the keys back on the desk and fell to her knees as Mother Sebastian marched into the room.

The Superior was surprised to find Sarah still kneeling where she had left her. 'Good heavens, Sister, did you think I meant you to stay there forever? Not that you don't deserve it. Go and pack. Pack everything. You leave tomorrow and it is not likely you will ever come back to St Cuthbert's.'

Forty-eight

The waiting train hissed steam as if impatient to be gone. Its whistle shattered the quiet countryside. Mick raced along the empty platform. Leaping aboard, he dashed down the corridor, eyes darting into each compartment until he propped in an open doorway. She was alone.

'Sister, where are they sending you?' Taking care not to step on her habit, he dropped onto the opposite seat tossing his hat down beside him. He leant towards her, his long legs bent at the knees almost as if he was kneeling. 'Promise me you won't let them send you to some god-forsaken corner of the world. I couldn't bear to think of you helpless in Africa. The missions aren't safe any more! Remember what happened in the Congo?'

Sarah stared at him, her eyes wide, her face pale. Slender fingers tightened on the closed prayer-book in her lap. 'Africa?' He had suggested a possibility that had not occurred to her — that the order might ensure her silence by sending her to some little-known outpost overseas.

'I'm sorry, Sister. I didn't mean to frighten you.'

She had hoped to untangle troubled thoughts in private as the miles raced away. But he had found her, this man who had befriended her and bewildered her, helped her and teased her. He made her nervous, a fact she thought he was well aware of.

'How come you're on your own, Sister? I thought nuns always travelled in pairs.'

'Mother Sebastian was so angry when she ordered me back to the Mother House. I think she's given up on me. Maybe she doesn't care what I do any more.'

'Mother Sebastian, yes…she was quite happy to tell me how much trouble you're in.

Concerned for Sarah following the publication of her letter, Mick had been on the phone to the convent in the early hours and Mother Sebastian had delighted in telling him of Sister Anthony's pending dismissal. His arrival at the station seconds before her train pulled out had startled Sarah. Now he was warning her that remaining a nun might mean a dangerous mission posting.

He had a point, she thought. Her superiors would be wary of further controversy. Leaving St Cuthbert's, she had not even been allowed to say goodbye to the children. She didn't want to leave them and she knew how much she would miss them. She would miss Sister Leo's kindly fussing and Sister Monica's cheerful smile. She would miss Sister Matthew's guidance and yes, she acknowledged with a private smile, she would miss her unlikely friendship with this committed atheist.

'Sister, I feel responsible. If it wasn't for me –' His hands hovered as if he wanted to grab hold of hers but thought you probably shouldn't do that to a nun.

'I knew what I was doing, Mr O'Mara. But you do seem to be the only one who doesn't think I've done something treacherous.'

'Treacherous? Heavens no! Heroic, more like.'

The train began to shudder from the platform. He made no move to leave.

Leaning forward again, he searched for her eyes. 'Sister, forgive me, but what made you become a nun?'

Sarah stared at her self-appointed companion. How could she explain her vocation to someone who didn't even believe in God? 'Well,' she began, then sighed and gazed out of the window as if the passing landscape might provide an answer.

*

In the Catholic schools of Sarah's childhood, priests and nuns from a mysterious place called 'the Far East' had planted the idea of a divine calling in fertile soil. They had Irish accents like her grandmother and they hushed spellbound classes of big-eyed children with tales of adventures to be had bringing Christ to the poor pagans.

Year after year, the missionaries visited the schools and at home, Sarah the eldest girl helped with her siblings and the housework each time her mother went into labour. Sarah's escape had been her world of books. Fact or fiction, she loved to read about good people changing bad worlds. She especially admired Caroline Chisholm, travelling three continents to educate children and help destitute women. Sarah wanted to be like her. She didn't want to be like her poor mother, stuck at home, up before the sparrows even in winter, school lunches packed before breakfast and every day the same boring grind of washing, ironing and cleaning.

At seventeen, Sarah had been quick to see that the missionaries offered a more exciting choice. They made a difference. They changed their world. It was then that she decided that God was calling her to a life of service as a missionary nun. She smiled, remembering her father's face the first time he saw her in the religious habit. His pride had sealed her determination to be a good nun. She had not imagined how difficult that would be.

As the train clattered south towards Melbourne, Sarah realised that her companion had given up on a reply. He had drawn his hat over his eyes and allowed himself to be rocked asleep by the rhythm of the train. His long legs were stretched along the leather seats opposite her. She dragged her eyes away to the rapidly changing horizon.

The train slowed into a small station and stopped just long enough for the single waiting passenger to board. It was raining now, the landscape blurred by fat drops splashing against the window. As the train lunged into motion again, the jolt of renewed movement woke Mick. He sat up, his hair more rumpled than usual and his rugged features flushed from sleep.

He grinned at Sarah. 'Sorry, Sister. I've done some boring interviews in my time but I've never put myself to sleep before.'

She smiled. 'I'm the one who should apologise, Mr O'Mara. Your question gave me a lot to think about. I'm afraid I forgot that you were waiting for an answer. But perhaps what I took for patience was more like cunning on your part?'

'Me? Cunning?' He pouted, pretending to be offended.

'Yes. You wanted to give me time to think about why I entered the convent because, for some reason, you don't think I should be a nun, do you?'

'I don't think anyone should be a nun,' he grinned.

'You don't throw these challenges at the other nuns, though, do you?

'Well, I can't see me getting anywhere with Mother Sebastian, can you? Perhaps I think you have more potential for seeing the error of your ways.'

She laughed and, feeling the heat in her cheeks, turned her face to the window. 'I've been thinking about what you said earlier, that the order might hide me away on a mission but I don't think they'll send me to Africa. We have a mission near Rabaul in New Guinea. I wouldn't mind a posting there. In fact, I'd quite like to go there. I entered, hoping to serve in New Guinea.'

'Why so keen on New Guinea?'

'Have you ever heard of the Kokoda Track?'

'Hmmm, let's see, jungle track across the Owen Stanleys, World War II, Japanese darn near taking Australia, pushed back by a bunch of brave diggers, that Kokoda?'

Sarah grinned. 'Yes, that Kokoda. Well, my father was one of those "brave diggers" but he talked more about the ones he called the real heroes of the track.'

'The Fuzzy-Wuzzy Angels?'

'Yes. He used to say, "They were our guides and our porters. They carried our gear and when we were wounded, hell, they carried us."' Sarah was silent for a moment, then she continued. 'Dad was wounded himself. The natives carried him all the way back to Rabaul on a stretcher. He felt like he owed them.'

Mick's eyebrows shot up. 'So! That's why you became a nun – to repay your father's debt. And now you can't leave the convent because you're afraid of disappointing him? Am I close?' He grinned as her mouth opened and closed again without a word.

The train had raced away from the rain of a moment ago. Overhead, a wedge-tailed eagle spread majestic wings, surfing beneath the clouds.

Mick leaned into the window. 'You know, if anything could make me believe in God, it would be these eagles. Why would you have a dove as a symbol of God, when you could have an eagle, eh? They soar so high, so powerfully, as if to say, Yes, Australia is a Spirit Land. We are its Guardians. Respect us and you will be safe.'

The sun emerged and their compartment filled with light.

Mick backed away from the window, shielding his eyes against the glare and noticed that Sarah was staring at him. 'Well, something like that,' he grinned. It was his turn to redden. He changed the subject. 'I've always loved trains. It's amazing the things you see from their windows.'

'Yes, I know what you mean. I remember a family holiday in Queensland. Our train was chuffing along through miles of sugar cane. Then there was a break and we could see this long row of curious little huts. They didn't look like anything I've seen anywhere else in Australia.'

'Oh, you mean the slave huts?'

'The what huts?'

'They were used to house the poor beggars that worked the sugar plantations. Of course we didn't call them slaves. This is Australia, right? But what else would you call people who were kidnapped from their homes and forced to work without pay?'

Sarah's eyes widened. 'Forced labour? Here in Australia?'

Mick raised an eyebrow. His amused smile alerted Sarah to the irony of what she had said.

She bit her lip and shifted on her seat. 'Well, you'd think someone would have demolished the huts by now, from shame at least.'

'Most people aren't so delicate about things like that, Sister. When

I was working on a story in Townsville last year, I was invited by a colleague who didn't know me better, to go on what he casually referred to as "a coon hunt".'

Sarah's jaw dropped. For a moment, she thought he was making fun of her. But he went on with such earnest indignation that she began to believe he was telling her no more than a shocking truth.

'This bloke had mates in the army. He said there was this place on the beach where the Aboriginal women – that's not what he called them by the way – where they liked to go swimming in the evening. He was boasting about how the soldiers had invited him along one night. They chased the poor women along the beach and herded them into a trap. Well, I won't spell it out, Sister. I'm sure you can guess what happened next.'

Mick pretended interest in the window again, so that Sarah could digest his meaning without having his eyes on her.

'This bastard – sorry, Sister – well, he thought it was real funny. He couldn't understand why I felt like thumping him. Started calling me a "boong lover" and stuff like that. So you see, a few dilapidated huts almost a century old are hardly going to embarrass a mentality like that.'

Sarah stared back at him in silence. Her cheeks were burning and this time she didn't hide behind her veil. When Mick looked back, he wasn't sure if she was shocked, embarrassed or both.

'But those huts…don't visitors, tourists, ever ask questions? Heavens, you can see them from the train.'

'We can be very good at not seeing things, Sister. And asking sensitive questions isn't what we do, is it?'

'Unless you're a journalist, of course.'

He grinned. 'Ouch. It's true, though. We have all these forbidden subjects, taboos and secrets galore.' His quick eye caught a subtle change in her expression. 'What did I say?'

She almost said, 'Nothing, Mr O'Mara, it was nothing,' but caught herself with a dry little laugh just before she proved him right. She stared at the window and a sigh escaped her. 'What you said about forbidden subjects. My life, my convent life, is a good example. People have no idea.' Her voice dwindled.

He leaned forward asking gently, 'Is that what happened to you, Sister? Did you have no idea?' There was genuine concern in his eyes.

Sarah found his kindness almost as unsettling as his teasing. 'I was naïve, I guess, but Mr O'Mara, there was never any real slavery in Australia, surely?'

He smiled and took the hint. 'Not "was", Sister. It still happens, don't you think?'

She blushed, aware of his meaning. 'But not like the African slave trade, with people shipped here from another country and all that sort of thing?'

'Well, not so different. Have you ever heard of "blackbirding", Sister?'

She shook her head. 'No. Well, yes, it was mentioned in one of the books you gave me but I didn't know what it was. I meant to ask you.'

'It was the term used for kidnapping labourers for the sugar plantations of Queensland. Ships would trick whole villages on board, pretending to trade and then set sail. Many died on the voyages or in the fields. Thousands of their descendants still live on the sugar coast.'

Sarah gave a rueful little smile and shook her head. 'I feel so ignorant.'

Mick stretched his cramped limbs. His arms reached high over his head and his long legs stretched out towards Sarah. 'Well, it's to be expected.'

She stared at him, green eyes full of indignation, then turned away, her chin in the air. When she looked back, he grinned at her. She pressed her lips together but couldn't stop a smile escaping. They both laughed. He noticed how her eyes lit up. She was far too pretty to be a nun. What a waste. If only she was any other woman. But how did one let a nun know, without offending or, worse still, frightening the hell out of her, that you wished she wasn't a nun?

Rushing to catch the train that morning, Mick had bumped into

Arthur Lawrence as he left his office. He had told the doctor of Sarah's dismissal.

The wise old man had scrutinised him curiously. 'Sister Anthony? The one who dropped a bomb on the orphanage? What an interesting young woman.'

Mick's answer had tumbled out unchecked and enthusiastic. 'Yes indeed, a very interesting young woman.'

'And a nun too, I believe.'

Mick had grinned at the doctor's tone. 'Yes, that too.'

The train devoured mile after mile, its passengers lulled by the thump-tee-thump of wheels on rails. Sarah and Mick turned their eyes back to the window, each lost in private thoughts. Sarah had taken out her Holy Office but it lay unread in her lap. This time, the hills and farms flew past without comfort. Her mind was racing faster than the train. In the gathering darkness, faces floated outside her window. Pearl's eyes, full of hope and agony; little Jamarra's big blue eyes, frightened and sightless with tears; Lily's proud, defiant eyes, full of hurt and confusion, staring at her through the glass. She saw the cane cutters' huts, cold, shorn heads and long lines of children, stretching their arms out to show her bowls that were empty. They were all blotted out as the train plunged into the darker darkness of a long tunnel.

They had almost reached Melbourne before Sarah thought to tell Mick about Mother Sebastian's files. As she explained to him what she had found and not found, Mick found himself thinking again that this young nun who casually confided to him that she had rifled her Superior's filing cabinet was, indeed, a very interesting woman.

*

When they reached Ballarat, misty rain and the chill of a spring evening in southern Victoria challenged even a nun's habit. Sarah shivered and tucked her rug around her knees.

As the train steamed into the station, Mick leapt up, glad to exercise his cramped legs. 'Can I get you anything from the canteen, Sister? Tea? Coffee?'

'No, thank you, Mr O'Mara. We aren't allowed to eat or drink in public.'

'Really?'

'Yes, really.' She smiled as he shook his head in disbelief.

'And you're doing this because…?' He disappeared without waiting for an answer.

Sarah decided to brave the cold and stretch her own legs on the platform. People cast curious glances at a nun alone in public. A bitter wind whistled through the station, making Sarah long for her abandoned blanket. As she hurried back to the comparative warmth of her compartment, she noticed a mother trying to wrestle a pram aboard the train. The young woman was making hard work of it, using only one hand, determined not to let go of the toddler she held by the other. The little boy was pulling in the opposite direction, eager to get closer to the engine. Other passengers were ignoring them and there was no sign of a porter.

Sarah was about to assist when an athletic figure dashed out of the canteen. She smiled as Mick handed the woman his coffee and a meat pie in a brown paper bag, and hefted the pram aboard. Then he hoisted the youngster into the air, making the child giggle and set him down on the train. He reclaimed his coffee and pie, tipped his hat to the young mother and handed her onto the train. Not noticing Sarah behind him, he loped along the platform and disappeared into their carriage.

When Sarah arrived, the hero of the hour was back in his seat, the pie demolished and the coffee cup stuffed into the mesh rubbish bag hanging under the window.

He stood up when she entered, then laughed and sat down again. 'Gallantry isn't going to work, Sister. I'll have to stay in my seat so that you can reach yours.'

Sarah wrapped her rug around her legs again and settled herself for the last stage of the journey. The drizzle that had welcomed them to Ballarat had now cleared. As the train raced across the rich alluvial plains of south-western Victoria, the landscape was a patchwork of hills, farms and livestock. Here and there, a house with smoke rising from its chimney signalled a cosy kitchen. Workers stooping in paddocks of potatoes stretched their backs and waved to the train. On dairy farms, pretty-faced jersey cows with huge dark eyes, stared lazily over stone fences erected more than a century before.

It was late afternoon before they reached Melbourne. When the train shuddered into Spencer Street station, Sarah closed her unread prayer book. She could see the nuns from St Magdalene's waiting as the engine hissed itself still. Mick handed down her suitcase. Comprehending the horror on her face when he offered to escort her to her waiting sisters, he disappeared into the mass of humanity flooding the station like a colony of frenzied ants.

Forty-nine

At St Magdalene's, Sister Daniel again led Sarah to one of the monastery's bedrooms. She checked that the water jug had been filled and that towels and face washers were in their place. Satisfied, she instructed Sarah, 'You may join the second sitting for dinner, Sister. Mother Anna is not expecting you tonight but she would like to see you after breakfast.' Her habit swished around the door.

Sarah listened to her footsteps echoing down the corridor and sank onto the bed, staring at the closed door. In this room, with this person, it was impossible not to remember that night.

That night of her reception ceremony, that Bride-of-Christ night when Sarah had responded to a late evening knock, opening her door to find Sister Daniel with a covered tray in her hands. 'May I come in, Sister Anthony?' Sarah had found the request as strange as being addressed by her new name. The sisters never entered each other's rooms. That night. however, Sister Daniel had hurried in and deposited her tray on Sarah's bed. 'I have come to cut your hair, Sister,' she whispered. Sarah still remembered how the words had disappointed.

As a postulant, she had always presumed that when she took the veil, she would wear her hair shorter. On her reception day, she had stepped onto the altar in her mother's wedding dress, ready for the sacrifice. Intoxicated by incense, surrounded by the Gothic grandeur of St Patrick's Cathedral and buoyed by the music of its great pipe organ, anything had seemed possible. But they had not cut her hair then. In a room hidden from spectators, senior novices had helped her out of her bridal finery and into the religious habit for the first time. They had simply unpinned the long auburn hair that she had worn in a braided crown, and let it fall down her back hidden by her new robes. She had been surprised and relieved. By the time Sister Daniel had arrived at her door in darkness, Sarah had not wanted to lose her hair.

Stifling her disappointment, she had removed her coif and veil and seated herself on the edge of her chair. As Sister Daniel lifted strands of her hair in one cool hand and reached for the scissors, Sarah clutched her chair. Inside the room, the only sounds were her breathing and the snips of the scissors. Outside wind moaned on the balcony, rattling the window. The cutting had seemed to go on forever. She had breathed a sigh at last as Sister Daniel replaced her scissors on the tray. She rubbed the boyish remnants of her hair and stood up with a sheepish grin, for the first time glad that there was no mirror in the room.

Sister Daniel had pointed Sarah back to the chair and bent her head forward till her chin rested on her chest. When the cold steel of the clippers touched the back of her neck, Sarah flinched, pressing her lips together. Her heart was pounding. Alarm gripped her as the clippers climbed higher. Sister Daniel stepped in front of her, taking Sarah's chin in those cool fingers and running the clippers over her temples. Sarah clenched her teeth and closed her eyes as the last of her hair slithered down her face. Her chest hurt. Without thinking, she grabbed at the black skirts in front of her. Sister Daniel made no move to resist the wretched plea. She had packed her tray without moving away from Sarah's hands. Only when Sarah released her did she fade back into the night, her footsteps echoing through the corridors. For a moment. Sarah had sat motionless, clinging to her chair. Then she had grabbed the bedside basin as nausea threatened.

The wind still clamoured at her window. She had huddled on top of her bed and fallen asleep without undressing. When she woke, still wearing her crumpled habit, for one merciful moment she had not remembered.

Fifty

Mother Anna studied the novitiate gardens through the windows of her parlour. In the centre of the room behind her, Sister Anthony was on her knees.

Sarah held her breath. So far there had been no mention of Africa.

The Superior spoke over her shoulder. 'This newspaper man that Mother Sebastian is so concerned about Sister, a Mr O'Mara?'

'Yes, Mother?'

'Do you have improper feelings for him?'

Sarah stifled a gasp. Her cheeks burned. What on earth had Mother Sebastian been saying? She answered a little too fast. 'No, Mother. I don't think so.'

Mother Anna was content to let the matter rest. Having asked the question, she knew that it was now something Sarah would have to ask herself. She addressed more pressing matters. 'And you, Sister, are you having doubts about your vocation?'

This time, Sarah felt sure she knew what the question was about. 'No, Mother, not about my vocation. I still want very much to be a Sister of St Frances, if I can. I believe that it is God's will for me. But I do have doubts about taking children from their parents.'

Mother Anna turned back from the window. She frowned across the room at the solitary figure kneeling alone on the floor. She seated herself in the window lounge and patted the padded seat beside her. 'Come, Sister Anthony.' The Superior waited while Sarah rose and joined her. 'Now then, Sister, don't you think the children are better off in our care?'

'Not in Mother Sebastian's care, Mother.' In her distress, Sarah blurted out her protest more abruptly than she intended. 'Mother Sebastian is not fit to be in charge of children. She humiliates them. She lies to them. She frightens them. She inflicts cruel punishments. She works them like little slaves.'

Mother Anna's eyes had widened in alarm.

Sarah lowered her voice. 'Mother, I'm sorry to speak like this but –' She shook her head and sighed, turning pleading eyes to Mother Anna's face.

'If what you say is true, Sister, it is shocking, shocking. Of course something must be done.' Recovering her calm, Mother Anna spoke as if a new thought had just occurred to her. 'Sister, I appreciate that you only accepted teaching because you were bound by obedience. I now believe that it may not be your true vocation. Mother Basil has asked for more trainees at the hospital.'

Sarah's eyes lit up. She took a deep breath, calming the excitement that fluttered through her.

Mother Anna's eyes didn't leave Sarah's face. 'I wonder if you would like to join them, Sister, in preparation for the New Guinea Mission?'

Fifty-one

On the east side of St Magdalene's manicured lawns, a wooded park was laced by meandering paths that were not much more than bush tracks. Sunlight filtered through the trees as Sarah strolled through the secluded little wilderness deep in thought. Around her, sparrows twittered an energetic chorus, wrens darted about in the undergrowth and blackbirds ploughed the earth in their ceaseless messy search.

In a stone grotto surrounded by bracken and funeral lilies, a statue of the Virgin Mary extended immaculate hands. Two marble seats enclosed a grassy space in front of the grotto. Sarah sat down and glanced around. She was quite alone. She slipped off her shoes and plunged black-stockinged toes into the cool grass. A magpie strutted his self-important walk only feet away, unperturbed by the presence of one more statue in the park. Sarah smiled at him. Her father was fond of magpies. She tried not to think about what it would mean to him if she were to serve in New Guinea. She dropped her head back, lifting her face and closing her eyes. Should she accept the golden carrot Mother Anna had dangled before her? Or should she return to St Cuthbert's under another Superior? Mother Anna seemed to have accepted at last that Mother Sebastian should not be in charge of children. St Cuthbert's could be a different place with Sister Matthew or someone else in charge. But nursing! Nursing and New Guinea.

The convent bell interrupted Sarah's reverie, announcing the midday meal. She slipped back into her shoes. As she left the trees and moved into the open gardens, a shadow fell across her path too quickly to be the movement of a cloud. She shielded her eyes and looked up at a majestic wedge-tailed eagle, wheeling in circles over her head. It stopped circling and hovered against the high blue of endless sky. 'We are the

Guardians. You will be safe.' Sarah smiled to herself, savouring a pleasant shiver of memory.

The park had been soothing but Sarah had found no answers there. In chapel, the sun had danced rainbows through stained glass windows but it had provided no inspiration, no Voice from above. When at last she closed her eyes on her pillow, a jumbled nightmare refused to let her rest. She saw Jamarra chained in the hold of a slaver, Pearl's bare feet tramping the dust of an endless highway, herself caught in a tornado, her habit corkscrewed around her body, binding her limbs, her veil blinding her, gagging her. Gasping, she rolled onto the floor in a tangle of bed sheets and blankets. When she dressed, her fingers fumbled with the buttons and ties of a habit that for years now she could have donned in the dark. She moved through the rituals of Mass and morning prayers like a mechanical toy. After breaking her fast with only a few forced mouthfuls of tea and toast, Sarah steeled herself for another visit to Mother Anna's parlour.

The room was bathed in early morning sunshine.

Again the Superior moved to the window sofa, her hand inviting Sarah to sit beside her. 'Good morning, Sister Anthony. You have been in my prayers, my dear.'

Sarah sat beside her Superior, her back straight, her head held high.

'Well now, Sister. Have you been guided to a decision?'

Sarah turned tired eyes to Mother Anna's face. 'Yes, Mother, I have. I'm afraid you will be disappointed.' She swallowed the ache in her throat. 'I'm disappointed in myself,' she whispered. 'I did think God wanted me to be a nun and I've tried, Mother I've really tried…but now,' Sarah sighed, 'I think I entered for the wrong reasons. When I realised how excited I was about going to New Guinea, I realised also that I had convinced myself of a vocation in order to please my parents.' She shook her head. 'Mother, I don't belong in the convent.'

'What makes you so sure, my dear? Even if you entered to please your parents, that may have been God's way of leading you to us, might it not?'

'Oh, Mother, I've told myself exactly that for such a long time. I have wanted so much to be a good nun. I've thought, prayed, done penance. This is not something I've come to lightly, Mother. I cannot renew my vows. I don't want to stay on until I've convinced myself that wrong is right, until I've convinced myself that taking children from their parents is "for their own good". I can't be a part of that any more, Mother, so I can't be a nun any more,' her voice faded away, 'not in New Guinea, not in Cobbs Crossing, not anywhere.'

*

In the parlour in which Sister Daniel had first welcomed her to St Magdalene's, Sarah found the suitcase she had brought from home and beside it a small overnight bag. The latter contained everything Vera Norton could imagine her daughter needing, even to the thoughtful inclusion of several headscarves and a pair of low-heeled shoes.

With unhurried hands, Sarah began to remove her habit for the last time. When she had first donned these garments in St Patrick's Cathedral, she had kissed each item and said a prayer of thanksgiving. Now it seemed as if she should be saying a different prayer, apologising to God for her failure. She lingered over each garment, separating and folding veil, guimpe, domino and coif, glad that there were no mirrors in the parlours.

She slipped into the dress her mother had provided. No matter how much she tugged at its skirt, she could not make it cover her knees. She hesitated over the scarves and decided against them. Her family might as well get used to her tomboy hairstyle from the start. Since taking her vows, her hair had no longer been cut by someone else. She had allowed it to grow into a short bob that was more fashionable than she knew.

As she prepared to leave the room, Sarah caught sight of her new self in one of the glass bookcases, a shadowy image that she did not recognise. With her hand on the doorknob, she looked behind her and rushed back to where her folded habit lay. She picked up the rosewood beads that had hung at her side for so many years, running her fingers over their glossy surface. They did not belong to the order. They had been a gift from her family. She opened her suitcase and nestled the beads between the scarves.

Picking up a case in each hand, Sarah stepped into the foyer. It was years since her family had seen her in anything but the religious habit. They stared, not quite able to disguise their shock. Henry could not trust himself to speak. He lowered his head in an awkward fashion as Sarah raised her face to kiss him. *He's disappointed. I've let him down.* Vera hugged her daughter but was also unable to find words. *I've let them all down.*

Ben grabbed Sarah's cases. 'I'm glad you're leaving this place, Sare. I'm glad you're coming home. Hey, Sare, stop hugging me. I can't breathe.'

As she started to close the doors of St Magdalene's behind her, music from the chapel echoed through the corridors. Sarah paused with her hand on the door, listening for the last time as the sisters she had not been allowed to farewell chanted their midday prayer.

'Come on, Sare.' Ben sounded as if he feared she would go back.

She closed the door and let him tug her down the steps.

Fifty-two

Margaret Rose, a grand old guest house at Lorne nestled its broad verandas between the beach and the rainforest. It had been established by Sarah's grandparents and named for the little princess who was then second in line to the throne. It was both the Norton home and their family business.

Sarah helped out and did her best to be gracious to guests, but as she tried to pick up the threads of the life she had left behind, she found that leaving the convent was in some ways more challenging than entering had been. Family friends who flocked to welcome her home asked endless questions.

'What was it like, Sare?'

'Was it hard, being a nun?'

'Why did you enter?'

'Why did you leave?'

More often than not, they couldn't understand the answers. Some seemed tongue-tied in her presence, afraid to say the wrong thing. Others talked about things she didn't understand. Like a soldier returning from battle or a prisoner released from jail, she found the world foreign and unfamiliar. She started making so many excuses to avoid guests that Vera began to lose patience. Julia dragged her sister off to the pictures once or twice but Sarah preferred escaping to the beach or anywhere she could be alone.

In the middle of her second week home, she searched her bedroom for something to wear that didn't make her feel naked. Her sister had insisted on unpacking her suitcase and Sarah was still trying to work out Julia's system. She rummaged through the shelves of her wardrobe. A book had been wedged between a jumper and a neatly folded cardigan. She pulled it out and gave a gasp of jolted memory as the world of Betty and Jamarra, Tommy and Peter came rushing back. She had not seen this patched and pasted copy of *The Little Black Princess* since she had smuggled it into her suitcase as she left St Cuthbert's. Technically, she supposed she had stolen it. It did belong to Mother Sebastian's library, whether she wanted it there or not. But leaving St Cuthbert's and knowing she might never be back, Sarah had not been able to leave the book behind. Every carefully restored page bore witness to the children's love of the story and their efforts to mend it.

She sat on her bed turning the pages with care, until she choked back a sudden sob. Her eyes filled as they fell on the children's last gift to her. Pressed flat between the pages of Bett-Bett's adventures, the open petals of the red geranium were now almost part of the paper. She closed the book, brushing a tear from her cheek. 'I will not forget you,' she whispered.

*

Christmas provided the distraction they all needed. Henry was in the church choir and the house took on a festive air as he practised carols for midnight Mass.

Harry was home on leave more handsome than ever in his army uniform. Sarah suspected that not all her girlfriends paid their visits out of fascination with her but she didn't mind. It was a relief to let Harry flirt with them. Someone mentioned a war somewhere in Asia. Thailand? No, Vietnam.

He dismissed it airily. 'We're not getting into it. Not the way the Yanks are. We're only sending advisors. That's all.'

Sarah noticed Ben staring at his big brother in undisguised admiration.

As the weeks passed, Vera began to believe that her eldest daughter was finding herself again. Sarah smiled and steered conversation away from her convent life but whenever she could, she still shoved a towel and a book into a bag and made for the beach.

Fifty-three

'You never used that word when you read the book to us. You must have censored it out, I suppose, as I did with the children.' Sarah and Vera were doing the dishes. Against her better judgement, Sarah had tried again to satisfy her mother's need to understand why her daughter was not still a nun. The conversation had led to a discussion of *The Little Black Princess*.

Vera put another plate on the drying rack. 'I don't suppose it was considered such a bad word back then.'

Sarah raised her eyebrows. 'Do you think there was a time when Aborigines liked being called niggers?'

Vera ignored the question. 'But you liked working with your little orphans, didn't you, Sarah?'

'They aren't orphans, Mum. They're taken from their families.'

'Well, that's sad, I suppose. But Sarah, surely it's for their own good, isn't it?'

Sarah shook her head with a mirthless laugh. 'No, Mum, it's not. It's to train servants for white bosses and to breed the blackness out of them.'

'Sarah!' The plate Vera had just washed slipped from her fingers and back into the sink, splashing hot sudsy water all over her apron.

'It's true, Mum. I've seen it. I was part of it, till I couldn't be part of it any longer.'

Vera dabbed at her apron with a dry tea towel. 'Oh, Sarah, I'm sure the holy nuns are only doing what's best for those poor little mites.'

'The "holy nuns", Mum, were stealing funds meant to feed those kids.'

Vera turned startled eyes on her daughter. 'Sarah, for goodness sake don't let your father hear you talking like that. Don't let anyone hear you talking like that.'

Sarah threw her tea towel down. 'Mum, that's just the trouble. No one ever talks about it. We never talk about what we're doing now and we never talk about what happened in the past, the massacres, the slavery –'

'Oh, for heaven's sake, Sarah, don't be so dramatic.'

'It's all there in the history books, Mum. All there for us to read, if we want to.'

'Written by Aborigines, I suppose?' Vera mocked. The dishes were forgotten.

'Well, no, not by Aborigines.' The books that Mick had given Sarah had left her hungry for answers. These days she was a familiar figure on the bus that bumped its way down the Great Ocean Road into Geelong and the library in Little Malop Street. 'At least, I haven't seen any books by Aborigines yet,' she admitted.

'And you won't.' Vera waved a finger in Sarah's face as if she was talking to a naughty child. 'I was being ironic, Sarah. Of course Aborigines couldn't write books.'

Sarah interrupted her mother with a despairing sigh. 'Oh, Mum!' She shook her head. 'There's no reason Aborigines couldn't write books.' Sarah had also forgotten the dishes. She gazed out the kitchen window across the grass that disappeared into the forest. A faraway smile lit her eyes. 'Lily was smart enough. I bet Lily could write a book.'

'Who is Lily?'

'One of the girls at St Cuthbert's.'

'What happened to her?'

The smile left Sarah's eyes. 'I don't know.'

Brisk strides crunching on the gravel outside announced Harry's military swagger. He removed his hat as he entered the house. 'Hi, Mum. Hey, Sare, Dad reckons he can trust me with the car. Want to come for a drive?'

Vera caught Sarah's glance at the dishes and waved her away. 'Go. I can finish these. Shoo. It'll do you good.'

In seconds, Sarah was sitting in the family's Humber watching Harry change gears with smooth confidence. She relaxed into the seat.

'Penny for 'em?'

'For my thoughts? I'm not sure they're worth a penny.'

'It's been tough? Coming home and all that?'

'I know everyone is trying to be nice but –'

'They don't understand?'

The car took bend after bend as they climbed away from the coast.

'No, they don't understand.'

'We can't, Sare. We haven't been where you've been. We, and you, need time to get to know each other again. It'll come good.'

Sarah stared at her twin. When did he get so grown-up? 'Maybe. At the moment I just feel, well, Dad's so proud of you... And me, I've just disappointed everyone.'

Without taking his eyes off the endless bends Harry smiled, guiding the car high into the rainforest. 'Julia told me that when they first knew you were leaving the convent, Dad said, "It'll be good to have her home." Seven whole words, Sare.'

'Really? He didn't say that to me. He didn't say anything to me. Why didn't anyone tell me that he said that?'

He gave her a cheeky grin. 'I just did.'

She went to punch his arm but remembered that he was driving. Around the next bend, he pulled into a wayside stop.

As they left the car, Sarah closed her eyes and took a deep breath. The air was fresh and full of the invigorating scent of eucalyptus. The great trees that gave the Otways its fame soared skywards. Bush tracks wound between the giants into their cool, under-canopy world of tree ferns, wildlife and waterfalls. A creek gurgled in the distance, competing with a noisy choir of birdsong.

Sarah threw her head back, laughing with delight. 'Oh, Harry! It's so good to be up here again. Thank you.'

They picked their way between twisted roots that had reclaimed patches of path and large moss-covered stones, half in and half out of the ground. Tree ferns spread dewy umbrella fronds over the track. Fairy wrens, so small they would disappear if held in a human hand, darted now in sun, now in shade. By the creek they found a fallen tree trunk and sat with their backs against it, watching the water cascade over smooth boulders. Light filtered through the forest canopy, sparkling on the water as if the creek bed was littered with diamonds.

Sarah closed her eyes again, giving herself up to the sounds and scents of the bush. She stretched, her contented sigh seeming to come right up from her toes. 'I love it here, Harry. It reminds me of when we were kids. Do you know, I used to think it was all ours, just us and the possums and the wrens.'

Harry laughed. 'It might as well be.'

She sobered as a different thought occurred. She sat up, watching the water rushing past their feet. 'I've been reading our history, Harry, not British history like we learned at school but real, Australian history.' She hesitated, shaking her head.

Harry pulled a handful of grass and threw it into the creek, watching the water swirl it away. 'Go on.'

'It was just horrible what the British – our ancestors, I suppose – did here. People were driven off their land, massacred, their children taken.' Her head dropped down and Harry only just heard her last words. 'Taking children, we still do that.'

He didn't know what to say, so he said nothing.

Sarah waved a hand around. 'I can't imagine how terrible it must have been, to have had all this taken from you. But at least Aborigines know that they belong here. We don't belong anywhere.'

Harry needed to move his legs. He perched on top of the log they had been leaning against and looked down on his sister's head, a puzzled frown creasing his forehead. 'We're Aussies, we belong in Australia.'

'Yes, we're Aussies but Australia isn't our country.'

'Eh? Why isn't Australia our country?'

'Because it was stolen; because our ancestors just pretended the Aborigines weren't here and took the land, no treaty, nothing, so really, Australia isn't our country.'

Harry cut in. 'So if the government ever wants me to go to war, I should just say, "Sorry, mate, Australia isn't my country." I wonder how that would work.'

'Harry –' She looked up and he shot her a half-hearted smile but the contented camaraderie of a moment ago was shattered. Sarah bit her lip. Speaking out hurt people she loved. Staying silent betrayed others.

Fifty-four

'Good news?' Julia poked her head around her sister's bedroom door.

Sarah had a letter in her hand. 'Uh, huh, I've received an offer to study nursing in Ballarat.'

'Ballarat! Why do you want to go away again, Sare?' Julia perched on the end of Sarah's bed.

'I don't want to go away. I want to start nursing. I'm twenty-two years old, Jules. I can't sit around here forever.'

*

Going on duty in Ballarat winters was a last-minute affair for even the most dedicated nurses. The students would make a furious dash across the lawns between their quarters and the hospital, crowding into the lifts with their red capes pulled tight around their shoulders. After six weeks injecting oranges and bathing rubber dummies, they had been released on unsuspecting patients and, at the end of each shift, a weary but happy Nurse Norton dragged herself off to coffee and crumpets in the nurses' lounge.

On her third day on the wards, an injection of penicillin was prescribed for one of Sarah's patients and she went in search of a senior nurse to supervise her. She spotted two stripes on the sleeve of a student who was bending over the steriliser. She started speaking to the nurse's back. 'I'm sorry to be a nuisance, Nurse, but –' She broke off with a gasp. As the nurse straightened, Sarah came face to face with Lily Matthews.

Lily's eyes registered unsmiling recognition. 'Sister Anthony,' she mocked.

'It…it's Sarah now, Lily. Lily, it's so good to see you…and here as a nurse, as you always wanted to be. How wonderful.'

Lily glanced at the badge on Sarah's uniform. 'What was it you wanted, Nurse Norton?'

Sarah's eager smile faded. She stepped back. 'I need someone to, um, supervise me while I give Mrs Jarvis –'

'Well, let's get on with it then.'

Lily swept away to the ward and Sarah scrambled to catch up, her mind awhirl. She had found Lily but Lily didn't want anything to do her. She bit her lip. I don't blame you, Lily. If I was you, I wouldn't want to talk to me. But Lily, I have so much to tell you.

Sarah's shift seemed longer that day. At last, she left the wards and dragged her weary body and wearier mind from the hospital to the nurses' home. In the first-floor lounge, she kicked off her shoes without untying the laces. While she waited for the jug to boil and her crumpets to brown, she stared at the toaster as if it might have an answer to the questions that had been haunting her all day. Lily here and a second-year nurse! Well done, Lily. I knew you could, if given a chance. But how did you get that chance?

Sarah flopped down into a big old armchair with her crumpets and tea and stared at the tiny television screen. It wasn't any more help than the toaster. She fidgeted about in the chair, trying to relax. Her mind was still talking to Lily. 'Mother Sebastian hated you so much. When she took you away, I bet she was looking for the most horrible placement she could find. But you've fought your way out of it and ended up here. I'd love to know how that happened. And I'd love to know if you have that birthmark. If you do, there's so much I could tell you.' Sarah sighed and nibbled on her crumpets.

*

After working a shift more demanding than usual, Sarah left the wards with her body begging for a nice hot shower. The shower block was almost empty. Only one other nurse was there, draped in a towel and bending forward to rub her hair dry. As Sarah walked behind her, the other girl straightened and shook loose a head of damp, black curls. She still had her back to Sarah but both recognised each other in the mirrored wall. As soon as their eyes met, Lily turned her face away. Sarah lowered her eyes and they fell on Lily's bare shoulder. There it was. Confirming all Sarah had suspected of Lily's identity, was the tiny blue-grey cloud shaped birthmark. Sarah couldn't help staring.

In the mirror, Lily followed the direction of her eyes. 'What? It's just a birthmark.'

'Not just a birthmark, Lily, a very important birthmark.' Sarah dropped her bag and towel on the bench, her eyes shining, her words tumbling out in an excited rush. 'Lily, I know who your mother is!'

'Oh, of course you do. And how long have you known?'

'Just a few seconds. You see –'

'Phoof, you're mad.' Lily's eyes were dark with scorn.

Sarah pressed on, determined not to give up now. 'Lily, it's the birthmark. Doctor Lawrence knows about it. Your mother didn't give you up. You were taken from her. She came to St Cuthbert's searching for you many times while I was there and probably ever since you were taken.'

Lily was shoving things into her shower bag, her face contorted with rage. Angry eyes drilled Sarah. 'You're mad and you're telling lies.'

'No, Lily, it's the truth. Ask Doctor Lawrence. He attended your mother. He knows the birthmark.'

'If my mother was looking for me all that time, why didn't you tell me?'

'Your mother always called you Tallara. Mother Sebastian had changed your name. I didn't suspect that you were Tallara until after you had been sent away. And I didn't know for sure until just now, when I saw your birthmark. You have met your mother, Lily. Remember the woman, Pearl, who helped you when you were lost in the bush? She's your mother, Lily! You have a brother, too. Do you remember the little boy, Joseph May? He's your brother.'

'Stop!' Lily tugged the string of her shower bag tight. Her eyes scorched Sarah with a blistering glare. 'Just stop it with your silly lies. You worked in those places. They were like hell for us and you stood by and did nothing. You watched bad things happen to us, and now you think you can fix everything? Well, you can't. You can't.' Lily was trembling with rage.

Sarah sank onto the slatted wooden seats surrounding the dressing room, staring at the floor. Her voice came in almost a whisper. 'I let you down, Lily. I understand you not wanting anything to do with me. I'm so sorry.'

'Sorry?'

'You've every right to hate me. You must feel –'

'You don't know one thing about how I feel.'

'No, of course not, but I can imagine –'

'Oh, you can, can you? Has anyone ever tried to rape you, Sister Anthony?'

An ashen-faced Sarah stared after Lily as she stormed away down the corridor.

Sarah didn't allow herself the long, relaxing soak she had planned. She showered in haste, and returning to her room, hurried to her dressing table and leafed through her writing folio for paper and a pen.

Dear Lily

Believe me, I feel every bit as pathetic as you could want me to feel, about writing this letter – even more pathetic that I will leave it under your door because you might refuse to take it from me.

Lily, I feel so foolish! How could I have thought that all I had to do was find you? So naïve! Of course you have every right to feel the way you do. But whatever you think of me does not matter. What matters is that what I told you was the truth and I can prove it. Pearl Marsh is your mother. She did not give you away. I know that she loves you and is still trying to find you. What you were told at the orphanage about your parents not wanting you was unforgiveable. Lies, Lily! Lies! I do not want to be a nuisance to you but neither can I forget your mother's desperation and my promise to her. If ever you change your mind – if ever you would like to meet your mother – I would be happy to help you.

Most sincerely
Sarah Norton

As soon as Sarah had sealed the letter in an envelope, she took up her pen again:

Dear Sister Matthew

I have wonderful news! I have found Pearl's Tallara and guess who it is? Someone who was with us at St Cuthbert's all the time. Sister, I now have proof that Tallara Marsh is none other than Lily Matthews! I know you will be delighted to hear that Lily is now a second year student nurse. You always had faith in her and you were right. I do not know how this happened as understandably, Lily is in denial and doesn't believe a thing I say – no wonder really. For this reason, I would ask you not to tell Pearl about this yet. I am hoping that you still have all those letters that Pearl wrote to Tallara. If you do, could you please send them to me? One day, Lily might let me give them to her.

My warm best wishes to you and all at St Cuthbert's
Sarah Norton (formerly Sister Anthony)

Fifty-five

In May Sarah had a four-day lecture break and she hummed to herself as she packed her case. She would be home for Mother's Day.

At Margaret Rose on Sunday morning, she served her mother breakfast in bed: tea, hot buttered toast, bacon and eggs and a small posy in a vase. Then she arranged an enormous bunch of white chrysanthemums in the parlour where Vera would see them when she came downstairs.

Now Sarah had time to prepare herself for Mass. The second Sunday in May was also Nightingale Sunday. On this day, the church honoured the nursing profession and it was traditional for nurses to attend Mass in uniform. Sarah grinned as she dressed, imagining the reactions of her family at seeing her jaunty cap and lovely red cape for the first time. She inspected herself in the mirror. She had taken extra care with every detail: shoes polished to military perfection; black stockings without ladders or holes; grey pinstriped dress with starched cuffs on the short sleeves; crisp white apron with Harry's watch pinned upside down on her chest; frilled cap set at just the right angle on her forehead and, of course, the cape. She turned this way and that in front of the mirror. Satisfied at last, she made her way downstairs.

Her father's was the first face she looked for and Henry Norton did not disappoint her. He loved the red capes. He had seen them worn over khaki uniforms on the battlefields of Africa and Europe, and persevered with in the steamy heat of Pacific jungles. The strong women who wore them had understood that the sight of their capes helped morale. They had comforted troops at Dafni and Athens. They had borne the heat of Alexandria and the humidity of Rabaul. It was, to his mind, noble work this nursing, and the way his face lit up when he saw Sarah in uniform, said so. 'Very nice, Sarah.' He put an arm around her shoulders then stood back, saying again, 'Very nice.'

Her eyes shone with pleasure. After parading for them in the warm room, she threw the front of her cape back over her shoulders and Julia spotted the watch.

'Harry's watch, you still use it, Sare?'

'Sure, I love this watch. Besides,' she laughed, 'nurses need to be on time, just as much as nuns do.'

'Speaking of the time, into the car, you lot, or we'll be late for Mass.' Vera herded them out of the room.

As the congregation filed into the white weatherboard church, the nurses waited outside.

Father Duffy approached them, beaming from one to another. 'Good morning, ladies.'

'Good morning, Father,' they chorused as if they were still in school.

'It's lovely to see so many of you this morning. Would one of you like to read the epistle today?'

The group in front of him seemed to shrink, the young women looking at each other or their shoes. A nervous giggle escaped one or two.

The priest caught Sarah's eye. 'Miss Norton, would you read for us?' She nodded and the rest breathed a sigh of relief.

The nurses formed a procession and entered the church in pairs, carrying the banners of the patron saints of nursing: St Catherine of Siena, St John of God and the Virgin Mary. The front pews were reserved for them.

The congregation shuffled to its feet as Father Duffy, now in liturgical robes, was led onto the sanctuary by two altar boys and Mass began. '*In nomine Patris et Figli et Spiritus Sanctus.*'

When the time came for her to read, Sarah tossed her cape over her shoulders and stepped up to the lectern. She took a breath and lifted her voice above the assembly. 'A reading from the epistle of the Blessed

Apostle James, chapter two, verses fourteen to twenty-six.' She read with confidence, her words steady and clear. 'If your brothers or sisters are in need and you say "I wish you well" without giving them the necessities of life, what good is that? If your faith is not accompanied by good works, it is dead.'

When the reading was finished, Sarah returned to her place in the pews, turning over the words of Saint James in her mind.

After Mass, the parishioners streamed into the churchyard, blinking against the brightness and rubbing dinted knees that had been too long on wooden boards. Few hurried away. Most hung back talking about yesterday's football games or the latest family to have acquired a television set. Sarah was both embarrassed and delighted by her father's eagerness to present her to his friends, as if they had never met her before.

Vera, mindful of the Sunday roast, was first to make a move.

As they walked to the car, Henry placed a hand on his daughter's shoulder. 'I didn't know you could read so well, Sarah. I'm proud of you.'

Her face shone.

Fifty-six

In January, Sarah faced her first-year examinations and added another stripe to her sleeve. While she worked and studied, *The Little Black Princess* sat on her dressing table where she could see it every day, a constant reminder of the children and her promise to Pearl. She wrote persistent letters to St Cuthbert's and St Magdalene's. Her letters to the orphanage went unanswered. Those to the Novitiate received a formal, uninformative response, Mother Anna claiming ignorance of the whereabouts of any Jamarra Marsh or Joseph May.

Pearl's letters to Tallara, which Sister Matthew had despatched by return post, were safely stored in Sarah's suitcase. Sarah now knew where and who Tallara was but she hadn't felt it safe to give the letters to Lily. Lily was still angry and Sarah was afraid that she might destroy the letters without ever reading them. Pearl would want her Tallara to receive those letters. Sarah was determined that she would make that happen.

Day after day on the wards, she saw Lily, always efficient, always capable Lily. And always ignoring Sarah, except when the good of a patient or the duty roster commanded cooperation. At such times, Lily was cool, professional and focused on the needs of her patient, no matter how undeserving that patient might be.

Mrs McCaffrey was such a patient. Sarah marvelled at Lily's patience and dignity in the face of racist slurs and the old woman's brutal refusal to be treated by Lily. She simply withdrew without complaint, leaving Mrs McCaffrey to Sarah. It was Sarah who protested. It was Sarah who objected. It was Sarah who, for the first time in her career, became angry with a patient. Nothing she said had any effect.

She shuddered as Mrs McCaffrey shouted loud enough to be heard all over the wing. 'Don't let that dirty Abo back in here, Nurse, or I'll tell her to her face!'

But not even Mrs McCaffrey's violent outbursts prepared Sarah for the revelations that would soon shock all Australia on the national news.

On a warm February evening, Sarah came off duty to a crowded nurses' lounge. More than a dozen young women still in their uniforms surrounded the television, all eyes on the images flickering across the screen.

The reporter's voice announced, 'Across New South Wales, a group of more than thirty students from Sydney University have travelled across country, exposing racial abuse suffered by Aborigines in Australian rural towns. These Freedom Rides are being led by an Aboriginal student, Charlie Perkins.'

The screen erupted as the students clashed with angry locals, who challenged them with loud voices and fists raised in threatening gestures. The coverage shifted to images of Aboriginal housing, living conditions that reminded Sarah of the River Camp at Cobbs Crossing. Then it shifted again, to show segregation signs on community venues in the town.

The reporter shoved a microphone at one of the students and she was happy to oblige. 'We've seen Aborigines refused service in shops; we've seen segregation in cinemas, swimming pools and hotels and bans in service clubs.'

'Service clubs? You mean the RSL? The Returned Services League?'

'Yeah, that's right.'

'Even though Aborigines have served in both world wars?'

'Yeah. In Walgett, for example, the vice president of the RSL, he said he would never allow an Aborigine to become a member.'

'You've had quite a few clashes with locals along the way, haven't you?'

'Yeah, well, when we see segregation, we protest, see, and picket these joints, you know? The locals don't want the world to see it, of course, so they get hostile. In Moree, we tried to get some Aboriginal kids into the swimming pool. A bunch of locals attacked us, very angry, very violent. Once, a heap of cars followed our bus at night. They ran us right off the road. That was scary, real scary.'

In the nurses' lounge, the newscast was met with mixed reactions.

One of the young women protested. 'They're making this up! We don't have segregated swimming pools.'

There was a general murmur of agreement.

The 'WHITES ONLY' sign at the Cobbs Crossing pool flashed into Sarah's head. She should say something. Across the room, Lily's raised brows shot a pointed challenge at Sarah. Yes, she should say something. She should. As Lily left the room with a just-what-I-expected smile of contempt, Sarah hung her head.

*

June ushered in the icy freeze of a Ballarat winter. As the nurses crossed the compound between their quarters and the hospital, a bone-chilling wind had them tugging their capes tight around shivering bodies.

Sarah reached the cloakroom and was hanging up her cape, when an orderly poked his head through the door.

'Craddick wants to see you, Sarah.'

She scurried down the corridor to the ward sister's office. Outside the door, she paused to straighten her collar and smooth her apron. She tapped twice.

'Yes? Come.'

Sarah stepped into the tiny room and stood before the desk.

'Ah, Nurse Norton.' Sister Craddick capped her fountain pen and picked up a folder from a pile on her desk. She handed it to Sarah. 'I am assigning you to '"special" a patient who came in yesterday – Mr Campbell Ross.'

Sarah's eyes widened. A patient placed in the care of an individual nurse would be very ill, or even dying. Nursing a 'special' was an assignment of responsibility and trust. 'Thank you, Sister. I'm glad you think I'm capable.'

Sister Craddick smiled. 'Don't worry, Nurse. You won't be on your own. You will share this duty with Nurse Matthews.' The ward sister detected a curious expression on Sarah's face. 'You don't have a problem working with Nurse Matthews, do you, Nurse?

'Oh no, Sister. I'm sure I can learn a lot from Nurse Matthews.'

'I'm sure you can. Familiarise yourself with that patient profile, then join Nurse Matthews. She's already with Mr Ross in D23.'

Sarah left the office eager for her new duty but biting her lip at the thought of her new partnership. Nursing a 'special' with Lily would be a challenge for both of them.

At morning tea, Lily briefed Sarah. Her manner left no doubt who would be in charge. She sat with the table between them and sipped her coffee speaking in a cool, detached way that conveyed, we are co-workers, not friends. At times, her instructions were almost patronising.

After going over their patient's condition and treatment as if she didn't believe Sarah could be trusted to read his file, she told her, 'Mr Ross has accepted that he hasn't long to live. He doesn't want us fussing about giving him a lot of false hope. He needs as much normality, as much care and dignity, as possible. Our job is to give him that for as long as it takes. It won't be long.' She picked up her cup and stood to leave, looking down at Sarah. 'It will require us to be strong, sensitive and, of course, dedicated professional nurses.'

Watching Lily's straight back walking away from her, Sarah sighed. It would require much more than that.

*

D23 was a private room which meant it had its own bathroom. It also had a window that looked out over the city to a glimpse of purplish hills. Not that the wasted man lying in the centre of the room could appreciate the view. Sarah was impressed by the bravery of her new patient. Campbell Ross was sometimes quite chirpy despite his frailty, as if he thought it was his job to cheer up the nurses.

He was watching Sarah now as she tidied his bed. 'Do you have a boyfriend, Nurse?'

She shook her head, smiling.

Her patient raised his eyebrows. 'I am surprised.' He turned to Lily, who was checking charts at the foot of his bed. 'I'm sure you must have a boyfriend, Nurse?'

'Just a friend, Mr Ross, not really a boyfriend.' Lily's tone was matter-of-fact but a pretty blush warmed her cheeks.

Sarah busied herself with the bed and tried not to look interested, hoping Ross would persist.

'Is he –'

'A Ballarat boy? Yes, he is.'

Sarah smothered a chuckle. Good on you, Lily.

Ross blustered. 'No, I meant –'

'I know what you meant, Mr Ross. Yes, Benny is an Aborigine.'

'I'm sorry, Nurse.'

'That's quite all right, Mr Ross. Time for some tablets, I think.'

The conversation had exhausted Ross. He accepted the pills from Lily and allowed Sarah to settle him back on his pillows. He was asleep before she had finished smoothing his blankets.

Sarah watched as Lily locked Ross's medicine cabinet. 'How did you meet Benny?' she ventured.

At first Lily scowled as if she was about to tell Sarah to mind her own business. Then she seemed to change her mind. 'There was a rally in town – Equal Rights for Aborigines. Benny was one of the speakers. He was really good. '

Sarah took heart. Lily was talking to her and not just about work. 'You were impressed with him?'

'Yes. He's a stirrer. I like that.' Without warning, Lily's mood changed again. 'But I don't like all these questions.' She nodded at their patient. 'He'll sleep for a while now. I'll sit with him. You can relieve me in half an hour.' She picked up a paperback novel and settled herself on a chair beside the bed.

Sarah risked another rebuff. She nodded at the book. 'Any good?'

Lily held the front cover up towards Sarah: *To Kill a Mockingbird*. 'Benny gave it to me.' She confused Sarah with a grin. 'You can read it when I'm finished.'

A few days later, Sarah was sitting by the bed of a sleeping Campbell Ross when Lily rushed into the room, her usual calm demeanour dissolved in a fluster of distress.

'Benny's been arrested!'

'Oh, Lily!' Sarah whispered, mindful of the sleeping patient. 'Why?'

Lily glanced at Ross and lowered her voice. 'He went to an anti-war protest in Melbourne. Some of the protesters made a fire in front of Parliament House. They were burning their draft cards, protesting against being conscripted to fight in Vietnam.'

'Did you know he felt so strongly about the war?'

'I know he felt bad about being safe while his mates were being sent to fight.'

'Safe?'

'Aborigines are exempt from the draft. They can volunteer to go, and some have, but not Benny. He hates the idea of killing people.'

A sleepy voice interrupted their conversation. 'But my dear, they're communists. They want to take over the world.'

The nurses turned towards the bed as their patient, now wide awake, joined the discussion.

Lily answered him. 'I don't mean any disrespect, Mr Ross, but Benny says all that taking-over-the-world talk is a lot of nonsense. He says the Viet Cong are only trying to get their land back. He says he'll be damned if he'll fight a mob that's only trying to get their land back.'

*

By the following day, Ross's coughing ceased only when he was asleep. His face was grey and his eyes were lifeless, even when he tried to be cheerful. His breathing was erratic and his efforts to be light-hearted were sometimes costly. Speaking was now a mammoth struggle, always punctuated by coughs and gasps for breath. He was only fifty-one, just a year older than Sarah's father, but he looked much older.

He managed an exhausted smile as Sarah smoothed his bedding for the umpteenth time. 'Some of our nurses in Alexandria were bobby-dazzlers,' he managed between fits of coughing, 'but I never thought I'd have such a pretty face to see me out.'

Sarah struggled to find the 'normality' Lily had spoken of. She pretended to be shocked. 'Mr Ross! Are you flirting with me?'

He chuckled but his weak little laugh collapsed into another choking, rasping cough and a struggle for breath. He slumped exhausted on his pillows.

Sarah filled his glass from the water jug on his bedside table and held it to his lips, holding him while he drank. When he was finished, he looked up at her, a grateful smile on the grey lips.

She settled him and drew up the chair beside his bed. 'You were in Alexandria, Mr Ross? My father was there, with the Sixth Division.'

'Was he? Well, I'm sure he told you how much we loved our nurses over there.' He started coughing again and took another sip of water from the glass Sarah returned to his lips. He tried again. 'In the drawer, Nurse, a little box.'

Sarah opened the top draw of the metal bedside cabinet and found a small velvet-covered box. She tried to place it in his hands but Ross pushed it back.

'You open it.'

She lifted the lid and smiled. Lying side by side were two beribboned medals she recognised, the Africa Star and the Pacific Star. 'I know these medals, Mr Ross. My father has both of them. He wears them every Anzac Day.'

'What ba-battalion?'

'He was in the Second First, the City of Sydney Battalion.'

'So was I!' There was a new light in the fading eyes.

Sarah could see that these memories comforted him. She sat down beside him again. So that he didn't exhaust himself with conversation, she did most of the talking, telling him all her father had told her about the exploits of Australia's legendary Sixth Division. He listened, nodding and smiling and managing an occasional breathless comment or a little laugh. His pale eyes were alive as they had not been for a long time.

When Sarah went to stand up, he clasped her fingers. 'Nurse, promise me, you'll be here, when –'

Sarah sat down again and took his hand in hers, feeling no shame in letting him see that she was close to tears. She squeezed his hand and said with a gentle smile, 'I promise.'

Soon after Lily had released her for a break, Sarah received a message asking her to call her family. The message said 'urgent'. The pay phone in the passage outside her room wasn't working so she ran downstairs to the reception desk.

Her mother answered the phone. 'Oh, Sarah, thank goodness. Can you come home straight away?'

'I don't know, Mum. What's wrong?'

'We're going to Sydney to see Harry off.'

'Harry? Where's Harry going?'

Her mother began to sob and her father picked up the phone.

'Dad, where's Harry going?'

'They're going to Vietnam, Princess, to the war. Can you get home right now and come up to Sydney with us?'

'Vietnam? But Harry said Australia would only send –'

'Yeah, yeah, I know, "advisors". Well, they changed their minds, Princess, and he got his marching orders. He's going.'

Julia called to her from the background. 'You have to come, Sare. We could go shopping in Sydney.'

Her father's voice was back again. 'He sails on Tuesday. Can you come home, Princess?'

Let Harry go to war and not say goodbye to him? Sarah twisted the cord of the phone around her fingers. There was a painful lump in her throat. 'Dad, I can't.'

*

It was two fifty-five a.m. by the luminous figures on Sarah's alarm clock. Almost three o'clock and she hadn't been asleep. There were too many hammers in her head. She tossed about, remembering Harry going to war, Campbell Ross dying and what Lily had said, no, what Benny had said about communist world domination being rubbish. At school, the nuns had filled her childhood with stories about the Red hordes and what would happen when they took over Australia. Communism was a danger to the free world, they were told at Mass on Sunday and by her father's favourite television commentator, Bob Santamaria. She had always believed it. Her father believed it. Almost certainly, Harry believed it. Sarah frowned at the darkness.

Campbell Ross died on the morning of the eighth of June 1965 with Sarah holding his hand. On the evening news, she watched the first contingent of Australian troops leave for Vietnam, knowing that Harry was somewhere among them. As the parade of heart-stopping slouched hats marched aboard HMAS *Sydney*, she watched every newscast, hoping to catch a glimpse of the one face she wanted to see, and wondered where on earth Vung Tau was.

It was not long before a letter from Julia brought news she had expected for some time: 'Ben has joined the army too now and of course Jack is itching to get into uniform. Mum is very upset.'

Fifty-seven

Towards the end of Harry's first year away, a rare letter, though welcome, weighed heavily.

> I don't go to Mass any more, Sare. I can't come at it. I know I'll go to hell when I die but, hey, it doesn't matter. I already know what hell's like.

Sitting on the edge of her bed, Sarah read and reread the last two lines until the words blurred. She unclipped Harry's watch from her apron, placed it in the envelope with his letter and changed out of her uniform. With the letter and watch in her pocket, she walked the few blocks to where the two great cathedrals of Ballarat stood opposite each other: St Andrew's with its steeple dominating the skyline and St Patrick's surrounded by date palms and iron lace.

Down the long centre aisle of St Pat's her high heels clicked echoes in the empty church. She knelt at the communion rail, her hands joined in prayer and Harry's watch and his letter clutched between them. 'Keep him safe. Please, dear God, please don't let him, don't let Harry…' She couldn't even think it. 'Keep him safe, bring him home.'

*

Sarah was now twenty-four years old and a senior nurse. Doctors sought her assistance on the wards, putting their faith in the three red V-shaped stripes on her sleeve. The addition of that third stripe was not as welcome as it might have been. Every time Sarah caught sight of her new insignia, she wondered where Sergeant Harry Norton was, how he was.

One morning at the end of winter, Sarah came off night duty and walked outside to cheerful, almost spring sunshine. She strolled towards the nurses' home, in no hurry to spend such a lovely day in bed. Daffodils flourished like weeds along the path and she stooped once or twice to pick a few. As she wandered into the foyer arranging her flowers, she squealed with delight as a waiting visitor rose to meet her. Her eyes danced at this unexpected visit but her father was not smiling.

Henry Norton avoided his daughter's eyes. He stood turning his hat in his hands, his shoulders slumped. He looked years older than when Sarah had seen him a month ago. The daffodils flew from her fingers, scattering across the foyer floor. Her hand clutched at the watch on her chest. She shook her head, delaying the moment she had to know.

But they did not know. It would not be like she had seen on television. There would be no flag-draped coffin for Harry. 'Missing in action' was a different kind of horror that plunged families into the nightmare of waiting for answers that did not come.

Fifty-eight

In January, twenty-five-year-old Sarah Josephine Norton graduated as a state registered nurse. She changed her frilled cap for a starched veil and the irony of being called 'Sister' once more, and packed her case for four days leave at Margaret Rose.

It was hard to be home these days. The house seemed full of Harry and empty at the same time. Ben, as Julia had written, was away in camp at Puckapunyal. Jack's hankering to join his brother reduced Vera to rage one minute and tears the next. It didn't help that Julia now had a boyfriend who was also in uniform.

Sarah soon sought out her old refuge at the beach. She found her favourite spot close to the water, a ledge of rocks worn smooth by the wash of waves. The sky stretched huge and cloudless into the distance. A little way from her, children digging in the wet sand ran shrieking when the tide filled their holes and washed away their sand castle walls. Seagulls circled, advertising their scavenging service with monotonous cries. In the distance, the Grand Pacific Hotel, icon of the region, dominated the skyline. Elevated on the cliff above the beach, it was the Norton family's main competition for the Lorne tourist trade. It was an elegant, old-world building, much larger than Margaret Rose, and Sarah had to admit that it was, indeed, grand.

She shaded her eyes, gazing out to sea at the vast expanse of deep blue water on the horizon. Closer in, the ocean rose in great green swells and formed foam-capped waves that raced each other to the shore.

Rolling out her towel on the sand, she relaxed against the sunbaked boulders. She stretched bare arms to the breeze that floated off the water and let her head fall back, closing her eyes, licking salty sea spray from her lips and listening to the surf rise and fall. Waves rolled in, rushing up the beach to bubble over her feet. She allowed her toes to be sucked into wet sand as they retreated.

Her latest read, *The Fatal Impact*, lay unopened in her bag. She didn't want to read it after all. Not here. Not in this place. She didn't want to imagine the lives of which it spoke. Those who had been here and had loved this place, long before her. She lifted her head, smiling at the happy squeals of the children on the beach, as they ran in mock terror from the waves.

Fifty-nine

In the days when Mick had swamped St Cuthbert's with newspapers, Sarah's interest in current events had been ignited. It now became an obsession as she kept watch for news of the troops in Vietnam. At Margaret Rose, broadcasts were all but banned because Vera couldn't bear to hear anything about the war.

As soon as Sarah returned to Ballarat, she resumed her vigils. Common sense told her that if Harry was found, the family would be informed. Still, she clung to a feeble hope that the face on the screen would one day announce lost diggers discovered or prisoners freed in allied action.

In the nurses' lounge one evening, she was about to switch off the television when a chat show host announced his next guest and mentioned 'blackbird' labour. The term conjured memories of a long-ago train journey and a disturbing conversation. Sarah moved across the room and turned up the volume. An attractive, well-spoken woman of a youngish middle age was being interviewed. From her complexion and features, Sarah imagined her to be Aboriginal but, no, she said when the compère put the question, her family was from Vanuatu in the South Sea Islands. She needed little prompting to tell a captivating story about her father's experience as a slave labourer in Queensland.

Sarah heard someone enter the lounge behind her but she didn't turn her head. 'Isn't this terrible?' she murmured over her shoulder.

There was no answer. She turned round.

Lily was standing in the doorway leaning against the jamb. She had just come off duty and was holding her veil in her hands, staring at the screen. Sarah looked from Lily back to the television, seeing the woman on the screen with new eyes, Lily's eyes. This must be the first time, she thought, that Lily had seen a black woman so strong, so impressive, and commanding so much respect.

Lily had graduated the year before Sarah and she presented an impressive picture herself these days. Glossy black curls framed blue eyes and glamorous, long lashes. The always spotless white of her graduate's uniform and veil set off the golden brown of her complexion. She was tall and slender and carried herself with aloof, straight-backed deportment on or off the wards.

She glanced at Sarah now, a mocking little smile about her mouth. 'Taking people from their homes and using them as slave labour? Terrible, really terrible.'

Sarah winced as Lily left the room.

The television blared on. The compère introduced another guest and another topic. A student from the University of Sydney was discussing a coming referendum, a referendum to change discrimination against Aborigines, he said. There was to be a rally in Sydney at which, the host announced, the previous speaker, Mrs Faith Bandler, would be present.

Faith Bandler. Sarah sat up, repeating the name of the woman who had had such an impact on her and also, she suspected, on Lily. There followed a promotion for another rally to be held in Melbourne. Sarah pulled a notebook from her pocket and jotted down details of the event. She left the nurses' lounge with a scary idea in her head.

Sixty

Tin trays rattled along steel counters. Crockery and cutlery rotated through dishwashers and clattered back into circulation. Young women laughed and chattered as they queued to be served. The noise in the hospital cafeteria was deafening each time a shift ended.

Sarah had settled at a table with some friends when Lily walked by carrying her tray.

A voice trilled above the café din. 'Look, ladies, a lovely brown tan all year round. That must be such an asset.' A graduate nurse in ward sister's veil was surrounded by sniggering friends, who seemed to think she had said the funniest thing in the world.

Around the dining room, a few others were shaking their heads in disgust. Most were pretending that they hadn't heard. Sarah was sure she had seen the speaker before. Yes, it was the girl from Mullanurra. Claudia? No, Cynthia! Cynthia Harris.

Lily strode the length of the cafeteria with her head held high. She passed through glass doors and onto an al fresco balcony, seating herself at an outdoor table. Sarah excused herself to her friends, picked up her tray and followed. As the balcony doors closed behind her, the noise of the cafeteria was muted.

Lily laughed at the distress on Sarah's face. 'Oh, don't worry about that lot. I've been called worse, believe me, Sister Anthony.'

Sarah winced. While Lily refused to be called Sister like other graduates, it wasn't the first time she had mocked Sarah by resurrecting her convent name.

Sarah pretended not to notice. 'Yes, I remember how Mother Sebastian used to –'

'Mother Sebastian?' Lily snorted. 'Mother Sebastian was only the start of it and far from the worst.'

'Sergeant Buchanan?'

'Him and others. Anyway, all that's a long time ago.'

Sarah took the hint and let the subject drop. She moved closer to Lily's table and stood without lowering her tray. 'May I?'

Lily returned her attention to her plate. She shrugged.

Relieved, Sarah slipped onto the opposite chair. 'It's nicer out here, fresh air and a lot quieter.'

Lily sipped her coffee without responding.

Sarah rushed on like someone who had decided to jump into a pool of ice-cold water. 'Lily, that speaker we were watching the other night, Faith Bandler?'

Lily's eyes flicked briefly to Sarah's face. They had seen Mrs Bandler on television several times during the week. Whenever the dynamic little activist was on the screen, Lily had seemed captivated.

'Last night she asked everyone to support the referendum rallies. There's to be one – a rally, I mean – in Melbourne.'

Lily said nothing.

Sarah plunged on. 'I thought I would go and, um, I was wondering if you would like to come with me.'

Lily's head came up with a jerk and Sarah shrank from the scorn in her eyes. 'Well, well, Sister Anthony, so that's how you're going to comfort your conscience. Doing good deeds for the poor blackfellas, eh? Getting us all counted in the census. And you want me along, why? So that you can show off your token blackfella?'

Sarah gasped. This was like walking on glass. The contempt in Lily's eyes, her mocking smile, threatened Sarah's resolve. She wanted to jump up and run. She wanted to slam the door behind her. Cheeks burning, she forced herself to look Lily in the face.

'You accused me of standing by and letting bad things happen, not doing anything, and you were right. I did that. But I'm trying to do something now, so I'm a do-gooder? Do you want me to support this fight or do you want me to go on doing nothing? I don't want "a token blackfella". I want someone to teach me how to avoid giving offence every time I open my mouth!' Sarah threw up her hands and dropped them again.

Lily was pressing her lips together like someone trying not to laugh. A grin relaxed her face. 'All right, Sister Anthony, let's go to Melbourne.' She laughed as Sarah glared a silent 'I do wish you'd stop calling me that' across the table.

Sixty-one

Sarah and Lily jumped aboard the early train to Melbourne with time to spare. They found an empty compartment and grabbed the coveted window seats.

Ever since Sarah's outburst in the hospital cafeteria, Lily's attitude towards her had shown signs of a cautious thaw but Sarah still never knew quite what to expect.

As the train jolted into movement, Lily seemed to realise for the first time that she was about to be alone with Sarah for a long time. 'I should have asked Katie to come with us.'

'Katie Steiner? She's your friend, isn't she?' When Sarah started nursing, Katie had been a senior in the same year as Lily.

'She's more than that. She's my sister.'

'Oh yes, of course she is. Twins, I suppose,' Sarah laughed.

'Well, adopted sister, of course,' Lily grinned.

'Was that the family Mother Sebastian placed you with?'

Lily snorted. 'Not likely, that old witch!' Her mouth twisted. 'She gave me to Sid and Harriet Muller. Harriet was pregnant and Rachel Steiner, that's Katie's mum, she was the district nurse. She started taking me out on my afternoons off. Huh! I didn't have an afternoon off until Rachel asked me out. Harriet didn't dare tell her that she had me working my bum off seven days a week. So from then on, I spent Sunday afternoons with Rachel and Katie. Katie was great fun,' Lily laughed. 'She played rock 'n' roll records and one day she asked me if I liked Elvis.'

It was Sarah's turn to grin. 'And you said?'

'"Who's Elvis?" Katie had hysterics.'

'I'll bet.'

'They had such a lovely house. Do you know the big house in Oak Street? It used to be the Cobbs Crossing hospital years ago.'

'Oh, I know the place. Is that Katie's home? Lily, it's lovely.'

'Yes, I know. It made going back to Sid and Harriet every Sunday so much harder.' Her brow furrowed into a forbidding frown and for a moment Sarah thought that the shutters would come down again but Lily went on, staring into space. 'I was a real slave in that place, no kidding. I had to light fires before they were up, cook meals, clean the house, do the laundry, feed the cats – they were everywhere – and even weed their garden.'

'Oh, Lily. Did they pay you?'

'Not a penny. Harriet was a slave driver but her husband was worse,' Lily looked away. 'Much worse.' She was quiet for a moment then she spoke again, gazing at the passing countryside and talking in a faraway voice, as if she was remembering a bad dream. 'My room didn't have a proper door. He used to come in whenever he liked. He used to call me "sweetheart". I hated it. Then he started leaving chocolates on my bed. That frightened me. I didn't understand why but I just knew it was wrong, you know?'

Sarah nodded. 'You were so young, Lily. How scary that must have been.'

In a movement so abrupt that it startled even Sarah's watchfulness, Lily straightened her back and lifted her head. 'What time will we be in Melbourne?'

Sixty-two

The rally had attracted a record crowd. As the marchers reached Parliament House, they spread left and right, milling against the wall of police that guarded the steps. Reporters hovered, notebooks in hand. A photographer stepped in front of the crowd and almost dropped his camera.

Through the lens, Mick spotted a face that was familiar despite the mass of auburn hair that now surrounded it. He forced his way through the crowd that was choking the road. 'Sister, Sister Anthony!'

Sarah recognised the voice. She and Lily both spun around. Lily thought that there was something familiar about the man pushing towards them.

Mick stopped in the middle of the road staring at Sarah, his camera forgotten. 'I'm sorry. I guess that's not your name any more but I didn't know what to call you.'

Sarah, pleased but confused by his sudden appearance, was for a moment speechless. Her hesitation disappointed him.

'I reckon you don't remember me.'

She remembered very well. She remembered the cheeky eyes and the irreverent grin and the way he towered over her. She offered him her hand as if they had just been introduced. 'It's Sarah. My name's Sarah Norton. How do you do, Mr O'Mara?'

As she said his name, Mick smiled. She did remember.

Lily looked from one to the other with an amused expression and Sarah realised that Mick had not released her hand. She pulled away, pushing a stray strand of hair back from her face and gave an awkward little laugh. 'Under the circumstances, Mr O'Mara, I'm amazed that you recognised me.'

Mick grinned, eyeing her hair. 'It's different,' he admitted. Her skirt, he noted, could hardly be called a mini. It almost covered her knees. He supposed current fashions would be difficult for her. The sixties must be the hardest decade ever for a girl who had just left the convent. On the other hand, the straight skirt of her companion's sleeveless shift, he noticed approvingly, was several inches above her knees.

'Lily, this is Mr Michael O'Mara,' Sarah introduced them. 'Mr O'Mara, this is Lily Matthews.'

Mick surprised her. 'Oh yes, Lily. I remember.'

'I don't think we've ever met, Mr O'Mara.'

'I hesitate to say so to a lady, Miss Matthews, but you're mistaken. I photographed you for the *Chronicle* when you topped your intermediate class at Cobbs Crossing High.'

Sarah raised her eyebrows at Lily. High school? Top of the class?

Lily was flattered. She rewarded Mick with a smile. 'I'll be going back to the Crossing soon. The hospital has offered me a place. My foster mother has a friend there, a Doctor Lawrence? I think he might have had something to do with it.'

It was the first time Lily had mentioned her plans to work in Cobbs Crossing. It said a lot for her attachment to her adopted family, Sarah thought, that she would want to go back.

'Yes, I know Lawrence well. He's a good bloke. In that case, perhaps you'd allow me to interview you again.' Mick turned on the charm, giving Lily a dazzling smile. 'I see a headline: "Local Girl's Triumphant Return".'

Lily laughed. Sarah looked from one to the other, envying the easy way Lily coped with his teasing. That had never been possible for her.

'And how do you two know each other?' Lily asked.

'We met at St Cuthbert's when Mr O'Mara was following the story of a certain young lady who had run away from the orphanage.' Sarah tilted her head to one side, grinning at Lily.

'Gosh yes, that's right,' Mick remembered. 'Lily Matthews! You're the runaway kid.'

Lily grinned at the pair of them. 'Good heavens,' she laughed, 'that's a long time ago, Mr O'Mara.'

Mick picked up the camera that hung about his neck. 'How about some photos? Then why don't we find somewhere to have a coffee, and see if I can't get you two ladies to stop calling me Mister O'Mara.' He positioned Sarah and Lily with Parliament House as a backdrop and chatted to distract them, while his camera clicked away. 'What did you make of the speakers?'

'They were great but,' Sarah shook her head, 'I felt so ignorant.' She was answering Mick but she was looking at Lily.

'And wanting to do something about it?'

She gave him a grateful smile. 'Yes, of course, that's why we're here. We would have loved to hear Faith Bandler speak, but she's campaigning in Sydney.'

'Not today, she isn't. She's about to address students at an open rally at Melbourne Uni, in about,' Mick looked at his watch, 'twenty minutes.'

'Faith Bandler! Here in Melbourne? Is it far? Can we walk?'

'Well, we could.' He grinned at the girls' high-heeled shoes. 'Probably not in twenty minutes, but if you would allow me to be your escort, ladies, my carriage awaits. We can drive there in ten.'

At the university, they had no trouble finding the theatre that was to welcome the famous activist. There were handmade signs stuck up everywhere. Mick led Sarah and Lily at a speedy trot from the car park. The venue was filling fast. He spotted three seats halfway down the auditorium and ushered his charges into them.

The warm-up speakers were students who had accompanied another civil rights campaigner, Charlie Perkins, on his famous freedom rides across New South Wales two years before. Finally, the moment everyone was waiting for arrived.

Faith Bandler was introduced by the president of ABSCHOL, a Melbourne University group that provided scholarships to Aborigines. 'Mrs Bandler,' he announced, 'is the director of the Vote Yes for Aboriginal Rights Committee, the movement which has resulted in this referendum. She has come all the way from Sydney to speak to us today. Please make her welcome.'

The tiny figure left alone in the centre of the stage waited in silence for the applause to subside. As the auditorium hushed, her unique voice rang out, remarkable for clarity and perfect diction.

'I have been thrown out of a Cairns hotel because of my colour,' she began. 'In Sydney, Aborigines are still being refused service in hotels.'

Lily glanced sideways at Sarah, who was leaning forward, brow furrowed in concentration.

Mrs Bandler went on. 'It doesn't matter whether we are educated or not. It is done for no other reason than the colour of our skin. It appears business people are afraid of losing other customers if they serve Aborigines. We are not asking to be "accepted" into white society. We are not asking for "tolerance". What we want is complete social and political equality.'

Her audience responded with deafening applause and again she waited for silence before continuing.

'The May referendum on Aboriginal rights is needed because Aborigines are not included in the census and live under six different sets of laws in Australian states. A Yes vote will end the buck passing of aboriginal problems from the state governments to the federal government and from state to state. As things stand today, Aborigines live in a vicious circle. An Aborigine can't get a house because he can't get a job. He can't get a job because he can't get an education, and how can he be expected to get an education and a job if he hasn't got a house to live in?'

Her listeners sprang to their feet, applause echoing around the auditorium.

As Mick drove Sarah and Lily back to the Spencer Street station, they passed another rally, noisier and more visible than the one they had just attended. Placards and chants vilified the war in Vietnam.

'Protesters,' Sarah sniffed.

'They've got a point of course.' It was a casual comment. Mick's attention was on the traffic.

Sarah spun away from the window, her forehead creased in a frown. 'What do you mean?'

'Well, I don't blame the troops. I think the protesters have got it wrong there. The troops are only doing what they've been told to do, their "duty", if you like. I blame the government and the church. It seems killing communists doesn't break the fifth commandment.'

'So you think our troops shouldn't be there, in Vietnam?'

Again, Mick's preoccupation behind the wheel prevented him picking up on the aggravation in Sarah's voice or the warning in her eyes. In the back seat, Lily held her breath.

Mick answered with his eyes on the road. 'I'm just not sure it's any of our business. We seem to be wasting a lot of young lives and I'm not sure it'll make any difference in the end.'

Sarah retreated into a chilly silence.

When they reached Spencer Street, Mick hopped out of the car. 'I'll see you to the train, ladies.'

'We're fine thank you, Mr O'Mara. Thank you for the lift.' Sarah's high heels click clacked away, leaving a stupefied Mick staring at her disappearing back.

He groaned when Lily whispered, 'Harry, her brother, is missing in action.'

Sixty-three

Back in the nurses' lounge at last, the exhausted travellers kicked off their shoes. Lily made a pile of hot buttered crumpets while Sarah boiled the kettle and found clean cups for coffee. As they relaxed with their supper, Lily caught Sarah watching her.

'What's on your mind, Sister Anthony?'

Sarah rolled her eyes but she smiled as she accepted a crumpet. 'Lily, it was nice to hear you call me your friend when we were talking to Mick today, a bit of a surprise, but nice.'

'Yeah, well, we all get carried away now and then, I guess,' Lily grinned.

Sarah sipped her coffee. 'You know, Sister Matthew always said that the only thing stopping Aboriginal kids learning like anyone else, was lack of opportunity.'

'Sister Matthew, yeah, she was good to us. She believed in us.'

'And you're proof that she was right.'

Lily snorted. 'I had to get darn near killed to do it, though.'

'I remember how badly injured you were when Sergeant Buchanan brought you back to the orphanage.' Sarah paused. 'I suppose he was the one?'

'Who tried to rape me?' Lily shook her head. 'No. It wasn't him. It was that disgusting old Sid Muller.' She pulled a face and stared into her coffee cup. 'One day, he grabbed me. God, Sarah, I was so bloody scared.' She shook her head, struggling with the memory. 'He got on top of me, hit me so many times I didn't think he'd ever stop.' She closed her eyes, feeling the explosions in her head all over again. 'There was a hoe on the ground. I managed to get hold of it. I hit him and he keeled over.'

'Good for you, Lily.'

'Yes, good for me but when I saw him lying there with his face all covered in blood, I was scared in a different way. I just ran. Harriet told Sergeant Buchanan about Rachel taking me out, so he turned up at the Steiner's house looking for me. As soon as he left their place, Rachel and Katie drove up and down the highway. They found me before he did, thank goodness. I ended up in hospital instead of the lock-up, with Doctor Lawrence looking after me and Rachel sweet talking Buchanan into backing off.'

'Backing off? So Sid Muller –'

'Wasn't dead after all. Buchanan was all for packing me back to Mother Sebastian, but Doctor Lawrence and Rachel insisted that I needed time to recover. So I went to live with Rachel and Katie and I never left until I came here.' Lily put down her cup. 'Sarah, Mick didn't know about Harry.'

Sarah sighed. 'Yeah, I know. I overreacted. But just think, Lily. If he's right, if this war is not any of Australia's business, then Harry should still be home. He should be safe. He should still be alive.' It was the first time that Sarah had allowed herself to accept that Harry might not be alive. A sob escaped her. She covered her face with her hands and the tears she had not allowed herself to cry, flowed.

Lily tiptoed away, resting her hand on Sarah's shoulders for a brief moment as she left.

Sixty-four

'Sarah, I'm sorry. I didn't know about your brother, about Harry.' Mick half expected her to slam the phone down.

'Of course you didn't. I was angry because I didn't want you to be right.'

*

Missing in action became missing, believed killed. Father Duffy offered a memorial Mass in place of a funeral service for the family that did not have a body to bury. RSL clubs swelled the ranks of mourners but their numbers could not console the family for the absence of a coffin. Ben was home on compassionate leave. Sarah caught Jack casting envious glances at his big brother's uniform. Vera's tears fell unchecked and Julia sobbed into her handkerchief.

Sarah sat dry-eyed and numb between her mother and sister, cradling the watch her twin had given her. 'Where are you, Harry? Are you dead or alive? Are you lost? Wounded? Are you a prisoner?'

She had read his last letter so many times she knew the words by heart: 'I don't go to Mass any more, Sare. I know I'll go to hell when I die.'

'No, Harry. I don't think you'll go to hell. I don't think there is a hell or a heaven. Mick was right. We just believe what we have been taught.'

When the Mass ended, Sarah's thoughts were far away. She didn't realise that she was the last one sitting in the church until Father Duffy appeared at the end of the empty pew.

'It's sad that Harry stopped practising his religion, Sarah, but we can always hope he made a good confession before he died, and we can pray for his soul.'

Sarah frowned. She picked up her bag and gloves. 'No, Father. What's sad is that if Harry is dead, he died so young and so far from home.' She pulled on her gloves. 'It's sad that he believed he was a condemned soul, headed for hell. I will never forgive the church for supporting this war.' She stood up and the priest stepped aside as she moved into the aisle. 'I won't be praying for anyone, Father. Prayer just stops us from getting things done.' Sarah swept out of the church without acknowledging the altar.

*

A gentle breeze and bright full moon played through the branches of the mountain ash that soared outside Sarah's upstairs window. They danced strange shapes around her room. As she began to doze, she could hear twigs scratching against the glass. The great tree began to sway as the breeze built into a wild wind, tossing its branches against the house with the force of a gale.

Sarah sat up in bed as the giant pulled up its roots and stepped away from the house. She ran to the window, throwing it open and leaning out into the storm. Rain stung her face. All around her, trees were picking up their roots with a squelch like boots pulling out of sucking mud. They sloshed towards a distant road.

First, in single file they went, then in pairs, then groups of three or four, then dozens and hundreds and thousands, as far as she could see. As they reached the road, they formed columns and trooped down the highway where they morphed into young men in uniform, who smiled and waved to her as they passed under her window. Harry went with them.

They marched past acres of felled timber and paraded across a rough, logged landscape. Here they began to stumble and one by one, to fall. Their slouched hats were gone, their uniforms shredded, their faces covered in blood and mud, the landscape a body-strewn battlefield.

Sarah woke drenched in perspiration.

The following day, a troubled Father Duffy arrived in the reception lounge at Margaret Rose. After paying his respects to Vera and Henry, he asked to speak with Sarah. She wasn't surprised by his visit and fancied she knew what was coming. She led the priest to cushioned chairs on an elevated deck at the back of the guest house. It overlooked her father's well-tended garden and the rainforest beyond it. The trees, she observed with a tired little smile, where all still standing.

The early morning sun was mild and the air was still.

Settling himself into one of the cane armchairs, Father Duffy raised watery eyes to the soaring giants of the rainforest. 'Such a lovely place we live in, Sarah. One can feel the Presence of God.'

A kookaburra filled the garden with raucous laughter. Sarah smothered a smile.

Father Duffy coughed. 'Ah, see? He agrees with me.'

The bird chortled again, louder than before and several others joined him in a deafening, full-throated chorus.

The priest abandoned his efforts to enlist the kookaburras as allies and turned to the purpose of his visit. 'God tests us, Sarah. We mortals don't know why He allows these things to happen, but He has His purpose.'

Sarah didn't interrupt. She sat listening in silence, while the platitudes washed over her like a radio no one was listening to. When he stopped and seemed to be waiting for an answer, Sarah shook her head. 'Father, I'm not turning my back on God in a huff because he allowed a tragedy to happen in my life. It's just that, well, I've spent so long smothering my doubts and now they won't stay smothered.' She lifted her chin. 'I don't feel guilty about leaving the church, Father. Sad maybe, disappointed certainly, but,' she leant back gazing at the sky, 'it will sound strange at a time like this, but in a way I feel more peaceful than I can remember.'

Father Duffy rubbed wrinkled hands together then looked at them palms up, as if waiting for them to be filled. 'You will find it isn't easy to live without faith, my child.'

Sarah sighed and sat up straight again, determined to stand her ground. 'I'm not leaving the church because I think it will be easy, Father. In fact, I expect it will be very hard and possibly,' she smiled at the irony, 'possibly the most challenging thing I've ever done. It's scary to accept that we are alone. It's scary to see evil in the world and not take refuge in the belief that a loving God will one day put things right. What could ever comfort us like faith? I will miss having faith, but missing it won't make me able to believe.'

'You really have lost your faith, haven't you, Sarah?' There was genuine grief in the old man's voice.

She shook her head. 'I can't think of it as losing faith, Father. It seems more like waking from a fantasy, recognising that I never had faith, only conditioning.'

They sat side by side, gazing at the forest.

The priest broke the silence again. 'What did you mean, Sarah, when you said that prayer stops us getting things done?'

She gave a grim little smile. 'It lets us off the hook, doesn't it, Father? It becomes an excuse for doing nothing. We substitute prayer for responsible action. Then we watch evil triumph and wonder why.'

'What things do you want to get done, Sarah?'

'I want to find Pearl's son. Pearl is an Aboriginal woman. Her son, Jamarra, was taken from her. I promised her that I'd find him.'

'How are you going to do that?'

'I don't know. But I won't just pray and wait for it to happen, Father. Not any more.'

He took her hand. 'Well, I still believe in prayer, Sarah. I'm going to pray for you every day. Goodbye and God bless.'

Sarah watched the priest depart with sad eyes. She would miss so much of her former life.

Sixty-five

Mick answered his phone to an indignant Sarah.

'Mick, Mother Sebastian is still in charge at St Cuthbert's. I've just found out and I can't believe it. I was sure I had convinced Mother Anna to replace her. No wonder my letters go unanswered. I don't particularly want to go back to St Magdalene's or St Cuthbert's but if I'm ever going to find Jamarra, I might have to. In the meantime,'

'Yes?'

'The rally on Friday, maybe we could help it along.' Fuelled by what she had newly learned about Mother Sebastian, Sarah's frustration spilled over. She told Mick all she knew about the taking of the children and the lies they and their parents were told.

Mick listened with the phone hunched into his shoulder, taking rapid notes in his own peculiar shorthand and asking a question here and there. 'Phew! This is good stuff, Sarah.'

'Do you think the Melbourne papers –?'

'Are you kidding? An insider story? They'll eat it up.'

There was silence on her end of the line.

He heard the hesitation. 'You are okay with this, Sarah?'

She fiddled with the phone's cord. 'Yes. People should know. It's just that,'

'You're worried about how your family might react?'

'No. Not any more. They won't like it of course but that's not what I'm concerned about.'

'What then?'

'This public opinion we're hoping to stir up. Mick, it could turn into a witch hunt, sweep up the good with the bad, you know? I'm thinking of people like Sister Matthew and young Father Conway. They really care about the kids and they do so much good. When these stories come out, I'm afraid all priests and nuns will be seen as ogres.'

'Well, you're right of course. Some people will react like that. Still,'

'Still, it must be told. But promise me one thing, Mick.'

'Anything.' He liked that she used his first name now.

'Just say that I worked in one of these orphanages but don't tell the world that I used to be a nun. I'm sick of answering dumb questions.'

Mick laughed.

'I'm serious, Mick.'

'OK. I understand. I promise. No nun story.'

Sarah glared a pain of death threat at the phone as she replaced the handset into its cradle but when Mick's article was published, she was satisfied. It ended with a promotion for the coming rally: 'Miss Norton will be one of the speakers at a referendum rally to be held at Trades Hall on Friday evening.'

The article drew a great crowd. As Sarah walked out in front of a packed hall on Friday night, her heart was racing. How on earth did Faith Bandler do it all the time? Remembering the example of the dignified white-gloved activist, Sarah waited until the crowd quietened. She took a deep breath. 'I suppose many of you saw my story in the Melbourne *Herald* a few days ago.'

A subdued applause rose and fell.

'I am here to tell you in person that every word of that report is true and that I am a witness to it.'

A more enthusiastic applause echoed around her.

'We have a great deal to put right in this country and we can start with this referendum. My friends, a No vote will tell the world that Australia does not want to give Aborigines a fair go.'

Sarah took another breath and spoke close to the microphone, keeping her voice low but steady. 'I grew up hearing my parents' generation talking about the Holocaust. They didn't just blame Hitler. They asked how such things could happen in a civilised country, without the support of the people.' She paused for the implication of her words to sink in.

The hall was hushed, all eyes on the slender figure on the stage.

'Make no mistake, that's what the world and history will say about us if we do not show now that we are determined to create a better future and see justice done.' Sarah's arm shot up above her head as she shouted into the microphone. 'Vote Yes for a fair go!'

Cheers from the crowd.

Sarah shouted again. 'Vote Yes for justice!'

More cheers.

'Vote Yes for Aborigines!'

The packed hall was on its feet, clapping and cheering.

Sarah continued to garner support for the Yes campaign, urging gatherings to consider their vote as an important step towards righting many wrongs. She spoke at rallies in Melbourne and travelled to centres throughout country Victoria. She stepped up to the microphone, often with Lily by her side, to tell of children taken from their parents and the conditions in which they lived. Their eyewitness accounts shocked listeners.

Sarah's auburn hair became a beacon people recognised whenever she stood on a platform. She lobbied politicians and wrote articles for the papers.

One day, Mick rang to congratulate her on her latest essay. 'Good job, Sarah, a well-written piece.'

She glowed with pleasure. 'Oh, Mick, I just want to make everything better straight away, but of course I can't.'

On the other end of the phone, Mick grinned. 'It's smart to know that. Accepting limitations has probably been the greatest frustration of all the world's activists.'

Sarah stared at the phone. She had not thought of herself as an activist.

Sixty-six

The office of the *Chronicle* was a humble establishment on Memorial Square, reflecting the small town circulation of the Crossing's only newspaper. A glass porch led into a cramped but well-lit room where Mick, if he was in, could be found behind a desk of organised chaos. The back door was open in all sorts of weather, allowing Bronko to come and go as he pleased. This evening he was curled up in one of the office's two lounge chairs, which he regarded as his own.

Mick was working late as he often did, his office light casting an eerie beacon into the empty square. He swayed on the back legs of his chair, his feet on top of his desk. He yawned and sighed as he sifted through photos that chronicled the lives of ordinary people in an ordinary town. He dumped rejects into a bin at his side and narrowly missed his coffee cup as he tossed anything useful onto a pile on his desk.

There were photos of Lily and Sarah at the Melbourne rally, pictures of the latest trophy awarded at Cobbs Crossing High, several shots of Cynthia Harris in a designer gown, receiving guests with her parents at yet another social function at Mullanurra, and the town's football heroes triumphant at Victory Park. A coloured photo of Lily landed beside one of Cynthia. The two faces looked up at Mick, startling him into a sitting position. He grabbed both photos, holding them side by side under his desk lamp. How had he not seen it before?

Cynthia's hair was blonde, long and straight. Lily's was a mass of short, black curls. But apart from their hair and a shade of difference in complexion, their faces were identical: the same arresting sapphire eyes, the same shape of face and features, the same determined mouth and proud expression.

He whistled and leapt to his feet. 'Gotcha,' he announced.

Bronko raised a sleepy head, looked around the empty room and snuggled down again.

A few days later, Mick unlocked his office, picking up the mail and Melbourne papers that had been delivered via a slot in the door. He tossed them onto his desk and made for his corner kitchenette in search of coffee.

Bronko had just taken possession of his chair when he sat up, ears erect and eyes alert, even before the phone rang.

Mick hurried back to his desk and picked up the receiver. 'O'Mara.'

'How could you! How could you do that?'

'Sarah?'

'I know journalists will sell their souls for a story but isn't anything sacred?'

'Sarah, what on earth are you talking about?'

'I'm talking about the front page of this morning's *Sun*.'

Mick pulled the phone along by its cord, looking for the offending paper among the ones he had dropped unread on his desk.

Under the headline 'RALLY STOPS SPRING STREET', a side leader proclaimed, 'Ex-Nun Supports Yes Vote'. There was a head and shoulders photo of Sarah above the article. She and Lily had been in the capital for yet another referendum rally the day before. Mick had gone down to cover it and caught up with them.

'I assume you're referring to the ex-nun story, and I gather that I'm guilty without a trial, is that it?' Mick thumped the paper down in front of him as he resumed his seat. 'I don't suppose you'd consider the possibility that you've jumped to the wrong conclusion, Sarah?'

There was silence on the phone. He waited without offering any further explanation.

'You're saying that you didn't give this story to the paper?'

'Yes, that's what I'm saying. I gave you my word, remember?' He sounded hurt. 'Do you believe me?'

'But…but you were the only one at the rally who knows that I was a nun and I know how long you've wanted to write a story about –'

'In the first place, if you think about it, I was not the only one at that rally who knows you were a nun. In the second, if I was going to expose you, do you imagine I'd give someone else the story to write? As you say, I'm a journalist. Look at the name under the article, Sarah. It sure as hell isn't Mick O'Mara, is it? And Sarah, I would never publish your story without your permission.' He dropped the phone back on the receiver.

Sarah was left biting her lip and listening to the disconnected buzz on her end of the line. She stared at the phone. She kept hearing the hurt in his voice and her fingers itched to dial again. She wanted to call him back and say, 'I believe you, Mick. Of course I believe you. I'm sorry.' She put the phone down.

Faced with Mick's denial, it didn't take Sarah long to work out the most likely other source of the story. Lily admitted that she had given information to another journalist. It had happened innocently enough. The reporter had been full of questions and Lily had supposed that Sarah's past vocation would lend weight to their support of the Yes vote.

'I'm sorry, Sarah, I didn't think you'd mind, or more likely I just didn't think at all. I'm really sorry.'

'Well, there's no harm done, I guess, except that I've already accused Mick of doing it.'

'Oh dear,' Lily grinned.

'Yes, oh dear.'

'Would you like me to talk to him…to explain? I'm starting at the hospital up there next week.'

'Cobbs Crossing?' Sarah had forgotten about Lily's plans to return to her home town.

'Yes, you remember Cobbs Crossing? The small town everyone wants to get out of,' Lily laughed. She was quickly serious again. 'Rachel Steiner is the closest thing I have to family, she and Katie. When she told me about the vacancy back home, I got the feeling she was missing having her girls around. She knows the Crossing won't see much of Katie any more. She's off in Melbourne now, at the Royal Children's and she just loves kids.' There was a wistful expression in Lily's eyes. 'I thought about going with her but I owe Rachel. If it wasn't for her, I wouldn't even be a nurse.'

'And Cobbs Crossing will be lucky to have you, Lily.' Sarah gave an enormous sigh. 'Don't worry about talking to Mick.' She rolled her eyes. 'I guess it's something I should do myself.'

'Good luck with that.' Lily laughed again as Sarah pulled a face at her.

*

It took all Sarah's courage to pick up the phone again. She doubted that Mick would still be angry. Even so, speaking to him again wasn't going to be easy. When he answered his phone, he had to say his name twice before she could speak.

'Mick, it's Sarah. I've been speaking to Lily.'

'Oh yes, Lily. How is Lily, Sarah?'

She screwed up her nose and covered the mouthpiece to smother a sigh. At least he wasn't still miffed, but he wasn't about to let her off lightly. She was glad she was out of range of the cheeky grin and the teasing eyes that she knew would be laughing at her.

'I owe you an apology, Mr O'Mara.' A chuckle greeted her nervous formality. She fumed at herself. 'I mean, Mick. Lily has explained everything. I'm sorry I said what I did about you chasing headlines. I should have trusted you.'

'Yeah, you should. I'm not that short on headlines, Sarah.'

'I know. I'm sorry, Mick.'

There was a moment of awkward silence then he remembered his discovery. 'Sarah, I reckon Lachlan Harris has two daughters.'

She breathed a sigh of relief as his voice dissolved the tension between them. 'Two daughters?'

'You've never noticed? Well, I didn't myself until the other night.'

'Noticed what?'

'That Lily and Cynthia Harris are almost certainly sisters – well, half-sisters anyway.'

Sarah gasped. 'Well, we know they don't have the same mother, so that means –'

'That they have the same father, yes exactly. I'll bet a penny to a quid, if we put it to Pearl, she won't deny that Lachlan Harris is the father of Lily.'

'If you're right, this could be just what we need.'

'For what?'

'Well, no matter how much she denies it, of course Mother Sebastian knows where Jamarra is. What we've needed all along has been a way to make her tell us. I bet she'll be so afraid of losing all that lovely Mullanurra money and another scandal attaching to St Cuthbert's that she'll tell us anything we want to know.'

He could hear the excitement in her voice. 'You're planning to blackmail a nun?' Mick sounded impressed.

Sixty-seven

Majik popped into Mick's office almost daily. He would sift through messages left for his delivery business with a comical expression as he struggled to decipher Mick's longhand scrawl. He always left with whatever newspapers Mick could spare for the river camp. The papers were often yesterday's news but they would be passed through the fringe-dwelling community, be read, reread and finally be used as fire starters or insulation.

Several days after the article for which Sarah had blamed Mick, Old George knocked on Aunty Mary's door. He handed Pearl a dog-eared copy of the *Sun*. Pearl took the paper to the kitchen, intending to leave it for Aunty Mary to read first. As she unfolded it and smoothed it out on the table, she stared at a face looking at her from the page. Snatching the paper up again, she hurried to the open door and scrutinised the photo in better light. She used her fingers to frame the face, covering the hair with her hands. 'Sister Anthony!' Aunty Mary's prior claim to the paper forgotten, Pearl pored over the 'Ex-Nun Supports Yes Vote' story. It promised more on page sixteen. Pearl began turning pages.

There was another photo of Sarah in a crowd scene with a younger woman standing beside her. Pearl thought she recognised the other woman. It had been some time but, yes, she was sure the woman in the photo with Sister Anthony was the girl who years ago had run away from the orphanage. Pearl remembered how she and Aunty Mary had found the girl wandering by the river and taken her in. She hadn't been with them a day before those coppers arrived and dragged the poor kid back to that place.

Pearl gazed at the photo and for a moment she stopped breathing.

A cry escaped her then she was sobbing and between sobs, choking out a name, 'Tallara!' The young woman in the photo wore a sleeveless shift, and on her bare shoulder was a mark Pearl would never forget. Tears blinded her, threatening the precious photo. She wiped her eyes and went looking for the kitchen scissors.

When Aunty Mary reached page sixteen, she raised her eyebrows at a gaping hole.

Sixty-eight

Despite all the affection lavished on him, Patch was a pup of questionable loyalty. He would seek out any of the children who might be hiding after a thrashing from Brother Leonard, lick tears from their faces and flop down beside them, placing his head in their lap. He would coax the boys back to activity by bringing them sticks to throw, racing off madly to fetch them again. He lay now at his master's feet, hoping for scraps from the table.

'Always wash your hands after touching the children. You never know what you might catch.'

'Yes, Brother.' The junior serving the evening meal stared as the principal put down his knife to scratch his dog's upturned belly.

Patch was a white fox terrier with a black blotch around one eye, hence his unimaginative name. The bigger boys delighted in telling the little ones that Patch looked like that because he had once been a pirate's dog. He was fed at the kitchen step and slept in a basket at the foot of Brother Leonard's bed. Whenever Brother sat down, Patch jumped into his lap to be patted or rolled on his back to have his tummy scratched. The pampered pup earned his keep catching rats around the out buildings, and fetching newspapers from the lawn to Brother Leonard's office.

As Jamarra frequently fell foul of Brother Leonard, he was often the recipient of Patch's unbiased consolations. He loved the mad little mutt as if Patch were his own. One day as they sat together at the front of the school, a stray ball from the playground flew past them and through the open gates. Patch leapt up giving chase as the ball bounced towards the highway.

Jamarra ran after him calling for him to come back. Barking wildly, Patch ignored him. He followed the ball into the path of a thundering lorry. The driver of the big truck seemed not to notice the crunch of tiny bones as he sped on his way. Jamarra stood on the footpath sobbing, as car after car rolled over the shapeless mess of fur and blood that used to be his friend. Boys crowded around, excited and frightened. When Brother Leonard discovered that Jamarra had been the last one playing with his pet, he decided that the boy had chased the dog to its death and the child's protests fell on deaf ears.

*

In the principal's office there was a low backed armchair well known to the boys of St Bartholomew's. On a hook behind the door hung a cane with which they had an even more intimate acquaintance. Jamarra, trembling before Brother Leonard, had given up trying to explain what had happened, but the manner in which his eyes darted about the room suggested he had not quite resigned himself to his fate. The words he dreaded descended on his ears.

'Bring me the cane!'

His small frame shrank further. He inched towards the door, making the distance last as long as possible. In clinging to the hope of an improbable reprieve, he succeeded only in prolonging his agony. Whereas most things at St Bartholomew's were out of his reach, the cane hung at a convenient height for small arms. He lifted it from its hook and turned back, the cane clutched before him in both hands like an acolyte bearing a cross. Brother Leonard waited with his finger pointing to the chair. Jamarra now resigned himself to the hopelessness of his situation and began to sob.

He bent over the back of the armchair into the seat, in the position he knew was required. His feet dangled above the floor. The cane landed on the little body, picking out shoulders, buttocks, thighs and calves with precision.

Jamarra's sobs turned into screams, punctuated by pitiful pleas. 'I won't do it again, Brother! I promise! I'll never do it again!' That he had not done anything to begin with was irrelevant. Thinking only of placating his tormentor, the child denied his own innocence.

Brother Leonard was impervious to his screams. When at last he tossed the cane on the floor, Jamarra stayed drooped over the chair like a rag doll someone had dropped there.

'Go to your dormitory. Stay on your bed. Do not go to dinner. Go!'

Unable to push his feet back to the ground, Jamarra pulled himself forward, his body protesting every movement. He crawled over the seat to the floor. Leaning on one arm of the chair, he got himself to his feet and stumbled towards the door.

In the empty dormitory, Jamarra collapsed face down on his stretcher bed. He ached for the only friend who might have come, the only creature that had made him feel loved in a long time. But this evening there was no Patch to comfort him. No warm, doggy body to snuggle down beside him. No affectionate doggy tongue to lick the tears from his face. The loss of Patch hurt more than his empty belly or his tortured back and Jamarra's heart-broken sobs wracked his little body again.

Even though he had gone to bed without his evening meal, next morning Jamarra had little appetite for breakfast. He had made several speedy trips to the toilet, not always making it in time. There had been another summons to Brother Leonard's office. Jamarra's first instinct had been flight but even his small understanding allowed this to be futile. Even delay, he knew could be fatal. He approached the principal's door praying for a miracle. He knocked. At the sound of Brother Leonard's voice booming an uninviting command to enter, Jamarra trembled, pressing his legs together.

He moved into the room, spreading his hands in an effort to hide the wet patch at the front of his shorts and keeping his eyes cast down. There were things he didn't want to see in this room. The enormous crucifix with its bleeding Christ terrified him. Even more frightening was the ghoulish statue of the martyred St Bartholomew, holding his own flayed flesh. Small boys had nightmares about that statue. Jamarra preferred to stare at Brother Leonard's desk. He fixed his eyes on a brass paper weight in the shape of a squatting camel.

Brother Leonard spoke with heavy, plodding emphasis. 'My dog was a good dog, a useful dog. He fetched my newspaper every morning and every night.' He regarded Jamarra with a paralysing stare. 'You are not good and you are not useful.'

Jamarra hung his head, trying to be as small as possible.

'You can, however, fetch my newspaper. You will fetch morning and evening papers from wherever the delivery boys throw them and bring them to my door. Do you understand?'

'Yes, Brother.'

'Go.'

*

St Bartholomew's Home for Boys was fronted by a vast stretch of lawn and shrubbery. Jamarra missed several breakfasts searching in bushes and garden beds for the morning paper before he realised that the trick to seeing into which particular spot the delivery boy lobbed his missile was to be there ahead of time.

The evening paper presented less of a problem as it arrived between the end of lessons and the evening meal. On wet days, it was necessary to be extra quick before the paper was spoiled. Twice a day, he delivered the paper as instructed via a brass slot in the door of the principal's office. Every time it fell with a satisfying thump into the wooden letterbox inside the door, Jamarra sighed with relief and knew a moment of triumph.

Sixty-nine

Arthur Lawrence stormed into Mick's office, allowing the door to bang behind him. He startled Mick with an uncharacteristic barrage. 'What on earth do you think you're playing at, man?' Like so many people who came through his door, the doctor was waving a copy of the *Chronicle* at Mick's head. 'Have you any idea what you've done?'

Bronko whimpered at the big man's raised voice and shrugged himself out of his armchair. He trotted through the open back door with his tail between his legs.

Mick could usually guess which article had given offence to any angry reader. In this case, he was mystified. What had he published that had Arthur Lawrence in such a lather?

The doctor spread the paper open on Mick's cluttered desk and slammed his hand down on its open middle pages.

Mick looked at the pages. He frowned. He still couldn't understand what the doctor was upset about. In an effort to help Sarah shake answers out of Mother Sebastian, he had devoted the social pages to two stories. On the left, a half-page photo of Cynthia Harris above a banal coverage of yet another dinner party at Mullanurra. Facing her on the opposite page, an equally large photo of Lily topped the story of her return to the Crossing as a nurse. Both photos printed in black and white made the likeness between the two girls all the more obvious.

'Very clever!' The doctor was leaning across Mick's desk on the knuckles of his large hands, his shoulders hunched and his eyes blazing. He drilled the open pages with his finger.

Mick had never before heard Arthur Lawrence raise his voice, except to challenge the umpire when free kicks were given against the Tigers at Victory Park. Now the doctor's deep voice rumbled at him as if it was coming from a crowd hailer.

'I take it you've known for some time that Lily Matthews is Pearl's Tallara?'

Mick nodded a bewildered assent. He still could not understand the doctor's anger. Lily had been happy to give him an interview and have her photo taken in her nurse's uniform. He had not told her that it would appear opposite her half-sister, the sister she did not know she was related to.

The doctor blustered on. 'Well, I only realised myself after that photo showing the birthmark appeared in the *Sun*.' He scowled at Mick as another thought occurred to him. 'You didn't plant that one too, did you?'

Mick raised both palms in a gesture of denial and shook his head.

The doctor rubbed his brow and looked around for somewhere to sit. He dropped into Bronko's chair. 'That birthmark was hard to miss. When I realised who Lily was, I consulted with Rachel Steiner. She and I recommended Lily to the local hospital. The idea was that she could live with Rachel and maybe also get to know her birth mother.' Doctor Lawrence shook his head. 'Everything was going beautifully and then you had to go and do this! What in God's name did you hope to achieve?'

Mick opened his mouth to speak, but the irate doctor stopped him with one flat palm raised in his face.

'Majik must have taken the papers to the camp early today. Pearl saw this article about Lily being here and headed into town on foot. I can't imagine how disoriented she must have been. Since she was fourteen, she's never worked or lived anywhere but Mullanurra, then finding herself thrown out like that, ending up living with strangers, Jamarra taken from her, and then the shock of finding out that her Tallara was right here in Cobbs Crossing. I suppose she might not have been too conscious of her surroundings in that state, or just unlucky. I'd hate to think it was deliberate.'

'What? What happened?'

'She was hit by a car and left by the road. Buchanan has just brought her in.'

'Bloody hell!'

'Yes, indeed.'

'How is she?'

'Not as bad as it could have been, but bad enough. She has concussion and a fractured tibia. She's in a lot of pain. We'll need to watch her for a while.'

Mick was on his feet, pacing back and forth. 'I didn't think about Pearl. I just wanted to help.'

'Help who? Who did you think you were helping?'

'I wanted to help Sarah.'

'Who?'

'Sarah. Oh, you'd remember her as Sister Anthony from St Cuthbert's. She left the convent. She's not a nun any more. She's been trying to find Jamarra and I wanted to help her.'

It was Doctor Lawrence's turn to look bewildered. 'And this story helps her how?'

'She's coming to the Crossing. Might be here already for all I know. She's planning to make Mother Sebastian tell us where Jamarra is. She thought it might loosen the old witch's tongue if another scandal threatened St Cuthbert's.'

'Are you telling me the story was... What's her name now? Sarah? Was it Sarah's idea?'

'Sarah? No. Heavens no, it was just me. Like you said, clever. Only, as it's turned out, not very bloody smart.' Mick frowned. 'But how do you know why Pearl was coming into town? And how would she know from this photo that Lily is Tallara? I know she's her mother but it's been twenty years.'

Mick's contrition seemed to mollify the doctor. 'I was in emergency when Pearl was brought in. She had two newspaper cuttings on her. One was this morning's photo of Lily, and the other was the one of her in Melbourne, the one showing her birthmark. Pearl just put two and two together.'

The click of high-heeled shoes turned their heads to the window. The doctor watched with some amusement as Mick rushed to open the door to a stylish young woman with lovely auburn hair. She wore a mint green shift and matching stiletto shoes.

'Sarah, come in. I was just telling Lawrence that you would be here soon. Do you two remember each other?'

Arthur Lawrence had risen from his chair with old- fashioned courtesy as Sarah entered the room. She held out her hand and the doctor took it, noticing the firmness of her handshake.

'Not as Sarah Norton,' she said. 'We met at the orphanage sometimes, when I was Sister Anthony.'

'Yes, I remember, Miss Norton. My pleasure.'

'Sarah, please.' She smiled and the doctor grinned.

It was easy to see why young O'Mara appeared so distracted.

Bronko had come bounding in at the sound of Sarah's voice, his tail lashing the sides of his body. She laughed as he pushed between her and the doctor. He nudged her with his nose, looking for pats. Mick hovered on the fringes of all this reunion.

Sarah refused his offer of a chair. 'Thanks, no. I just popped in to let you know that I've given my family the phone number of the *Chronicle* until I book into the hotel.'

'What, you didn't fancy asking Mother Sebastian to put you up?' Mick grinned and the doctor chuckled.

Sarah screwed up her nose at them then smiled as if she was tolerating naughty children. 'Your office was the only place I could think of. I hope you don't mind?' She had already turned back to the door.

'No, of course I don't mind. But before you go, there's something you should…' His voice trailed away as he turned forlorn eyes towards the door.

Sarah and the doctor followed his gaze through the glass lobby. Two elderly female heads were approaching. Mick groaned. Arthur Lawrence grinned. The Misses Klein, wearing their greying hair in identical Jacquie Kennedy bobs, marched into the office. Miss Mary had a roll of cardboard under her arm. The doctor, feeling like a wind-up toy, vacated his chair again.

Mick introduced Sarah. The women acknowledged her with quick impatient smiles and Miss Mary rushed to their news.

'We've heard about the pre-season match, Mick, and we have a great idea for the banner.'

The sisters were the Cobbs Crossing Tigers' most loyal supporters, creating crêpe paper banners for every football match. Each Saturday, a new banner was ready. Miss Mary and Miss Constance never minded their week's work being destroyed as the young gladiators burst through their slogans and onto the field.

The doctor's eyebrows shot up. 'What pre-season match, O'Mara?'

Mick snorted. 'The VFL fancies itself against a combined Mallee team at Victory Park.'

Doctor Lawrence grinned from Mick to the sisters. 'Oh, I see. So you two have decided to make a new banner, right?'

'Right, and we thought…'

'…that there could be only one slogan…'

'…for a match against the south.'

With a flourish, Miss Mary unrolled the cardboard. Mick grinned. The doctor roared with laughter. Sarah stared at the prototype banner. It declared, 'The Mallee Doesn't Crack!'

Mick answered Sarah's raised eyebrows. 'During the last dry season, a city journo claimed that the Mallee would be "nothing but dry, cracked earth". He was swamped with replies from irate locals telling him, "It's soft, this red earth. It doesn't crack like the claypans of the south. Everyone knows that the Mallee doesn't crack."'

Doctor Lawrence was dabbing his eyes with a handkerchief. 'The expression caught on with blokes who thought of themselves as tough Mallee men. It became a popular slogan here in the north-west.'

Mick nodded to the sisters. 'Miss Klein, Miss Constance, it's perfect. I'll take a photo for the *Chronicle* before the match.'

The sisters left, glowing in the approval of their hero. Mick glared at the grinning faces in his office.

As Sarah started to leave again, he remembered what he had to tell her. 'We have some bad news, Sarah.' He exchanged glances with the doctor. 'It's about Pearl.'

'Pearl? What about Pearl?'

'She's in hospital. She was hit by a car this morning.'

'What? Oh, good grief, poor Pearl.' Sarah looked from Mick to Arthur Lawrence. 'How bad is she, Doctor? What injuries?' She searched the doctor's face, her own full of concern. 'Will she be all right?'

'Well, it's early days but I hope so. It might help if she knew her daughter was nursing her.'

'Lily! Yes, of course, Lily's here already, isn't she?'

'Yes, and I believe she still doesn't know who Pearl is. You know her better than any of us, Miss... Ah, Sarah. Should we tell her, do you think?'

Sarah frowned. 'It's hard to know. We might only make matters worse. Lily is still very angry about the mother she thinks gave her away. I've tried to broach the subject several times and been warned off. We can't know what might happen if we try to force things.'

'Indeed.' There was a surprising coolness in the doctor's tone.

Sarah caught a puzzling exchange between the two men but neither said anything further. She thought Mick looked uncharacteristically mortified.

The doctor took his leave. 'I must be going. Mrs Lawrence will be waiting. We're leaving for Treasury this evening. It's been a pleasure to meet you again, Sarah. O'Mara.' He picked up his hat and was gone.

Sarah raised her eyebrows at Mick. 'What's Treasury?'

'It's their holiday home in Victor Harbor. I've heard Mrs Lawrence complain that going there with the doctor can hardly be called a holiday.'

'How come?'

'Well, apparently he never forgets that he's a doctor and even when he's away, he's generous with his time. Mrs Lawrence says the Victor Harbor hospital knows him as well as we do here.'

'He's a good man.'

'He is.'

There was an awkward silence in the little office.

Sarah moved towards the door. 'I'd better be going as well.'

Mick put a hand on her arm. 'Can you spare a moment more? There's something I should show you.' He turned to the copy of the *Chronicle* that Doctor Lawrence had left on his desk. 'I had this brilliant idea, see.' He pointed at the side-by-side photos of Lily and Cynthia with a sheepish grin. 'After what you said about getting Mother Sebastian to talk, I thought I could help.'

Sarah was staring at the open paper. 'Oh, damn.'

'I didn't know nuns used words like that.'

'I'm not a nun. Do you know what you've done?'

Mick sighed. 'Yes, Lawrence has already given me the rounds of the kitchen. He was very explicit. The last thing I intended was to hurt Pearl. I've been kicking myself.'

'What's this got to do with Pearl?'

'Oh, I thought that was what you meant. It was how the accident happened. Pearl headed into town looking for Lily as a result of this photo.' The way Sarah was shaking her head at him suggested she found such stupidity hard to believe. Mick was comically contrite. 'At the risk of hearing more about my own folly, may I ask what you did mean, then?'

'I planned to threaten Mother Sebastian with this story, you knew that.' She frowned at the offending pages. 'But if she knows that the cat is already out of the bag, I've lost that leverage. Damn.'

Mick was keen to redeem himself. 'It's only this morning's paper. St Cuthbert's, as you know doesn't have a daily delivery, only the bundles I take out there.'

'Tell me you haven't made a delivery to St Cuthbert's this morning.'

'I have not.'

'Could you, would you, mind driving me out to the orphanage?'

'Now?'

'Yes, now. No, wait. I'd like to visit Pearl first. I'll only be a minute. Wait for me, please.' Before Mick could reply, Sarah had left his office, all thought of finding a place to stay forgotten.

He picked up the suitcase she had left behind and rushed after her. 'Whoa, Sarah, you just got off the train. You must be exhausted and even you have to eat,' he grinned. 'Let's get you booked into the hotel and let me buy you lunch. You can visit Pearl and then I'll drive you to the orphanage.'

Sarah didn't resist. He was right. She was tired and hungry and, though she would never admit it, having someone take care of her felt good.

*

Pearl's room was in semi-darkness, its blinds pulled down against the bright Mallee sun. A nurse sitting by the bed raised a finger to her lips as Sarah entered. Pearl lay motionless, her eyes closed, black curls tangled on the pillow. Her forehead was bandaged and her face was cut and bruised, one eye puffed into a purple ball. The bed bulged where a cradle protected the cast on her leg from the weight of blankets.

Pearl's head shifted a little. One eye half opened, unable to focus. Sarah blinked away a tear. She was used to hospital wards and sick beds but this was Pearl. She waited but Pearl did not seem to register that she was there.

'It's Sarah, Pearl,' she whispered. 'I'll come back when you're stronger.' She made her escape, ashamed that she was glad to be out of the room.

In the corridor, she almost collided with a nurse carrying a covered tray. 'Lily! I'm so glad you're here. It will be so good for your mother.'

'Yes, Rachel's very happy about it. Come around later. We can catch up. I have to give Mrs Marsh her medication now.'

Lily disappeared into Pearl's room leaving Sarah biting her tongue.

Seventy

It was mid-afternoon before Sarah and Mick left Cobbs Crossing. When they turned into St Cuthbert's drive, Sarah clutched the edge of her seat. Mick knew it had nothing to do with his driving. As he pulled up in the car park, she let out an audible sigh. He left the keys in the ignition and got out. Sarah hadn't moved.

He leaned back through the window. 'You don't have to do this, you know. If it's too scary, we can go.'

She jumped out at a speed that had him grinning.

Standing on the path to St Cuthbert's front door, Sarah stared at weedless rows of red geraniums and clean, raked gravel. Visions of little bodies labouring on hands and knees rose up from the stones. She drew another deep breath and rushed up the bluestone steps. Before Mick caught up with her, she had pressed the brass doorbell.

Whilomena was still St Cuthbert's permanent portress. She looked softer than Sarah remembered and pleased to see Sarah again. 'I almost called you Sister Anthony,' she smiled. 'It's Sarah, isn't it? I never knew your surname, though. How should I introduce you to Mother Sebastian, Sarah?'

'It's Sarah Norton now. Sister, it's lovely to see you again.' Sarah meant it.

Whilomena acknowledged Mick with a smile and he nodded, removing his hat. She led them into the great hall. As they crossed the threshold, Mick's jaw dropped as he stared at the lavish interior of St Cuthbert's. Sarah and Whilomena exchanged startled smiles as his whistle echoed through the hall.

Whilomena showed them into an airy parlour opposite Mother Sebastian's study. On one wall there was a painting of the Virgin Mary's triumphant entry into heaven and at the other end of the room, a window overlooked the front veranda. A rosewood table was surrounded by bentwood chairs. Sarah perched on the edge of one of the chairs. Mick stood by the window with his hat in his hands. Even though they were alone, they waited in silence like patients in a doctor's waiting room.

Sarah was not surprised to be kept waiting. She sat straight-backed with her feet neatly together. One hand clutched the fingers of the other in her lap. From his spot near the window, Mick could hear her breathing. He smiled at the determined line of her mouth and the resolute tilt of her chin. Her eyes never left the open door.

At last, they heard a door open across the hall, followed by the rustle of a habit and footsteps. With a grim glance at Mick, Sarah came to her feet like a convent school girl. He grinned to himself. Old habits die hard. Mother Sebastian appeared and seated herself without inviting her guests to sit.

Sarah had never expected this meeting to follow the rules of courteous conduct. She resumed her seat and took the initiative. 'Good afternoon, Mother. I'm now called Sarah Norton again. You know Mr O'Mara, of course.'

Mick nodded without moving from the wall he was holding up. Mother Sebastian ignored him. Stiff-backed and stony-faced, she stared across the table at Sarah without acknowledging the introductions.

Unperturbed, Sarah launched her objective. 'Mother, you may not know that Lily Matthews is now a state registered nurse.' Sarah had rehearsed her opening statement with care. She took no trouble to hide her delight in describing Lily's success.

Mother Sebastian gave no sign that she was impressed. She continued to stare at her guest without changing her expression.

Sarah ignored the look that was meant to reduce her to jelly and continued. 'Lily now has the backing of a prominent family in the community. She has the support of professional friends and she is in secure employment. Under these circumstances, she is well able to support her mother and her brother. So, on behalf of Lily and her mother, Pearl Marsh…' Sarah was rewarded at last, as a shadow of disquiet flickered in the eyes that hadn't left her face. She pressed on like someone delivering an ultimatum and confident of achieving a result, '…I've come to ask where Joseph May was taken when he left St Cuthbert's.'

Recovering her composure, Mother Sebastian sniffed. 'And what makes you think I would give you that information?'

'You might think it would be wise.'

'I can't imagine why.'

'Then let me explain. We know that Mr Lachlan Harris of Mullanurra is St Cuthbert's benefactor and we know why. He pays you to hide his unsavoury secret, doesn't he, Mother? How long do you think his generosity would last if the secret wasn't a secret any more? If the whole world knew what he's paying you to hide? I'm sure the *Chronicle* would be happy to tell them.'

Mother Sebastian's eyes shot towards Mick for the first time. He winked at her, nodding.

'You're guessing. You know nothing.'

'Oh, but we do know, Mother. Doctor Lawrence has identified Lily's birthmark, and Pearl has admitted that Lachlan Harris fathered both her children.'

Mick knew that Pearl had not been able to tell Sarah anything, but he nodded his confirmation with a solemn face. Mother Sebastian paled.

Sarah offered a solution. 'Mother, if you were to tell us where we can find Jamarra, the boy you named Joseph May, perhaps Mr O'Mara would lose interest in the story and your funding might remain secure.'

Mother Sebastian fumed. 'Don't threaten me, Miss Norton. I know your friend here has been doing his best to cause trouble.'

Sarah almost laughed as Mick adopted an expression of injured innocence.

Mother Sebastian took no notice. She continued, 'However, it's unlikely that even the *Chronicle* would risk libelling a prominent member of the community without more proof than the word of an Aboriginal woman.'

Sarah tried another tack. 'Lily Matthews bears an amazing resemblance to Cynthia Harris, Mother, as I'm sure you've noticed. What do you think would happen if the *Chronicle* ran side-by-side photos of both girls?' Sarah didn't dare look in Mick's direction. 'How much proof do you think Mrs Harris would need of something she probably already suspects? Pearl isn't dependent on Mullanurra any more. She is free to tell her story, a story the gossips would love, and I'm sure Lily has some interesting tales to tell about her time at St Cuthbert's.'

Confronting her Superior of so many years was more intimidating than Sarah had imagined. Composed at least on the outside, she hurried on, determined to get what she wanted before a phone call alerted Mother Sebastian to the photos already published in that morning's *Chronicle*.

Mick was impressed by her tenacity. He nodded at everything she said, his regard for her growing by the minute.

Sarah played her final card. 'There's something else you might like to consider, Mother. If this coming referendum returns a Yes vote, the government may exercise its new powers with an inquiry into the care of Aboriginal children. People with secrets they don't want uncovered would be better off making friends than enemies.'

As Mother Sebastian digested the new threat, her self-assurance gave way to apprehension. Mick turned his face towards the garden, grinning his admiration of Sarah's inventiveness. He had heard of no such intention on the part of the government.

Sarah had played all her trumps. She sat straight and still, a mask of confidence defying flutters of anxiety as she waited for a reply. She pulled Harry's watch from her pocket, cradling it in her lap for comfort.

On the other side of the table, Mother Sebastian's eyes glinted. She adopted a more genial tone. 'Could we have a word in private, Miss Norton?'

Mick raised his eyebrows at Sarah.

She shrugged and nodded.

He pushed himself off the wall, ramming his Akubra back on his head. 'I'll go check on the car,' he said, as if the FJ was a Ferrari he had left in a dangerous neighbourhood.

Mother Sebastian waited in silence while his long strides echoed across the great hall. As they heard the front door close, Sarah wished she could run after him. The parlour seemed much smaller now.

Mother Sebastian pulled out her own timepiece and regarded it with a sigh. 'Miss Norton, I find it very hard to remember the comings and goings of this great establishment, when I have to depend on such an unreliable little watch as mine.' Sarah gasped but Mother Sebastian showed no trace of embarrassment. 'If I had a watch like yours, I'm sure my memory would improve.'

Sarah's fingers closed over the gift her missing brother had given her. She couldn't. No, not Harry's watch. Through the open parlour door, her eyes fell on the filing cabinet in Mother Sebastian's study. A lump rose in her throat. Her fingers were cold and numb as she fumbled to unpin the watch's chain from the inside of her pocket. With a reluctant hand, she placed watch and chain on the table. The beautiful silver timepiece gleamed against the rosewood surface for just a second before it was snatched away.

Mother Sebastian swirled towards the door. With her back to Sarah she hissed, 'Joseph May was sent to St Bartholomew's Home for Boys, in Adelaide.'

Mick was stretched out on the bonnet of his ute, enjoying the sun that filtered through the dappled shade of stringy barks. He looked up as the convent door opened and watched Sarah walk towards him. He jumped off the car as she reached the trees. 'What was that all about?'

She avoided his eyes. 'I guess she didn't want to give in, in front of you.'

'You mean it worked? She told you?'

'Yes. Jamarra's in Adelaide.'

'You did it! Well done, Sarah. I'm impressed.' He opened the passenger door for her, shutting it as she seated herself. As he climbed into the driver's seat beside her, he frowned. The distress she had refused to let Mother Sebastian see was now all over her face. He put a hand on her shoulder. 'Sarah, what's wrong? What did that old witch say to you?'

'Let's get out of here, Mick, please.'

He paused, watching her for a second, then he nodded, turned the key in the ignition and planted his boot on the accelerator.

Before the FJ's dust had settled in St Cuthbert's driveway, Mother Sebastian was on the phone. 'Brother Leonard, you are about to receive a visit from some people looking for Joseph May. I regret they have discovered his whereabouts. Heaven knows what wild story they will concoct. They are not to be trusted. Whatever they claim, it is my certain knowledge that they intend reuniting the child with his Aboriginal mother. Be warned.'

As Brother Leonard put down the phone, he looked across the room at the empty letter box inside his office door. The mention of Joseph May reminded him that his evening paper had not arrived.

Seventy-one

It was a wet night a few weeks into Jamarra's life as Patch's replacement. He patrolled the front veranda, his eyes straining into the gathering darkness for the evening paper that had failed to arrive. When the dinner bell rang, he stayed at his post, his fear of Brother Leonard's armchair stronger than the gnawing in his belly. The front door opened and the principal appeared, looking for his paper.

Jamarra glanced up, his heart thumping. 'It hasn't come, Brother. I've been here all the time, honest.'

Brother Leonard was about to deliver a disbelieving tirade when Jamarra was saved by the arrival of the paperboy. He puffed as he pushed his bike against wind and rain. As he drew level with the figures on the veranda, he sent a rolled-up newspaper soaring above a path of muddy puddles.

Jamarra ran along the veranda. Keeping his eyes on the flying paper, he hurled himself into its trajectory, reaching high above his head to pluck it out of the air. He stepped back to earth like a defending full-back, with his trophy clasped to his chest. Anywhere else, the feat would have been greeted with applause.

Brother Leonard merely reached for the paper. 'You'd better see if there's any dinner left. Hurry yourself.'

Jamarra took off. He scampered around to the back of the building, leaping puddles and skidding as he took the kitchen corner too fast. Picking himself up and brushing muddy knees, he pushed on past the kitchen to the back door, keen to be out of the rain. It was locked. He rattled the handle and banged on the door but it stayed locked. He could smell the evening meal being served as he raced back to the kitchen where Patch had been fed on the steps. This door was locked as well.

Jamarra circled the building again, trying windows as well as doors. When he passed the kitchen for the second time, he began to fret, seeing a cold, wet night ahead and a lot of explaining to do in the morning. He wandered about peering into the darkness, looking for a place where a boy might shelter for the night. He wished Patch was here. Patch would know where there was somewhere warm and safe.

Patch! Jamarra's eyes lit up and he grinned to himself in the darkness. Barely able to see now, he stumbled back to the kitchen door, his heart pounding. Yes, there it was, the little dog door Brother Leonard had installed so that his pet could come and go at will. Jamarra got down on his hands and knees and butted the flap with his head as he had seen Patch do. It moved inwards over the flagstones of the kitchen passage. He crawled forward. His head went through but his shoulders, small though they were, were too wide for the tiny opening. He dropped his left shoulder and raised his right one, angling his body across the space. This gave him a little more room but not enough. He could not move any further. He was debating whether to call for help, when a pair of sandaled feet and the skirt of a brown habit appeared at the level of his eyes.

'Well, well. I didn't realise boys could use that door, as well as dogs. I'd better have it boarded up.' Brother Leonard pattered away, his laughter floating back behind him.

Jamarra wriggled and strained but he could get no further. Then he tried to back out. The flap that Patch had managed with such ease was now lodged into the back of his neck, between his head and his shoulders. He couldn't get his head under it, even with his face flat against the flagstones, and with his arms trapped under him, he couldn't push it outwards again. From the shoulders down, his body was exposed to the night air and the rain was getting heavier. After trying every twist and turn without success, Jamarra collapsed and sobbed himself into an exhausted sleep. Rain soaked him and wind howled around him.

He was frightened awake by an unknown noise and screamed as he felt something licking his legs. He kicked as hard as he could, startling the kitchen cat. It fled with a screech. For the rest of the night, he fell into fitful bouts of sleep, waking sometimes to struggle to free himself, only to give up in despair and fall into a tearful sleep again.

On his way to the kitchen in the early dawn, Brother Gabriel stared down the dark passage towards the back door, at what he thought was an animal trying to enter the building. He hurried towards it, making shooing noises. When he realised it was a child, he ran. The boy appeared to be unconscious.

Brother Gabriel patted the little face, the skin pale and as cold as the flagstones it lay on. 'Joseph? Joseph!'

Jamarra moaned and shivered. Brother Gabriel grasped the little body by the shoulders and tried to pull it towards him. It would not budge. He saw the problem and edged the dog door backwards. Rushing outside, he took hold of the cold little legs and, stretching one hand forward under Jamarra's face to protect him from the stones, he eased the child back. As soon as the boy was free, he scooped him up in his arms. Ignoring decorum and the rule of silence, he ran to the infirmary, the urgent patter of his sandals on flagstones echoing through the corridors.

Seventy-two

'Pearl, why didn't you tell anyone what was going on? Doctor Lawrence, perhaps. He would have helped you.' Sarah was sitting beside Pearl's hospital bed.

This time, they were alone and the blind was up letting light into the room. Pearl was still very weak but today she was conscious. As Sarah had predicted, she now saw no reason not to name the father of her children and the name she gave was no surprise.

'Mr Harris said if anyone found out, I'd go straight back to the orphanage.' Pearl turned her face away, tears of shame in her eyes.

Sarah fumed at herself. 'Oh, Pearl, I'm so sorry. It wasn't your fault. It was never your fault. You were only fourteen, just a child. I can't imagine how trapped and frightened you must have been.' Sarah paused. 'You're safe now, Pearl,' she soothed, 'and I'm still trying to get your children –'

Pearl twisted back glaring at Sarah. 'No more promises, Sister Anthony! You promised before. You said you wanted to help but you didn't really want to help. You worked in that place when they took my boy. You knew things and you kept secrets.' She coughed and sank back on her pillows.

Sarah had never heard Pearl raise her voice. She hung her head. 'I'm sorry, Pearl.' She wondered how much to say. With Lily still not wanting to know and Jamarra not yet safe, it was too soon to raise Pearl's hopes. 'There's no reason for you to trust me, Pearl, but I will not give up. For you and Jamarra and Tallara, I will keep trying.'

Pearl did not answer. She had turned her face away again.

Sarah stood up to go. 'Goodbye, Pearl.' At the door she paused. 'I will keep trying.'

In the corridor outside Pearl's room, Lily was leaning against the wall. 'I heard. Well, I listened,' she admitted with a rueful grin. 'You're a brave soul, Sarah.' She straightened up. 'There's something else.' She beckoned Sarah down the corridor to a visitors' lounge. It was empty. Lily sat down and Sarah sat beside her.

Lily dug in the pocket of her uniform and fished out a wad of folded newspaper. She handed it to Sarah. 'Look what I found under Mrs Marsh's –' she swallowed '– under my mother's pillow.'

Sarah raised her eyebrows, delighted to hear Lily call Pearl 'my mother' but puzzled by her obvious distress. She unfolded the papers and gasped, 'Oh, Lily!'

The newspaper cuttings were the ones Doctor Lawrence had seen. There was Mick's article about Lily's return and photos from the rally, including a bare-armed Lily with her birthmark visible and Sarah standing beside her.

'She knows,' Lily whispered. 'Sarah, she knows who I am. She's probably waiting for me to say something. I can't imagine what she thinks of me.'

'What she thinks of both of us, Lily. So this is what she meant about me knowing things and keeping secrets. Poor Pearl, she must think we've all betrayed her.' Sarah put a hand on Lily's arm. 'Lily, it's good that you know she's your mother. You must have many questions. I'll be happy to answer them, but not right now. If you want to, you can help Mick and me do something that will make her very, very happy. Listen.'

Seventy-three

Sarah, Mick and Lily sat in front of Brother Leonard's desk. They had answered endless questions, all of which seemed designed to defeat their purpose. Sarah and Lily exchanged dispirited glances. Mick sat with one leg tucked against his chair and the other stuck out in front of him, turning his hat in his hands. His eyes roamed around the room and he gaped in astonishment at the macabre statue of St Bartholomew.

Brother Leonard claimed Mick's attention. 'O'Mara? That's Irish, of course?'

The significance of the question was not lost on Mick. He answered in his best imitation brogue. 'It is, Brother! Michael Patrick Francis, me dear mother called me.'

Sarah kept a straight face.

'A good Catholic home, then?'

'Mass every mornin' o' the week, Brother, and twice on Sundays.'

Sarah pressed her lips together so hard it hurt.

'And what is your interest in the boy, this Joseph May?'

Sarah was sure there must be a limit to the hoodwinking Brother Leonard could swallow. She jumped in before Mick could carry the act too far. 'We're here on behalf of the child's mother, Brother Leonard.'

'And where is the mother?'

'She's in hospital recovering from an accident.'

'The boy has enjoyed a costly upkeep with us for more than five years. Why has the mother not applied for custody before this?'

'That would have been difficult, Brother, when she was lied to and denied information concerning his whereabouts.'

Brother Leonard regarded Sarah with narrowed eyes. 'Indeed? That's a very serious allegation, Miss Norton. Can you substantiate it?'

Sarah met his challenge without flinching. 'I was a Sister of St Frances Cabrini, assigned to St Cuthbert's before Jam, before Joseph May arrived there. Many times I opened the door to his mother and just as often I heard Mother Sebastian deny that she knew him.'

Brother Leonard pursed his lips and sniffed. Ignoring Sarah's evidence, he turned inquisitorial eyes on her, asking as if she had confessed a crime, 'May I ask why you left your order, Miss Norton?'

A warm flush coloured Sarah's cheeks but she held his gaze. 'We are here to talk about Joseph May, Brother Leonard. His mother has always —'

'Ah yes, the mother. Is she employed?'

'She has been employed since she was fourteen and with her experience, will no doubt find work again very soon.' Sarah could see Jamarra slipping away from their grasp. Desperation made her reckless. 'Pearl is in every way a capable mother. It seems that the only mark against her is that she's black!'

Brother Leonard turned amused eyes on her. They always gave themselves away, these bleeding hearts. He leaned back in his chair, shaking his head. 'So you are suggesting that we return the child to an unemployed, incapacitated, single mother? Impossible! Brother Gabriel, please show our guests out.'

Mick jumped to his feet with a thunderous scowl. He looked as if he was about to leap across the desk and help Brother Leonard to a more sympathetic understanding of the situation. Sarah laid a hand on his arm and shook her head. He rammed his hat on his head and stalked out of the room, followed by Brother Gabriel and the two women.

In the doorway, Sarah paused. 'We will be back, Brother Leonard.'

In the passage outside Brother Leonard's office, Brother Gabriel placed a finger to his lips. Instead of escorting them to the front door, he beckoned them to follow him down a side corridor.

'Where are we going?' Mick whispered.

Brother Gabriel again signalled for silence, glancing behind them as if in fear of discovery. As they hurried after him, Sarah and Lily froze as their heels clattered like kettledrums on the flagstones. They removed their shoes and sped on over the chilly paving in their stockinged feet. The four silent figures passed through a labyrinth of corridors until Brother Gabriel led them into a long, narrow chamber. His sole patient was sleeping, tucked up with extra blankets.

At the foot of Jamarra's bed, Sarah and Lily exchanged glances, shaking their heads at the unnatural colour of the child's face.

Jamarra murmured in his sleep, turning over and throwing off the bedcovers. Sarah smiled and blinked away a tear as Lily leaned down to replace her little brother's blankets. She was startled by a gasp. She and Mick pressed closer to see what had alarmed Lily. Jamarra's thin pyjama top had ridden up as he turned in bed. His naked back was exposed and they looked in horror at red welts snaking across his body.

Mick, his eyes blazing and one hand balled into a fist, grabbed a startled Brother Gabriel. 'Where is he? Where is that mongrel?'

Sarah rushed between them, her palms against Mick's chest. She shared his outrage but common sense must prevail. Mick released Brother Gabriel, muttering an apology.

Lily drew the pyjama top down. Almost blind with tears, she replaced the blankets, tucking them into place. She smoothed Jamarra's curls from his face and kissed the little forehead that was warm with sleep. Straightening up again, she directed a meaningful glare at Sarah, her eyes full of defiance, reckless intent written all over her. For one mad moment, Sarah too wanted to scoop Jamarra up and run. She hated leaving him here. But she knew they needed a more permanent solution than kidnapping him, or having Mick locked up for assaulting Brother Leonard.

Leaving the monastery, Mick looked back to see Sarah whispering to Brother Gabriel on the steps. The young brother was listening and nodding. When they parted, the two took each other's hands, not a handshake but a clasp of four hands intertwined, in the way people do when there is something between them. Mick looked away.

Waving goodbye, Sarah ran down the steps and hurried to catch up with the others. She stopped as a shadow fell across her path. Shielding her eyes, she smiled up at an enormous wedge-tailed eagle circling in the big skies overhead.

Lily greeted her with a despondent sigh. 'I'm glad we didn't tell Pearl we'd be bringing Jamarra home.'

Mick was kicking the tyres of the FJ as if it had done something to him. 'I hate going back without him, Sarah. I hate leaving the poor little bloke in this godforsaken place. Surely there's something we can do?'

'I think there is. But we need reinforcements.'

'Reinforcements?' Mick grinned, despite his anger. He shook his head, smiling. She used to be so timid.

'Doctor Lawrence. We need to talk to Doctor Lawrence.'

'Why go all the way back to Cobbs Crossing? Surely a local doctor –'

'A local doctor wouldn't have a personal interest in Jamarra. Besides, we don't have to go back to the Crossing. Didn't Doctor Lawrence say that he and Mrs Lawrence would be at their holiday house in Victor Harbor?'

'Treasury! Yes, that right.'

'Well, that's where we need to go. I've got an idea.'

'Of course you do.'

Sarah was determined to be optimistic. 'It's going to be all right, you know. Didn't you see your friend up there?' She grinned at Mick.

He laughed and nodded, causing Lily to raise a curious eyebrow as she followed his eyes towards the clouds.

Seventy-four

They took to the road without stopping to rest or eat and Treasury opened hospitable arms to receive them. Martha ushered them into a dining room reserved for special guests and sat them down to a welcome meal of her famous home cooking.

As they ate, Sarah explained that they had seen Jamarra and why they were unable to bring him home. She and Lily filled the doctor in on his condition.

'He's clearly malnourished.'

'He has been horribly beaten, poor little soul.'

'And suffering from exposure, too. Brother Gabriel said he had been locked out overnight.'

'Good God.' The doctor knitted bushy eyebrows. 'Hypothermia?'

'I think not. It was wet but, as you know, the autumn nights have been mild. Brother Gabriel has taken good care of him. I believe he has a real concern for the boys but he's limited by his circumstances. Thank goodness it wasn't winter.'

Martha paused in the middle of pouring cups of tea, her motherly face full of distress. 'Poor little boy. You had to leave him there? Couldn't we tell the police, or report the place to Welfare?'

'Sadly, it was the police and Welfare that put him where he is.'

'There must be some way we can get him out of there, Sarah.'

'Well, I think there might be.'

The others stopped eating, all eyes on Sarah.

She grinned around the table. 'Brother Leonard will never release Jamarra to us. He made that clear.' She lifted her cup to meet Martha's teapot. 'We made the mistake of letting him know that we want to re-unite Jamarra with his mother. Of course he's against that because an

287

Aboriginal mother would be such a bad influence, you know the kind of thinking. On the other hand,' Sarah turned to the doctor, her eyes dancing with the cleverness of her plan 'if respectable you and Mrs Lawrence turned up when he was expecting a return visit from us, which I threatened by the way –'

The doctor's eyes twinkled as he interrupted her. 'He might be happy to have the boy spirited away into "a good Christian family" before you came back?'

'Yes, yes, that's it.' Sarah smiled her delight at the doctor's perception. She rushed on as if he had confirmed his acceptance of the mission. 'You should not express any particular interest in Jamarra, Doctor. Just ask to see some boys about nine or ten and then pick him out. You might feel it your Christian duty to take the sick one, seeing you're a doctor and all that.'

Mick and Lily grinned at each other.

Sarah beamed as she laid out the details of her plan. 'Brother Gabriel has promised to make sure Jamarra is in the line-up and to indicate him to you, if you don't recognise him, though I think you would. Apart from his diminished physical condition, he hasn't changed a lot. He's not even all that much bigger. Oh, and Doctor, I suggest you use your Victor Harbor address. Don't mention Cobbs Crossing.'

The doctor chuckled. 'What a devious mind you have, Miss Norton.' He turned to his wife. 'What do you think, my dear?'

'Of course we must try, Arthur. Do you think we stand a chance, Sarah?'

'With Brother Gabriel as our accomplice, I think we have a very good chance.'

The doctor smiled at her eager face. 'Imagine returning the lad to his mother after all they've been through. We'll do our best, Sarah.'

As soon as their visitors had been waved goodbye, the doctor phoned St Bartholomew's. He made an appointment for himself and Mrs Lawrence to see Brother Leonard, taking care to introduce himself as 'Doctor Arthur Lawrence, of Victor Harbor'.

Having set in motion a plan to rescue one child, a determined Sarah, intent on saving others, overcame her reluctance to return to St Magdalene's. She confronted Mother Anna with a firm, unsmiling ultimatum, threatening to expose the embezzlement of Welfare funds if Mother Sebastian was not removed from child care for good. Mother Anna had little choice. She capitulated at last and Sister Matthew became Mother Matthew, Principal of St Cuthbert's Convent and Orphanage School.

Seventy-five

It was mid-morning when Brother Gabriel showed Doctor and Mrs Lawrence into the principal's office. The doctor's finest suit, for once minus his football club tie, presented a picture of respectability. Martha, in her Sunday best and her grey hair in a tidy bun, was an image of matronly decorum. They stared at the statue of St Bartholomew and grimaced at each other behind Brother Leonard's back as he ordered tea for his guests.

When he returned and seated them in the same chairs that Sarah, Lily and Mick had occupied the day before, the doctor explained their hope to adopt a child.

'Mrs Lawrence is delighted at the prospect of having a pupil again, Brother. The child we choose will receive a good education, no doubt about that.'

'And of course, a good Catholic home, Brother,' Martha assured him.

Brother Leonard was delighted to have this impressive couple look over the age group they favoured. When he ordered the boys paraded for inspection, Brother Gabriel was faithful to his pact with Sarah. Jamarra was with them.

While her husband pretended no particular interest in Jamarra, Martha played her part to perfection. 'I think we should take the sick one, Arthur. What better than a doctor's family for him? It's our Christian duty.'

Brother Leonard acknowledged her remarks with a condescending smile and a slight bow of his head. Yes, indeed. A doctor could keep the boy alive long enough to ensure that no scandal attached to St

Bartholomew's. And the child would be out of reach of the trouble-makers that Mother Sebastian was concerned about.

Without waiting for the doctor to respond, Brother Leonard manoeuvred the conversation as if a decision had been made. 'Very well. It will take a few days to organise his transfer with Welfare but, with my recommendation, your credentials, Doctor, and those of Mrs Lawrence,' another bow to the lady, 'I don't anticipate any problems.'

'Thank you, Brother.' Arthur Lawrence rose from his chair with an energy that seemed to fill the room. He reached across the desk to shake hands with Brother Leonard. 'My wife and I will wait for your call. This is our number.'

Martha marvelled at her husband's charade of outward calm. She knew he must be a bubbling cauldron on the inside. As they walked to their car, she placed a hand on his arm, her voice lowered to a whisper. 'Arthur, I think we should not call him Jamarra. Not yet.'

He waited for her to explain.

'That name is sure to trigger memories for the child. The first person he hears it from should be his mother.'

Arthur nodded. He patted the hand on his arm and gave her an adoring smile. 'You're a good woman, Martha Lawrence.'

They returned to Treasury as if they had been condemned to limbo. Every time the phone rang, the doctor snatched it up, hoping he wasn't going to hear Sergeant Buchanan's voice dashing their hopes. If Mother Sebastian rang Brother Leonard again before their mission was accomplished, it would be doomed.

At last the call came. Brother Leonard was brief and to the point. 'Everything is arranged Doctor, for you to foster the boy with a view to adoption. You won't need to worry about getting the mother's consent. I'll ask the police to have her sign the necessary papers.'

The police! Doctor Lawrence swallowed his alarm. If Ed Buchanan heard who wanted to adopt Jamarra, their chances of bringing him home would melt like butter on a hot muffin. 'The police?' The doctor cleared his throat. 'Brother, we wouldn't want the mother to know our name. Mrs Lawrence and I wish to raise the boy in a civilised Christian environment. It would be counterproductive to have his Aboriginal mother turning up, willy-nilly. I hope you understand.'

Martha watched her husband roll his eyes as he played on Brother Leonard's prejudices. She understood the desperate game he was playing.

'You're quite right, Doctor. Of course the mother won't be given your name.'

'But even the police, with the best of intentions, Brother, they might let our name slip.' He held his breath.

'I understand your concern, Doctor. The police only need to know that the mother's signature is required.'

'Thank you, Brother. I appreciate your discretion.' Arthur put down the phone, muttering, 'Damn! I should have thought of that. Now I may have ruined everything.' He started pacing up and down, shaking his head in self-deprecation.

Martha was following her husband's agitated movements with sympathetic eyes. She nodded. 'We did our best, dear. You mustn't blame yourself.'

At the other end of the room, the doctor paused, one outstretched arm leaning on the mantelpiece. 'I thought adoption would be more persuasive than foster care, to Brother Leonard's mind. I didn't give a thought to the need for parental consent, let alone the police getting involved, or Pearl's panic if she's asked to sign her son away. Oh my god! Pearl!' He dashed back to the phone and snatched it up again.

*

'Sarah! Great timing.'

She had walked into Mick's office unexpected and unannounced. 'I couldn't wait in Ballarat,' she said. 'I wanted to be here.' He gave her such a delighted grin that she added rather too quickly, 'I mean, I wanted to be here when news arrives from Victor Harbor.'

'Well, there are phones, you know. Or didn't you trust me to ring you?'

Ignoring his teasing, Sarah accepted the chair he cleared of papers and sat down with exaggerated dignity. 'You said "great timing". Has something happened?'

'As a matter of fact, yes.' Mick relayed Arthur Lawrence's concerns. 'The police? Oh, Mick.'

'Yeah, not good.' He frowned. 'Sarah, Pearl needs to be prepared. I know we didn't want to raise her hopes until we had Jamarra safe, but now that Brother Leonard has thrown a spanner in the works, I reckon we have no choice.' His face relaxed into a grin. 'It's great that Lily's nursing Pearl, though. I can't see Buchanan bullying Pearl on Lily's watch.'

Sarah was on her feet again. 'You're right. We must warn Pearl and put Lily on guard. And there's something personal I need to see Lily about. If you don't mind, I'll go on my own, Mick. See you later.' Sarah whirled out of the office leaving Mick staring after her.

She ran to her hotel room and rummaged in her suitcase. Her fingers closed on a bulky bundle wrapped in brown paper and tied with string. She sped back down the stairs two at a time.

At the hospital, she found Lily at the nurses' station. Lily left the desk and steered Sarah into a drab little staff room. As they sat down, Sarah deposited her parcel on the chair beside her.

Declining a cup of coffee and some rather stale-looking doughnuts, Sarah relayed Doctor Lawrence's message. 'So you see, Lily, we need to prepare Pearl for a visit from Sergeant Buchanan.'

Lily nodded. 'Yes, of course.' She gave a wry little smile. 'I'm afraid I've been an awful coward, Sarah. I haven't told her yet that I know she's my mother. I've been telling myself it's because I don't want to excite her in her fragile condition. It seems this would be a good time to stop making excuses, don't you think?'

Sarah picked up her parcel. 'I've been minding these for ages, Lily. It's time they reached the person they were written to.'

Lily raised her eyebrows as she accepted the packet. Unwrapping it, she gaped at dozens of faded letters all addressed in the same laboured hand, 'Tallara Marsh, Saint Cuthbert's Orphanage'. Turning them over, Lily gave a little cry. The sender address on letter after letter was 'Pearl Marsh, Mullanurra.' She wrapped them up again and tucked the parcel under her arm. She stood up, facing Sarah with a nervous little smile. 'Will you come with me?'

*

Pearl stirred, taking a moment to focus as they entered her room. Grasping the triangle above her head, she pulled herself up, looking at Lily with eager eyes.

Lily hurried over and sat beside the bed. 'Mrs Marsh, you know who I am, don't you?' There was a lump in her throat as she whispered, 'I believe you used to call me –'

'Tallara!' Pearl's eyes filled with tears. 'You're beautiful, girl.' She stretched out a hand to touch Lily's face. 'I knew you would be beautiful. You were such a beautiful baby, Tallara.'

Lily smiled. 'It sounds strange to be called that. Nice, though. Tallara, what does it mean?'

'It means "rain". You were born during a big storm. It was my mother's name too.'

'So you called me after my grandmother, Mrs –'

'Can you, only if you want to, Tallara, can you call me Mum?'

Lily thought about all those letters. 'It will take a bit of getting used to…Mum.' The last word was managed with a soft, self-conscious little laugh.

Sarah had waited just inside the door, not wanting to intrude on their precious moment.

Lily beckoned her forward. 'Mrs Marsh –' she corrected herself with another awkward little laugh '– Mum, Sarah has something exciting to tell you.'

Pearl pulled her eyes away from her Tallara. Sarah moved a little further into the room, shaking her head. 'Why don't you tell your mother, Lily?'

'It's your news, Sarah. You deserve to be the one to –'

Pearl turned exasperated eyes from Sarah to Lily and back again. 'Well, is someone going to tell me?'

Both of them laughed. Lily urged Sarah on with a smile and a vigorous nod.

The mood lightened by Pearl's impatience, Sarah hurried to the foot of the bed. 'Pearl, we've found Jamarra.'

Pearl gave a gasp that was almost a scream. She looked back at Lily, eyes wild with excitement. Lily nodded, dabbing away at damp lashes.

'Where?'

'He's in a boys' home in Adelaide.'

'Adelaide! Why? Why so far away?'

'Doctor Lawrence has gone to Adelaide, Pearl. He and Mrs Lawrence are trying to bring Jamarra home to you.'

'Doctor Lawrence, he's a good man.' Pearl started to cough. She sank back on her pillows.

Lily poured a glass of water and helped her to drink. 'Well, it was really Sarah who found Jamarra, Mum. Sarah made Mother Sebastian tell us where he is, and she was the one who asked Doctor Lawrence to go to Adelaide.'

Pearl turned her eyes to where Sarah was standing at the foot of her bed. She didn't miss the uneasy glance that passed between Sarah and Lily. 'What?'

Sarah took a breath. It had to be said. 'Pearl, Doctor Lawrence told the people at the home that he wants to adopt Jamarra. He only said that so that he could bring Jamarra home to you. But the police will be here soon, asking you to sign some papers...papers that say you give your consent to Jamarra being adopted.'

Pearl stared at them. 'Say that someone else can have my baby?' Her startled eyes were wide with horror. 'All these years, I never gave my consent. I never gave my baby away.' She turned to Lily, her face wet with tears. 'I never gave either of my babies away.'

Lily blinked away a tear and squeezed the hand that still held hers. 'You don't have to sign, Mum.' The word was sounding more natural. 'I'll be with you.'

Sarah pulled up a chair across the bed from Lily. Laying a calming hand over Pearl's trembling fingers, she whispered, 'No, you don't have to sign. Doctor and Mrs Lawrence can still bring Jamarra home as his foster-parents.' Sarah leant forward to emphasise her next words. 'But Pearl, if Sergeant Buchanan finds out that Doctor Lawrence wants to bring Jamarra back to you, he will stop him. It's very important not to mention the doctor's name to the police.'

Pearl signalled her understanding with a nod. 'I'll remember. I won't say Doctor Lawrence's name. Thank you, Sister Anthony.'

Lily grinned across the bed. Sarah rolled her eyes and grinned back, shaking her head.

Lily spread the letters out on the bed. 'Look, Mum. Do you remember writing these? Sarah gave them to me just a few minutes ago. I'll have a lot of lovely reading to do tonight.'

Pearl stared at the envelopes, then at Sarah.

Sarah gasped at what she saw on Pearl's face. 'Oh, Pearl, I didn't steal your letters! Mother Sebastian ordered them destroyed but Sister Matthew saved them. She didn't know then that Lily was your Tallara. She just kept the letters safe, hoping to find Tallara and give them to her.'

'How did you find out?'

'Doctor Lawrence told a friend of mine about Lily's birthmark. But I didn't see the mark until I started nursing with Lily.'

'Why didn't you give her the letters then?' Pearl demanded.

'That was my fault.' Lily looked sheepish. 'I wouldn't let Sarah tell me.'

Pearl understood. She patted Lily's hand and turned back to Sarah, taking her hand. 'You kept your promise. You found my babies. Thank you, girl.'

Sarah couldn't speak.

Lily leaned down. 'We've exhausted you, Mum. We're going to leave and let you sleep. I'll be back when you're awake. Meantime, I've got my letters to read.'

Pearl reached her hand out to Lily. 'Don't go.'

'We must, Mum. You need your rest. You have to get strong again, to meet Jamarra.'

Moving towards the door, Sarah glanced back and saw Lily kiss her mother's face. Pearl was still smiling as she closed her eyes. She gave a contented little sigh. Sarah scrambled in her bag for a handkerchief.

*

Sergeant Buchanan loomed at the foot of Pearl's bed with his feet apart and his cap tucked under one arm. Lily stood by Pearl's bed and met the sergeant's scowls with cool determination. She refused to budge, insisting that her patient was not well enough to be left alone. He had to accept Pearl's firm 'No' and leave with his papers unsigned.

Seventy-six

Brother Leonard scowled at the police report. The foolish mother had refused a fine opportunity for her child. Still, even though they would be denied the right to adopt, the doctor and his wife seemed willing to go ahead with a fostering arrangement. They didn't seem the sort to hand the child back at the first hiccup, as Alf Braachs had done. He would have to be satisfied.

*

Brother Gabriel helped settle Jamarra into Arthur Lawrence's car, where Martha was waiting to bury him in blankets and a motherly hug. It was snug and warm bundled up beside her like a caterpillar in a cocoon.

Jamarra was sorry when the car stopped and it was time to get out. He was put to bed in the biggest bedroom he had ever seen. The cheerful little woman brought trays loaded with good food. She brushed his curls, smiled at his big blue eyes and sighed over his thin little arms and legs. The deep voice of the big man who read him stories, reminded him of something from long ago.

Doctor Lawrence would not attempt the journey to Cobbs Crossing until Jamarra had regained his strength. He phoned the hospital and explained to Pearl why it was necessary to delay Jamarra's return. Despite her eagerness to see her son again, Pearl trusted the doctor. She wanted only what was best for Jamarra. Still, every day of waiting seemed longer than the last.

On a mild, late autumn afternoon, Lily pushed Pearl's wheelchair out into the hospital gardens. She arranged a pillow behind her back and tucked a rug around her legs. Pearl patted her daughter's hands away. Pretending impatience at being fussed over, she tut-tutted to disguise the pleasure it gave her.

She leaned back. It was good to feel the sun on her face again. Across the freshly mowed lawns, she spotted Doctor Lawrence standing on the veranda. She raised her arm to wave then dropped it with a gasp. Her blanket fell to the ground unnoticed and her hands flew to her face. A small head had appeared from behind the doctor, looking uncertain. Doctor Lawrence coaxed into full view a child smartly dressed in new clothes. He took the boy's hand and led him halfway across the lawn. Then, with his hands on the child's shoulders, he gave a gentle push, encouraging him to walk forward alone. Lily wanted to run to her brother but she stayed behind Pearl's chair, tears streaming down her cheeks.

Jamarra took a few steps. Doctor Lawrence had told him that the lady in the wheelchair was his mother but he didn't recognise her. He looked back and the doctor nodded him forward. He took another tentative step.

Pearl stretched out her arms, laughing and crying. 'Jamarra! Oh, Jamarra, Jamarra!'

As she called to him, Jamarra's head came up and he moved closer. He allowed her to put her arms around him and the scent of her was more familiar than her voice. He was content to let her hug him and she hugged him as if she would never let him go.

Seventy-seven

'How is he, Pearl?'

It was a blue sky morning two weeks after Jamarra's return to the Crossing. Sarah was enjoying a coffee with Pearl on Martha's back veranda. Jamarra was searching for snails in the garden.

Pearl couldn't take her eyes off him. She gave a rueful little smile. 'He calls me mummy but I'm not sure if he really remembers me.' She sighed. 'I think he's got a big knot in his belly, might take a while to shift. He has bad dreams, Sarah, real bad dreams, crying out in the night.'

Jamarra had abandoned his search for snails and climbed into one of the doctor's apple trees. He was swinging from a branch and making funny faces at them.

Pearl laughed. 'He's a happy little fella when he's awake, though.'

Jamarra dropped out of the tree and somersaulted on the grass.

Sarah smiled at his antics. 'I suppose it will take time. When he's been safe for long enough, maybe he'll be able to sleep without nightmares.'

Pearl nodded. 'Well, at least he's here now, here where he belongs.'

Sarah put down her cup. 'That's something I envy you, Pearl. You, Jamarra, Tallara, Aunty Mary, Majik and Old George, all of you are, as you say, where you belong.'

Pearl grinned. 'And you don't belong because you have no blackfella blood? So you're going back to England some day soon, yeah?' she teased.

Sarah laughed. 'Probably not.'

Under the apple tree, Jamarra was sorting the contents of his pockets – snails in one pile, stones in another.

Pearl's adoring eyes followed his every move. 'Look down there. Look how happy my boy is. If you weren't here, I might never have seen him or Tallara again. You did that, girl. You were meant to be here.'

'That's very generous, Pearl, but if we, Europeans I mean, if we weren't here, they would never have been taken from you in the first place.'

'And they would never have been born, either!' Pearl gave an exasperated snort. 'Oh girl, you think too hard. You'll get a sore head thinking like that. Sometimes, what's good and what's bad gets all mixed up together.' She took Sarah's hand. 'Sometimes, Sarah, my people talk about "being on country". They talk like it's such a great thing, this being on country, like it makes them feel good. I don't know where I was born, but you, girl, don't you feel that kind of belonging in some place that's special to you? Some place that makes you feel good, just to be there?'

Sarah's thoughts raced away to her last happy days with Harry in the Otways. She smiled a grateful smile at Pearl. No words were equal to such generous absolution.

*

'It's great to see them together at last, isn't it, Sarah? Martha had kept busy indoors to allow her guest some private time with Pearl. Now she smiled at Sarah's contented face as she came into the kitchen.

'It is, and it's good of you to have them here, Martha.'

'Of course it isn't. Where else would they go? Back to the river to wait for another visit from Sergeant Buchanan?' Martha slid her baking tray into the oven. 'Lily is looking for a house that the three of them can share. Until she finds one, I've got them all to myself.' She sounded as if Pearl and Jamarra were doing her a favour. 'The doctor and I have asked Pearl to be our housekeeper – when she's recovered of course – and she has accepted.' Martha updated Sarah in triumphant bulletins. 'They'll have a home and an income. Pearl will have the support of her daughter, who is also employed. Jamarra will live with his mother and sister but on paper he will be our foster-child.' She waved her rolling pin. 'Let's see Sergeant Buchanan cook up a charge of neglect out of that!' Martha looked fierce enough to lead the charge of the Light Brigade.

Sarah laughed and clapped her hands. 'Perfect!' She perched on a kitchen stool and watched Martha fill the kettle. 'Jamarra seems comfortable enough around me. I'm not sure if he remembers me from the orphanage. I haven't been game to ask him.'

Martha ceased her bustle. 'Sarah, my dear, you were placed in a situation not of your making. You made sacrifices and took risks to put things right, as far as you could, and just see the result.'

They looked to where Jamarra was parading his snail collection for Pearl's inspection.

'It's time for you to forgive yourself.'

Sarah accepted the cup of tea Martha offered. 'Pearl tells me he's having nightmares every night.'

Glancing back at the garden, Martha whispered, 'Well, it's to be expected, isn't it? It must have been so frightening for the poor little mite in those dreadful places. Oh, my dear! I'm so sorry. What a foolish old woman I am.' Martha hurried around the kitchen bench and took Sarah in her arms, stroking her hair and never once telling her not to cry. When Sarah pulled out a handkerchief and dried her eyes, Martha replenished her cup of tea.

By way of distraction, she proceeded to tell her what the town gossips were saying about Mullanurra. 'The property has become the centre of their divorce settlement. Apparently, it was a wedding gift from Amelia's parents and people always said that Harris was more married to Mullanurra than to his wife. That was why he was so generous to St Cuthbert's. Her family are very religious, and what most people might shrug off, they seem to consider a great scandal. Now they're wielding their considerable wealth to see that the entire property is returned to them. Harris could end up with nothing at all.' Martha finished with a smug smile. 'His wickedness could cost him the two things he cares about most – Mullanurra and his reputation.'

'I can't say I'll lose much sleep over that.'

'No. Not many will, I imagine.'

Sarah looked out to where Jamarra had gone back to searching for snails. 'Martha, would you be happy to have a puppy here?'

Martha followed Sarah's eyes into the garden. 'Now, why didn't I think of that? That's a wonderful idea, Sarah!'

Seventy-eight

On the twenty-seventh of May 1967, Sarah dressed as if she was going to church. The campaigning was done and referendum day had arrived. She set out to vote, her mind full of the great activists who had worked for this day. They had inspired her. They had galvanised a nation and their names were famous: Faith Bandler, Charlie Perkins and all the others who had made it happen.

The polling booths were set up in the grounds of the Cobbs Crossing Primary School. A queue of early-morning voters trailed across the playground and down the footpath outside the gates. Sarah studied the faces in the queue. Miss Constance and Miss Mary Klein, side-by-side as usual, were chatting to their neighbours. Would they vote Yes? The sight of Doctor and Mrs Lawrence brought a smile to Sarah's face – two certain Yes votes there.

Sergeant Buchanan and Lachlan Harris were leaning on the top rail of the fence, their heads close together like players in a football huddle. Sarah sighed. A No vote would be a disaster, making the situation worse than before. In one of her many broadcasts, feisty Faith Bandler had warned, 'The eyes of the world are on Australia, to see if the white Australian will take with him the black Australian.'

Further down the line, Majik's showy cowboy gear stood out. Beside his son, Old George in his faded army uniform held his head high. Sarah smiled at the medals pinned across his chest as if it was Anzac Day.

'You're looking very formal today, Miss Norton.' Mick's voice startled her out of her reverie. He grinned at her gloves and the tiny, emerald green pillbox hat perched on her auburn hair.

She tossed her head. Why did he find everything she did so amusing? 'It's a very important day, Mr O'Mara.' Her tone implied that any reasonable person would understand that formality was to be expected.

'It is,' he conceded, sobering like a reprimanded schoolboy. He tried to redeem himself. 'You seemed far way just now. What were you thinking about?'

Sarah's ruffled feathers were easily unruffled. 'Oh, I was looking at George's medals. I was thinking it's good that they, Aborigines I mean, can vote today.'

He shook his head. 'Not all of them. The whole of the Northern Territory can't vote in a referendum because it's not a state – that's around four thousand Aboriginal votes lost.'

'Oh, Mick!'

The distress on her face made him feel like a brute. He rushed to reassure her, putting an arm around her shoulders. 'Hey, it's not as bad as it sounds, Sarah. See, it's not only Aborigines – no one in the Territory, black or white, can vote today.' He gave her an encouraging smile. 'That means that there won't be any No votes from there either.'

Her small smile acknowledged his effort to console her, but her eyes showed how much she feared that No vote. His arm was still around her. Sarah noticed that people were watching them and she eased away.

The queue progressed and they found themselves in the school's assembly hall. It was dominated by the national flag draped high on a wall above them. Cardboard booths had been installed beneath it. Plastic chairs were stacked around the walls. Voters crossed the bare boards to officials seated at tables on the opposite side. Sarah's name was found on the electoral roll and marked off. Her high heels echoed through the hall as she hurried to the nearest vacant booth. Controlling a trembling hand, she wrote 'Yes' in large, bold capitals. As she left the school grounds, she raised anxious eyes at an uncertain sky. Waiting for a result was going to be torture. Thank goodness for Rachel's party.

Rachel Steiner refused to believe that the Yes vote would not be successful. With determined optimism, she had invited her friends to share in a celebratory meal, even before the polls closed.

Doctor and Mrs Lawrence were the first to arrive, bringing Pearl and Jamarra with them. Katie, home on a four-day break, invited them into the living room, where she and Lily made a fuss of Jamarra. He was becoming more relaxed around people but his journey back to himself was taking its time. Pearl still had to soothe away nightmares in which a big leather armchair chased little leaden legs.

Sarah arrived not long behind them. She looked stunning in a sleeveless, figure-hugging dress of emerald green. The hat and gloves she had worn to the voting booth had disappeared.

Jamarra ran to pat the tiny bundle she was carrying. Sarah lowered it into his arms.

He giggled as the puppy licked his face. 'What's his name?'

'He hasn't got a name yet. I thought you might like to give him a name. He's your dog, Jamarra.'

Jamarra looked as if he thought he had heard wrong. He stared at Sarah and as the puppy snuggled into his neck, he gasped, 'To keep? Forever and forever?'

'Forever and forever. What will you call him?'

'Patch!'

The others had crowded around to admire the puppy. As Jamarra announced his name without a moment's hesitation, they looked at each other with baffled faces. Patch? The puppy was a smooth, glossy black with no patch of any other colour to be seen. They looked at Pearl but she shrugged and shook her head, as mystified as the rest.

Doctor Lawrence bent down to pat the puppy. 'That's an interesting name, Jamarra. Why is he called Patch?'

Jamarra just smiled a shy, happy smile and buried his head in Patch's warm body.

Sarah found her hostess in the kitchen.

Rachel smiled a welcome, admiring her attractive guest. 'That's a lovely dress, Sarah.'

'Thank you, Rachel. I'm still not quite comfortable in these short skirts, though,' she laughed. 'What can I do?'

Rachel tossed her an apron and nodded towards the end of her long kitchen table. A damp tea towel covered a bowl of savoury muffin mix. 'If we keep those cooking, the smell will make sure everyone is hungry,' she grinned.

Sarah tied the apron around her waist and found herself some muffin trays and a measuring spoon. 'Who else have you invited, Rachel?' She tried to sound casual.

'Don't worry, Sarah, Mick's coming.' She laughed at Sarah's whatever-do-you-mean expression. 'You like him, don't you?' she prodded.

Sarah grinned. 'A bit,' she admitted, 'but I always feel kind of uneasy around him.'

'You're not frightened of him, surely?'

Sarah scoffed at the idea. 'Heavens no, not frightened, just sort of irritated most of the time.' She paused halfway to the oven with one of the trays. 'Mother Anna asked me once, if I had "improper feelings" for him.' She screwed up her nose as she repeated Mother Anna's cryptic phrase.

'Whatever they might be,' Rachel laughed. 'What did you tell her?'

'I said I didn't think so.'

'You wouldn't lie to a nun now, would you?'

Sarah and Rachel both spun round. Mick was leaning in the doorway, grinning. Sarah hurried to the oven, thankful that it was on the opposite side of the kitchen, and ignoring the chuckle that followed her. She exchanged her tray for the muffins Rachel had been baking before her guests arrived. The tantalising smell of hot cheese filled the kitchen as she transferred the muffins onto serving platters. Mick perched on the end of the table and watched her. Green certainly was her colour, he decided.

As long as Rachel was flitting about and chatting to Mick, Sarah was content to work around him in silence, avoiding his eyes. She dreaded to think how much he had overheard. When their hostess picked up two plates of muffins and disappeared, a vacuum seemed to need filling. She looked up from her trays, determined to say something light-hearted before he could disconcert her with a teasing remark.

She nodded at the football tucked under his arm and tried to sound nonchalant. 'I'm guessing that's not for me.' It was so new that she could smell the leather, despite the aromas of the kitchen.

Before he could answer, they were interrupted by what looked like a walking mushroom hugging a puppy. Jamarra was visible only from the chin down, under a cowboy hat several sizes too big.

'That's a great hat you've got there, Jamarra.'

The little neck craned backwards to look up at Mick from under the silver studded brim. 'Majik's come. He gave it to me.' He held the new Patch up for a pat. 'Look what Sarah gave me! He's mine.'

Mick patted the pup and allowed Patch to lick his hand. 'I don't suppose you can hold a puppy and a football?'

Jamarra's mouth fell open. He stared up at Mick with his neck so far back that the hat fell from his head. It hung down his back by its cord. 'For me?'

'For you, mate. How about you, me and Majik have a kick after dinner?'

Jamarra nodded and the hat bounced about on his back. 'Thanks, Mick!' He hugged the ball to one side of his chest and Patch to the other, and tore off to show the others.

Left alone with Mick again, Sarah busied herself with the remainder of the muffin mixture. She pushed a wayward lock of hair from her forehead with the back of a floury hand.

Mick grabbed a hot muffin from the last batch that had left the oven. He did speedy justice to the mouth-watering morsel of cheese and bacon. 'It's a good job it's not Friday,' he said, licking his lips.

Sarah looked up from the tray she was filling. 'Why?'

'You wouldn't be able to eat any of these,' he grinned. 'They have meat in them.'

Sarah sniffed. 'Well, it wouldn't matter now,' she said loftily. 'I'm not a Catholic any more.'

'You're not?'

'No, I'm not.' An impish grin made her eyes sparkle. 'But you are still a Mick.'

Mick groaned. 'Sarah, that is about the worst joke I've ever heard,' he laughed, 'but I suppose I'm going to hear it for the rest of my life.'

'The rest of your life?'

He moved around the table and took the measuring spoon out of her hands. As his fingers touched her forehead to brush away a dab of flour, Sarah remembered how cosy they had been in the schoolyard that morning.

He put his arms around her. 'Would that be a problem, Sister Anthony?'

Sarah glared at him. 'Well, that depends. Are you going to think of me as a nun for the rest of your life?'

He grinned at her indignant expression. 'Well, perhaps not all the time.'

She could feel her cheeks burning. She answered too quickly. 'Well, it won't be a problem for either of us for much longer. I've been accepted by a hospital in Rabaul. I leave in two weeks.'

'New Guinea?' His smile disappeared. 'You're kidding!'

Sarah regretted her blunt delivery. 'No, Mick. I'm not kidding.'

'Why?'

'I have a debt to pay, remember? But like you said, running away from problems here isn't a solution. I'll be back.'

'Did I say that?'

'Didn't you?'

'It sounds like something I would say but I don't think so.'

'I must have dreamed it, then.'

'Nice to know I'm in your dreams.' His arms were still around her. 'New Guinea, eh? For how long?'

'I've signed for two years.'

'Two years?' He sounded crushed. Why on earth?'

'You know why.'

'Oh, Sarah, you don't owe anyone! You've already sacrificed years of your life to this debt you think you have to pay. Are you sure this is about repaying that debt or is it just your excuse?'

'My excuse?'

'Your excuse for running away. Are you sure you're not running away, Sarah?'

'From what?'

'From me – from those "improper feelings".'

She couldn't look at him any longer. 'It, it's something I have to do, Mick.'

He released her, shrugging as if it was no longer any of his business.

As he backed away, Sarah felt a pang of regret. Part of her wanted to tell him that she would stay. 'I'll look you up when I come home, shall I?'

He looked back at her but didn't answer.

'First stop, the *Chronicle* office, I promise,' she coaxed. One of his cheeky grins or even some teasing remark would be a relief.

'I won't be here.'

It was Sarah's turn to look anxious.

Mick's voice was matter-of-fact. 'I was going to tell you that I'm going away myself but you beat me to it. The *Herald* has finally realised that it can't do without my extraordinary talents. I'm off to Melbourne next month, so it seems we'll be a whole continent apart, unless – oh, Sarah, why don't you come to Melbourne too? I know you love working with kids. What about working at the Royal with Katie?'

Sarah bristled. He had made his plans and hers too, it seemed – oblivious to any plans she might have had. 'You're asking me to give up something I've dreamed of doing ever since I was a little girl. You question my motives but I'm not the only one who thinks debts should be paid. I'm not the only one who would like to be working at the Royal.' Sarah lowered her voice to almost a whisper. 'Lily would love to be down there, working with Katie. Did you know that the only reason she returned to the Crossing is because she feels she owes Rachel? Well I've always felt that my family owes this debt and I've always known that I would be the one to pay it.' Sarah was resolute.

Mick shook his head.

Rachel leant into the kitchen. 'Come on, you two, time to eat!'

The guests had left the head of the table for their hostess. Sarah found a place waiting for her between Martha and Katie. The doctor sat opposite his wife with Pearl and Jamarra. Mick seated himself at the bottom of the table between Katie and Lily. Not that he had them to himself. Sarah noticed with a smile that Majik had claimed a chair on the other side of Lily. Jamarra sat between his mother and Majik, saying little and watching the food as if it might disappear. He rewarded with beautiful big smiles anyone who put something on his plate.

Doctor Lawrence raised his glass. 'We have two triumphs to celebrate today. First of all, we are absolutely going to see a Yes vote win hands down in the referendum.'

'Hear, hear!'

'And secondly, we applaud the mighty Mallee's success against the VFL. Never was a place more appropriately named than Victory Park, largely due to Cobbs Crossing's very own football heroes, Majik and Mick!'

Everyone raised their glasses. 'Majik and Mick!'

Mick acknowledged the toast with an uncomfortable grin. Majik leapt to his feet. Sweeping the cowboy hat from his head with a flourish, he bowed like Walter Raleigh before Queen Elizabeth.

As the laughter died away, Martha claimed Sarah's attention. Under cover of conversation with the doctor's wife, Sarah watched as Mick flirted now with Katie on his right and then with Lily on his left. He looked up once and caught her watching him. He winked down the table and turned back to his companions.

The doctor and his wife were full of their plans to sponsor Jamarra to one of the very best schools in the district. Pearl had been consulted and she was happy. Jamarra would be a day pupil, home with her every night.

Katie whispered to Sarah. 'If Aboriginal kids like Jamarra can go to state or even private schools, why were they taken to an orphanage in the first place?'

Sarah looked at her plate. She supposed there were going to be lots of questions like this in her future. 'Well, they were taken more to separate them from their parents than because of much concern with their education. In local schools, they would be too accessible. They were placed in remote institutions to make contact by their families difficult or impossible, even sent to another town or state for the same reason.'

'Shhugar!'

'Yes, indeed. Sugar.'

Martha addressed Lily across the table. 'I read yesterday that Charles Perkins is organising an Aboriginal debutante ball. The doctor and I would be happy to sponsor you, Lily, if you'd like to make your debut in Sydney.'

'Thank you, Mrs Lawrence. You're very kind but I prefer to wait until we can all attend balls together.'

Mick raised his glass in salute. 'Quite right, Lily. It's a disgraceful irony that even some places campaigning for a Yes vote are still barring Aborigines.'

'But we will get a Yes vote,' Rachel insisted, 'and things will change then, Lily. Things will get better, you'll see.'

Lily shrugged. 'You think so? Do you really believe the government will make all those changes we've talked about?'

'If the vote is conclusive enough, they'll have to take notice.' Sarah pushed an unoffending pea around her plate. 'They'll have to.'

Bibliography

100 Years: The Australian Story – ABC www.abc.net.au/100years/EP4_4.htm

Bandler, Faith: *Turning the Tide: A Personal History of the Federal Council for the Advancement of Aborigines and Torres Strait Islanders.* Aboriginal Studies Press. Canberra, 1989

Dickens, Charles: *Oliver Twist.* Richard Bentley. London, 1838

Docker, E.G.: *Simply Human Beings.* Jacaranda Press. Brisbane, 1964

Faith Bandler at Melbourne University: *The Sun* (Melbourne), Friday 19 May 1967, page 13

www.nma.gov.au/.../faith_bandler_new_south_wales_director_of_the_vote_yes_for_aborigines_campaign

Gordon, Harry: *The Embarrassing Australian.* Lansdowne Press. Ltd. Melbourne, 1962

Gunn, Jeannie: T*he Little Black Princess: a true tale of life in the Never-Never land.* Melville and Mullen. Melbourne, 1905

Initial Conference of Commonwealth and State Aboriginal Authorities Held at Canberra 21st to 23rd April 1937. http://nla.gov.au/nla.aus-vn118931

James 2:14

Lake, Marilyn: *Faith: Faith Bandler, Gentle Activist.* Allen & Unwin. Sydney, 2002

Mark 16:16

Moorehead, Alan: *The Fatal Impact: the Invasion of the South Pacific.* Hamish Hamilton. London, 1966

Neville, A.O.: *Australia's Coloured Minority – Its Place in the Community*. Currawong. Sydney, 1947

Lee, Harper: *To Kill a Mockingbird*. William Heinemann, 1960